# FAMILY REUNION

The train from Liverpool came puffing in and stopped with a shuddering crash at the buffers. Soon Mary's tall slim figure was stepping off the train. She was quite an imposing sight, despite the confused scared expression in those lovely green eyes. Much careful planning had gone into the completion of her traveling attire. Dainty hands had fashioned the lace jabot at the neck, and the smart straw boater, which had been left behind by a visiting American cousin, was now retrimmed and decorated with a scarlet rose.

It was the hat that Tim spotted first as he tore down the platform. Holding her little son by the hand, Mary stood looking anxiously about.

"Mary! Mary, me darling!"

They fell into each other's arms and stood in a silent embrace. The big knobbly pin that secured the hat fell out and her hair came loose as the boater rolled along the platform. But Mary did not care. She walked along with her Tim holding his arm, her dark hair hanging free . . . as they all made their way home to Autumn Alley.

**Books by Lena Kennedy**

Autumn Alley
Kitty
Maggie

Published by POCKET BOOKS

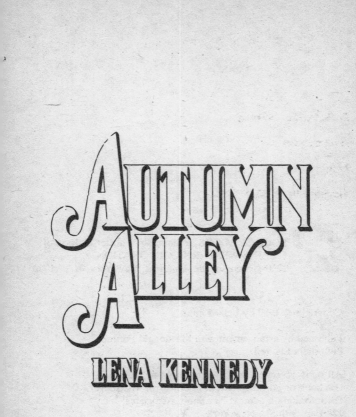

# AUTUMN ALLEY

## LENA KENNEDY

PUBLISHED BY POCKET BOOKS NEW YORK

POCKET BOOKS, a Simon & Schuster division of
GULF & WESTERN CORPORATION
1230 Avenue of the Americas, New York, N.Y. 10020

ISBN: 0-671-42559-5

Originally published in Great Britain in 1981
by Macdonald Futura Publishers Limited

First Pocket Books printing December, 1982

10 9 8 7 6 5 4 3 2 1

*To my friend Frances,
and Aunt Mollie*

# BOOK ONE

# Autumn Alley

It was 1894, the age of gaslights and horse-drawn buses, large flowery hats and trailing skirts. The country was witnessing the start of many exciting new enterprises. Some of them were great engineering projects, like the new tunnel that was to pass under the River Thames at Black Wall Point.

Once work had begun on this tremendous task it attracted hordes of immigrants from the poorer countries, and particularly Ireland. Here was work, highly dangerous but well paid; it would provide cash to send home to hungry families in Ireland, so many of which had been evicted from their small farms by the land-grabbing gentry. They came in droves. Some were exiled with a price on their heads, and some were just honest young men seeking a better living, but all were making for the East End of London to work on the new tunnel.

One Saturday night two such Irishmen sat side by side on the spray-washed deck of the cargo ship S.S. *St. Bridget* as it battled with the huge waves of the Irish Sea. Both were twenty years old and they were cousins by birth. One was big and husky with a mop of red hair; the other, small, dark and thin, with very Irish blue eyes. The former was Timothy Murphy, and the latter, Daneal Fitzpatrick—known to all as Dandy Fitz. They had grown up together, from village school to farm, but now they had left their native land and sailed the ocean in search of work and success.

"Be Jasas, pull yourself together, man," protested Dandy to Tim, who moaned and groaned beside him. Dandy's voice was a deep, rolling brogue.

"Oh, 'tis hell," cried Tim, "Every time she heaves the whole of me stomach goes wid her."

"Didn't I tell you to stick to the hard stuff, not to keep on swilling all that cold beer?" Dandy admonished.

"By God, Dandy, you've the innards of an old donkey," groaned Tim.

When Tim and his cousin arrived in Liverpool they began the long trek to London, walking every step of the way, sleeping by the roadside to eke out the little money they possessed. Eventually they arrived, footsore, weary and broke.

Obtaining a job on the new tunnel was easy enough but holding it down on empty bellies was a harder task. All day, every day, they were up to their knees in wet clay, and each night they slept in the dosshouse run by the Salvation Army—men packed into a room on straw pallets on the floor, riddled with lice and bugs. They used their boots as pillows in case they should be pinched during the night. Drunken bullies were anxious to pick fights with these green young men. So many, many times that first week they longed for the bright peat fires and the hot potato cakes back home across the Irish Sea. Then Friday came and in their blistered palms were placed two golden sovereigns—almost a fortune, never had either one earned so much money in a week. They never forgot the warm feeling after that first visit to the coffee shop with its high-backed seats and its scrubbed wood tables, hot mutton stew and dumplings served by a roguish looking blonde.

"This is real living, Dandy, me boy," exclaimed Tim, loosening the belt on his green corduroys.

"Indeed, 'tis right ye are," replied Dandy mopping his lips carefully with a red spotted handkerchief, his bright blue eyes shining with satisfaction and pleasure.

"Yes, 'twas foine," declared Tim. "Tastes almost like me

old mother's stew back home. Well now, 'tis toime for a few pints of porter, then I am away to find some new lodgings. Those darn bugs nearly ate me alive last night."

"Aye," agreed Dandy, "'tis no rest up there with those devils roaring and fighting all night." Then shyly he asked: "If you get a grand place will you bring Mary over?" When Dandy thought of Tim's lovely young wife Mary his heart always missed a beat.

"Yes," said Tim, "I'll bring her over, and the child, as soon as we get a decent place."

"It will be nice to settle here where there is good money to be made," said Dandy.

As they were leaving the coffee shop, the blonde proprietress, whose name was Rosie, counted out their change with her rough, red, work-soiled hands. A lovely smile was on her mouth showing white teeth and it lit up her merry brown eyes. It was a striking contrast to the pile of brassy blonde hair caught up in a white fish net snood.

"'Ow was it?" she inquired, with the flat intonation of a Cockney born within the sound of Bow bells.

Dandy remained silent—he was always awkward with women. But Tim, so polite and so good to look at, replied in his soft brogue: "It was a foine good hot meal, madam, and very nicely cooked."

Rosie's eyes twinkled, her teeth flashed another winning smile. "Get away wiv yer old blarney, but for that I'll take a tanner orf the bill. Looking for lodgings, ain't yer?"

"Yes," replied Tim, "but I have in mind getting a house and bringing my wife over."

"Well," said Rosie, busily pouring tea for the next customer, "there's a room upstairs you can have for a week. It belongs to a paddy that's gone home to bury his ma, but you're welcome to it."

"'Twill be better than the old dosshouse," urged Dandy.

Tim hesitated. His mind was set on getting a house for Mary.

Rosie's eyes ran over Tim's rippling muscles and red hair. "Wait a bit and I'll take you up and show it to you," she suggested.

Rosie was as changeable as the wind in her love life. In business she was an astute hard-working Cockney, but in bed she was weak and very willing. Often she would be seen red-eyed and weeping as she filled the big mugs with tea, her tears falling for that last Irish laddie who had just left for home. But the next day she would be bright and smiling again, ready to welcome her new man. At the moment her mind was focused on the red head and strong arms of Tim.

She escorted them up the rickety stairs and showed them the narrow uncomfortable looking bed. "Don't know if it's big enough for both of you," she remarked, rolling her eyes roguishly. "Got a big double bed meself, next door."

"'Tis foine," said Tim, "we'll manage nicely." With a provocative swing of her hips, Rosie went downstairs again.

That night Dandy slept tight, dreaming of himself with Tim's Mary high up on another planet with God and all his holy angels. But Tim remained on a more earthly plane, for when Rosie tweaked his big toe he left the little bed to share with her fat comfortable shape next door, and Dandy did not even notice the extra draught on his back.

"Me Gran's got a lot of property around here," Rosie informed Tim a few days later. "I'll see if I can get a house for you and Mary." She grinned. "After all, Patsy boy, you did earn it."

On Friday she handed him a huge key. "Here ye are, Tim. It's down the road in a little alley. It's five bob a week and don't let 'er put up the rent."

Tim took the key, smiling his thanks to Rosie. She winked her eye. "I'll be seeing you, then. Come in for dinner some time."

Dandy was overjoyed and praised all the saints in heaven for this stroke of luck. There was a certain twinkle in his cousin's eye as he thought how little the heavenly saints had had to do with this transaction. With their few possessions in a canvas bag, they set off down the road to find their new residence.

Autumn Alley was at the end of a long winding lane that ran beside the Regent's Canal—or the Cut, as it was called for some unknown reason. It was no different from the hundreds of other alleys in the maze that was London before the First World War. It was a blind alley, its rear end blocked by the canal. Two round concrete posts were planted at the entrance to the alley. Their purpose was somewhat obscure; perhaps they were for hitching horses or for layabouts to lean on, no one ever found out.

There were six dwellings: three one side and three the other. The small windows stared out like sightless eyes at the cobbled stones of the street. Each front door had a round iron ring with a griffin's head on it for a knocker.

Tim and Dandy stood at the entrance to the alley hesitating, very impressed by its neat orderliness. Directly on the corner was Rosie's gran's shop. It was an ordinary house but the front room window displayed fly-blown tins of toffee and several lop-sided packets of merchandise. All over and around the window were chalk-written signs: "Firewood sold here"; "lemonade sold here"; "bread and potatoes very cheap." It seemed that Rosie's gran, who was known as old Sal, catered for all and sundry in her front parlor-cum-shop, and maintained a thriving business.

As the two men stood looking, a voice called from the dim depths of the shop.

"Hi! there." It was a dry cracked voice but very loud.

Peering into the gloom they could just see old Sal sitting at the homemade counter which was just a couple of boards tacked together with a kind of flap to enter.

"Come in 'ere," ordered old Sal. They went in at her invitation, through the small low doorway that almost scalped Tim. Old Sal sat on a stool behind the counter, so obese that for her to leave the premises would have been an almost impossible feat. Tim stared at the face that in its prime might have been like Rosie's but was now wreathed in fat. Four chins hung below it, and wispy locks of hair stuck out around it, beneath a black woolen cap that Sal wore pulled well down over her ears. Her eyes shone out like black boot buttons. All about her the shelves were packed tight with a muddled array of merchandise—tins, bottles and packets. For many years old Sal had sat in this same spot with her beady eyes fixed on the wooden drawer in the counter that held the takings. And always there was the big blue jug beside her, full of beer.

"Come in 'ere," she croaked. "Let's take a good look at yer." She pulled Tim forward with the curved handle of the walking stick that she occasionally used to assist her ungainly shape to rise. "Micks, ain't yer?" She screwed up her face as she scrutinized them. "Renting No. 1 opposite. Don't know as I like Irish, they're trouble. Bring the bobbies down here Saturday nights with their fighting and arguing."

Tim raised his cap politely.

" 'Tis a pleasure to meet you, madam," his soft Irish brogue rolled on, "and you're as lovely as your granddaughter Rose."

Old Sal smirked. "Bit of a ladies' man, ain't yer?" she cackled. "Well, give me ten bob a week in advance, and you can sleep with whoever you bloody well please."

Tim's white teeth showed in a cheeky grin as his eyes rested on the blue jug. "Shall I fill the jug for you, gran?" he asked as he handed her the ten bob.

Quickly old Sal grabbed the money and pushed it well down into the canvas pocket she wore about her waist.

"Boy after me own heart," she chuckled. "Here's two bob. Git me jug filled and have one on me. Quart of black beer, that's me poison."

Tim carried the blue jug across the main road to the local, the Railway Arms, which stood in the shadow of a big arch formed by the iron bridge that carried the new railway north. The huge steam trains roared overhead day and night shaking the little pub like earth tremors.

"It's not such a bad little alley," remarked Dandy to Tim as they waited for the blug jug to be filled and they drank a pint of porter each.

"Come on, me boy, let's go see our new house," said Tim, finishing his beer.

They returned the jug full of foaming liquid to old Sal.

"Don't suppose you got any furniture," she remarked. "There's an old bed out in the yard. Bugs have left it by now—it's been there all through the winter." She had taken a fancy to Tim, that was definite.

"That's most kind of you, madam," said Tim as they left. Once outside they youthfully gave way to their mirth.

"Well now, if that's not the funniest old gal I ever did see," announced Dandy.

"By God, Dandy, you're not joking," cried Tim, holding his sides and shaking with laughter.

They crossed the cobbles and put the key in the door of No. 1 Autumn Alley.

"Well, if it ain't me old friend the devil," jested Tim, giving the griffin's head a friendly pat.

"Hush now," whispered his superstitious cousin as he turned the key in the lock. Their heavy boots sent sounds echoing through the house as they trod the bare boards in the narrow passage.

"Smells a bit," remarked the fastidious Dandy wrinkling his nose. The odor of stagnant water came up from the canal and pervaded all the houses in the alley.

"'Tis a foine big front room," said Tim as he peeped in. "Holy Mary! Look at all this!"

In the corner of the room there were empty bottles by the dozen—beer bottles, wine bottles, medicine bottles, jam jars and pickle jars. There were also bundles of old newspapers and a terrible smell of tom cats.

"Someone's in the collecting business," muttered Dandy. "Get a farthing for jars and a penny on bottles. I wonder who it is?"

"Whoever it is is moving out right now," declared Tim, taking off his coat. "This house is mine."

Between them they cleared out all the rubbish and put it in the back yard. Worried little faces peered over the back yard wall at them. Suddenly a tousled head popped up and a squeaky voice asked: "Can we have our bottles back, mister?"

Tim's long lean body bent over the low wall that divided the houses. Crouched down behind it were four young boys, pale-faced and ragged.

"Oh, so *you're* the businessmen then." He held out a big hand to them. "Come on, hop over."

"No, we can't," whispered the eldest. "We don't want our farver to see us."

Tim's blue eyes twinkled.

"Well now," he said, "we'll have to be a bit careful then, won't we." Four heads nodded in agreement. "I'd better have your names," said Tim with mock seriousness, "seeing that we're going into business."

"That's John, he's George, this is Billy and I'm Arfer," piped up the shrill-voiced youngest.

Tim carefully placed a sixpence on the wall.

"Here's a bit to be going on with, and tonight when it gets dark you can come in and shift this lot. And mum's the word." He put a finger to his lips and four pairs of youthful eyes gazed up at him in dumb gratitude.

While Tim had been negotiating with the boys next door,

Dandy had been busy cleaning the room and lighting a fire in the rusty old grate. When Tim returned they carried the bed over from old Sal's back yard, wading knee deep through rubbish to find it.

"Don't throw much away, these Cockneys," muttered Dandy. "Hope the bugs aren't still in it," he added nervously.

The exuberant Tim only laughed. "Don't be silly, man, them red devils only live where it's warm. A drop of the old turps and she'll be as clean as a whistle."

Dandy looked as if he hoped it was true as they struggled to put the old mattress on the bed. Its four brass knobs were green with neglect.

Eventually they had it in position. "It's not so bad," said Tim contentedly as they lay down on it, covered by their coats, for their first night in Autumn Alley.

They rose at five the next morning to walk the mile down the road to their work on the tunnel. Tim strode along whistling, his shirt open at the neck and his red hair waving in the breeze. Dandy walked more slowly, coughing slightly, for the smell and the damp of the alley had upset him, and he longed for the green meadows of the Emerald Isle. Tim gave him a terrific thump on the back. "Buck up, boy. I'll send for Mary next week. She'll look after us now we got a foine house."

A month had passed and No. 1 Autumn Alley had received a new coat of paint inside and out. It was now a lovely battleship gray—the paint, unknown to them, had been acquired from the naval dockyard and their next-door neighbor, Bill Welton, had obligingly let them have it very cheap. His little sons had also been very helpful, offering to fetch newspapers or bottles of beer. But on this bright Saturday morning with all decorating complete and the bare necessities obtained, they were off to meet Mary. The train was due to arrive at St. Pancras Station at ten o'clock.

Tim and Dandy stood together leaning on the parapet of the long iron bridge that spanned the brand new station.

"'Tis like a palace," remarked Tim, staring up at the immense glass-domed roof and the network of iron girders. It was the first time they had ever been in a mainline railway station.

"It's a clever man that thought of all this," agreed Dandy.

"That's what I'd like to do, build a bridge, something indestructible."

The train from Liverpool came puffing in and stopped with a shuddering crash at the buffers. Soon Mary's tall slim figure was stepping off the train. She was quite an imposing sight, despite the confused scared expression in those lovely green eyes. Much careful planning had gone into the completion of her traveling attire. Her nimble fingers had spent many hours sewing in dim lamplight to make the navy serge dress she wore. Dainty hands had fashioned the lace jabot at the neck, and the smart straw boater, which had been left behind by a visiting American cousin, was now retrimmed and decorated with a scarlet rose.

It was the hat that Tim spotted first as he tore down the platform. Holding her little son by the hand and her straw traveling basket in the other, Mary stood looking anxiously about her in the milling crowd.

"Mary! Mary, me darling!"

They fell into each other's arms and stood in a silent embrace. The big knobbly pin that secured the hat fell out and her hair came loose as the boater rolled along the platform. It was retrieved by Dandy who then stood in embarrassed silence holding little Timmo by the hand. But Mary did not care. She walked along with her Tim holding his arm, her dark hair hanging free. Behind them trailed Dandy with the little boy as they all made their way home to Autumn Alley.

# Neighbors

To the demure country-bred Mary, her next-door neighbors were a bit of a shock. Bill Welton often paraded up and down the alley. He was short, thick-set and very surly. With his hands clasped behind his back and a measured gait, he looked like a bobby patrolling his beat. Bill, however, had no desire to ape the cops—they were his deadly enemies. He thought himself a chap to be reckoned with and he ruled his family with a rod of iron; when provoked he was extremely violent. Lil Welton, his wife, had been only seventeen when she married this tough-necked man and after twelve years of poverty and four sons she had plenty of regrets. In the evenings she worked in the local bar to keep the home fires burning. Bill found it very difficult to hold down a regular job and, being a compulsive gambler, the bookie or the pub got what little he did earn. As his boys grew older they had begun to hate him, and Lil used to long for the time when he would disappear for a while and leave them all in peace.

Living next door to them, with only thin plaster walls to keep out the sound, was no joke. Mary used to wonder what on earth they all found to quarrel about. There was always someone getting a beating, Lil screaming insults or Bill returning them with blows.

On top of all this, a dreadful smell drifted out of their front door and traveled up the alley. It was quite a while before Mary discovered the source of it.

The mystery was solved one day when Lil invited Mary to join her for a cuppa. On entering the dimly lit passage way she almost turned and ran out again, for confronting her was a line of glassy staring eyes. To the simple Irish girl they looked like a line of supernatural beings.

"It's only the ole man's 'addicks," the fair, faded Lil reassured her as she led her past them. "They don't 'alf stink, don't they?" she remarked pleasantly.

Bill Welton loved fish. In fact, he believed firmly in its ability to keep him fit and virile. He would bring home fresh haddocks from Billingsgate and smoke them over a wood fire in the back yard and then hang them all along the narrow passage to dry. So when the front door was open the fishy smell almost knocked flat anyone passing. His boys would yell "fish face" at him as he rolled home drunk, and they would dive over the canal wall to hide.

In the Weltons' poor and bare back kitchen Mary drank the first of many cuppas made for her by Lil, and surveyed her new friend whose small square hands laid out the two best cups and saucers—the only survivors from a wedding gift. Lil's dung-colored hair was drawn back in a bun with one strand that always escaped and dangled against her faded cheek. She had probably been quite a good looker years ago, thought Mary, but as Lil herself explained, "Life with my Bill takes it out of yer a bit."

Mary admired her straight features and her wide smile, though her teeth were yellow with decay. She was a little taken aback to see Lil drink her tea from the saucer with loud slurping noises, but she warmed to her happy-go-lucky approach to life.

Having seen Lil that morning in a shapeless, grubby blouse and skirt, Mary was amazed to see her in the evening on her way to work, arrayed in a fairly smart black dress, with a velvet choker around her neck from which a brilliant locket dangled. Her hair was piled high with two frizzy side burns, she wore large imitation pearl earrings and her lips and cheeks were reddened with carmine.

"I just could not believe my eyes," Mary commented to Tim. "She looked a different person."

"It's the old paint pot what does it," jested Tim. "Don't let me catch you at it. I like my woman natural."

Apart from little setbacks, Mary's existence was bright and colorful down in Autumn Alley. It was very far from the peace and beauty of her homeland but Mary loved it. Each day she took Timmo down to the nearby Roman Road market and sometimes she brought back little knicknacks to brighten up her home. Then she would go next door for a chat and a cuppa with Lil after which she would return to her own home to cook for the two men in the evening.

Mary's sweet personality radiated happiness and it began to spread through the alley. There were just three houses on the Irish family's side: Mary's on the end, Lil next door, and right at the end near to the canal lived an old man still brooding over the wife he had lost a year ago. He would sit outside, cat on his lap, his bald pate shining. He had bushy gray eyebrows and was known as old Charlie. He had time for no one except his old tom cat.

On fine days Lil would sit on the narrow window ledge of the front room window, arms akimbo, and hold long conversations with Mary who would stand in her front doorway with little Timmo on the step beside her. The younger Welton boys played down by the canal wall.

"Who lives opposite?" Mary asked Lil one afternoon as they watched the children play. The house directly facing hers, the only one with a brass knocker, interested her. She seldom saw the front door open but occasionally she caught a glimpse of the pale face of a young girl, peeping nervously out of the window.

"No. 5, yer mean?" asked Lil, sucking her teeth. "Them, they're all potty over there," she declared. "Only come out on Sundays."

Mary's soft lips trembled into a smile at Lil's forthright Cockney manner.

"Do you mean they have all gone mad?" she asked.

"No," said Lil, "just barmy, religious barmy. He stands down the Roman Road market jawing about Jesus. Our boys pelt him with spuds."

"He's a preacher, is that what you mean, Lil?"

"Don't know what he is," snorted Lil, "but to my mind

he's a funny old cuss and on Sundays the whole bloomin' lot of them spend all day up at the Mission Hall."

"Everyone has their own creed, that doesn't make them mad," countered Mary. "But who is the little girl?"

"Ellen. Proper little skivvy, she is. Does all the housework. There's two boys as well, a bit older than my John." Lil began to cackle very loudly. "Wait till yer sees them," she bawled. "Proper bloomin' freaks, Peter and Paul, both as ugly as sin and like two peas in a pod."

Mary stared across the road hoping for another sight of that little girl. Lil was off on a running commentary on the rest of the residents.

"No. 4, that's Becky and Sam Lewis. Jews they is. Don't 'alf fancy 'erself. Got a fur coat and goes up west in a cab." This last remark was uttered in tones that conveyed Lil's disgust.

Mary, however, was very impressed. Lil's hoarse voice broke into her thoughts.

"'Ere's your men coming down the road. I'd better get ready for work. Gawd knows when my old sod will come 'ome."

Tim and Dandy came down the alley looking very tired, their boots covered with wet clay.

After supper, when little Timmo was in bed, the men went to the local for a drink while Mary washed dishes, did her ironing and then wrote letters to her folks back home.

Hers was a happy house. But the atmosphere at No. 5, that house directly opposite, was far from convivial. The whole exterior seemed to shed gloom even though the knocker shone like glass. A small girl's thin hands polished it vigorously each day. Without a glance in either direction, she stood there, dressed in a brown linen smock, reaching up to rub the knocker as hard as she could, before darting inside again. This was Ellen Brown, owner of the pale countenance that often peeped out of the window. For her the rest of the alley did not exist. She was not allowed out to play and she seldom went to school although her education was not neglected; many hours were spent studying and reading the huge family bible that was propped up on the parlor table, looking so unwieldy amid her mother's dainty china, framed photographs, shell boxes and other bric-à-brac.

"Evil clap trap," her father would snort as he surveyed the room, "one day I'll destroy the whole lot."

Ellen would shiver, and there would be a sick feeling in the pit of her stomach. She knew that her mother's sanity depended on those few treasures, remnants of her past, and she clung to them as the last vestiges of her youth. At forty Mrs. Brown was old, her body and her mind shriveled. She sat all day by the fire crocheting or just staring into space. Her hair was as white as the driven snow, and her shoulders rounded. From beneath her voluminous skirt stuck out a huge surgical boot and above it a thin twisted leg. Hannah Brown had been born a cripple. She had grown up used to the idea of not being able to run and play as others did. She had not wanted to marry, and had been happy in the protective bond of her Quaker family. But in her late teens her mother had died and a dogmatic father had insisted on her marrying. His belief was that it was right to continue the line of followers that had existed since the seventeenth century. Reluctantly she had wed Jacob Brown, also a Quaker, and unwillingly borne him children. Her thin twisted body had suffered the torture of hell as she gave birth to twin boys. They were lusty screaming babies and she had always hated them. Ellen had only been a tiny baby and had always been a great comfort to her. Now her health had broken down completely and she made no effort to get well; she just sat muttering her prayers in preparation for the next world.

Ellen swept, cleaned and dusted, cooked and waited hand and foot on her mother. She was now eleven and this had been her life ever since she could remember. Strict discipline and blind obedience were enforced on them all by their fanatical father. Ellen's dark eyes and pale face showed no sign of rebellion as her brothers' did, for behind that pallid look she lived in a fairytale world all her own and on tiny scraps of paper, hidden all about the house, she scribbled her innermost thoughts.

Just before ten o'clock each night Jacob Brown would arrive home from his preaching and so-called good works. He was a short stocky man with hair as black as jet matching the waxed moustache whose ends stuck out so stiffly that they received the nickname of winkle pickers. He always wore a dickey, a sort of stiffened shirt front seldom seen in the working-class alley, and adorning the dickey was a small stiff black bow tie. A long tailed jacket, striped pants and a sombre looking bowler hat finished off this natty outfit. On his short legs he would march through the alley every evening.

To the boys sitting idly on the canal wall, Mr. Brown was an everlasting source of amusement. They would call out to him and make rude remarks about his appearance. Little Arfer's tousled head would pop up and his squeaky voice proclaim: "Hi, mister, yer dickey's hanging out!" As Mr. Brown walked slowly and solemnly toward them, they chanted a street song that went: "We will arse ole Brown to tea." Lewd titters and loud chuckles would accompany him to his front door. Mr. Brown only smiled at them benevolently and raised his hand in the manner of a bishop giving his blessing. But if they had looked closer they would have noticed the glowing fires of hatred in his narrow eyes, signs of the volcano that smoldered beneath that seemingly calm exterior.

Once he entered his home, the front door would close quietly behind him and the silence it breathed combined with a sad melancholia as if the whole house cried out its woe.

On Sunday mornings the whole family would emerge from the house together: the father went first; his lanky sons walked behind carrying the huge books of the Lord tucked under their arms. They were identical twins. Peter may have slouched a little more than Paul but both had the same mincing gait, wore thick specs and had black frizzy hair. Last in the line was Ellen laboriously pushing a bathchair containing the huddled shawl-draped figure of her sick mother. The procession would pass slowly down the alley. All eyes would be watching them from the windows. "Funny lot o' buggers," was the general comment from over the way.

One Sunday when Tim and Mary were coming home from Mass they encountered this strange cortège. With his usual friendliness, Tim raised his hat in greeting.

"Good morning, neighbors." His white teeth showed in a jolly grin and his red hair shone in the sun.

But the little cavalcade passed slowly by, not a head raised, not a glimpse of a smile on any face, just a benign wave from the master leading them.

"Holy Mary!" exclaimed Tim. "What a cheery lot of blighters."

"Hush, Tim," remonstrated Mary, "don't swear. We've just left the church."

"But they stay there all day," muttered Tim, staring after them with a puzzled expression.

"Come along now." Mary pulled at his arm impatiently.

"I don't think it does them much good either," continued Tim. "I'm bloody sure I've seen that old fella rooting about the brothels in Gable Street."

"Do be quiet, Tim," begged Mary, shocked at such a suggestion.

Recently she had met Becky at No. 4. She was a dark-haired lively woman, with the tongue of a shrew, and she quarreled incessantly with Lil over the mischievous antics of the Welton boys. Becky often wished she were back in Black Lion Yard next door to her momma. She should never have moved here amid all these *shiksas,* she would say.

"Didn't I warn yer that yer wouldn't like it?" her husband Sam would reply.

"So what? I like the house," Becky would screech, and a battle royal would begin, mostly in Yiddish. The rest of the alley folk would hold bets as to who would shut up first. It was usually Sam.

He was really quite a mild little man. He was a fat, hard-working bespoke tailor who spent most of his time at his shop in Whitechapel hemmed in by Becky's host of relations who lived in the vicinity.

Becky was rather lonely in the alley and would swoop down on Mary as she came home with her shopping. First there would be a long tale of woe regarding the misdeeds of the boys from over the road, then in a more cheerful vein, a long account of the comings and goings of her family in the East End. "My life, Mary," she would say, "if you should see that bride, Princess Alex never looked so good, and my momma, she was dressed like the queen." Then a long description would follow of the food which had been eaten at the wedding she had attended. Mary, pregnant with her second child, would stand first on one foot then on the other, wearily waiting for the end of this long tale.

"I suppose I should be honored," she said to Tim, "for I believe she's related to the queen. But oh, how it plagues me."

"Don't let her worry you, darlin'," responded Tim, "a

couple of kids is what she needs. What the hell's up with old Sam?"

So life continued on down in Autumn Alley. The new tunnel slowly stretched out under the Thames, and men still sweated and toiled. More immigrants came to join them but now jobs were not easy to get; the tunnel would soon be finished and unskilled laborers were not needed so often. The unlucky ones hung around in groups, unshaven, lean and hungry, some with ragged scraps of military attire on their backs—relics of the First Boer War. Tim and Dandy were lucky for they still had regular jobs and by sheer hard work and will power they hung on to them, trying not to notice the hungry faces of their less fortunate compatriots.

Toward the end of the year when the tunnel was almost completed the two cousins received an extraordinary stroke of good luck. Working one day on the entrance to the tunnel, stripped to the waist, their bodies glistening with sweat as they laid the heavy paving stones end to end, they were noticed by Sir John Ward, the big man on the tunnel project. He had a lot of property and had recently bought a grand new house in the suburbs. His shrewd eye had settled on the huge pile of masonry—paving stones broken in transit, and entirely useless for the purpose intended—and it had given him the idea of landscaping his new garden, a patio, paths, perhaps even a lake—that would please his wife. And here were two likely lads, just the fellows to build it.

"Come here, my man," he beckoned to Tim. "How would you like to earn a bit of extra cash at weekends?" he asked, scraping the dust with his walking stick, and avoiding Tim's wary eye.

"As long as it's honest," replied Tim.

"Oh, it's honest enough, but we don't want everyone to know, do we? I want some work done at my home in Finchley. Bring your friend and I'll make it worth your while."

# Our Arfer

THE SUMMER HAD PASSED AND GIVEN WAY TO A
very cold winter. Life in the alley was much harder in the cold
weather; there were coals and boots to keep out the rain to
buy. All the summer the Welton boys had run around
barefoot, happy, carefree and, in spite of the beatings dished
out regularly by their father, hardy enough. But winter
proved an endless source of worry to their mother Lil. The
boys would scrounge fruit boxes from the market to keep the
house warm. Bill became over-fond of his bed in winter and
seldom got even a casual job. So little feet got blue and noses
red and the boys were forced to stay indoors in the small
confines of the living room. They got under Lil's feet all day
long, and when eight o'clock arrived she would plod off to her
job behind the bar mentally and physically exhausted.

Mary did the best she could to help her neighbor. There
was never a great deal to spare but both Tim and Dandy gave
her good housekeeping money, and Mary was thrifty—
nothing was wasted. She remembered so clearly that feeling
of hunger back home and the dreadful tales her mother told
of the hungry forties, when little children dropped dead of
starvation.

So she would put that extra bit of mutton in the stew and always plenty of vegetables and gravy. At dinnertime she would call softly over the wall that divided the houses: "Lil, Lil, there is a wee bit of stew left. Will the boys eat it up for me?"

The boys came out of their house like a shot to collect it, having been sniffing hungrily as the appetizing smell of Irish stew came drifting in.

Each day Lil put on the same act. "They might, I dunno. They've had their dinner. Greedy hogs, never stop eating."

As the boys were gobbling up the steaming food Lil would take herself off to the front door and stand, arms folded, unable to stand the aroma of food on her empty stomach.

"Why don't you eat a bit, Lil?" Mary would ask.

"No, thanks," Lil would reply, "I never eat till evening, then missus up the pub gives me a glass of stout and a sandwich." So Lil maintained her pride and her family survived.

The boys laughed and giggled, and fought each other in bed at night. Mary listened, for she could hear almost every sound. She marveled at their tough resistance to life and the way they clung together.

John was the eldest and almost twelve, a thin hatchet-faced boy with the sly look of his father. He was mild in temperament but a shocking thief; if something was missing the whole alley could be sure that John had pinched it. George was two years younger, slow and dreamy with a mop of almost white hair. Every day he sat by the canal fishing with a bent pin on a string, just idly dreaming.

Billy was a lot like John, two years younger and very aggressive. He was always throwing stones, knocking tin cans about and making a general nuisance of himself.

The youngest of all was Arthur, or Arfer, as he called himself. He was everyone's favorite and quite a character. He was only six but big and forward for his age. He had rosy cheeks and eyes like bright blue marbles but one eye wandered off into a corner which gave him an odd, rather comical appearance. He was always grinning, exposing as he did so a wide gap in his teeth. He had thick brown hair that grew wild and shaggy and was forever in need of cutting. It was Arfer who did most of the talking, and he was very advanced— nothing missed the odd eyes or the big ears of little Arfer.

To Mary this little lad with his wet nose, so like an affectionate puppy, was a great source of amusement. She wanted to fuss and pet him, but Arfer was not used to such mollycoddling. Nevertheless he treated Mary as an equal, a sort of grown-up friend, and was ever ready to run errands for her.

In the mornings he would get straight out of bed and present himself at her front door with his hands stuffed in ragged pockets. "Shall I pop dahn the Roman for yer, Mary, and get yer a nice new loaf?" he would say cuffing away the dewdrop on the end of his nose with the sleeve of his grubby jersey.

Each day Mary would say, "Come in, Arthur, come and play with Timmo for a while." Arfer would saunter in and play with Timmo on the floor while Mary served the hot oatmeal porridge from the kitchen range that always had a roaring fire.

"Shall I make some toast, Mary? Got any stale bread, 'ave yer?" Then with a long wire toasting fork he would make toast, roasting himself at the fire, always making that bit extra knowing Mary would say: "Why now, there's a piece too many. I'll stick a bit of marge on it and you can take it for Billy." Arfer was always concerned about Billy, his much loved brother, and shared all he managed to scrounge with him. He would dash next door with the hot toast but was soon back in Mary's house. She would say softly and tactfully, for Arfer could easily be offended: "Now, there's a bit of butter on your chin, Arthur. Wash it off under the tap." In this way she managed to get him to put a drop of water on his dirty face.

His runny nose was another matter. Mary would regularly pin a clean hanky onto the grubby jersey. "There now, how's that? Mind you don't lose it." Arfer never lost the hanky; he would return it in the evening, crumpled but unsoiled, his jersey sleeve still accommodating that little dewdrop. With a deep sigh Mary would thank him for returning it, then start again the next day. Because if anyone had dared say that he was a dirty boy Arfer would have been extremely annoyed and Mary valued her friendship with him.

There was one occasion when Arfer presented himself at the local church school but returned an hour later using many unmentionable words.

"You know what she said?" he declared indignantly. "I ain't going there any more." He struck a pose that was the living image of the school teacher holding her pince-nez to her nose. He stood with a finger pointing at Mary.

" 'Bring out that dirty boy. Where is your handkerchief?' 'I ain't no dirty boy,' I said. 'You are a dirty old cow.' And wiv that I came home and I ain't going back no more."

Mary was shocked but found it impossible not to laugh at Arfer's antics. But Arfer did not return to school for a long time.

During that long winter when Mary was heavy with her second child, she did not know what she would have done without Arfer. Generally she went each day to the market to buy bread because under no circumstances would she buy it from old Sal's filthy shop.

Tim had defended old Sal for he liked her.

"She's not such a bad old gal. Got a heart of gold really."

"Nevertheless, I will not buy food from that dirty shop," declared Mary.

So now Arfer had the job of getting Mary's bread from the market. He loved that trip down the Roman Road and instead of a piece of bread to make up the weight he received bread pudding. The woman in the shop always saved a piece for him because he was a regular.

Old Sal sat like a huge spider—shop door open—missing nothing that went on in the alley. As far as she was concerned it was her alley; she owned the houses and was getting five bob a week for each one but she liked her tenants to buy at her shop. They could have goods on the slate, get in arrears with the rent but what did really upset her was if they took their custom elsewhere. So each morning on his way back, Arfer with the air of Sherlock Holmes himself, his mouth full of bread pudding and Mary's loaf stuffed up his jersey, would creep carefully past old Sal's shop. "Come here, you sod," she would yell at him. But Arfer turned a deaf ear; he had to get Mary's loaf past unseen to protect her—she could turn quite nasty, could old Sal.

The foolish Lil was always in trouble with old Sal. She ran up big bills for groceries, borrowed money from Sal for Bill to gamble and paid it back at a terrific interest rate. In fact, every Friday Lil handed most of her wages over the counter to old Sal and received only insults in return. Sal's boot button eyes under that wool cap would glint greedily as she reached out for Lil's money.

"That all?" she would grunt. "Suppose that drunken old man of yours had the rest of it."

Poor Lil would gabble a long line of excuses, her eyes full of tears. She had a lot of pride and the old woman really made her squirm.

"Put less bloody paint on yer face and yer might have some more to pay me," Sal grumbled. Then she relented at the sight of Lil's worried face and said: "Send one of those bleeding boys over to help me and I'll knock off a few bob."

So on Saturdays, while his brothers played ball, John was forced to work in that dingy shop. John having worked hard all the week in the flour mill now spent weekends helping old Sal. Reluctantly he shifted heavy sugar sacks and restocked the high shelves, her beady eyes on him all the time. At heart he was a willing boy, though he pinched little bits here and there, and he hated old Sal. She really brought out the worst in him.

"Getting like yer bloody farver," she complained. "Lazy old git he is."

John's head hung low but he never answered back.

"How's yer Uncle George?" she would cackle, rubbing salt into an open wound. Uncle George was a sore point. But John worked hard and did not argue; that burning hate of her was kept bottled up inside.

# Uncle George and the Departure of Dandy

It was in the New Year that Lil mentioned casually to Mary that George was back.

"Who's George?" asked Mary.

"He's my old man's brother; he's been very good to me," replied Lil, strangely reticent.

"Where's he been?" asked Mary scenting some secret.

"He's a tinker," said Lil, "got a pony and cart and goes up and down the country sharpening knives and mending pots and pans and such like."

Mary had been quite sure she knew what a tinker looked like until she met Uncle George. He was a little spritely man with a ruddy face and mop of white hair. He had bandy legs that did not seem to fit his body. He jogged along as if he was much happier in a saddle than on foot.

He always called at lunchtime, and Lil would be practically bursting with excitement at the sight of him. Together they would retire upstairs for the rest of the afternoon. On a piece of waste ground near the canal the pony and cart would be tethered and the boys played with them all the afternoon.

Mary was expecting her second child any day now and usually took a rest in the afternoon. But today there was no rest. The boys were kicking up a dreadful shindy so she rose to see what the noise was all about. Outside the door was Arfer, tears streaming down his face, holding his hand under his armpit and screaming blue murder while Billy was trying to cuff him into silence.

"Whatever's wrong with you, Arfer?" Mary cried. "Leave him alone, Billy."

"He wants to go indoors," said Billy. "He hurt his hand larking about with Dolly, Uncle George's pony."

"She trod on it," roared Arfer. "I fink it's broken."

"Well, why can't he go in?" asked Mary.

Billy stared at her horrified. "Because he can't!" He jerked his thumb in the direction of the Welton's front window and began winking his eye in a frenzied manner.

Mary began to think that Billy had lost his wits. But then he announced in a loud whisper:

"He can't 'cause *he's* in there."

"Oh, dear," sighed Mary, still unable to fathom out what was going on.

"Come in with me, Arfer," she said kindly. "I'll bandage it for you. God knows what Billy's getting at, for I'm sure I don't know." Mary dried Arfer's tears and he trotted inside with her.

On examining his little hand she found it had a huge black bruise where the pony's hoof had obviously pinched him. She bathed the hand and wrapped a piece of clean linen rag around it.

"Aw, fanks, Mary. It didn't 'alf hurt."

"It will be better soon," she said. "Now sit still and I'll cut you a nice bit of bread and jam."

Arfer munched his bread and jam and was then in a mood for a conversation.

"All I wanted to do," he explained, "was put it under the tap and that rotten Billy wouldn't let me go in, just because Muvver's having a lay down with Uncle George."

Mary, spreading more homemade jam onto a thick slice of bread, suddenly stopped stock still. Her neck got red and a blush came up over her ears.

"What's up, Mary?" demanded Arfer. "What yer stopped doing me bread and jam for?"

Mary's head was spinning. "She wouldn't—she couldn't—

surely she would not be such a fool." Mary decided she must
ignore this as just childish prattle. Repeatedly she told herself
that Lil would not do such a terrible thing, but she could not
erase it from her mind. The thought of what might be going
on next door disquieted the pious Mary.

But each day Uncle George came ambling down the alley,
parked his pony and cart, and disappeared into Lil's until four
o'clock when he would come out, untether his pony, and ride
off very perkily. Mary asked no direct questions but she
became very cool with Lil. Lil was the same as ever, though
she looked a little better than usual. She had acquired a new
dress and a long rope of artificial pearls.

One afternoon as Uncle George left Mary caught a glimpse
of Lil in the passageway, all starry-eyed and disheveled.

"Oh, come in, Mary," pleaded Lil. "Don't go past my
house as if you don't know me."

So Mary relented and over a cuppa Lil told Mary of her
complicated love life.

"It's been going on years," she said. "Oh gawd, what that
little ol' fella does to me . . ." She rolled her eyes in a
ridiculous manner.

Mary stared at her, white-faced and very shocked.

"Surely, Lil, you would not commit adultery," she cried.

"Can't help meself," replied Lil quite unabashed. "Should
have married him, I suppose, but being young and foolish I
thought my Bill was the big tough man. But believe me,
Mary, it's old George who thrills me. My young George
belongs to him," she admitted proudly.

"Well, I simply can't believe it of you, Lil," said Mary
prudishly.

"Don't be silly, it happens—could easily happen to you.
Don't you think we can't all see the way old Dandy fancies
you?"

That was too much. Mary got up to go.

The following week Mary gave birth to a lovely dark-eyed
baby girl. It was Lil who ran for the midwife and who made
her a nice cuppa afterwards. Looking into Mary's reproachful
eyes she whispered: "It's all right, love, old George has
hopped it again." Mary squeezed her hand and they were firm
friends once more. Lil fussed and cooed over the new baby,
who was called Mollie, and took care of Timmo. In a couple

of weeks they were out together again walking down the Roman Road with Lil pushing the baby along in her brand-new basinette.

Tim and Dandy had been working hard for the last eighteen months, and had a thriving part-time business that often took them away at the weekends. Sir John had been very satisfied with his well-paved garden and had recommended Tim and Dandy to his influential friends. So they went out at weekends to dig pools and lay paths—little jobs that were well paid and profitable. Mary had begun to save for a holiday back home in Ireland.

Having children had matured Mary. She had begun to fill out and now wore her dark hair bound up in loops and curls. She often noticed Dandy looking at her in a certain way that made her feel uncomfortable.

"Sometimes," she said to Tim, "I wish Dandy would find himself a wife."

"Be Jasus, that dry old stick? Don't think he's ever had a woman," replied Tim.

"There's no need to be coarse, Tim," reproved Mary. "All I meant was that he's wasting his life being so bound up with us."

"Don't fret, love. He won't marry. We used to call him the parson back home," jested Tim.

But Mary felt uneasy. Was it Lil's nasty remark? Not entirely. When Dandy passed her by, he often put his arm about her waist, and if she was sad, right away he would ask: "Is there anything wrong, Mary?" He was always ready to help her, and she was fond of him but determined that there should be no bad things in her own life. Tim was her man, she told herself firmly.

She busied herself about the house polishing the furniture until it shone like glass. She was never bored—there was always plenty to see and hear in the alley and always new familes arriving from Ireland to settle in the neighborhood. She met them at church. She had become a member of the Catholic Women's Guild, always ready to help someone in need.

At the center of this web of humanity sat old Sal, a grotesque parasite reaching out to suck a few shillings from one house, a fragment of gossip from another. They were all hemmed in tight by the murky web of that obese landlady who seldom moved from her stool except to go to her bed in the back room.

Her one surviving relative was her granddaughter Rosie, who occasionally left the coffee shop in the main road to visit her. "Better go and give old Gran a clear up," she would say to her latest man friend. Then Rosie would sail down the alley like a ship in full sail, her best dress very full and flowing, her huge hat loaded with artificial fruits and flowers. "Looks like bleeding Covent Garden market," was Lil's cryptic comment from her perch on the windowsill.

Having set aside her finery, Rosie would don an old sacking apron and an overall, and proceed to clean up the premises and tidy the stock.

All the time old Sal would complain. "What are you doing there? Don't move that! Like to be able to put me hands on things."

"Crikey, Gran! I must clean up a bit or you'll be getting the food inspector down on you."

"He don't bother me," returned old Sal. "He knows what side his bread's buttered, plenty of pound notes gone in his direction."

"Still, he might retire, and if you get a young bloke who can't be bribed you won't find it so easy," warned Rosie.

"Balls on them all," muttered Sal. "Don't care about any of those thieving bleeders."

"Well, I say you should put all your money in the bank," protested Rosie, "not sit on it like a broody hen."

This upset old Sal. "What?" she snarled. "Can't get yer hands on me money quick enough. It's all them fancy men you got that you want to squander it on." Her little black eyes glared suspiciously at her granddaughter, and the gnarled hands clasped the canvas pocket tied about the wide waist under the black apron.

"Aw! shut up, Gran," cried the exasperated Rosie. "You'll get interest from the bank and I won't have to worry so much over you."

"Worry over me?" jeered Sal. "That will be the day. Too busy with them blokes."

"Now, give over, Gran," begged the soft-hearted Rosie, very near to tears.

"Soft, soft as shit," declared Gran, "just like your mother

was. It's a good job I got me head screwed on all right—it's all up there." She pointed a bony finger toward the black woolly cap that she wore continuously.

On such an evening Tim popped in on his way to the pub. "Hello, Rosie." He greeted her like an old acquaintance. "Give us the ol' jug, Sal, I'll fill it up for you," he offered.

"Now," said Gran, "there's a man for you. Worth all the rest put together."

Rosie, all gooey-eyed, agreed, but apart from an offer of a glass of stout that was all Rosie had got since Mary had arrived.

"He ain't got time for me, Gran," she said, "not since his wife came here."

"Stuck up bitch, she is," the venomous tongue of old Sal wagged. "Too posh for the alley dwellers, and thick with that Lil Welton, she is—you know, the one who knocks it off with her brother-in-law. She's a saucy madam, that Mary. Got a lodger, supposed to be Tim's cousin. Never tell with these hoity-toity ones, worse than the other sort, they are."

With her work now done Rosie sat greedily absorbing the gossip which would be transmitted across the coffee shop counter the next day. Then, having made Gran as comfortable as possible, she got ready to leave.

"Don't shoot them bolts," called out Gran as Rosie closed the door. "Leave the string hanging down inside so I can open it with me stick."

"Aw gawd, Gran, you don't 'alf take a chance, always having the door on the latch." Rosie was often really worried, for Gran kept every penny she owned tied about her waist. If anyone else knew that she was bound to get robbed. Rosie sighed and went home to her new man friend, big Barney, and tried not to think about her obstinate old Gran.

Mary's cool, calm independence aggravated old Sal. "Fancy herself, don't she?" she would exclaim loudly when Mary was in earshot. "Live like pigs where she comes from!"

Because Sal was a very old woman and Tim respected her, Mary kept her temper and did go to the shop occasionally for odds and ends. One afternoon accompanied by Timmo and the persistent Arfer, Mary went over to the shop. Old Sal, determined to make Mary wait, got up slowly from her stool and, holding onto the wall, went slowly into the dim regions behind the shop. Mary, who only wanted some tobacco for Tim, waited patiently, while Arfer eyed the sweet lollies.

"Where's she gorn, Mary?" he asked.

"Out the back, I suppose, Arthur," replied Mary.

"No, she ain't! She's got a pot under there. I'll show you."

Scarcely taking in what he had said Mary looked under the counter to where Arfer's little finger was pointing.

"Glory be to God!" she exclaimed, her face flamed scarlet. "Let's go, Arthur. We'll not wait."

Tim laughed his head off when Mary announced later: "Something has got to be done about that dirty old Sal. She has a full chamber-pot under the counter!"

"Oh, don't take on so, love, she's an old gal," he said.

But the sight of that pot had really sickened her and Mary never went inside old Sal's shop again.

Arfer was saddened to find that there were no more trips to the shop. It meant no gobstoppers, large, hard, round sweets which you popped into your mouth, and sucked and sucked, and they came out a different color each time you looked. Many a pleasant afternoon he had passed contentedly sucking a huge gobstopper while he played with Timmo and kept an eye on baby Mollie. Now Mary had stopped going to the shop so there was no treat.

One Saturday, when Tim and Dandy were away working, Arfer sat on Mary's doorstep casually tossing a ball out into the road while Timmo, chuckling madly, retrieved it again and again. He wondered whether he should go down to the Cut to play with the other boys. He was feeling very moody.

"Shall we go over the shop?" he asked Mary hopefully.

"No, not today, Arthur."

"Shall I go and get Timmo some dolly mixture?" he persisted. His little old-fashioned face stared up at Mary in such a reproachful fashion. She knew he was longing for the sweets.

"All right." She gave in. "But I'll wait here. Here's some money for sweets." She handed him a penny and his wide grin returned.

"Aw, fanks, Mary. What shall I get for Timmo?"

Mary, suddenly remembering the chamber-pot, said: "Get him a stick of barley sugar that's wrapped."

Arfer trotted off and from the other side of the street Mary watched him disappear into the shop. Framed in the doorway of the shop was the lanky shape of Peter, one of the twins from No. 5. He held up a slip of paper and, gesticulating wildly, was reading out loud from it. Arfer darted under his arm into the dim regions of old Sal's abode. He saw that old Sal was very angry. She was yelling and cursing, waving her stick at Peter who stood reading loudly from a religious tract. "Hop it, you barmy bleeder," she screeched. But Peter read on.

"Thou will be saved. Repent, you sinner," he yelled.

Old Sal whacked the counter with her stick and gasped for breath. Her mouth hung wide open exposing her one remaining tooth, yellow with age.

"Sling yer hook. Wait till I sees yer father. He'll take a stick to yer."

"Repent," hollered Peter, "the hand of the Lord is nigh."

Hearing the rumpus and wondering what had happened to Arfer, Mary crossed the road, and peered through the shop doorway, past Peter. Behind the counter in the back room she caught a glimpse of another shadowy shape almost identical to the one in the doorway. She stood perplexed for a moment, then suddenly Paul was beside his brother and the two lanky boys fled up the alley to the main road. Sal was very annoyed and slapped Arfer's sweets on the counter. She sat down to regain her breath.

"Hurry up, Arfer," called Mary as he came running out, cheek bulging with a gobstopper. "What the dickens was old Sal yelling about?"

Mary had to wait while Arfer transferred the gobstopper to the other cheek. "Those twins was turning her over," he stated, with cold unconcern.

"Doing what?" exclaimed the astounded Mary.

"Pinching fags. They do it every Saturday," said Arfer.

"But they are Quakers. They don't drink or smoke. I'm quite sure they would not steal."

"All right, then," said Arfer, hands on hips, "don't take no notice of me but I tells you now, them two is crooks."

Mary tut-tutted impatiently and pushed Mollie's pram indoors.

"Can I go now, Mary?" wailed Arfer. "I wanna go dahn the Cut and play wiv Billy."

Mary knew she had offended Arfer but dismissed it from her mind. She would make friends with him later on.

Mary put the baby to bed, bathed Timmo, and watered the bucket of the Virginia creeper that had begun to climb up the back wall. She was immensely proud of this little bit of green among the bricks and high walls of the alley. She knew Tim would be late. He always went for a drink with Dandy on Saturdays but she did not mind, her man would return when the pubs had shut. Contentedly she went off to bed.

For Tim and Dandy it had been a long dry journey in the horse-drawn bus from Barnet. They had a few pints when they changed buses at the Archway then again at Aldgate. They had plenty of money in their pockets having just been paid off for the spare-time job.

"Now just one more for the road," suggested Tim.

Dandy, already tipsy, was not so keen. "Mary will have dinner waiting," he protested.

"Well, one more will make no difference to me appetite," jested Tim, pushing open the door of another dreary pub. His hat on the back of his head, his face very red, he strolled in boldly with Dandy walking more slowly and cautiously behind him. Sitting on a long wooden form, all alone, was blonde Rosie from the coffee shop. Her fruit-burdened hat was all to one side, her brassy hair awry. With numerous gins inside her she sat and wept, her eyes red-rimmed, her wide mouth drooping dolefully. She made a very desolate picture.

"Well, well," burst out the jovial Tim, "if it ain't me little Rosie all ready and waiting." But Rosie only wagged her head in a kind of grotesque way and brought forth a fresh flood of tears.

"Good God! What's up, love?" asked Tim, surprised to see the happy-go-lucky Rosie so depressed.

"It's him," wailed Rosie, "gorn off with all me savings he has."

"Who, Barney?" inquired Tim. This was no shock, for big Barney had a record for this sort of thing.

"'I'll take you home to Ireland,' he said," grizzled Rosie, "now he's gorn wivout me. Fifty quid I give 'im."

Tim put an arm around her. "Now don't cry. You're better off without a scoundrel like that. Get her a double," he called to the disapproving Dandy.

During the next hour Tim consoled Rosie with sugary words and a considerable quantity of gin. When the pub closed Tim guided Rosie's wide unsteady shape down the road toward the coffee shop. Dandy, very drunk and rather disgruntled, went on home.

Mary was half asleep when an unsteady figure entered her bedroom. "Is that you, Tim?" she called.

A slurred murmur was the only answer.

"Oh dear," she sighed, "you've had more than enough to drink, Tim. Don't wake the children."

As she turned on her side to settle back to sleep Dandy catapulted from the corner of the room onto the bed, muttering drunkenly as he pressed close to her. "Love me, Mary. Tim doesn't love you as I do."

The words seethed through her bewildered mind. With a sudden jerk she broke free and leaped out of bed. Tall and majestic, she stood over him.

"God in heaven, what are you about, Dandy Fitz? Where is Tim?" she demanded.

From his seat on the floor where Mary had pushed him, Dandy was too embarrassed to reply. He crawled slowly back to his own room.

Her face livid with temper, Mary grabbed her shawl and went down to look for Tim. There was no sign of him and the clock on the mantelpiece showed it was well past midnight. She gave a little gasp, she was shocked after her encounter with that drunken Dandy. Then she sat down to wait for her erring husband.

With zig-zag steps Tim managed to propel Rosie to the coffee shop. Finding her latch key, he pushed her stout body in front of him down the narrow path through the shop with its high-backed seats and well-scrubbed tables to the little room behind the shop. He deposited Rosie in a basket-weave chair which creaked loudly each time she moved, her befuddled voice singing: "The old dun cow is dun for now, got no whiskey, got no gin, next week we're going to have the brokers in!"

"It's all right, Tim," she slurred, "you're a real man. Not like that worm Barney. Took me lot, he did!"

Tim put the kettle on. "I'll make you a nice cup of tea, Rosie, then I'll have to be going, my love," he added kindly.

But Rosie whimpered: "Don't go, Tim. Stay with me like

you used to, love. Remember that night when you first came over?"

But Tim wanted very much to forget it. He was getting worried about Mary. "I must go home, love," he told her. But Rosie had dropped off, mouth wide open, fat legs wide apart. He reached for an old coat behind the door, covered her up, took the kettle off and crept toward the door.

Strolling along the deserted streets whistling a merry tune, the church clock struck one o'clock and Tim began to hurry. By the time he reached his house he was panting heavily.

He was bending down to take off his boots so as not to wake Mary, when her cold voice called from the parlor. "Don't bother with the old boots, Tim, I'm down here."

She sat very straight and erect, fully dressed in her gray outdoor dress, her hair in a neat roll on top of her head. Beside her was the straw traveling basket she came over with, all packed up with her own and the children's clothes.

"Where are you going?" demanded Tim in amazement.

"Never mind where I'm going. Where have you been all night?" she inquired coolly.

"But, Mary, it is only one o'clock," stammered Tim.

"It's late enough," she said, "seeing that the pubs shut at twelve. But that's not what I'm annoyed about."

Tim came toward her very contrite. "I'm sorry, me darling."

"So am I," said Mary crisply, "and you will be more so if you don't get that damned cousin of yours out of this house before morning."

"Dandy?" exclaimed Tim. "Why? What's he done?"

"It's not what he's done, it's what he was about to do. And with no man to protect me." Tears came into her eyes.

"You mean . . ." Tim could not utter the word, let alone believe it. ". . . not old Dandy." He just stared at her in disbelief.

"Are you calling me a liar, Tim?" Mary's temper rose. "Tomorrow I'll leave and take the children. You can have your old cousin. Bad cess to you both."

In all their years together Mary and Tim had never actually quarreled but now their voices rose in anger and each one could not believe it was happening.

"He never meant no harm," cried Tim. "He had a few drinks. Could happen to any man."

"But not in my home," stormed Mary. "Either he goes or I do."

So the battle raged on, until down the stairs came a very bleary-eyed Dandy. "'Tis all right," he said quietly, "please don't quarrel, I'll go." He stood there so sad, his few belongings in the pack on his back.

"I'll be hanged if you will," roared Tim. "I'll be master in me own home."

Mary stood tall and ashen-faced.

"I'll get the children up," she said. "We'll go home."

Tim sank down in a chair, his head in his hands, almost weeping.

Without a word Dandy left, his footsteps echoing on the cobbles. Mary took off her shawl and went silently from the room. Tim never moved but tears trickled through his fingers and over the backs of those hard-working hands.

Early in the morning Mary got the children up and took them to Mass. Tim still sat silently in the parlor and as soon as the pub was open he went over there. From the pub he went to the coffee shop to see how Rosie had fared. He did not return until nightfall by which time he was very drunk having scoured all the East End pubs in a frantic search for Dandy. But it was in vain, for Dandy had taken the early boat train to Liverpool and was now on his way home.

On Monday morning Mary's face was still pale and very rigid. She had no intention of giving in. Tim with a dreadful hangover made no attempt to get to work and remained in the Railway Arms all day.

In her good-hearted way Lil pleaded with Mary. "Make it up with him, love. Don't want him to become a layabout like my old Bill."

"I'll handle my own husband, if you don't mind," replied Mary tartly.

For more than a week Tim boozed it up with Bill Welton. His pride had been shattered and Mary still remained cold and aloof.

In the local pub there was always plenty of trouble. The Boer War had broken out again that year. British settlers and soldiers were being massacred and besieged, jingoistic newspapers provided lurid propaganda, and the alley dwellers, along with the rest of the local working-class community, took sides. In the Railway Arms Bill Welton's voice could be heard shouting loudly about all the bleeding foreigners that came here taking the bread from poor people's mouths. England was for the English and he would fight any man who was not a patriot. Many Irishmen from the surrounding districts used the pub and more often than not their sympathies lay with the Boers—had not Ireland been subject to the same tyrannical persecution for many years? Many fights broke out as they resorted to fisticuffs to settle the disputes.

The climax came in May when the news of a British victory came. Folks lit bonfires and danced about. The pubs were filled to the brim. There was still an uneasy tension between Mary and Tim, but he had at least returned to work.

This evening Mary sat watching the boys playing about the bonfire. The children had a street party—cake and jelly served outside in the alley—and there had been a most congenial atmosphere. Tim and his now close companion, Bill Welton, swilled pint after pint in the Railway Arms. By closing time a full-scale battle was in progress. The police came in a horse-drawn wagon to break it up and carry several away, including Tim and Bill Welton.

Mary had heard the sounds of breaking glass and the shrill screams of Lil, and had left the children to investigate, arriving just as the wagon drove off.

With her sleeves rolled up and bespattered with blood, Lil shouted to her: "Too late, duck, they took 'em."

"Took who?" asked Mary, amazed at the shambles left behind.

"Your Tim and my Bill—in the bloody black maria."

Mary gazed pathetically after the police wagon that contained her husband.

Lil put a protective arm about her. "Don't worry, love, they'll let 'em out in the morning. Let's go and have a cuppa."

"Blimey, what a fight!" said Lil later as she poured the tea. "Funny that for once your old man and mine should be on the same side. Of course, it was my Bill who started it all," she said proudly. "Very patriotic, he is."

Mary sat silent. She did not like or even understand these violent goings-on.

Lil poured her tea into the saucer. "Like it nice and hot," she said conversationally.

"Whatever were they fighting about?" inquired Mary.

"It was this big bloke that came in. He's called Bob. He kept hollering about us pinching Africa and something about Home Rule for Ireland. Well, it really upset my Bill, it did," said Lil, nodding her head emphatically. Then, noticing Mary's weary face, she said kindly: "You get off to bed now, love, we'll go down in the morning before they comes up in front of the old wig."

Back home Mary buried her face in her pillow and placed her hand on that empty spot beside her. "Oh, I'm so sorry, Tim. Come home safe, darling," she wept.

The next day, leaving Lil's boys in charge of the children, and arrayed in their Sunday best, Lil and Mary went down to Bow Court to hear the charges read out. It was a new experience for Mary but Lil was quite unperturbed; married to Bill she had become used to attending court.

"Dunno what he'll get this time," she muttered. "Been up three times before. Got three months last time."

Mary looked very worried.

"Do you mean they might go to prison?" she asked anxiously.

"No, not your Tim—it's his first time," replied Lil with a knowledgeable air. "But I bet me old man goes down." She wagged her head with its frizzy sideboards.

Sitting in that dingy courthouse among the many frowsy unwashed bodies, Mary felt sick and faint.

The wig, as Lil called him, was a famous East End magistrate whose name was a household word. He was used to these Monday morning sessions, but, having also celebrated the previous night with much vigor, he was in a lousy temper.

They shuffled in, these errant subjects, in twos and threes—unshaven chins; caps in hands. The wig reprimanded them, fined them or sent them down in rapid succession and these hard-drinking, hard-fighting men went like sheep without comment. However, it was an entirely different case for Tim and Bill. Tim had noticed Mary in court and was looking very shamefaced but Bill Welton, like a small fighting cock, was in his element; no great actor could have risen to the occasion better.

"Do you plead guilty?" asked the wig of the downcast Tim.

"Yes, sir. Indeed I do, sir," muttered Tim.

"Just one moment, your honor," Bill held up his hand. "Have I your permission to defend my case?"

"Go on," said the wig wearily.

"Well, sir," began Bill, very ponderously, "we are accused of fighting, but *why* was we fighting?" His beady eyes swept the court. "For our queen, that's why," he shouted. "Defending her from the insults of those rebel Irish louts."

The wig took off his specs and stared angrily at Bill. What did he want to bring up matters like that for? Was he trying to make it a political issue instead of an East End pub brawl? He looked at Tim very puzzled.

"But you are an Irishman, Murphy."

"I am, sir," said Tim quietly, looking worried. What was old Bill Welton up to?

The wig suddenly decided against pursuing this inflammatory subject; it was too complicated and would take up too much valuable time.

"All right," he said abruptly, "two guineas fine for you, Murphy. Don't let me see you here again."

With a sigh of relief Tim left the dock and went over to put his arms around Mary.

"Oh, crikey!" said Lil. "What's my old man up to now?"

Bill was still in the dock laying down the law. The constable was about to remove him forcibly when the wig called him back.

"Wait a moment, Welton. As you are still on probation by the right of the law you should go back to prison. However your patriotic fervor has greatly impressed me. So if you will cross the road to the recruiting office all charges will be deferred," pronounced the wig. "Otherwise I might find it necessary to impose on you the extreme penalty that your conduct has incurred."

Bill's mouth dropped open. He had talked himself into the army and with a bloody war on too!

"Well, of all the silly sods!" cried Lil, as they marched him over the way to take the queen's shilling.

On the way home they stopped at a pub for a few beers and

Mary took a glass of stout. By this time Bill had recovered his pride.

"Don't worry, me ol' mates, war will soon be over once Bill Welton gets out there. Fit as a fiddle, I am. Army doctor said I was in great shape for a man of my age and they could do with more like me."

The next few weeks life in the alley was rather hectic, and there was a long succession of farewell parties. By now Mary had forgiven Tim and life was back to normal at No. 1, Dandy Fitz was never mentioned and peace was restored. Bill, due to sail for South Africa any day, bunked home from the Chelsea barracks every other night to drink with Tim in the Railway Arms. Over a cuppa Lil confided in Mary. "Like a bloomin' honeymoon couple, we are. I do believe I'm going to miss him."

"Well, dear, that's just the way it should be—he is your own lawful husband," replied Mary.

After Bill's final farewell party the floorboards in the Welton's front parlor took a slope downward as a result of the hectic knees-up. But everyone was happy that spring when Bill with his bandoliers and shiny brass buttons came to say his goodbye to the alley.

Tim had managed to get a good job on the great new road running north and took Lil's John to work with him and learn the trade. Young George moved on into the vacant job at the flour mill, and with an army allowance Lil was better off than she had been for years.

Four weeks after Bill had left, while Mary and Lil sat over a cuppa, Becky from across the way burst in on them, her dark eyes shining joyfully.

"My life," she gesticulated, "I must tell someone, I can't keep it a secret any longer."

"Well, spit it out," said Lil crudely, supping her tea loudly from her saucer.

"He's done it!" exploded Becky. "After nine years, I'm pregnant!"

Mary looked at Lil and in unison they cried: "Congratulations!"

"Tell her she ain't the only one," cackled Lil.

"Oh, you too, Lil? How lovely!" cried Becky. Everyone was her friend this morning.

"And Mary," said Lil, giggling loudly.

"Oh, such news," cried Becky, "three new babies to grow up together. God is indeed good."

Mary sat very silent; she was not so overjoyed. Mollie was not yet two and Timmo still very young, but it was God's will and she had to abide by it.

# Murder in the Alley

WHILE THE THREE WOMEN ALL AWAITED THE BIRTHS of their babies, the days grew longer so the boys played down by the canal much later.

Suddenly things began to happen.

At first there was just one small incident—old Charlie from No. 3 was taken off to the workhouse, no longer able to care for himself, and his old cat, Tigger, was given away. Everyone was so sad at this happening and that empty house at the end of the row looked derelict and gloomy.

One night when Lil was out working at the bar, before Tim had reached home, Mary sat placidly sewing. The boys next door began to make a terrible noise and she could hear little Arfer crying, so she got up and went next door.

"Whatever's the matter, Arfer?" she called.

He came creeping downstairs in a long striped nightshirt, his face pale with fright. "There's a ghost next door, Mary," he whimpered.

"Now don't be silly, Arthur. You don't believe such things," she scolded him.

"Listen, listen then," urged Arfer and held up a trembling finger.

From next door came the weirdest sounds, scratchings, thumps and thuds. Mary felt very frightened. Arfer dived under her skirt and hung on to her legs crying: "Don't let him get me, Mary."

"Hush," she said, wishing it was not so dark and that she was not so afraid. "Bring a candle, Billy. We'll go and see what it is."

Arfer made a dive for the kitchen and hid under the table. "I ain't going in there," he whispered.

Billy, shivering a little, brought a lighted candle and together they entered the empty house next door.

"Who's there?" Mary called timidly up the passage. The strange howls ceased and there was a moment of tense silence. Then something brushed against her ankle. She jumped.

"What was that?" she whispered. But Billy had fled with the lighted candle leaving her in complete darkness.

Her heart thumped like mad. Suddenly from the gloom came that familiar "miaow" and a soft purring sound. Putting her hand down she felt the furry body of that friendly old cat.

"Why it's old Tigger," she exclaimed and picking him up she carried him home with her.

"'Tis only poor old Tigger come back to look for Charlie," she informed the frightened boys huddled under the table.

She fed the hungry animal and placed him in front of the fire. She was relieved but that sick frightened feeling in the pit of her stomach lingered on for days.

Mary was unusually listless for the whole time she carried her third child. In his boisterous manner Tim did not notice the change in her. Then in June came a terrible tragedy that was to lift Autumn Alley from obscurity into a world of notoriety.

On Saturday afternoon Mary sat on the windowsill while Timmo played marbles on the cobbles with Arfer, and little Mollie slept peacefully in her pram. George lolled on the canal wall, his white hair blowing about in the wind while Billy tossed a ball against the wall, catching it deftly each time. In spite of the breeze that drifted down the canal the air was hot and oppressive.

From the Browns' house opposite, the twins, Peter and Paul, emerged in black suits and stiff collars, and black shiny bibles under their arms. Off to the mission, thought Mary as she watched them pass by.

The hot day passed and the babies were tucked up in bed when Tim came home to his supper.

"I'm so pleased you're home early for once, Tim, it's been a funny sort of day," Mary remarked.

"Cheer up, love," said Tim kindly. But there was an anxious look in his eyes. Did Mary suspect why he was always so late on Saturdays? It was only a couple of drinks he had with Rosie, surely no harm could come of that? After all, she was very good company and Mary was always so tired and depressed these days. A man needed a bit of relaxation after a hard week's work.

But tonight he had come home early because he was worried about young John. The Saturday before he had left him at Aldgate and the boy had stopped out all night and lost all his wages in a gambling house. Tim felt responsible for young John, what with his father being away at the war.

The next morning had been the customary haircutting session. With a huge pair of shears and a high chair Tim would give haircuts to the boys next door as well as to his own son. Haircutting Sunday always went with a swing—the boys hung about the back yard, awaiting their turn. First a tuppenny all-off, then a good scrub with carbolic under the tap in the back yard, "just in case anything walked," as Tim put it.

Arfer kept everyone amused. Often he would produce a long-haired friend.

"Will you cut my friend's hair, Uncle Tim?" he would ask.

"It'll cost him threepence," Tim would retort with a grin.

Hands on hips, Arfer was prepared to haggle. "But he's only got tuppence."

"All right then," Tim would reply, "put him on board."

The ragged boy with neglected hair and things that crawled in it would receive a short hair cut and a good scrub with strong soap that left him almost unrecognizable.

Arfer, knowing well that Tim would not take any money, would wait outside until the little lad came out. "Come on, halfsey," he would demand, and receive a penny commission.

"Good gracious me," Mary would exclaim, "don't bring those lousy kids in here, Arthur."

Tim, setting light to the contents of the dustbin, would jest: "Burn the buggers, that's the way to get rid of them."

John Welton, who was not yet sixteen, had hung about the yard with a long miserable face.

"What's up boy?" inquired Tim. "You look as if you've lost a shilling and found a farthing."

"It's worse than that, Tim, I lost all me wages."

"You did what?" Tim stared at him in astonishment. John earned five guineas a week for Tim always made sure he got good overtime.

"When you left me at Aldgate last night, Uncle Tim, I went to Solly the Turk's and I lost all me money."

"Who the devil is Solly the Turk?" yelled Tim, for he was no gambling man.

"It's card playing and roulette school, and I lost," whined John.

"Well, of all the bloody fools," cried Tim. "I told you to go straight home. I never dreamed you couldn't be trusted to." He produced his wallet. "There's a couple of guineas to pay your ma, but don't do it again," he warned. Tim was seldom angry with the boys next door and John knew that this time he had really got Tim going—his jaw was set in a stern line and his blue eyes gleamed angrily.

"I'm not the only one that goes down there," said John hoping to turn Tim's mind in another direction. "Guess who I saw there?"

"I don't know and certainly don't care," retorted Tim angrily.

"Them twins from over the road," said John excitedly. "That's how I knew where it was."

Tim stood still and looked shrewdly at John to see if he was lying.

"Don't surprise me," he suddenly retorted. "I spotted them for a couple of rogues a long time ago. All that bible punching don't fool me. Now hop it, John, and don't do it no more."

It had been with John on his mind this particular Saturday that Tim had popped into the pub to inform Rosie that he would not be staying late. Rosie sat on her regular seat, a new hat perched on her blonde curls—this one had a very fetching bird of paradise sitting on top.

"Ow, just one little drink, Tim," she wheedled. So he relented and stayed awhile.

When Tim emerged from the pub, John was not standing on the corner where he had left him with instructions to wait, so he walked along the Old Ford Road looking for him. Tim began to worry.

"To hell with that boy," he muttered. "If he's gone routing off down the gambling dens again, I'll thrash him when I get him."

At two o'clock that morning there was trouble at Solly the Turk's gambling house. The twins, Peter and Paul, slipped out quickly and managed to avoid the police raid. Two tall thin figures ambled along the deserted streets, white shirts and spectacles gleaming in the moonlight.

"We've done it tonight," muttered Paul.

"Hope little Nell used her head. Don't want the old man to tumble us," murmured his brother.

"You know we've lost all the collection money," Paul informed Peter.

"I know," said Peter. "We're supposed to hand it over in the morning."

With doleful expressions they went on in silence. Their shirts bulged where the bibles were resting.

Soon they came under the arch and turned the corner of the alley.

"Got any fags?" asked Paul.

"No, ain't you?" queried Peter.

They both glanced toward the shop on the corner and the high wall that ran alongside. Without hesitation they dropped lightly over the wall into the muddle of old Sal's back yard. A sudden noise made them start. Her back door was open and swinging in the wind.

"Let's get some fags," said Peter as they crept silently toward the door.

The moon sailed from behind a cloud and cast eerie shadows into that back room where old Sal lay on her back, snoring like an old badger. Crouching down low they crept past her into the shop where they proceeded to fill their pockets with packets of cigarettes.

It was Paul who pulled out the wooden drawer in the counter; it contained only a few shillings which he hastily slipped into his trouser pocket, but as he pushed the rickety old drawer back into position it squeaked and fell to the floor, echoing loudly through the night. Then like the croak of a bullfrog, old Sal's voice rang out:

"Who's that?"

Those were the last words she ever uttered. The heavy three-legged stool that she had sat on for so many years came down on her face. Peter went berserk and kept hitting and hitting that helpless old body as it lay on the bed. His brother hung on desperately to his arm trying hard to restrain him, until with a sickening thud and a squelch the fat lifeless body rolled off the bed onto the floor. Tied about her waist was the old canvas pocket stuffed with money—sovereigns and bank notes. Peter stood back against the wall still holding the blood-smeared stool, mouth gaping, eyes wild and rolling. His blood-drenched shirt stuck to his shivering body. Not a word was spoken as Paul slowly and calmly took out his penknife, cut the string that held the canvas pocket, and stuffed it inside his shirt.

They both backed toward the door pausing only for a second in the back yard to remove Peter's shirt and wrap it in a piece of old newspaper together with the bible. They leaped over the wall and stood for a moment pressed to it.

"Fool!" hissed Peter. "We should have gone over the wall on the other side into our own back yard."

But Paul put a cool restraining hand on him. "Walk slowly," he instructed, "as if nothing has happened. I've got the key. We'll go in by the front door."

On the other side of the alley little Arfer was wide awake. He often lay awake at night conjuring up all sorts of wild dreams. When brother John threw pebbles up at the window it was little Arfer who went down to let him in.

"Where've you been?" he demanded of John. "You wouldn't 'alf cop it if the old man was home."

"Mind your own business," said John who had drunk wine and beer and was feeling very carefree. He started trying to tell Arfer about the twenty pounds he had won at Solly the Turk's before the police raid, from which he had also escaped, but his little brother had lost interest. Arfer had lifted the flap of the letter box and was spying out into the street. A strange sight met his eyes. Down the alley came the twins, one with a white shirt on and one without. Peter carried a newspaper parcel and Paul bulged out in front as if he had a fat tummy.

Arfer made no comment about what he had seen, but just turned and followed his brother up the stairs. "How much are you going to give me for not telling how late you came in?" he asked.

"Here's two bob. Now shut up and let's get some sleep," said John.

But another pair of eyes had looked out of the window earlier to see John being let in by little Arfer. Becky suffered with insomnia during her pregnancy, every movement of the child kept her awake.

"Come back to bed, Becky, you'll catch cold," Sam called out.

"How am I supposed to get any rest with these boys of Lil's out half the night?" she grumbled.

Then gradually the alley settled down for the rest of the night, none knowing the secret that the darkness held or the tragedy the morning would reveal.

Even when Tim was not working on Sundays he rose early. It was a habit. After giving Mary a cup of tea in bed he would stroll over to old Sal's shop for his tobacco and newspaper. Sal always made sure of her customers. If they wanted the *Irish Times* or the *Jewish Chronicle,* she ordered it. "No need to go up the road," she would say. "You just tell me what you want and I'll get it for you."

First down the alley was Sam in his carpet slippers and round skull cap to collect his *Jewish Chronicle.* Behind him in a more leisurely fashion strolled Tim, his striped shirt sleeves rolled up to the elbows showing strong freckled arms. As Tim crossed the road he stopped to pick something up out of the gutter. It was a holy picture, the kind that children put inside their bibles. Thinking he would give it to little Mollie, he slipped it into his trouser pocket. Then his attention was drawn to Sam who stood outside the shop pointing to the ground, his face ashen, his mouth hanging open, speechless with fright. Tim looked down and from under the shop door came a dark red trickle of blood which ran slowly down into the gutter. He stood amazed for a second, then with one long stride he burst into the shop and threw wide the shutters. On the floor in the back room lay old Sal's huddled shape and the floor swam with her life blood that had oozed out all night. A short sharp gasp came from Tim as he turned her over and saw the battered, almost unrecognizable face.

"Call for the cops, Sam!" he yelled. "She's been done in."

An hour later crowds had gathered to watch the dark blue horse-drawn police cart take the body away. Bobbies endeavored to move the crowd on and ropes were stretched across the entrance of the alley and no one was allowed to leave or enter as the police began their investigations.

Three women stood on their doorsteps—Lil, Mary and Becky, each one almost five months pregnant, Mary so pale, Becky on the verge of hysteria, and Lil mostly aggressive. "Don't want to look dahn 'ere," she told the bobby. "No one dahn 'ere dun that ol' gal in. If my Bill was 'ere he would tell you lot where to go," she added belligerently.

The small boys were chasing in and out thoroughly enjoying the excitement of it all. Only the door at No. 5 remained closed, windows shut tight, heavy curtains drawn close as usual. Tim had gone with the police sergeant to bring Rosie from her coffee shop for her to identify her grandmother. Two plain clothes men went from house to house with notebooks. "Where were you between twelve and three last night?" they inquired. The general answer was: "In bed."

Now Becky was being held down as she was having an attack of screaming hysterics and the doctor had been sent for. Poor old Sam looked distracted.

The noise from outside brought John from his bed. He came out with no shoes on his feet and his hair all awry.

When Becky caught sight of him she let out a high-pitched shriek. "He done it!" she screamed. "I saw him come in. I knew he would come to a bad end."

They carried Becky inside but the constable gazed with interest at John. John had the usual innate mistrust of coppers, so when he saw him coming he backed against the front door.

The policeman edged his way toward Lil.

"Is that your son?" he asked. "Where was he last night?"

"In bleeding bed," retorted Lil. "Where do you think he was?"

But the policeman was not satisfied. He had to talk with John, who came forward white-faced and scared.

"You were out a bit late last night, were you?" the policeman questioned him sharply.

"I was down the East End till early this morning," muttered John, hanging his head.

Two more policemen entered and went upstairs where they began searching the bedroom. Under John's pillow they found a wad of notes.

"Do these belong to you?" asked the inspector wagging them under John's nose. Sweat appeared on John's brow; his eyes squinted foxy-like, as did his father's when cornered.

"I won it," he whispered, looking from side to side like a caged animal.

"Better come with me, lad. Might need you to help in these inquiries." He spoke kindly putting his hand on the boy's shoulder. Terrified, the boy backed away.

Lil waded in shouting and screeching. "Where's Tim," she yelled, "they're taking my John!"

John broke away and quickly darted upstairs and locked himself in his room. Whistles were blown and more policemen came running. Women cried and children shouted adding to the din. The inspector called upstairs for John to surrender and a little lad pulled at his sleeve. It was little Arfer.

"He ain't done it," his squeaky voice informed the inspector, "it was them twins over the road."

But the policeman firmly moved him aside.

"Hop it, son," he said, "you might get hurt. Get all them kids out of here," he roared to the bobby in the doorway.

While this was going on, the Sunday morning parade emerged from No. 5—the twins in their best black suits, their frizzy hair plastered down, led by the stocky upright Mr. Brown, and behind them a pale-faced girl pushing an old lady in a bathchair. Slowly, without looking either way, they made for the entrance of the alley.

The harassed constable standing there surveyed them curiously. "Sorry, sir," he said, "but no one is allowed to leave or enter."

Mr. Brown politely raised his hat. "We are God-fearing people, we have nothing to hide," he said. "When I return from the house of the Lord later on, I shall do all in my power to assist you, but now my congregation awaits me."

The young policeman dithered for a moment; then he lifted

the rope and the procession went out in the direction of the mission hall.

Suddenly the crowd of onlookers in the street saw that something was happening. John had got out of the window and was walking in his bare feet over the flat roof of the back kitchen toward the canal, the police in pursuit. Balancing very precariously, his slim shape crossed the sewer pipe that bridged the canal, then with a sudden leap he landed on the railway bridge and began to climb up the long supporting struts. The onlookers held their breath as the distant sound of a whistle told of an oncoming train. It came tearing past puffing and belching steam, and John was lost in a misty cloud. A few seconds later when it had passed he could still be seen perched on that iron parapet, high above the road outlined against the quiet morning sky. The police were getting nearer, approaching from each side of the bridge. The crowd fell silent and held its breath. John stood up, balancing like a tight-rope walker. Then suddenly he stumbled and with a terrible cry his body came hurtling down into the road.

At that moment Tim was on his way back from Rosie's, accompanied by the police sergeant. Tim reached John as the last convulsive shudder came from his body and he lay still. Tim's strong arms went around the boy and through pale stiff lips John whispered: "I never done it, Tim." Then he was suddenly limp.

For the second time that morning Tim had made contact with death. He took off his hat and knelt beside John, made the sign of the cross and offered up a prayer for this young lad, so full of life a moment ago, and now just an empty shell. All around there was silence as people went down on their knees on the cobbles, men and women united in prayer, such sadness was felt by all.

At the inquest the coroner decided that the police had been overzealous as there had been not the slightest bit of evidence that this youth had been connected with the murder of old Sal, and a verdict of accidental death was set down on the record. Local newspapers demanded that his mother should be compensated. But what compensation was there for the loss of an eldest son?

In her perverse manner Lil blamed Becky whom she was sure had put the police onto her John, and with terrible screaming and cursing she told her so. Becky was so upset that she went away to stay with relatives and the two did not speak to each other for many years.

Arfer sat on the canal wall in his old ragged jersey, hair standing on end. "I told them who done the murder," he muttered to himself, "it were them twins, but nobody didn't take no notice of me." But then who took any notice of poor little Arfer?

John and old Sal were buried in Bow Cemetery on the same day. People came from miles around to watch the funerals. Mary and Lil clung to each other and the mourning in the alley was deep and genuine.

Tim did all he could to help Rosie, for she was just a bag of jelly and relied on him for everything. Three weeks after the funeral he was still sorting out her affairs. Old Sal had left plenty of money but all tied up in slum property. The cash from the canvas pocket was never found. As Rosie said at the inquest, John's twenty pounds was nothing—there had been at least five hundred pounds tied up in that pocket Sal had worn about her fat waist. Not a trace of the culprits had been found and Sal's murder remained unsolved.

There was an unusual happening the day the hearse took John from the alley. The door of No. 5 slowly opened and a young girl came out and stood among the rest of the children, right next to George who stood looking tearfully after his brother's body. Then this little girl began to cry. Sobs shook her thin shoulders and kind-hearted George put his arms about her. "Don't cry like that," he said tenderly.

So for the fist time a hand had reached out across the alley, a soft kind hand. Ellen grasped it like a drowning man grasps at a straw, her mind unable to understand the dreadful torrent of fear that was surging about her. They stood close together, his white curly head close to her neat brown braided one. The fine glass hearse, drawn by four coal-black horses decked with black plumes, was escorted by men in high silk hats. It carried the battered body of old Sal, on her way to her last resting place. Only three mourners sat in the carriages behind: Rosie, all veiling and black feathers; Tim, solemn faced, bowler hat on his red hair; and a young newspaper reporter who stared curiously at the crowds that lined the streets. Behind there was a little space and then a less sumptuous cortège. John's insurance money had not run to the expense of a glass-framed hearse, so he had just a pinewood coffin and a hearse with open sides. But there were flowers everywhere, huge floral tributes from the local traders, small bunches from his playmates, flowers from the poor back streets where they had collected a penny a time. One carriage followed with Lil and Uncle George and a distant uncle and aunt, and behind them a long line of mourners on foot would form up—John's workmates, his childhood friends and all the children from the surrounding district.

As the hearses passed down the alley the mourners fell in behind—Ellen and George, hand in hand, then Billy and little Arfer. It was a moment they remembered all their lives as they moved slowly toward the ancient gates of Bow Cemetery.

Mary had not felt well enough to attend the funeral. The terrible quarrel that she had been forced to witness between Lil and Becky had just about finished her. They tore into each other, Lil calling Becky a treacherous dirty Jewess, and Becky in return calling Lil a whore, and all this while a young lad lay in his coffin in the front parlor. Mary's sensitive heart ached amid all this misery; her rosary was her only comfort. Tim was so preoccupied with Rosie he did not see the dark shadows under his wife's lovely eyes.

Mary watched sadly from the window at the solicitous way in which Tim looked after Rosie and the possessive way she clung to his arm. Mary passed her hand wearily over her eyes. She must not think such thoughts. Had there not been enough unhappiness in the alley? After all, that was her Tim, always there when he was needed, she should be grateful that this generous man was her own true husband.

Taking a white sheet with her she went next door to prepare the tea for the returning funeral party. Lil's front room had been cleared; only a few flower petals on the floor remained now that the coffin had gone. But the smell of death was still in the house, not one of fear, but of perfect peace. Mary picked up a little bunch of violets that had been left behind and pressed them to her lips for a moment. Then she set the table with the snow-white sheet and went into the kitchen to make tea and cut sandwiches.

The first to return was Arfer.

"What we got for tea, then?" he asked, sniffing about the table. Mary kissed the top of his tousled head.

"Pack it up," said Arfer, embarrassed by the affection.

"Give us a cake, Mary." She popped a cake into his grubby hand.

"Go and play with Timmo and give eye to Mollie and I'll save you something very nice," she cajoled him.

Munching his cake he retired next door to play with Timmo in the passage.

"Look at them!" cried Timmo pointing at the black horses bringing home the mourners.

The knowledgeable Arfer replied: "That's a funeral, Timmo. Our John's gone right up in the air."

Timmo stared at the ceiling. Seeing only dingy paintwork he looked back at Arfer for confirmation, and Arfer passed the time telling Timmo all about it.

In the heat of the afternoon the children had stood quietly through the long ceremony, watching the coffins being lowered into the ground, and listening to the sobs and moans of the mourners. Then, as children do they lost interest and began to drift away. Ellen stood with a white tear-stained face beside George whose hand held hers very tightly. They left together, walking silently. The rest of the children scampered past, anxious to get back to their play. Taking a short cut, George and Ellen walked toward home along the winding lane that bounded the cemetery. Tall gloomy factories lined one side, the grass verge bordering the canal bank the other. Less than fifty years ago this lane had been notorious, so many children had died in the slave mills. There were still three mills there—a flour mill, a lead mill and a match factory. The law now stipulated that a child must be thirteen before entering a factory, but conditions were still very far from satisfactory.

George pointed out to Ellen the flour mill where he worked. His job was to drag the sacks of grain along a tunnel once they were unloaded from the barge. He had taken over John's job when he had left to work with Tim. The two small figures stood looking up at the huge dirty brick building.

"I wish I could go out to work." Ellen spoke slowly and quietly as if unsure of herself.

George turned and stared at her aghast. "You wouldn't like it there," he said.

"Why?" she inquired. "I work very hard at home."

"It's not the same. A nice girl like you wouldn't like it. They swear and do a lot of things you'd never understand."

Ellen's hazel eyes looked at him with immense feeling and somehow it embarrassed him. They walked on in deep silence. When they came within sight of the alley she began to get very nervous.

"What are you so edgy about?" he asked in his straight-forward way.

"I don't want my brothers to see me," she whispered, "they will tell my father."

"Why don't they let you out to play?" asked George. "I never saw you in the street before."

"My father is a very religious man and does not believe in indulging in pleasures."

"He must be barmy," declared George. "Anyway, I don't believe in all that Jesus stuff."

She pulled her hand away from him and tears sprang to her eyes.

"Please don't say such things," she begged, "because we can never be friends if you do."

"Who cares?" cried George. He turned and went slouching off, his hands in his pockets.

Ellen ran to the front door of No. 5, while George sullenly resumed his seat on the canal wall.

Inside, Ellen paused for breath. The hall walls were covered with dark red embossed wallpaper and the smell of floor polish and wax candles pervaded the house. She stood listening and then her mother's thin wavering voice called from the front parlor: "Is that you, Ellen? Where have you been?"

"Only to the shops," she replied, biting her lips. She hated to lie to her mother—poor old lady, so pitiful and always in pain. Ellen was very fond of her.

When Ellen went into the room, she found her mother sitting in the half light. Her white hair was drawn tightly back in a bun, her skin yellow and wrinkled from lines of pain, a deep purple crochet shawl lay about her frail shoulders, and her small white hands held her knitting on her lap.

"I'll make you a nice cup of tea," said Ellen.

"You have been quite a long time," remarked her mother looking at her curiously. "Whatever is going on out in the street?"

"Nothing in particular," Ellen lied once more. "Why do you ask?"

"I don't know, but I thought it seemed strangely quiet, and I could not hear the children playing."

"It's nothing for you to worry about," said Ellen as she put the kettle on.

The cares of the outside world were always kept from Hannah Brown: no visitors, no newspapers; her world revolved around that stuffy parlor and her family photographs.

As they sipped hot tea, Ellen's attention was focused all the time on the big grandfather clock in the hall. Its monotonous tick tock seemed to grow louder and louder as confused thoughts tumbled through her mind. If Peter or Paul found out about her new found friend—the boy from across the street—they would tell Papa. She had better not see him again.

The brass pendulum swung to and fro; ten to six; five to six; soon they would be home. Ever since last Thursday when she had found a parcel behind the lavatory cistern there had been a sick feeling at the pit of her stomach. She was now terribly afraid of them. The parcel had contained a blood-stained shirt and Peter and Paul had caught her in the act of unwrapping it. She shuddered. She could still feel the point of that sharp knife Paul had held at her throat; there were still bruises on her back where they had pushed her so brutally against the wooden mangle out in the yard threatening to put her hand through the clothes wringer. She had always been nervous of Peter, he had broken her only doll and killed her puppy, but Paul, who had always been kind, suddenly became an ogre and threatened her with a knife.

She watched the hands of the clock reach six. At any moment they would be home. A cold shiver went down her spine. They had committed the murder, she was sure of it, and poor young John had paid for their crime. It was a wicked world. How was she to live with this dreadful secret?

"Read to me for a while." Her mother's sickly complaining voice broke in on her thoughts. She rose, went over to the huge family bible propped up on the table. Red velvet bookmarks hung from the bible and she turned the familiar pages to the Psalms that her mother never tired of. Her gentle tones filled the room and her mother's eyes closed and peace reigned on her countenance.

"The Lord is my shepherd, I shall not want . . ." Knowing

the lines by heart, Ellen's mind wandered. "He maketh me lie down beside still waters . . . ," she imagined herself down beside the canal and there was George sitting on the canal wall.

"Get on with it," grumbled her mother. Ellen continued and the beauty of those ancient words gave her courage. She did not dread the twins' homecoming quite so much.

However, the twins did not come home. At seven o'clock Mrs. Brown's worried voice inquired: "Why are those boys not home yet, Nell?"

"Don't worry," Ellen consoled her, "I expect they've gone off for the evening." She knew only too well that every night as soon as the evening meal was over they escaped out of the back window and did not return until after midnight.

She assisted her mother into bed, and then sat patiently waiting for her father to come in. He would arrive at the stroke of ten, as he always did, and then there would be the usual performance, the same every night. She would sit on her normal spot at the bottom of the stairs, her sad face outlined by the yellow glare of the gaslamp in the alley. Mr. Brown would enter, not a hair out of place, no change in his attire or expession—summer or winter. "Boys in bed?" he would ask, short and very sharp. He never wasted a word on Ellen, she was a woman and quite unimportant, a drone worker, necessary but dispensable. The boys were his world; in this very religious hive they were future preachers to bring the light of the Lord to the people.

Ellen would remain seated on the stairs until her father had gone past her into the kitchen. His eyes would inspect the house, looking for dirt; an unforgivable tea leaf in the sink, or an unemptied bin would set Ellen's knees quaking. She had learned at an early age to cope with the cold disapproval and punishments that were meted out—no supper next night or prayers to be copied out with cold stiff fingers in a fireless bedroom. At fifteen she was older and wiser, knowing exactly how to cheat him and how to protect the rest of the family from his wrath. Each slice of bread, each piece of meat was rationed out by Mr. Brown. No army quartermaster did his job as thoroughly as he, no one was allowed to waste; what you did not eat came back on the table the next day. Ellen often wondered how he managed to survive, he ate so little, but a certain blonde waitress in a city restaurant could have explained that Mr. Brown was a regular customer, and quite a gourmet.

On this particular night Ellen looked at the slices of cold beef on the kitchen table. Even though she was very hungry she would not dare touch their food. At ten minutes to nine, when the twins had still not arrived home, Ellen had crept upstairs to her own room and sat with her elbows on the windowsill staring out across the alley to the house over the way. She could see the last of the funeral party lingered in the front room at Lil's; red of face and loud of tone, the guests sat swilling beer. It was the close relations only who remained and in slurred speech they discussed the merits of the late John. Boozily Lil wept and Uncle George comforted her. Ellen watched Tim leave with Rosie who swayed down the road like a huge black galleon against the wind, as Tim guided her back to the coffee shop while Mary with sad eyes watched from her own window.

Young George who had sat on the canal wall all the evening and missed very little was filled with a yearning to get away from this narrow smelly alley over the sea to a land of big rivers full of fish, a blue sky and golden sands. He had seen a picture of such a place in a book on one of his infrequent visits to school. As it grew dark he left the canal wall and went inside the house. At the foot of the stairs he found Billy and Arfer. Billy, looking very green, puffed at the butt end of a cigar discarded by Uncle George, and Arfer's tummy was distended from guzzling the dregs of beer from the large jugs. From the parlor came the drone of intoxicated voices. Leaping over his brothers, George dashed upstairs to the room that he shared with them. There were two beds in it, he and John slept in one and Bill and Arfer in the other. On the windowsill was a half-finished model of a boat that he had been working on. A dreadful sadness welled up within him. He pressed his face close to the window pane and tears fell like rain. Another pale sad face was looking toward him from across the way. He opened the window and leaned out motioning to Ellen to do the same, but she shook her head and pressed her face to the glass.

She did not hear the key turn in the lock.

"Ellen, where are you? What are you doing?" thundered Mr. Brown. "And why did the boys waste their supper?" A torrent of questions poured out. Ellen stood petrified unable to answer.

"Where are those boys?" He stormed up the stairs to find them, and pushed open the door of their room. A moment later he staggered out of the room—his face purple with rage and shock. In his hand was a letter from his fine upstanding sons. The letter told him plainly that they had left home for good and in unrepeatable language they told him exactly what he could do with the bibles which were half torn up and scattered over the room.

Suddenly with a maniacal screech he threw the letter away and came charging into his frightened daughter's room.

"Jezebel!" he screamed. "Evil lives within the walls of my house!"

With the speed of a whippet Ellen ran quickly into her mother's room. She locked the door and struggled to push a heavy chest against it.

All through the night Jacob Brown patrolled the passage, praying and reading aloud from the Old Testament. "When the Lord God shall deliver them before thee, thou shall smite them, they shall turn thy sons from following thee. He shall build a house in thy name, he shall be thy son, ye shall be his father."

On and on, he ranted and raved until the break of dawn. Ellen lay all night beside her mother's thin shivering body, trying to pacify her. Mr. Brown's house, built in the name of the Lord, was becoming very shaky at the foundations.

Ellen pressed her lips together. "I hate, I hate," she said repeatedly. "It is like George said—how can there be a good God if he allows such misery in our lives?"

# A New Generation

AFTER THE MURDER OF OLD SAL AND THE DEATH OF John, the alley slipped into a fairly quiet period. The recent excitement had been a letter to Lil from the War Office stating that Private Bill Welton was reported missing—not in action, he had disappeared while his ship was docked at Cape Town and he was now posted as a deserter. Lil consoled herself with several bottles of stout and sat out in the windowsill red-eyed and weeping. "Just like that old devil to do a thing like that," she grizzled. "If I was a widow I'd know what to do, but I'm only a grass widow and they stopped me bleeding army pay."

Lil, her time getting near, had become very untidy, her skirt bursting at the seams, her beer jug always beside her. There she sat casting ugly glances over the road at poor old Sam as he went back and forth to work, his house cold and empty now that Becky was in a nursing home for the last months of her pregnancy.

As always Mary was full of sympathy and she tried hard not to argue with Lil. But some days she was insufferable, and lately Mary had been feeling a little down herself. Tim was still working hard but he was also drinking hard. Money was always scarce and he was often down at Rosie's coffee shop sorting out some problem or other for her.

One dreary November morning, Arfer went scooting up the road for the midwife while Lil, her loud yells resounding through the alley, gave birth to a ten-pound daughter. Her hair was a beautiful shade of auburn and she was a lusty, kicking, healthy baby with perfect limbs and fair skin.

Mary sat beside Lil holding the cup while she drank the hot tea from the saucer in her usual way.

"Christ," Lil exclaimed, with flushed face and a smile that smoothed those pain lines from her forehead, "that was hard work, but worth it. I always wanted a little girl, I've had enough of bloody boys."

They watched the midwife wash the baby in a big tin bowl.

"Ain't she got lovely skin?" said Lil proudly, "and her hair is just like your Tim's. It's a good job yer knows me," she giggled.

Mary smiled sadly. "She is lovely, Lil, but I think her hair will be darker than Timmo's."

"I hope you have another little girl, Mary," said Lil. "They'll grow up together." Lil looked at her friend with affection beaming from her homely face.

Mary looked down at her tummy where her child kicked feebly.

"I'm not very big this time, so it might be a girl."

The midwife handed the newly washed baby to Mary who dressed it in a vest and nightgown. Over this she put the woolly jacket she herself had knitted. Her soft dove-like eyes looked down at this lovely child.

"What are you going to call her?" she asked.

"I'll call her Colleen after that song your Tim sings," she said shyly.

" 'On the Colleen Bawn!' " exclaimed Mary. "A lovely Irish ballad. She'll grow up charming and clever, I'm very sure."

No mention of the missing father had been made so far—nor even of Uncle George. This was Lil's baby and she did not care who fathered it.

A few days later Mary was waiting anxiously for Tim to come home. Looking out of the window she saw him get out of a cab and she caught a glimpse of the blue-black plumes of

Rosie's hat. Tim staggered drunkenly down the road and the cab drove off.

"I'm sorry I'm late, me darlin'." He gave her a rough bear-like hug, but the whiskey fumes made her pull away from him. "Wassa matter?" he slurred. "Oi've only been up west with Rosie. She had to see her solicitor, Mary, me love," he said conversationally. "You should see the way folk live up there—it's really opened my eyes to what fools we are grubbing away for a few shillings."

"Tim," said Mary sharply, "if you are sober enough fetch the nurse, my time has come." Wearily she went up the stairs to her bed.

Immediately Tim ceased his rambling and swayed down the road to get the nurse.

In less than half an hour a small squalling little body lay on the bed beside Mary, a yellow little babe with a wrinkled face that looked as old as Adam. Mary looked down and felt sad for this little one. She did not know why, the baby just did not seem like the other children. I must think of a different kind of name for her, thought Mary, as she lay there, pale and exhausted. She ran through a long list of names in her head. Then she picked up the novel she had been reading. The heroine was called Abigail, a name quite unfamiliar to Mary. So her little girl assumed an identity.

The next evening Tim was on his way to the pub to celebrate the birth of his third child when he met Sam who was almost bouncing along the street. He wore black curly side-whiskers and a wide brimmed hat and his portly figure seemed almost buoyant as he came down the alley.

Tim touched his hat. "Evening, Sam."

It was customary for Sam to say "Good evening," and continue on his way. Tonight, however, he lingered, grasped Tim by the hand and announced with shining eyes: "I'm a father at last! Got a lovely son after ten years." He was positively jubilant.

"Well, congratulations, mate," responded Tim. "I've got a new daughter, so let's have a drink on it." He took hold of Sam's arm as if to steer him to the local, but Sam hesitated.

"No offense, Tim, but I've never gone into a public bar. You are welcome to join me any time in a glass of wine at my home."

"It's all right, old son," Tim gave him a hearty whack on

the back, "every man to his own taste. I'll come in and see you tomorrow." Leaving Sam on the pavement, Tim went into the pub and settled in his usual spot for the evening.

Owing to the excitement of the last two days Tim had been a trifle boozed and carefree. On the mantelpiece was a letter that had come the previous day and had so far remained unopened.

"Remind Uncle Tim that he's got a letter," said Mary to Arfer, who had come in to see the new baby and linger for a while.

"I'll get Uncle Tim to send me for some nice fish and chips," volunteered Arfer. "Nice and hot they are down at Coren's and he gives me cracklings for meself."

"There's a good boy," said Mary, "and here's extra money for you to buy chips. Don't eat them oily old cracklings."

After his tea Tim read his letter. Arfer just pushed it under his nose, then ran up the stairs to Mary.

"It's from old Dandy!" Tim burst out excitedly as he read it. "And guess what? The old devil has got himself married. Well, I'll be damned!" Tim was beside himself with pleasure at hearing from his cousin again.

Mary's cool slim hand took the letter. Tim watched her anxiously, wondering at her reaction. She read:

Dear Tim and Mary,

I am sorry I did not write to you before but you were never far away from my thoughts. I have found a wife while home in Ireland, she is a distant cousin born in the United States of America. I know both Mary and yourself would like to meet Maud. We are coming to London in a few weeks time and would very much like to visit in the alley, if we would be welcome.

My love to you both and the children.
Dandy Fitz

"Well," said Mary calmly as she perused the letter, "that's the best news I've heard in a long time. Dandy settled at last!"

"He will be made welcome, Mary darling?" Tim inquired anxiously.

"Don't be such a softy, you know he will," she replied.

"I'll get the back bedroom fixed up," decided Tim, "a nice bright bit of wallpaper."

The rest of the week, while Mary was still in bed, Tim spent his time preparing a room for his guests, whistling and singing, and buzzing in and out with jugs of beer and newspapers. Mary was content, sewing dresses for her new baby and listening to Tim's rich baritone as he sang songs of their homeland.

Tremendous preparations were made for the return of Dandy Fitz to Autumn Alley. Mary was very anxious to welcome this new bride properly, for she felt slightly guilty of the fuss she had made over that one small misdemeanor. In the past Dandy had been a good friend to her as well as Tim's inseparable companion.

That Dandy's wife was an American caused much debate in the alley. No one had ever had an American visit them before. The boys gathered on the canal wall to discuss the matter, as to how she would look, and every day Aunt Maud gained in stature and untold wealth, until she was a cross between a painted feathered Red Indian and a beautiful actress dripping with jewels.

When the cab halted that Saturday afternoon of their arrival, the boys stared open-mouthed at the tall, rather plainly dressed lady who alighted, a black felt hat pulled low on her brow. She wore a dark tailored suit. "No jewels, no furs, no fevvers," said Arfer sadly, "just some old bat all dressed in black." The boys' disappointment showed on their grubby faces. The tall fair lad who got out of the cab with her chanced to get George fair and square on the nose with a shot from a peashooter as his mother fussed with the cabby, who she was convinced had overcharged her. This attractive curly haired boy was called Larry—Maud's son by her first husband. He was a very precocious child and the apple of his mother's eye.

Dandy looked very smart with a square, hard hat and a coat with a fur collar. He was still very shy and quiet—marriage had not changed him. His wife on the other hand was like a breath of strong Atlantic breeze as she blew into the alley. She was more than thirty years old, tall and angular. Her short-sighted blue eyes would stare hard and then light up in merry humor. She had a wide mouth and uneven teeth. Mary liked her instantly but Tim, he was not so sure.

"She's like some old battered squawking hen," he remarked to Mary in the privacy of the kitchen.

"Oh, Tim," pleaded Mary, "don't be so unkind."

"Well," he groused, "surely old Dandy could have done a bit better than that."

"She is quite well off, you know," said Mary. "Love isn't everything."

"But attraction goes a long way," muttered Tim very disgruntled, for what aggravated him most was her voice; it was loud and vibrant, she drawled in that Yankee manner and pronounced each word with hefty vigor.

"My first husband, I divorced him," she told Mary quite unashamedly.

Mary surveyed Larry whom she found very charming and wondered where he fitted in.

"Never wanted to marry again," Maud announced in a loud tone, "but that old roué over there got me pregnant." Acutely embarrassed Dandy stared down at the floor. There was a moment of silence. Then, remembering her duty as a hostess, Mary said: "Well, now, Maud, how nice, when are you expecting?"

"In seven months!" shouted Maud, "I was two months gone before I got married."

Out in the street the kids heard every word for Maud's voice carried so well. Inside they all sat down to high tea—boiled ham, spuds, salad, and plenty of sweet things and cakes. The atmosphere was slightly uncomfortable at first but it soon eased, as it was impossible not to enjoy the forthright conversation of Maud Fitzpatrick. The mass of mat-like hair piled high made her head look rather large, and underneath the mass she wore a kind of artificial bun that was supposed to make her hair seem even more plentiful. This unruly mass bobbed and shook as she regaled them with endless stories of the folks back home.

She told her avid listeners about how her parents had emigrated to America from Ireland some forty years before. She herself was born in Boston when her father had become quite well-to-do. At the age of nineteen she married a flashy but unreliable American who swept her off her feet and gave her a son. But soon the marriage was in ruins, and much to the shame of her family Maud obtained a divorce. To escape the disapproval she took her young son across the ocean to

Ireland where her relatives gladly took her in. And it was there that she met Dandy Fitzpatrick.

"I'll never go back to the States," she informed them. "And now I ain't so popular in the Emerald Isle either. That darned old village priest didn't like the idea of remarrying a divorcee, so we crossed to Liverpool and got spliced in one of them registry offices."

Mary was terribly shocked but there was something about Maud, and Mary's generous heart went out to her. And Maud adored Mary on sight.

The evening could be considered a reasonable amount of success. Lil and Uncle George came round, and Tim and Dandy brought back beer and port wine from the pub. Jigs and reels were danced and many Irish songs were sung, the star of the evening being Arfer, who blew out his chest manfully and rendered an almighty chorus of "Land of Hope and Glory."

Tim was in a strange mood, but his blue eyes gleamed in amusement at Arfer.

"Be Jasus," he asked, "who teaches that stuff? Ain't they pinched enough territory, those bloody imperialists?"

"Hush, Tim," remonstrated Mary, "'tis what the children learn at school."

"Bad cess to the blighters that teach them," grumbled Tim.

"No, they don't," piped up Arfer, "'cause I never go to school."

"Don't go to school?" broke in Maud. "Why not?"

"Don't like it," said Arfer grabbing some biscuits and making off.

So the conversation turned to politics. Maud stood up to Tim—she was against these new-fangled socialists. Tim objected to the way the Americans cornered the money markets —capitalist swine, he called them—so Mary decided it was time to break up the party.

Later in bed she reprimanded Tim. "It's not nice to argue with a woman," she insisted.

"Some woman!" snorted Tim. "Let them keep their place. All this talk of votes for women and equality when there are not enough jobs to go around for the men. They'll cause plenty trouble, women like her."

"Oh, shut up, Tim!" snapped Mary wearily turning on her side. She did not really understand it anyway; her home and her children were all she cared about. But Maud was certainly very forthright—whatever had made placid little Dandy choose her for a mate?

From December to February Dandy and Maud occupied Mary's spare room and Tim stayed out of Maud's way. Mary got on well with Maud. She would rise very early and clean the whole house, giving Mary more time to devote to her sickly child. Then Maud would march down the road with a big shopping bag and, regardless of the expense, buy enough food to fill up the larder. She cooked and washed, and kept an eye on every move the kids made out in the alley.

Larry had now joined the boys on the canal wall. He was full of mischief and had plenty of pocket money. George, who was nearly fifteen, took Larry to see the sights up in town and found him pleasant and amusing company. For a ten-year-old, Larry knew a lot about girls and gave George some advice with regard to that girl over the road who was so shy and unapproachable. He knew plenty and brought fun and variety to our alley and even vied with Arfer for popularity.

When Maud acquired the empty house at the end of the row from Rosie, Tim was relieved; he was so glad to get her out of his own house.

Maud's black-clad figure had swept into the coffee shop and taken Rosie by surprise.

"How much are you asking for that damned old house?" inquired Maud in her raucous voice.

"Well, Gran charged five bob a week. When I got around to having it done up, I was going to put the rent up a bit . . . Let's say six," said Rosie determined to let this odd-looking woman know she was in business.

Maud dived deep into her capacious handbag and brought out a velvet purse.

"In here is seventy-five gold sovereigns. Do you want them or not? I'll buy that old dwelling lock, stock and barrel."

Rosie's eyes gleamed greedily. Who had that sort of money these days? "Well, let's sit down," she said. "I'll think on it."

"So you ain't selling then?" asked Maud, starting to stuff the money back into her handbag.

"I never said no," gasped Rosie.

"Well, then?" demanded Maud. "What's it to be?"

Speechless, Rosie just nodded her head.

"Right then," declared Maud grabbing Rosie's hand and

pumping it up and down, "bargain's made. Here's the money. I'll send my solicitor around tomorrow to make it legal. If you can't write, put a mark of some sort on this here piece of paper—just in case."

Rosie's stubby fingers wrote her name slowly in Maud's notebook and then Maud bustled off out again, the first owner-occupier in Autumn Alley.

In no time she had the windows ripped out and replaced by larger ones. Then the floorboards were repaired. In two months the house had completely changed. Wrought-iron railings now surrounded the house, concrete posts with Grecian urns on top stood outside the front door, and the back yard was freshly paved. Indeed, there seemed to be no end to the improvements she was making. When finally it was finished, it looked very smart, with lace curtains and an aspidistra in the window and carpet going all the way up the stairs, held in place with shiny brass stair rods. The crowning glory was a bathroom, an unheard of thing in the alley, built on at the end of the scullery.

While the work was in progress, Maud hovered about like a huge bat, making more noise and creating more tension than half a dozen workmen. Lil was green with envy and Becky, who was now back home wih her fat cuddly baby boy, could not believe her eyes. Mary was not bothered, she had other things on her mind; she worried over Abigail, a whining, grizzling little baby who would not take her food and had spasmodic attacks when her limbs went stiff and her eyes seemed unable to focus.

"I'm afraid, Tim," Mary confessed one day. "I don't like the looks of those attacks."

"Don't worry, my love," he consoled her, "she's probably got my Irish temper—that's what the screaming's all about."

So Tim, not much bothered, went off to drink with Dandy; now they were both at work together, and Tim saw much less of Rosie. Mary sat beside the crib watching every movement of that little child.

"Stop watching her," Lil would say. "She'll thrive—just look how my Colleen has got on."

Mary would look at the lovely Colleen sitting up chewing a crust with a ready smile for anyone who passed by, and she would get even more anxious for her sickly baby.

Lil looked very well these days. Uncle George had now

taken up permanent residence with her, and even parked his cart outside the door while his pony still grazed on the wasteland beside the canal. He was kind and good to Lil and patient with the boys and very fond of the new baby. Life was much easier next door. Lil left off swilling stout and wore a new dress and walked with Mary in the park along with all the children. Sometimes they passed Becky, proudly wheeling her son Lesley. With his black curly hair and brown healthy limbs, he was a bonny boy. Mary would stop a while to praise him but Lil would sniff loudly and go straight on.

The months passed by and still Abigail made little headway.

"It's no good, Tim, I can't stand it any longer, I must get proper medical advice," cried Mary. "I'll take her to the new clinic up in the city. I've heard that they're very good."

The young doctor at the poor man's dispensary looked admiringly at this tall good-looking woman with her gentle manner and the small crying baby on her lap.

"Any epilepsy in the family?" he asked.

Mary looked afraid. "Do you mean fits?" she asked.

"Well, something similar," he replied, "it could be hereditary or something else—we just can't be sure."

"Oh, dear God!" burst out Mary. "Do you mean she won't live?"

"No, no, she'll be all right," he assured her. "The child might even grow out of them, but she's going to need a lot of care until she's about seven."

"Oh, my poor little darling," wept Mary, holding her baby close.

"No, don't get so upset," he advised her, "she will sense it and this child must have a very peaceful existence. You seem to be a very good mother, the battle is not yet lost and we will help you all we can."

That night Mary sobbed her heart out in Tim's arms. "To think I brought a little one into the world to suffer, I simply can't bear it."

"Pull yourself together, Mary," he begged. "Remember there are two other children to be considered. The little one may come through all right, but we're still young, there's plenty of time for more children."

"I will never have another child," Mary declared emotionally.

"Calm down, love, of course you will," said Tim rather dismayed.

"Oh, 'tis fine," she cried, "to tell us to have children for the faith, but that old priest does not have the heartbreak and worry to bring them up. I'll have no more."

That the gentle Mary was actually rebelling against her church Tim just could not believe, but she was adamant. From then on the marriage bed became a cold, unwelcoming place. Convinced that she could not fall for a child if she was unroused, Mary lay passive like a sack of potatoes when Tim tried to make love.

"It is the will of God, Mary," he tried to convince her, "if you are to bear children. Such an attitude will make no difference."

But Mary was determined and would not give in and finally Tim cooled off and left her alone.

The children grew, and even little Abigail began to toddle; the care and the medicine were taking effect. Sometimes she went into a fit but her mother was always there to hold down her tongue with a spoon and to cuddle her until the fit had subsided. Mary's whole being was wrapped up in that child. Both Lil and Becky noticed the change in her. She had grown very thin and seldom laughed nowadays. And she was always up at the church, little Abigail beside her.

Maud Fitzpatrick had given birth to a little girl whom she called Patricia—a pretty little thing with jet black hair which Maud always tied up with a scarlet bow. Larry had gone away to school in America, and Dandy was now his own boss. Outside their house was a painted board that read: "Fitzpatrick Ltd, Road Contractors." Maud had set him up in business. It was a freelance road repairing firm and Tim worked for him.

Now that school had become compulsory Billy and Arfer were forced to attend and with George working all day in a factory, the alley was fairly quiet during the day. The new generation were put out in their prams: there was Patricia with a scarlet bow in her hair; and Colleen just a bit older with a blue bow in her hair—Lil was not allowing Maud any advantage; over the road lay Becky's fat lusty kicking baby, Lesley. All were now in the second year of their lives and gurgling; baby talk was the order of the day. Only little

Abigail lay quiet, her strange eyes seeing very little, her mouth constantly drooling and dribbling. Mary watched her all the time.

Since that dreadful murder, more than two years ago, the shop on the corner had remained empty. The boys used to play in it, pretending they had seen a ghost. It was a big surprise when workmen arrived and pulled the front down and rebuilt it, put in big glass windows and over the door painted a sign which said: "Rosie's Transport Cafe." Inside it was furnished with marble-top tables, and a counter with a tea urn on it. Rosie had come back to the alley to live. She modernized the flat above the shop and moved in. From her front door Mary could see Rosie's fat arms and flowered overall as she poured out cups of tea for the wagon drivers who worked for Carter Paterson and the railway whose depots were all on the main road. Mary's sad eyes watched Rosie's blonde hair shining in the sun and she heard her loud voice as she called out to Tim on his way to work. Mary was not sure why but for some reason it made her feel uncomfortable.

The outside world was changing but the pattern of life in the alley went on just the same. A cafe on the corner now instead of a shop, three ever-open doors and women gossiping, prams outside three houses and the boys still playing on the canal wall. Only one house remained with curtains drawn and was as silent as the grave—No. 5—where Hannah Brown quietly faded away, getting thinner each day. No longer was her daughter her willing slave; more times than she cared to remember she awoke to find the house empty and had called in vain for a glass of water to quench her parched throat. Ellen had discovered a secret life of her own and could be found most evenings sitting in the park with George, hand in hand, heads close together.

# *Young Love*

AT SEVEN O'CLOCK THE FACTORY HOOTER SENT OUT a shrill cry, the wide gates opened and the grimy workers poured out. One of these was George. His white curls were obscured by a greasy cap and the black oil on his face emphasized the broad grin and the white teeth as he saw Ellen waiting on the corner as she did each evening.

She was a slim little figure in a long, old-fashioned brown coat and a plain straw boater. Her long plaits were now twisted into a neat knot at the nape of her neck. In her hand was a little parcel (she never came without one). This was George's meal—neat sandwiches and a piece of homemade cake.

Her face lit up as he came toward her, then hand in hand they walked to the park. It was very secluded in the newly opened park which had been named after the late queen. There were miles of open space and little creeper-covered arbors where lovers could leave the world behind.

Ellen would watch George rather hungrily while he scoffed the food. Little did he know how careful she had to be to get so much food from that parsimonious home. With her head on his greasy shoulder they would talk until he finished

72

eating. Then in the shadow of those tall trees their love and need for each other overwhelmed them. Making love in the long grass was a form of entertainment that cost nothing and it was all they did these days. All fears and religious scruples were forgotten; they were just two healthy young beings and very much in love.

At fifteen minutes to ten they parted. Ellen's slim figure skipped along in front and George's stocky shape came several yards behind. No one should see them together—that was a pact that they had made. Ellen was still terribly afraid of her father and George was bashful, he must not let that little monkey Arfer see him with Ellen.

But Arfer seldom missed a thing and one night while his brother was undressing for bed, Arfer's squeaky voice came out of the dark: "Got a tart, ain't yer? I saw yer in the park."

"Be quiet, you nosy little swine," hissed George, putting his hand over his brother's mouth.

"Give us a tanner and I'll not tell," came Arfer's muffled voice. So he got his blood money and he never told, well, not many people—just his close friend and brother Billy, Mary next door and some kids at school. Thus it became generally known that George Welton was courting that skinny Sunday school teacher from over the road.

Ellen felt so guilty whenever the thin wavering voice of her mother called out: "Where have you been all evening? I was calling out for you to get me a drink."

"Only for a walk, Mother," Ellen would reply softly.

Hannah lay silent. She sensed that something was going on and prayed that her daughter would find the happiness which had always eluded her.

The two young lovers had been meeting in secret for almost three years. They were young and immature but each taught the other so much. George in his sweet shy way had guided Ellen from her narrow Quaker upbringing to a world she had only dreamed of. On Saturdays they walked along the tow path, beside the canal, the smooth green oily water flowing placidly past them. Every so often there came a long barge pulled by great shire horses, their massive muscles bulging as they strained at the ropes, little children waved from the gaily painted barge, Ellen and George stood hand in hand just looking.

"That's just what I'd like to do," said George, "be a bargee."

"Well, why not?"

"It's not so easy," replied George, "most of those chaps have been born on those barges."

"It would be a lovely life," said Ellen dreamily.

George agreed. "At least they're moving, not stuck in a dirty factory all day. Don't think I'm going to stand it all my life," he muttered gloomily.

"If my mother dies," declared Ellen, "I shall run away. I hate my father."

George put a protective arm about her. "We will run away together," he told her, "to my island, that island of my dreams, where there are blue skies and golden sands and the sun shines always."

With love shining in her eyes, she drew close to him. "Don't ever go away from me, will you, George?"

"No, darling, I promise I'll never leave you," he vowed. "As soon as I'm nineteen we'll be married and travel the world together." Rash promises of youth.

They paused under a low bridge against the cool damp wall, pressed close together away from the prying eyes, lost in that dreamland of lovers.

On Sunday Ellen still attended the mission hall where she gave religious instruction to the poor children of the district. They came in from the cold to listen to the words of Jesus. Ellen's voice was soft and soothing and she made the Bible stories interesting. The elders of the chapel disapproved of her flowery speech and the lighthearted manner in which she taught the children, but were forced to admit she was popular and brought the local children into the chapel where they deposited their farthings and halfpennies into the plate. Arfer was a regular, being chased out of the house on Sunday afternoon as his mum still liked to have a lay down with Uncle George. Arfer would sing the hymns lustily cuffing that everlasting dewdrop from his nose all the time. When the service was over he would collect the hymn books, informing his friends in a loud whisper that the Sunday school teacher was his brother's tart.

Ellen's pale austere face seldom relaxed, but there was often a glint of amusement in her eyes at Arfer's antics. It would disappear quickly as she caught a glimpse of the red choleric face of her father as he sat in the entrance with the green baize collecting plate always in front of him. Since the twins had left home he did not often address Ellen or her mother. He kept himself remote, except for the occasional outbursts of ranting and raving.

To Ellen those black beady eyes seemed always to be watching her. If she chanced to level her gaze to his she shivered, so afraid was she that her secret would be disclosed. Hannah Brown was now too sick to attend the mission and lay at home worrying over Ellen and mourning the loss of her twin sons.

The rest of the alley constantly discussed the young lovers.

"Stay away from those barmy buggers," Lil was heard to yell at George, "that gel will only bring you trouble."

"Funny affair, that odd-looking girl and young George," Tim remarked to Mary.

That winter Hannah Brown passed on. Not much interest was shown in the alley, most of the residents had not seen her for years. The only difference seemed to be that Ellen Brown now wore a black dress instead of a brown one. Her father had taken to marching up and down the market with a sandwich board on his back that called on all to repent because the end of the world was nigh. Only Arfer knew that Ellen and George never made love in the park these days. He had seen George's blond head come over the wall just before ten each evening having spent the time in Ellen's house, but Arfer took his tanner and said nought. Now that he was older there were always plenty of diversions for him in our alley on Saturday evenings. When the barrel-organ man came and one and all gathered to listen to him, it meant big business for Arfer; he took the white pocket around to collect the pennies while the wrinkled old man turned the handle that ground out the music. Men, women and children gathered to listen and all the children danced, including the three youngest, Colleen, Patricia and Lesley, or Lew, as he was called for short.

Lil was still happy with Uncle George; he catered for her every need, bought her pretty things, took her out to shows and was kind and understanding. Often well boozed he would waltz with her around the barrel organ.

It was such a night as this in early summer, all the alley was out of doors—the men on the corner, the women at their front doors, all the children sat on the curbside to watch the show. Tim had given them money for sweets, and Arfer, in bare feet and short, ragged knee-length trousers, was master of ceremonies. The old organ grinder was refreshed by an occasional beer and a good time was had by all. At ten o'clock the old man picked up the shafts of the organ and trundled off while the children went home to bed.

Mary lay awake until after midnight. She was worrying over Abby. Had the excitement been too much for the child? Would she have a fit? Tim snored beside her as his wife lay wide-awake in the dark listening for the slightest movement from the cot in the corner, when along the cobbles of the alley came slow ponderous footsteps. Mary listened intently; they had a familiar sound. Tim was home, and so was Dandy. Who could be out so late? The footsteps stopped next door, she heard the turn of a latch-key, a moment's suspense. Then an unearthly screeching, yelling and bumping came from next door. Mary did not have to be told. After more than five years of absence, Bill Welton had returned to find his brother in bed with his wife. In his inimitable fashion, Bill took the law into his own hands and proceeded to beat both of them up. Lights came on, the whole alley was aroused, all watching from their windows the mêlée going on in the Weltons' house. Loud cries and oaths could be heard as Bill and George fought it out in the passage. Arfer dashed out into the street barefoot wearing only a baggy pair of underpants. Billy and young George seemed to be trying to prevent Lil from dashing in to protect her lover. Suddenly, like a rat from a trap, out of the front door sprang Uncle George with his long-tailed nightshirt streaming out behind him like a sail in the wind. He made off down the alley with Bill a yard or so behind him waving an old service revolver. The neighbors held their breath but George had a head start on Bill who was not in such good condition. Little Arfer had run like the wind in front of them, and getting to the horse first, the boy roused the old mare and put her into the shafts so that Uncle George could make a quick getaway.

Pale and breathless, George was limping on to the cart when up blundered Bill. He fell over the dangling reins and the pistol went off. This was too much for the mare; she bolted, tossing Uncle George upside down in the cart, his bare backside exposed for all to view, as he, the horse and cart disappeared out of the alley. For little Arfer hiding in the grass, that was the last look he ever had of Uncle George.

Bill Welton picked himself up and charged off using the most dreadful swear words. Windows were flung open and the population of the main road came over to watch the uproar until the men in blue arrived and took Bill down to his old abode, Bow Road Police Station.

"Gee," said Arfer to his brother, "it wasn't 'alf exciting—just like Buffalo Bill."

But it did not end there. Early Sunday morning the police let Bill out. He came straight home and started to beat up Lil. The two older boys tried to defend her while Arfer danced up and down uttering shrill cries just like a monkey.

Tim was trying hard to get some well-earned sleep. It had been a hectic night. The child had had a bad fit and Mary, pale and wan, was walking up and down with the whimpering girl in her arms. Then they began again next door, shrieking, fighting, crashing and banging. Without a word, Tim got out of bed, heaved on his pants and stuck his feet into his slippers. Walking with slow determination, he went around next door. There was a frightful scene. Lil lay on the floor and Bill was aiming heavy kicks at her. George was hanging on to his father's back and Billy was making feeble efforts to spar up to him. In two strides Tim was inside and with one quick upper cut he knocked Bill Welton out cold.

"Look after your ma," he said to the boys. "Now perhaps we'll all get some sleep."

Mary smiled quietly when she saw him come back and climb slowly into bed, no temper, just calmly assertive. She thought how lucky she was to have a man who never raised a hand to his children. There was nothing violent about him, and only under extreme provocation would he fight.

She laid the child, now sleeping, in her cot and went next door to attend to Lil.

So with a series of big explosive disturbances Bill Welton returned to the alley. For a time all was peaceful. He did not work but spent most of the day standing on the street corner or in the pub. Traveling overseas had changed him very little; he was broader, a little fatter and as sly and as villainous as ever. Somewhere he had acquired a new suit in flashy checked cloth with a new style high-necked waistcoat. Over his pot belly he wore a big watch chain at the end of which was an enormous gold watch. With his hands behind his back, Bill would stand looking pompous at the edge of the pavement watching the pub door and repeatedly taking out his magnificent watch to look at the time, picking on whoever showed the slightest interest to tell them fantastic stories of his supposed exploits in the Boer War. Tim, on his way to and from work, would eye him contemptuously. "Won the war yet?" he would call out with a smile.

Like a bantam cock, Bill would strut and squawk. "Fought for me country, I did," he would shout in reply. Then, when Tim was safely out of earshot he would add: "Not like you Irish bastards, coming here and pouncing on it."

Eventually the gold watch went to the pawn shop and Bill back to his old gambling haunts in the East End. Lil heaved her backside, which was gradually getting fatter, off the windowsill and went up the road to work in the match factory, and the kids were left to play in the street.

# An Unhappy Climax
# for Mary

THE YEARS HAD NOT BEEN KIND TO MARY. SHE HAD aged considerably since Abby's birth; there were silver patches each side of her temples and a hollow in the slender neck that had once been so elegant. Those large greeny eyes, that Tim used to say were as deep as the lakes of Killarney and forever changing color, had lost their sunshine and were now so sad. More and more Mary was tied to the home while Tim spent less time there. All week he was away, working with Dandy who had recently obtained a good contract for the new Great North Road, and at weekends he boozed with Dandy in the Railway Arms or spent his time in the cafe chatting to Rosie who still drifted from lover to lover but always had a smile for Tim.

Mollie was six and Timmo twelve. They attended the local Roman Catholic school and both were pleasant, well-behaved children, though very independent. They had to be, since Mary was always so tied up with Abby, and Tim so seldom at home. Timmo was a young edition of Tim; the same strong build and the same red-gold hair. He was a roamer and always off out somewhere; he belonged to the scouts and served as an altar boy in church on Sundays. Dressed in a long white surplice, his hair gleaming in the candlelight, he no longer seemed to need them. His reaction to Abby was very strange; he avoided her, pretending not to notice her.

Mollie, very pale with dark eyes, was a silent moody child who stared resentfully at this screaming sister that made her mother so unhappy. Mollie did little things to help Mary—made tea, ran errands—but she would never look after Abby. She was afraid of her. Mollie did not know why but she often felt an awful terror when, lying awake at night, she heard her father's faltering footsteps climbing the stairs. Then it would begin, whispering and rustling, her mother's voice pleading, then loud curses from her father until he dashed downstairs and out of the front door. From the bedroom would come the sounds of her mother's heartbreaking sobs. Little Mollie would lie there in her bed, sweating and shivering. What was this terrible thing that went on?

All the next day Mollie would sit and watch her mother intently. With anxious eyes, her mouth tight and unsmiling, Mary would say: "Why don't you go out and play, darling?" But Mollie stuck tight as if afraid to leave her mother.

Tim and Dandy got drunk most nights, Dandy valiantly assisting his friend to drown his troubles.

After Mary had had one long harassing Saturday with the children, they arrived home drunk and very boisterous. They had bottles of whiskey in their pockets and several of their drinking companions in tow, one being Lil who had recently acquired a taste for gin. "We will have a bit of a party," said Tim. "I've bought you some stout, Mary."

His wife's pale face stared unsmiling at him but in his alcoholic haze he did not even notice her disapproval. The chairs were all put out in the passage and the front window thrown wide open. The party got under way and Dandy, in a very inebriated condition, scraped out tunes on his old fiddle, and jigs were danced until the boards in the parlor creaked. Then, in his rich baritone, Tim sang all his favorite songs. All the alley kids left their beds to peer in through the window. The whole street was roused. Amid all this sat Mary, as still as a graceful statue, a whimpering child on her lap. There was a peculiar tension in the air.

Tim began a heart-rending ballad from the Emerald Isle:

> "I'll take you home again, Kathleen,
> Across the ocean wide and wide,

*To where your heart has ever been,*
*Since first you were my bonny bride.*
*The roses all have left your cheek,*
*I've watched them fade away and die.*
*Your voice is sad whene'er you*
    *speak,*
*And tear drops fill your loving eyes."*

Suddenly Tim's voice broke and he realized that he and Mary were the only two people in the room. A world of tears washed over them. Mary sat still and silent clasping the sick child to her breast. As she stared at Tim the song died on his lips and he stood in the middle of the room just looking at Mary.

"Well now, pull yourself together, Tim," he muttered drunkenly. "The old beer has destroyed me voice for sure."

But the party had fizzled out.

"What's the matter with Mary?" inquired Lil of Dandy as they made their way to their own homes. "She looked very funny tonight. Do you think she's found Tim out?"

"What are ye jabbering about, woman?" snarled Dandy, who was often very nasty in drink.

"Oh, you know, you crafty old sod," yelled Lil and went in and banged her front door. But she was worried about Mary, there had been a strange look in her eyes. In spite of Mary's disapproval of her dissolute ways Lil cared very much for her.

Mary also still had a great champion in little Arfer. Now very grown up, he no longer sniffed. The council school had rigged him up with some steel-rimmed specs that had straightened his eye. He still loved Aunt Mary, memories of a hot fire and buttered toast remained with him. He came each day to tell her of the happenings at the council school. Mary would make him a cuppa and find him a piece of homemade cake and he lingered, helping to amuse Abby, bringing a smile to Mary's sad face.

Mary would trust no one but Arfer with Abby. He would guide the child around the small paved yard, straps holding her up on her wobbly legs. "Come on," he would say, "let's play gee gees," and the child's frail little legs would go up and down and she would gurgle and dribble with pleasure. Mary would watch them through the back window, the window that was now bordered by the splendid Virginia creeper that she had planted in a bucket when she first came to the alley more than ten years ago, the window where Mary spent many hours looking out, dreaming of the green meadows back home.

That night after the unfortunate party it was Arfer who returned to wash the glasses, tidy the room and chase all the kids back to bed. Mary lay in bed, sleepless, deep in thought. Tim did not go upstairs but stretched out snoring on the kitchen floor. Arfer turned out the lights and closed the front door. His heart was heavy; something was definitely wrong with Aunt Mary.

On Sunday morning Mary still lay silent and wide-eyed. Tim came up very sheepishly with a cup of tea.

"Here ye are, me darlin', a nice cup o' tay."

She sat up, her large eyes looked at him with deep reproach. Tim looked away.

"Don't get up for early Mass, dear, I'll take the children." He was falling over himself to please her and was not quite sure why.

Then from a tight drawn mouth came the words, "Tim, I want to go home."

Tim was flummoxed for a moment, then he said: "Of course, me wild darlin'. We'll go on a holiday in the New Year, when the job on the North Road is finished."

She shook her head. "No, Tim, I mean forever."

"Don't be silly, Mary, I can't get a living in me own land. How am I supposed to support you all?"

"Let's go back to Ireland," she pleaded, "live in an old shack, anything but this soul-destroying misery." Mary's voice broke as she spoke but Tim was annoyed and rose from the bed.

"Look here, Mary, it's got to stop. You're making life hell for us all over that child." He looked down at the sleeping Abby.

"You're a heartless man, Timothy Murphy," she reproached him. "I'll take her home myself and may God in His mercy make her well once I leave this den of drunkenness and iniquity."

"Stop this nonsense," he said abruptly. "We all know the child won't live. For God's sake, why can't you accept it?"

Mary put her hands over her face as if to shut out the sight of him. "Go!" she sobbed. "Leave me alone. I hate you!"

Tim went off to find Dandy who had already left for church, then after Mass they retired to the pub.

Mary was still lying in bed at twelve-thirty when Lil bustled in.

"Ain't you well, Mary?" she asked. Her moon face looked so worried; it was not like Mary to sleep late, nor Abby. Lil looked down at Abby lying in the cot. There was something different about the child but she passed no comment to Mary and offered her a small bottle. "Have a drop, love. It's gin, it'll buck you up."

Mary refused. "I'll get up, Lil, and we'll have a cuppa."

Outside, Colleen, still in her nightie, was repeatedly jumping down the last three stairs. Mollie sat disconsolately at the bottom.

"Get out in the bleeding street!" Lil screamed at them as she went to put the kettle on for Mary.

At last, dressed and with her hair pinned up neat and tidy, Mary emerged and came slowly down the stairs.

Lil looked at Mary in admiration. "Gawd," she said, "you don't 'alf look smart—even when you first gets up. I wish I could."

Mary did not laugh gaily as she normally did, she just sat very still while Lil poured the tea.

"Cheer up, love," coaxed Lil. "What's on your mind? Get it off your chest, and it won't hurt so much."

"I'm going home to Ireland," Mary said quietly.

"Forever? All of you?" Lil's cow-like eyes nearly popped out of her head. "Oh no, Mary! Don't go away!" Lil was quite incoherent with shock.

"I'm convinced that Abby will get well if I take her home."

"Don't torture yourself, love," cried Lil. "Those children seldom live to their teens."

"Oh dear God!" burst out Mary. "Leave me alone, Lil. You're as bad as Tim."

Lil began to look very miserable. "But Tim loves you, Mary, and you're so cold to him. He's only human after all," Lil made excuses for Tim; no one was ever brave enough to mention Rosie.

"Kindly mind your own business," said Mary tartly and Lil, with tears in her eyes, went home.

Around two o'clock the alley grew quiet. It was time for
Sunday dinner; the pub had shut and all had gone home to
eat. On this crisp November day it seemed more than usually
silent. Mary was still sitting at the kitchen table and there was
no sign of dinner. The hungry children had congregated down
by the canal wall.

Mary roused herself suddenly to realize that Abby was not
awake yet and it was lunchtime. Terrified, she ran upstairs but
the little one lay white and still. One last fit had ended her
misery. Mary snatched up the still body and tried to breathe
air into the tiny lungs. Then she ran frantically down the stairs
and held the child's head under the tap. In a terrible panic,
she ran out into the alley carrying the small, slowly stiffening
body in her arms. Scream after scream issued from her—
terrible heart-rending screams that rose up and up encircling
the alley. All around windows were flung open, the children
stopped playing, and Mary stood with her hair streaming out
behind her and the dead child in her arms. Rosie's window
suddenly opened wide and the blonde tousled head appeared.
Blouse undone, bosoms exposed, she hung out of the window
staring in amazement at Mary. From her side door dashed
Tim. He had no shoes on his feet and pulled up his braces as
he ran. All eyes went from Mary to Tim and several dropped
their heads in sympathy. Mary, still clutching the child,
crashed to the ground just as Tim reached her. Lil was on her
doorstep and Becky on hers; both cried real tears for Mary
and her little one.

After the ambulance had taken Mary and the dead child
away, Lil, full of gin and her sleeves rolled up, banged on
Rosie's door and challenged her to come out for a fight.
"Bloody whore! I'll paste the daylight out of yer," screamed
Lil. Rosie, however, was hiding. Stupid with drink, Lil wept
for Mary and her little one.

When Mary came out of the hospital her hair had gone
almost white and there was a nervous twitch to the side of her
mouth. She went about her duties in the house with a
zombie-like indifference. It was as though Mary had gone
with little Abby and there was only the frame left. After
several miserable weeks Tim was so desperate that he sent
Mary and little Mollie back to Ireland to live with Mary's
mother, and the neat house became silent and neglected.
Timmo, now aged fourteen, started work on the road with his

father. They lived on pease pudding and faggots, or fish and chips in newspaper, and they muddled along.

Maud and Lil wept together in earnest when they talked about Mary and the death of little Abby.

"That whore over the road, all her fault," announced Lil venomously.

"Poor gentle Mary," whispered Maud. "Wait till I get that bastard Tim."

"Loved her like a sister, I did," wept Lil, downing the brandy Maud had given her.

"Don't worry, Lil," Maud consoled her, "I'll have that fat Rosie from her den."

# *George Goes Away*

ELLEN BROWN RAN DOWN THE ROAD TO MEET George. After her mother died she had got herself a job as an assistant in a newspaper office in the city. She had just been given a raise, and with her earnings in her bag, she felt she had a small fortune. Now she and George would be married and they could leave that dreary alley and live in a nice flat facing the park. Once she was married she would never go near that grim house ever again.

With all these thoughts buzzing about in her head she went to meet her lover. Since he had lost his job, George always came to meet her too. Ellen had egged him on to ask for a raise and the result had been instant dismissal. George, a very willing, conscientious boy, had worked hard since he was twelve and was still only earning thirty shillings a week at eighteen. Ellen wanted to be married and so did George, but when he asked for sufficient money to live on he got the sack and a younger lad replaced him. For the last three months he had decorated the opposite side of the street to the one his father lounged on and whiled away the long evenings by walking to the city to meet Ellen. He had grown shabby of late and there was a kind of hang-dog look about his fine features; his complexion had been destroyed by the dirty factory and his skin was now a mass of pimples and enlarged pores. That once attractive youth had become a rather seedy-looking character as he approached manhood.

George was leaning against a wall, very downcast, cap over his eyes. She wished he had more go in him but never mind, she thought, now she could earn for them both. Hugging her secret tight as she approached, she looked forward to giving him the news of her raise, of their little nest egg; it would cheer him up. A thrill passed through her at the touch of his hand as he took hers. They went on their regular walk. Ellen wanted to chat but George was peculiarly excited; he wanted to talk as well.

"Guess what?" he said. "Me mother's heard from Uncle George."

"Really?" she replied. "Is he all right?"

"Yes, he's fine—he's out in Australia, and he's asked me to come over. Got a good job for me, he says. Runs a blacksmith's business out there. Wants me to work with him—what a break, eh?" His voice rose excitedly.

Ellen's face paled, her voice trembled.

"Go over where?" she asked.

"To Australia, my love, the land of milk and honey."

"But, George, dear, I thought we were going to be married at Christmas?"

"We will, darling, but just give me one more year and I'll build the grandest home for you out there. Think of it—blue sky and fresh air—you'll love it."

"Can't I go with you, George?" she queried.

He looked down at the pavement and said:

"I'm sorry, love. I must be single to get the government grant, but I promise I'll send for you as soon as I'm settled out there."

Ellen nodded sadly but she had complete trust in him.

"I might even get over before this Christmas if I can get ten pounds for the fare. I was thinking of asking old Rosie to lend me the money."

Ellen sighed and clutched her little bag very tight. He was going to borrow the fare; he could not get away from her quick enough. She could not bear it. Tears of self-pity ran down her cheeks.

George swept her into his arms and held her close. "Don't

cry, my love. I won't go. I couldn't bear to think of you fretting."

"It's a good opportunity for you," she sobbed, "you must go."

"I was thinking of the job you see. If I don't go soon I might lose it. Old George might take on someone else and forget about me," he said pathetically.

Ellen stared at him. He was so sincere, he could not help being so. She opened her bag and produced the money.

"It was for our wedding, dear, but I'll wait."

"Ten pounds!" he gasped. "How did you manage to save all that?"

Ellen never got a chance to explain for George was off into his dream world once more. "I'll buy some land and build a house in my spare time—that's what they all do out there." She held tightly onto his arm as they walked home to the alley and kissed goodnight on the doorstep.

Ellen went into the gloomy house with its dark red curtains. She felt numb. How was she going to get through a whole year without him? She must work hard, she thought, extra hard. A slight cough from the parlor reminded her that she was not alone; her father still lived, but there was nothing left there—he grew more remote every day.

Once she was in bed, Ellen tossed restlessly. How she wished she was like the girls at the match factory; practically all of them had to get married, and came out of church with big stomachs. Then a terrible thought crossed her mind; she might be barren, never bear a child; after all, she and George had been lovers for more than a year. And if she did bear his child how could she be sure George would return to her? Or would he change his mind about leaving her? "Oh God, how wicked I am," she cried into her pillow, "but, I love you so, George."

The setting sun was like a red ball of fire floating in a sea of black storm clouds and the dome of St. Paul's stood out starkly against the horizon. Ellen leaned over the balustrade of Tower Bridge to get a better view down river. She was dry eyed; there were no more tears, she had cried them all out as she had watched the ship glide down the Thames to the open sea; she could still see the little puffs of smoke it had left in its wake. On board was her lover, kind, gentle George, off to a new world to seek a living, something he had found impossible in the land of his birth. It was all wrong somehow. Why was life so hard on the young? They only needed to eat, love and be together. Quietly she dreamed, thinking of the hundred other wives, sweethearts and mothers who had watched their loved ones sail away; she wondered how many would ever meet again. The last three weeks had been wonderful—she might even bear his child. But it did not matter, she would work hard and eventually join him.

She slowly turned toward home and the alley. It was cold. Her hands and feet were chilled. The people who passed her looked cold also. There was so much poverty and it always got worse in the winter. Now the miners were on strike and coal was in short supply. Little children ran past her with blue bare feet, red noses and faces mottled with cold, running back to some verminous tenement they called home and shared with numerous brothers and sisters. Surely there must be a way to change all this, the rich so rich, the poor so poor.

In the main road stood the brand new free library—one of the feeble attempts to improve the working-class minds. It was much warmer in the library than at home and this was where Ellen spent the best part of her leisure hours that winter, voraciously consuming books on every subject. That lonely winter passed more quickly, from office to library and from there home to a cold bed. George had been gone two months and it was now Christmas Eve. Ellen wended her way home through the city and watched the population get into its festive spirit. The shops were well lit and there was holly and mistletoe decorating the windows but she did not dally to look at the splendid display. In a long shabby coat and an old woolen tam-o'-shanter pulled well down over her ears, she plodded on through the snow. She saw a beggar in a doorway shivering and a blind man selling matches. It depressed her and she wondered if she should have stayed with her office companions and partaken of a few pleasures at their celebrations.

"Stay for a drink, Miss Brown," Ronald had begged. Ronald was the young son of the boss who spent his university vacations learning the business.

"No, thanks, I don't drink," had been her reply.

"Well then, for Pete's sake, take the bus home," yelled
Emm. "What the hell she wants to walk all that way for, I
don't know."

Emm was rather boyish and at this moment quite aggressive having already had more than her fair share of the port.
She wore baggy tweeds, stamped her feet as she walked, and
swore. She had come to the *Argus* only recently but already
everyone knew she was there. Emm was a photographer's
assistant, and she helped Ronald bring in the news in a very
efficient manner. She came from a good family but they let
her do as she pleased, realizing that they would not be seeing
Emm take a husband; she was too masculine in her ways.
Ellen liked Emm but was shy of her. "You are barmy, Miss
Brown," Emm had said, "wasting your time with that bloody
Cockney boyfriend." Ellen only smiled and went on her way.

As she walked home through the snow, she recalled Emm
waving a bottle and loudly begging her to stay and she felt a
slight regret. The alley when she reached it seemed deserted,
but Lil's door was open and the sound of raucous voices came
from within. There was also music and singing from Rosie's;
she was entertaining a new lover.

Ellen looked hungrily for a sight of George's blond head
but saw only white snow lining the canal wall and ice floating
on the water. With a quick shiver she ran indoors. In the
kitchen she poured hot water over an Oxo cube and drank the
dark liquid down. That was her dinner and supper combined.
She then went up to bed to read until dawn. Ellen supposed
she should go up to the chapel soon but her interest in religion
had waned in this thirst for knowledge. It would have been
nice to have heard from George but perhaps he had not
reached his destination yet.

About midnight things began to liven up in the alley. Lil,
aggressively drunk, had decided on a couple of rounds with
Rosie.

"Whore!" yelled Lil. "Come out and I'll spliflicate yer."

Rosie, drunk and dishevelled, appeared at the window.

"Hop it, yer dirty ol' cow," she yelled at her before she was
dragged in by her lover, a little street bookie known as 'Arry
Smiff.

Then Lil seated herself on the windowsill and began to
wail: "Oh my poor Mary. Look what that whore did to my
poor Mary." She changed her tune for one second when

Becky, Sam and fat Lew hurried by. "Bleeding Jews," she howled. "Crucified Christ, you did, and told on my John. Judases, all of yer!" Becky and Sam went swiftly indoors dragging their fat son after them.

Eventually the bells rang out the good tidings and the alley settled down. A cold clear moon came out and shone on the bedroom wall as Ellen lay listening for the stumbling feet of her father but they never came.

In the slippery snow in the market Mr. Brown lay face down, his sandwich board splintered and blood-stained. He was stiff and cold. He had stumbled against a wagon and fallen under its wheels. The carter, going home drunk, had not noticed him. It was a policeman on his beat who discovered him.

Just as others were sitting down to the traditional Christmas fare of turkey and plum pudding, Ellen was standing in the mortuary beside her father's corpse. She had been called by a church elder to identify her father. She looked dispassionately down at the still face of death. She felt no sorrow or remorse, just curiosity. The rosy cheeked preacher from the mission placed a kind hand on her arm.

"Do not grieve. He has found peace at last. Pray for his soul, do not be sad."

Ellen did not reply. She was desperately trying to overcome the desire to giggle. The thought that he had campaigned so long to get there crossed her mind.

The kindly holy man looked at her shabby clothes.

"We will take care of everything," he said. "Your father was a devoted servant of our chapel."

Ellen did not even attend the funeral. From her reading of Freud and others she had emerged almost an agnostic and convinced that most of her close family had been insane. Perhaps it was just as well that she did not bear a child, healthy plants did not grow from rotten roots. That Christmas a deep dark melancholy overcame her. She returned to the office very wan and preoccupied.

# *Maud Imprisoned*

THE YOUNGER GENERATION WERE GROWING UP: THE loud-voiced, red-haired Colleen; the pretty but temperamental Patricia; and fat happy Lew. In the street they played an endless game of dressing-up. Passers-by would see the well-formed seven-year-old Colleen dressed in a long gown and bustle (once the property of Aunt Maud), a lace curtain adorned with a paper rose on her head, and a limp bouquet of the cowslips or dandelions that grew beside the canal wall clasped firmly in her podgy hands. Behind her trailed the rotund shape of Lew attired in a pair of red flannel drawers and fancy waistcoat that had once been Tim's Sunday best— Lew's part was that of train bearer. Tall, slim Patricia, in an old jacket, her long hair bundled up under a trilby hat, played the male lead. They went back and forth up and down the alley, the performance only being varied at times by Colleen's acrobatic feats. With her skirts tucked into her knickers she would do handstands, high kicks, the splits, the lot. Her supple young body would twist and turn in all directions. Once Aunt Maud came into the alley and found Colleen upside down; the young acrobat received some hearty whacks on the backside from Maud's umbrella for her pains. Patricia fought, kicked and screamed as her mother's umbrella descended again and again, her wayward daughter refusing to desert her friend Colleen. Eventually Maud gained hold of Patricia and dragged her through that prim front gate. After that the trio was broken up for a while—but not for long.

Recently Maud had been acting strangely. Every day she flapped up and down the alley in her large hat and long flowing black dress, her cheeks flushed with color and her eyes bright with a hidden excitement, as though hiding some dark secret. Where she went each day was a mystery to all in the alley except one. Every lunchtime Ellen Brown would leave her office in the city and wander through the streets, watching the pigeons and the people hurrying to and fro. At St. Paul's there was often a meeting of the women from the suffragette movement. Munching her lunch—an apple—Ellen would sit and listen to these well-bred women, pioneering for the cause of all women.

One day Maud's familiar black-clad figure appeared on the platform, her strident voice haranguing the bystanders to rise up in the cause of the suffragettes. Ellen stood, half-eaten apple in hand, gazing up fascinated by Maud's eloquence. This ungainly woman whom the folk down the alley laughed at, held the crowd spellbound. One moment she drew laughter as she made fun of the police and the prime minister; the next she drew tears when she spoke of the mothers of England who had given their sons' lives for the imperialistic warmongers and were unable to utter a word of complaint or whisper a protest. The shy retiring Ellen was momentarily uplifted and inspired. Then suddenly the mounted police charged down on them. Ellen scurried away like a tiny mouse to its hole, back to Cheapside where her gloomy office was situated. Her last glimpse of her neighbor was of Maud minus her hat belaboring a young policeman with that black umbrella.

In the dusty, paper-strewn cubicle that was her particular spot in the office, Ellen usually spent the day writing endless letters and addressing envelopes. Today an intense excitement gripped her. With still more than half an hour left of her lunch break, she took up a pad and pen and began to write. She had memorized Maud's speech and described the scene at

St. Paul's vividly, adding her own opinion on women's suffrage.

She was still engrossed in her writing when her office companions returned. Ronald looked over her shoulder.

"What are you doing, little Nell?" he asked.

"It's nothing," Ellen stammered, trying to hide the page under the blotter. But Ronald had it and he began to read. She sat nervously biting her lip expecting him to burst out laughing. But he was not such a bad boy, Ronald.

"Gosh!" he cried, "this is great stuff, Miss Brown, where did you get it?"

"I was only amusing myself," she said, brushing aside his enthusiasm.

"Can I borrow it?" he begged. "Just to show the old man?" Before she could answer Ronald was already on the way to his father's office.

That evening in Autumn Alley outside the open window of Maud's home Colleen was eavesdropping. Inside sat Dandy and his cousin Tim. Dandy's long thin drooping moustache looked even thinner than usual and his long face even gloomier. Tim's red head glowed in the shadows and his deep rolling tones drifted through the window.

"Should have given her a good beating, Dandy, me boyo. That would have stopped her!"

"Nothing stops Maud," said Dandy. "She's like a God-damned steam roller. But it's the child I'm worried over. What'll she think? Maud'll get three months at least. Dear God, 'tis such a disgrace to have your woman in prison," moaned Dandy.

"Maud's tough enough to stand it," said Tim. "Don't brood, lad. Now come on." Tim took his arm and guided him to the local.

Two bright eyes and two long legs quickly scampered away as Colleen dashed off to inform her friend. Patricia was sitting outside Tim's house looking very bored when a shrill whistle came from Colleen's pursed lips—the signal. Pat dashed over and the two girls made for the canal where they proceeded to do what was known as "head and heels," walking precariously on their hands along the top of the canal wall.

"I know a secret, Patsy Pat," announced Colleen from her upside-down position. (This name was a private joke between them. "Patricia Fitzpatrick?" Colleen had scoffed, "blimey, what a mouthful." Ever since then she had referred to her friend as Patsy Pat.)

"Well, spit it out," urged Pat.

"Your mum's in the nick," exclaimed her friend, jubilantly.

Pat's legs wobbled but fortunately they came down on the right side of the wall.

"What did you say?" She stared in disbelief at Colleen who sat on the wall swinging her legs nonchalantly.

"It don't hurt," Colleen said. "Me dad's been inside, I heard me mum say so."

"What's she done?" gasped Patricia.

"Murdered a copper, I think," replied Colleen, her vivid imagination running riot.

"But she'll get hung," exclaimed Pat in horror.

"I expect so," replied Colleen, quite unconcerned.

Pat was off like a shot. "I'm going to ask Uncle Tim," she cried, and headed in the direction of the Railway Arms where she had just seen her father and Tim go.

To Tim Pat ran, not to her father. From early days Dandy had had little connection with his lovely daughter; her mother monopolized her. This thin broody man was only there to poke fun at, he was never a father figure. Now Pat's little face peeped in at the pub door and her voice called out in anguish: "Come out, Uncle Tim, I want to speak to you."

Tim placed his pint on the counter and went out to her at once, his tall body bent double as he crouched to hear her tale of woe.

"Colleen says me mum's done a murder and she's going to be hanged," she sobbed.

"Oh, she did, the spalpeen." Tim looked to where Colleen was lurking. "Wait till I get me hands on her. Come to Uncle Tim." He picked her up and cuddled her.

"Where is me mum?" demanded Pat as he put her down. "Is she really in the nick?"

"Your mother is being detained for a while but she'll be home soon," he assured her. "In the meantime you shall stay with us."

"But I want to know!" Pat wriggled away from him and stood with her dark eyes flashing. He thought how pretty she was.

"Well, all right, I'll tell you. She is in prison, not for doing wrong, but for sticking to her principles. Do you know what that means?" he asked.

"Oh, I know, suffragettes." A broad smile crossed Pat's face. "Did they catch her?"

"Little devil, you knew all the time," said Tim.

"I knew about the meetings, I heard her talking about them. Thanks, Uncle Tim." She skipped off to play with Colleen who was lurking in the background.

A series of cartwheels and they were down by the canal once more. "It isn't true, Colleen, me mum is in the nick but she's not going to be hung," she informed her best friend. "Let's go tell Lew about it."

Outside Becky's house sat her rotund son, a self-satisfied expression on his podgy face and his mouth full of sweets.

"Guess what! Her mum's been nicked," yelled Colleen, simply bursting to tell someone.

Lew did not seem all that interested.

"What's up with you, soppy date?" demanded Colleen.

"Both shut your eyes and I'll let you see my birthday present," said Lew.

"It's not until November, same as mine," insisted Colleen.

"But I got it today," explained Lew. He dashed inside the house and opened the front room window. Two heads peered in and two voices gasped: "A real piano!"

With all the style of a professional, Lew seated himself on the piano stool and ran his fingers up and down the keys—a look of rapture on his flaccid face.

"Play something, Lew," urged Pat.

"Like this," said Colleen. She tapped out a few steps, her arm linked in her friend's, and her rich young voice sang: "Daddy wouldn't buy me a bow wow," while Lew picked out the tune quite easily by ear. Colleen's full-toned voice rang out and she and Pat kept in step:

> "I got a little cat,
>  And I'm very fond of that,
>  But I'd rather have a bow wow wow."

So it all began that day; Lew, a born musician, forgot about the music academy that was training him and began to knock out tune after tune, and the children sang and danced the days away.

Colleen lay on her back in the passage, her long legs stretched up against the wall. She wiggled her toes. She loved this form of exercise, but today she was feeling fed up. Lil was still mooning over Uncle George and missing her friend Mary. And her father had done his usual disappearing act. But worst of all, her poor friend Patsy Pat had been stuck in that convent since her mother had been sent to prison.

Fat greedy Lew stayed indoors most of the day, stuffing himself with sweets, but when it got dark he and Colleen would sneak down to the convent to see if they could see Patsy Pat. The convent school adjoined the park. Through the iron railings it was possible to see the high brick wall of the convent. On several afternoons lately Pat had climbed over that wall to chat with Colleen while the old nun in charge of the girls dozed on a bench and while Lew narked out for them.

They had discussed ways of helping Pat to escape from the school. There was no definite plan of action as yet and the trio had argued long and hard about it. But now fat Lew was backing off making out he had to go up to London for his music lesson. This annoyed Colleen; she was determined not to let her best friend down.

As she lay there in the passage, brooding, her legs against the wall, Colleen was suddenly startled by a shout from over the road. It was Lew at the window. He was wearing a long white nightgown.

Colleen sprang up and ran over the road to join him. "Look proper daft you do," was her first comment.

"It's all right," whispered Lew, "I've got me clothes on underneath. I've been making out I've got a sore throat."

"Where are they?" whispered Colleen furtively. She was scared of Becky.

"Gone to me cousin's bar mitzvah. Won't be home till after midnight," said Lew with a grin.

"Come over to our house and we'll make plans," said Colleen.

They huddled close together in Lil's passage whispering and giggling until big brother Arthur (he had long outgrown the urchin "Arfer") chased them out. He was studying for his matriculation and wanted peace and quiet in the house.

For a while they played ball in the park, and then they went over to the convent wall.

"Cooee, cooee"—that was the prearranged signal. A few seconds later came the answer, a shrill "cooee" in return, and over the wall came the long black-stockinged legs of Patricia and she descended on top of them. For a while they all crouched down by the railings.

"Where're we going?" asked Pat. "No one is going to miss me. They're all having a grand pray up."

"Let's go up to London," Colleen suggested. Lew and Patricia readily agreed.

Lew produced a mouth organ and put it to his lips and struck up "John Brown's Body." Jubilantly three small figures marched out of the park and along the main road, singing very loudly: "Glory, glory, hallelujah."

After several close scrapes crossing the busy London streets, they eventually found themselves in Shaftesbury Avenue where the theater queues were forming. A man stood on the pavement rattling soupspoons up and down his leg and people threw money at him; another bound himself up in chains and then thrashed about on the ground until he was free. To Colleen, Patricia and Lew this was an enchanted land, there was so much to see and hear.

"I ain't 'alf hungry," said Colleen, after a few hours wandering about. "Anybody got any money?" They shook their heads.

"Let's go home," wailed Lew. "I'm starving."

"Shut up," said Pat, giving him a pinch.

"I've got an idea," said Colleen. "Give us your cap, Lew." Obediently he handed it to her. "Now you play and we'll dance and perhaps people will put money in the hat."

People were queuing for the second house at the theater and they laughed at the fat boy blowing furiously on a mouth organ, the slim dark girl who did graceful high kicks and the acrobatic feats of the red-haired girl. The pennies came rolling in; Lew's cap was filled to the brim by the time the queue moved on into the theater. Picking up the takings, they dived around the corner. Then it was chips, hot pies, lemonade and roasting chestnuts—just anything they fancied.

"Let's go to the World Fair," suggested Lew.

"We don't know where it is," returned Pat.

"I do," said Lew proudly. "Come on, we'll get on a tram."

In those days an underground tram serviced London; it went down under the embankment and came up at Kingsway.

They had so much fun. They went upstairs in the tram and slid along the polished wood seats, crouching down close together when it went down into the dark tunnel, holding their breath and wondering if it would ever come into the light of day.

When they reached Kingsway, they jumped on a bus to Islington.

Once a year an annual fair was held in the Agricultural Hall in Islington. It was a huge domed building which most Londoners had visted at some time. Once past the turnstile, where everyone pushed together to get in, the three children were in another world.

In the center was a huge circus tent. They peered through the cracks in the canvas to watch the performance that had already started inside. The lions roared, the clowns fooled and the crowds clapped—never before had they seen such wonderful things. It was all so overwhelming—the cries of the audience and the star-spangled acrobats swinging precariously to and fro high in the air.

When the show was over, the trio dashed off to inspect the sideshows. They saw the smallest man, the fattest lady and the bearded lady; they were such sights to behold that the three were held spellbound. Rooted to the spot they stared at the dancing girls who threw up their legs and wiggled their hips, and they were disappointed when a rough man in a top hat and waving a stick said: "Hoppit! You ain't old enough."

Then there was the hall of mirrors and the scenic railway— there was no end to the excitement and pleasure until the money ran out.

Toward ten o'clock the hall began to empty, and the trio was ushered out by a man in a uniform.

Once outside, tired, very happy and very dirty, they looked in dismay at the deserted streets.

"It ain't 'alf late," said Colleen.

"I don't care," said Pat defiantly, "I ain't going home any more."

Her two friends stared at her, open-mouthed.

"You can't do that, you're not old enough," Lew explained slowly—he knew about such things.

Pat held herself up to her full height.

"I'll make out."

Colleen's mind, however, was on more practical things. "How much money we got left?" she asked.

"None," said Lew. "We spent it all."

"Well, then," said Colleen, "we'll have to walk and it ain't 'alf a long way." In her determined way she stepped out with Lew at her side and Pat trailed along sulkily behind.

The streets were empty and a cold frost gleamed on the pavements. Occasionally parties of drunks chivied them and Colleen gave them the sort of saucy answers she had heard her mother use. Through lonely back streets they plodded. Lew complained of feeling sick. Pat was very nervous, and looked up at the gloomy slum dwellings with real fear in her eyes. But Colleen, brave as a young lioness, carefully read the street names and planned the long route home.

Then an ugly-looking lout stepped out of a dark doorway. He grabbed Lew by the collar. "Where are you going, fat Jew boy?" he demanded.

Colleen, with a quick command to Pat to start running, lifted her skirt and aimed a kick at the lout who let go of Lew; she had caught him well below the belt and left him doubled up. Dragging Lew, who seemed paralyzed with fright, Colleen soon caught up with Pat, and all three ran and ran until they were exhausted. They sank down in the doorway unable to go any further.

Lew was blubbering; Pat, white and trembling, hung on to Colleen. "I'm so scared, let's go on," she begged.

"We can't," said Colleen, "we're lost. I don't know where we are." They all began to cry. Suddenly, the yellow gleam of a policeman's lantern shone into the tear-filled eyes. "'Ullo, wot 'ave we 'ere?"

"We're lost," chimed three small voices together.

Later, in the police station, they sipped hot cocoa and told their tale of woe. "We only went to the fair," they explained, "but all our money got spent so we were walking home to Bow."

"Autumn Alley, you said? That's on my way home," said

the constable. "Wait till I come off duty and you can walk through the park with me."

Dawn was breaking as three very tired children were escorted home by the kindly bobby. Little sparrows twittered in their nests and the grass was wet with dew.

"Doesn't it give you a nice feeling being out so early in the morning?" whispered Pat.

"Not me," said Colleen. "I'm too tired and I'm wondering what me mum will do to me."

Down in the alley a conference of mums and dads was being held in Maud's best parlor. Becky was weeping loudly and Sam, Tim, and Dandy were contemplating the next move. The three children had been missing all night; every hour their parents had become more and more concerned. Tim had reported it to the police who said they would drag the canal at daylight. So morose was Dandy with his thin whiskers drooping. Whatever would Maud say? A young nun had brought the news of Patricia's flight from the convent school. Lil stared aggressively at the weeping Becky who blamed Colleen for leading her son astray. The air was full of tension.

Then along the cobbled street came the sound of footsteps. Everyone dashed out to be confronted by the bobby and the three weary absconders. Pandemonium broke out. Lil dashed at Colleen screeching like an angry hen; Becky grabbed her fat son calling on the Lord and all his blessings that brought him home safe, her voice a wailing crescendo, just like a ship's siren. Pat stood looking shyly at Dandy and he stood looking at her with that selfsame expression. Then she dashed into Tim's arms to sob her heart out. Dandy put his long clay pipe back in between his straggly whiskers; the child was home safe, now he could face Maud.

Later Tim tucked Pat up in her own little bed.

"Don't let them take me back, will you Uncle Tim?" she pleaded.

"No, me darlin', you're staying here. Uncle Tim will look after you," he promised. Her worried dark eyes closed and she slept peacefully.

Not having had much sleep no one bothered to go to work that next day. Instead they lounged about in Maud's front room. Timmo sat with his feet up on one of her very shiny antique side tables reading the racing paper, while Dandy knocked out his pipe on the polished hearth. Tim rested his huge body against the marble mantelpiece and took an occasional swig from a bottle of beer.

"No doubt about it," he said, "we've got to get a woman."

Dandy's blue eyes gleamed with humor. "Bedad, 'tis all you're short of, Tim, a woman!"

"Don't be an old fool," said Tim. "What I mean is someone to mind the child and cook us some grub." He laced his hands inside his wide leather belt. "I'm getting too blowed out with all that pease pudding and faggots."

"If I eat any more fish and chips, I'll grow fins," broke in Timmo.

"Doubt if the old woman would like it," said Dandy, referring to Maud.

"She's still got two months to do, and let's face it, me boy, they won't let her out of there till she quietens down."

"So she won't know," chimed in Timmo, who liked to be involved.

"Who'll we ask?" queried Dandy. "Not that boozy old cow next door."

"No," said Tim, "but I know just the one: the Callaghan boy's sister. She came over a while ago but she detests that hotel job she's got."

In no time the final arrangements were made and into the alley came a new face, a smiling happy face with irregular features and long golden hair. Only five feet two and built like a short broad pixie, her name was Bridie.

From the moment Bridie entered Autumn Alley she was popular with the male population—old and young. There was a certain air about her and something sexy in the way she walked, sticking out her small bosoms and wiggling her wide hips. Laughter rippled from her wide mouth and good humor shone from those roguish eyes.

She carried a little straw traveling basket with her when she came and plonked it down in the hall. "Now then, what is it you're after having me do?" she asked cheerily. She proceeded to put in order the disarray of both Maud's and Tim's houses, cleaning them thoroughly, humming a little Irish tune all the while. That first evening they all sat down to dinner in Maud's well-equipped kitchen. "I've cleaned the parlor, no more eating in there," Bridie told them, "and it's dirty boots off when ye tread me kitchen floor."

The kitchen table was laid with a sumptuous feast—a grand sight for those hungry men who had roughed it since their women had left them. The traditional Irish meal, boiled ham, spuds boiled in their jackets and cabbage boiled in the bacon water. There were all those tastes and savory smells that they had missed so much, and the golden, freckled, smiling Bridie to serve them.

"Cooee, Bridie, can Colleen come in?" called Pat from the front door.

"To be sure, darlin'," said Bridie, "there's plenty for all."

Colleen, who had never been allowed in Maud's house, sat goggling beside her friend.

It was a merry meal, the first of many happy evenings while Bridie ran the house.

After dinner they played cards and Bridie pretended to tell the girls' fortunes. When Tim and Dandy retired to the pub, she entertained the girls with ghost stories and tales about the leprechauns.

Young Timmo lay on the rug and listened intently, his lithe young body stretched out. His hair looked more fiery in the glow of the fire. He reached out and touched Bridie's ankle.

"Stop that, you naughty boy," she rebuked him. A tremor ran between them. Not yet sixteen years old, Timmo for the first time felt the need for a woman and he was sure from the very beginning that Bridie would oblige.

# Bridie

MAUD MIGHT HAVE BEEN WORRYING OR EVEN PINING for her lovely daughter, but Patricia did not miss her mother at all, she was having too good a time. Colleen now ate and slept with her, and Bridie was so easygoing, she let them play their dressing-up game from morning to night no matter what inconvenience they caused. In Maud's bedroom they had discovered untold treasures, a real jet-trimmed cape, ropes of beads and long Victorian earrings. Most of the day they played royal families, roping Bridie in for the small parts.

Pat had gone reluctantly back to day school at the convent on Tim's instructions. Bridie took her each day and walked to meet her every tea time, ogling the policeman on his beat as she walked past swinging her sexy hips. "Top of the morning to you, Bridie," he would say, and she would giggle and remark to Pat: "Well now, just look at him, he's eating me with his eyes."

"She don't 'alf fancy herself," Pat told Colleen. Colleen agreed. "Me ma says she's very sexy. What's that mean?"

"Mean to say you don't know?" asked Pat in a very superior tone.

"Well, I'm not sure. Someone said it meant making love, but I ain't never seen anyone doing it," Colleen said.

"I wonder what she does with Timmo when we've gone to bed," pondered Pat.

"Let's watch them tonight," suggested Colleen.

Every evening after dinner Timmo sat around, his nose glued to *Sporting Life*. When Tim and Dandy retired to the pub and the girls to bed, he and Bridie retired to the parlor and the long leather sofa. Timmo was desperately immature and so anxious to prove his manhood but each time Bridie foiled him. Passionate kisses were quite permissible but that was all. Suddenly she would pull down her skirt and say firmly: "Now that's enough, Timmo."

He was very puzzled. He had heard Tim and Dandy joke about her.

"Bedad, she even gets me going," drawled Dandy. "Keep 'er off me," cried Tim, "I'm in enough trouble."

It was young Arthur who weighed her up correctly. Looking her over he said: "Don't fancy her meself, she's too much of a tease." He was dead right, for Bridie at nineteen was still a virgin and intended to remain so; a golden ring she was seeking.

To the girls peeping through the keyhole that night it seemed very funny business.

"Oh, go on, let me," pleaded Timmo.

"No, no, you naughty boy, you've gone far enough," they heard Bridie reprimand him.

"She won't let him," whispered Colleen.

"Let him what?" asked Pat.

"I dunno' he's lying right on top of her, that's all I can see."

"Shall we try it on Lew?" suggested Pat.

"Then maybe like that we could find out."

"Don't say nothing to Bridie," returned Colleen looking worried. "She might not take us to London."

Bridie took them up to the music hall each week. High up in the gallery they sat, looking down on the performers who looked like dolls. The moving lights shone on the painted faces, and all the audience joined in the choruses of the songs. They munched peanuts and sucked oranges, and watched Marie Lloyd, George Robey and the long line of dancing girls. It was a weekly delight for these stage-struck youngsters.

Bridie always had plenty of money and was very generous with it. She had a special method of obtaining money for the treats. To Dandy she would say: "Butcher was here today. If you eat good meat it must be paid for." Dandy would hand her some notes. To Tim, who was even more generous, the same tale would be told. Having conned them all, even Timmo, she would take the kids out on a spree. Everyone loved Bridie, except the butcher and the grocer, who never got paid. The bills would be presented to Maud on her return.

So life progressed down in the alley and everyone was happy except Timmo. He surprised them all by saying one day: "I'll come up to London with you next week. It's my treat."

"Wonder what he's after," said Colleen with a wink.

"Make out you don't know," whispered Pat.

The previous week they had invited Lew over. He was used to being pushed around by them so did not protest when Colleen dragged him onto the floor and Pat lay full length on top of him. But when she pressed her full red lips onto his, he went wild. "I want me mum!" he screamed. He fought madly to get away and then fled home.

"He didn't like it," said Pat in surprise. "Can't say I go much on it either."

However, Lew turned up punctually for the week's outing to the music hall. Bridie and Timmo sat close together. His arm was around her and constantly he looked at her bosom. Pat nudged Colleen who nudged Lew whose mouth was full of popcorn at that moment and he nearly choked.

The way home was through the park. It was dark and deserted. Lew showed the girls a bright shiny coin in the middle of his palm. "Timmo gave it to us. We got to start running as soon as we get past the shelter and not to stop till we get home."

"What's he want us to run for?" the girls asked.

"He's going to kiss Bridie, silly fools," whispered Lew.

Swiftly they fled, not heeding Bridie when she called them to stop.

"Let them go, Bridie. We're alone at last," said Timmo. His strong young arms went about her and bore her down to the wet grass.

"No! No! Stop it, Timmo!" protested Bridie.

But there was no stopping Timmo this time, he was the son of his father. Bridie fought for a while, then she gave way. They lay close together caring little for the cold or the dampness of the grass.

When Timmo released her, Bridie put her face down on the grass and wept. "Oh, Timmo!" she cried, "why did you do that?"

"But I love you," he declared valiantly, slightly nonplussed. He had not realized that Bridie had been a virgin, he had no idea that she had just been playing him along. She was three years older than him and he had been sure she had had plenty of men. "Did I hurt you, darling?" he wept, his tears mingling with hers.

"Is that you, Bridie?" called the girls when she arrived home.

"Go to sleep, darlings," called back Bridie in a choked voice.

"Don't she sound funny," said Pat. "I think she's drunk."

"Don't be silly," said Colleen, "Bridie don't drink." But it was mysterious they both agreed.

After the initial shock of the ten months' sentence imposed on her, Maud soon settled down in Holloway and made plenty of friends there. Some quite influential women of good families were also there, enrolled in this fight for freedom that the male population seemed determined to regard as ludicrous. At first Maud had been worried about Patricia until Dandy wrote to say he had sent her to the convent. As for that drunken fool Dandy, he could fend for himself. So Maud continued her campaign within those walls. She lost all her remission, and was forcibly fed or in solitary confinement most of the time. Maud bravely suffered these indignities, and was loud and very courageous in her protest. No one from the alley had visited her but Maud did not fret, and she was very surprised one day to be told she had a visitor.

In the visitors' hall she saw the pale skinny Sunday school teacher from the alley, Ellen Brown, who with a beating heart and full of fear, had braved the terror of that grim place to obtain another report on women's suffrage. Maud stared at Ellen with some hostility and did not know what to say.

Ellen smiled sweetly and asked how she was. Maud only

frowned in response, wondering what was the purpose of her visit.

"Your daughter is well," said Ellen.

Immediately Maud softened up. "Behaving herself, is she?" she asked with a broad smile.

Ellen noticed how thin Maud had become and how yellow her skin was. She put her lips close to the wire cage that separated them. "I want to help," she whispered. "I work for the *Argus* and they'll print any news you can give me."

Maud's face lit up. "You're most welcome, my dear," she muttered. In a deep whisper she told of the constant battles inside the walls, the bad treatment, the forced feeding and gave Ellen the names of the suffragettes in there. With a handkerchief over the pad on her lap, Ellen noted it all down and completed her second assignment for the *Argus*. Her boss had given her ten pounds for the first one and promised ten more pounds if she could get any news from the prison first hand.

It was Ellen on her second visit to the prison who unwittingly let Maud know of Bridie's presence in her home. A note from Maud to Ellen asking her to visit had been smuggled out of prison and left at the *Argus* office. Maud, recently released from her solitary confinement, was eager for news. Ellen was shocked at the change in her. Maud seemed to have shrunk in size and her hair was a kind of pepper-and-salt mixture; it had been cut very short, a style which certainly did not suit that big horselike face.

Maud's eyes like steel gimlets looked straight at her. "All right," she croaked, "I know I'm not as able bodied as I was, but I am still okay upstairs—my brain is still ticking over."

"I'm very sorry," stuttered Ellen.

"No need," replied Maud crisply, "I only asked you to come because I want news from the alley."

"Does no one ever write to you?" asked Ellen.

"I only got one letter from Dandy saying that Patricia refuses to stay at the convent. But I don't want letters, I want to know what's gone on. Who's taking care of Patricia?" she demanded.

"I'm not sure, but I believe you have a housekeeper," returned Ellen.

"What? Another woman in my house? I'll kill that bloody

Dandy," roared Maud, her old self once more. The attendant warden raised a warning finger.

"I'll take a message to your husband if you like," said Ellen.

"No, you don't, my girl," said Maud in a loud whisper. "Just keep your trap shut. I'll be out in three weeks and I'll settle with them all then."

Ellen returned to the office wishing she had not got so involved.

"Buck up," said Emm, giving her a hard thump on the back. "I bet you haven't eaten all day. I'll bring you some coffee and a sandwich."

Ellen smiled warmly. What a good pal Emm was. Between the boisterous Emm and the strong-willed Maud she felt weak and insignificant and longed hungrily for her George.

Tonight it was evening classes. Both she and Emm had been sent on courses to learn the new skills of typewriting and shorthand. It was very interesting and she was making good progress but Emm larked about all the time and tormented the other pupils. The class consisted of nice neat young ladies, all anxious for a commercial career, but because of Emm they avoided Ellen. Emm sat on top of her desk, smoked and passed comments on the other girls' appearance. Ellen was always watching and wondering about Emm.

Ellen still spent a great deal of her time reading and studying. Her nose was invariably deep in a book.

"Let's go and see a play or a film," Emm pleaded with her one evening.

"I can't afford it," Ellen replied tartly.

"Get away," retorted Emm, "you got your pay and the extra for the little bits that go in the paper."

"I'm saving up to get married," Ellen explained.

"Married be blowed!" cried Emm. "You'll probably never see him again."

Ellen's eyes filled with tears. "I'm getting married next Christmas," she said firmly, "and I'm having red roses and white velvet."

"Here we go," jeered Emm. "That bloody wedding is becoming an obsession with you. Roses in December? Don't make me laugh!"

For a while after that they did not speak, but it was not long before Emm became her normal good-tempered self once more. Ellen quietly and promptly made it up, she had missed the company of tomboyish good-natured Emm.

After that night out at the music hall, Bridie had gone about for a week with red-rimmed eyes and a downcast face.

"What have you girls been doing with Bridie?" asked Tim.

"It wasn't us," they replied and collapsed into giggles.

Timmo stayed up at the job all week and did not come home for meals but Tim saw no connection. "Always was a moody little devil," he complained.

"Missing his mother," suggested Dandy, "but he won't admit it."

After a week Bridie cheered up and worked over the house, dusting and polishing with great gusto. She was back to her old tricks too, ogling the local copper on his beat. One morning she opened the parlor window and, waving a checked duster, she pretended to flick the dust from the sill knowing only too well the young bobby would stop for a chat. He was Irish and straight out of the bog, as they used to say, so when two roguish blue eyes twinkled at him, he lingered. A cab from the main road turned into the alley, the old nag's hoofs clip-clopping on the cobbles. It halted and the driver helped out a feeble old lady who walked with a stick. Slowly she walked toward the house where Bridie and the copper were chatting. They did not notice her until a voice like a squawking hen shouted: "Shut that bloody window!" Maud had returned to find a brazen hussy leaning out of her window, holding a conversation with a dirty copper. It was not a good beginning for Bridie; Maud detested the clinging type of woman that ogled men as much as she detested policemen. "Sling your bloody hook," she growled at the constable. "Don't want your lot nosing about down here."

The young policeman, though slightly disconcerted, did not argue. He just sauntered away. Shoving aside Bridie, who had opened the front door, Maud went rampaging inside, weak and tottery on her legs but her temper more vile than ever.

"Shall I make you a cup of tea?" suggested Bridie nervously.

"Not tea, hot milk," said Maud. "And if Dandy has left me any there should be a bottle of brandy in the sideboard."

Bridie got busy and Maud sat down and surveyed her home. The kitchen was clean, bright and shiny and there was plenty of food in the larder. Her steely eyes examined every nook and cranny. Keeps the place nice, she thought, give her credit for that. But she's a sexy bitch. I wonder what's been going on in my absence. I'll soon find out when Lil gets home from work, meantime I'll hold my horses, she decided.

She kept Bridie busy for the rest of the day, running up and down stairs with her things. Maud had decided to sleep downstairs. She had hurt her leg in a scuffle with authority and it had stiffened up and she did not want to climb the stairs.

When Bridie met Pat from school she was very depressed and her legs ached. Pat came skipping out, her plaits flying, a scarlet bow on the end of each one.

"What's up?" she asked when she saw Bridie's face.

"Your mother's home," said Bridie glumly.

"Oh, is that all?" said Pat. "And she's been having a go at you, I suppose. Don't get upset, she'll love you like we all do when she knows you," Pat tried to reassure her.

While Bridie prepared the tea, Pat sat with her mother, hugging and kissing her. "Poor Mummy," she said, "what have they done to you?"

Maud's good humor returned at the sight of her pretty daughter glowing with health. "I'll buy you some nice things tomorrow," she promised. "Now tell me what you have been doing while I was away."

"I was bored in that nasty convent, so I ran away. That's why Bridie is here," Pat informed her. "You do like her, don't you, Mummy?"

"If you do, darling." Maud was noncommittal.

"Dad loves her, so does Uncle Tim," pouted Pat.

"Oh, he does, does he?" Maud pursed her lips. "And what does Uncle Tim do?"

"He eats here, so does Timmo. They all share Bridie.

Maud was stunned. Out of the mouths of babes and sucklings, she thought. Wait till I get my hands on them.

"Go and have your tea, love, but first ask Lil to come in and see me." She would hear the rest of it from Lil if she was not mistaken.

Lil waddled in. She had grown very stout and the gin had begun to destroy her eyes. She stared at Maud.

"Christ! what have they done to yer?" she said. "You look twenty years older."

"But I ain't dead yet," retorted Maud dryly. "Pour yourself a drink and give me all the news.

"What about this sexy piece they've installed in here?" she inquired.

"She ain't so bad and she's ever so good to the kids," said Lil.

"Never mind that," said Maud. "How is she with the men? That's what I'm interested in."

"No, Maud, I don't think so." Lil shook her tousled head. "Tim's behaved himself since that last business. He wants Mary to come back to him. And as for your old Dandy . . ." Lil began to cackle obscenely. "Don't think he's a decent fuck left in him."

"We'll see about that," said Maud grimly. "Thanks for putting me in the picture, Lil. Take the rest of the bottle with you and welcome." Maud wanted to get rid of Lil before the men came in from work.

Bridie's soft hands helped her bathe and put on clean clothes. The old black dress she had been arrested in was thrown out. "Burn it," said Maud, "it stinks of that horrible prison."

"Will you let me arrange your hair for you, Mrs. Fitzpatrick?" asked Bridie politely.

Maud stared at her perplexed. Bridie's downcast eyes made her look so unhappy. Maud's generous nature came to the fore. "Don't look so bloody miserable," she said, "I won't bite. If you can do anything with this mane you're welcome to try."

With a brush and curling tongs and infinite patience, Bridie made Maud look much younger. In her best beaded dress, long ropes of pearls and dangling earrings, Maud was once more her old self. Pat buzzed about excitedly and Bridie began to smile again. When the men came home they welcomed Maud warmly and they all sat down to a good chicken dinner cooked and served by Bridie. Maud had decided to bide her time; this girl was clean and useful, there was no sense in causing an upheaval just yet.

It had been a strange meal. Pat was full of jovial chatter; Bridie was silent, her golden freckles shining out on her pale face; Dandy was shy, and Tim was awkward and afraid that

Maud would upset things. Maud watched them all with suspicion.

That night Maud retired early to sleep on the sofa in the parlor. Pat also went to bed and Tim and Dandy went to the pub. Bridie was in the kitchen washing the dishes, and the house was quiet except for the rattle of plates as she stacked them in the cupboard.

The kitchen door opened slightly and Timmo's head appeared. His long arm went around her.

"I've come back. Love me, Bridie," he begged.

She put her arms about his neck, standing on tip toe because she was so short and he so tall.

"Hush, the missus is back," she whispered and together they crept out into the back yard.

Maud was restless. "Not enough room on this damned sofa," she muttered. She had many things on her mind, among them a letter from her first husband in America, who now took care of Larry's schooling. He was insisting that she give up her position as trustee of Larry's estate. Maud had no intention of losing track of her son or of the legacy his grandfather had left him.

Maud was turning this over in her mind when she heard unmistakable sounds from the back yard. It took her a while to hobble to the window, but she was just in time to see a red head disappearing out of the back gate.

"Are you out there, Bridie?" she called.

"I'm in the lavatory, Mrs. Fitzpatrick," Bridie called back demurely.

Maud was convinced that it had been Tim out there with Bridie. Why, the dirty old rogue, she thought, he won't get away with it. I'll catch him out, then God help him.

Within a few weeks Maud had begun to be more like her old self. She put on weight and her old energy returned. She watched Tim like a hawk but so far had not caught him in any compromising positions. She told Dandy that Bridie had to go. But he only put her off.

"Can't send the lass away, she has nowhere to go. Her brothers have left for Canada. I've promised to take care of her until they settle and then they'll send for her."

"Now that is extraordinarily nice of you," said Maud sarcastically. "How about Tim? Is he going to assist you?"

"What the devil are you getting at, woman?" complained

Dandy irritably. "Has that damned prison warped your mind?"

Then they started to quarrel. Maud's voice was very shrill, Dandy's slow and grumbling. In the kitchen Bridie put her hands over her ears ashamed to hear the things they were saying to each other.

Then one afternoon Maud got up and walked over to the cafe. Rosie was making pies, and up to her fat elbows in flour. She looked rather scared as Maud marched in. 'Arry Smiff, a little weasel of a man, sat in the corner totting up bets.

"I want a word with you," said Maud loudly. "Get rid of him." She jerked a thumb in the direction of 'Arry.

Rosie's foolish mouth dropped open, but plucking up her courage she said: "He's my fiancé, 'e stays 'ere." Then like two old battered warships, they lined up for battle, the tall scraggy Maud and the fair fat Rosie.

"How much do you want for those broken down slums in this alley?" Maud demanded.

"If you mean the property that I own, I've no intention of selling," replied Rosie haughtily.

"Well, you might as well sell, because by hook or crook I'm having you out of here," Maud informed her aggressively.

Rosie pushed the bowl of flour angrily away from her and began to wipe her fat arms on a towel. "Who do you think you are? Bloody old hag, coming in here telling me what to do. Just out of prison, ain't yer?"

"Yep, that's right," returned Maud briskly, "fighting for the rights of real women, not floosies like you."

"How dare you!" screamed Rosie, losing her temper.

"Ladies! ladies!" implored 'Arry Smiff, vainly trying to calm them.

"You sit down!" cried Maud, giving him a shove. "It's got nothing to do with you. By the way, you owe me six quid from that bet that came up yesterday."

"Just checking 'em now," muttered 'Arry, wishing he'd kept his mouth shut.

"Well, hand it over," said Maud, holding out her hand for the money. "I'm not here to argue with the likes of you," she said, turning to Rosie again, "but to warn you. Get out peaceable or by God I'll drive you out of here, I promise you that."

"This is me own property, left to me by me Gran. You can't do anything," jeered Rosie.

"Can't I?" threatened Maud. "Just you wait and see." She strode off and Rosie burst into tears.

"There, there, never mind, my love," 'Arry Smiff comforted her. "What she got on you, that old battleaxe?" he asked.

"She thinks I carried on with Tim and that's why his wife left him," she wept. "But it's not true. We was only friends," wailed Rosie.

"I know, love, don't cry." The wily little bookie had had an idea. "Why don't you get married?" he suggested. "That would keep 'em guessing."

"Who to?" said Rosie, tears fast disappearing.

"Why, to me, who'd yer think?"

"Do you mean that, 'Arry? Ain't you got a wife?" she asked anxiously.

"No, love, been dead years." He was not really sure that she was.

"Right then," said Rosie, "I'll bloody well do it. I'll show 'em I'm a respectable woman. It'll be a real smack in the eye for 'em," she cried jubilantly. 'Arry smiled slyly; he was well pleased with himself—nice little bank account and some property to play with.

Rosie resumed her pie-making. "That old cow wants to drive me out of here so that her mate Mary will come home. That's her game, I can smell it a mile off. Trot round to the registry office and put up the banns tomorrow, 'Arry."

She washed her arms under the tap, they were all floury and mottled, just like two huge legs of lamb. Rosie then plonked her fat backside on 'Arry's small lap.

"'Ow about a little bit of love to go on with," she said.

Nearly all the residents of the alley were outside the town hall to see Rosie emerge as a blushing bride. There was Tim and Dandy, and Lil throwing confetti and yelling out coarse comments; there was Becky and her sister Sophie from Aldgate who had a passion for weddings, Jewish or otherwise. Then there were the children all lined up, eager and very curious—Pat, Lew and Colleen. Arthur, wearing a huge checked cap tilted to one side and a white carnation in his buttonhole, was in charge of the transport—a smart pony and trap borrowed for the occasion.

The only people who were not there were Maud, who sat at home writing letters—Rosie's wedding made not the slightest difference to her, she still campaigned to get rid of her—and Bridie who was not feeling well.

As Colleen and Pat informed everyone later on: "It was a topping wedding."

"Rosie didn't 'alf look smart," declared Colleen. "She had nine diamonds, a green fevver and a veil on her big blue hat."

"Good God!" cried Maud. "What else did she wear? Ballet tights?"

"No, Mother," Pat ignored her mother's sarcasm, "she had a beautiful dress covered with beads. They're all in the pub now. Can I go and wait outside?"

"Indeed not," said Maud. "Go upstairs and tidy your room and you, Colleen, can hop it."

Behind her mother's back, Pat stuck out her tongue but she still obeyed her and went upstairs. She leaned out of the back room window as far as she could and Colleen leaned out of the one next door. In this precarious position they proceeded to gossip until Bridie came to put Pat to bed.

Rosie and 'Arry Smiff went to Brighton for their honeymoon and Arthur was installed in the cafe, taking the bets and pouring large mugs of tea. Just by chance 'Arry Smiff had discovered Arthur's ability to count. "'E's a mathematical wizard, that boy. Reckons up bets better than anyone I ever knew." Arthur was definitely a lad after his own heart. So 'Arry began to bribe Arthur with a few shillings and instead of doing the studying that was necessary during the last two months at school if he was to further his education, Arthur sat up late into the night checking bets. So the rot set in. The boy strained his already weak eyes in a dimly lit room reckoning up doubles, trebles and threepenny-each-way bets. He was so tired in the morning that he often missed school or dozed off during lessons and was a perpetual disappointment to the headmaster who had had great hopes for him. However, Arthur was happy over at Rosie's. He was a natural busybody and liked to be among people and Lil did not nag him quite so much when he parted with some of the money 'Arry paid him or some he had won on the horses. So he poured out the tea for the wagon drivers, discussed the gee gees with them and put all thoughts of university or college from his mind.

The fact that street betting was illegal bothered no one and 'Arry had the cops well buttered. It was a thriving business and nearly all the alley had an occasional flutter. Tim and Maud were regulars and Bill Welton, when he was at home, hung about the cafe all the time, scrounging tips and borrowing a tanner here and there to put on a "cert" that seldom came home. When he did have a win, it all went straight back on again, for he had a compulsive gambling streak. Maud gambled in pounds and fivers and was extremely lucky. 'Arry appreciated her custom but had yet to find out how lucky she was.

Rosie returned from her honeymoon as red as a boiled lobster from lying in the sun. She had several new dresses and, accompanying that shiny golden band, she had a quite enormous diamond ring. Arms akimbo, she stood in the shop doorway each day to allow the alley dwellers to gaze on her beauty. In her opinion this was more recognizable now that she wore a wedding ring. 'Arry lurked furtively on the corner, his cap over one eye, on the look-out for the prospective client or strange coppers.

Back and forth several times a day through the alley went Maud. Her ungainly appearance was not enhanced by the fact that a walking stick replaced the old black umbrella as her knee was inclined to give way. When she saw Rosie, a vague secret grin would distort her features and make Rosie feel very uncomfortable. "Some people!" Rosie would mutter as Maud's bat-like shape disappeared from view.

Maud was very busy. She had made various influential contacts at the town hall, one being the recently appointed sanitary inspector. His duty was to try and improve the lot of the slum dwellers. When Maud first approached him, he was very wary for he felt it did not do to go poking your nose in those back alleys. However, Maud was so insistent that finally an appointment was made for him to inspect all the houses in the alley that belonged to Rosie.

On the appointed day, before the inspector arrived, Maud paid one of her infrequent visits to Lil.

"I'm here to do you a favor," she declared. "How long is it since you had a bit of paint or wallpaper in this damned rabbit-hutch?" She screwed up her eyes in disgust at the greasy walls and the filthy paintwork. "And I'll bet your toilet is all bunged up. I can smell it." Notebook in hand, she marched through the house like a sergeant-major. Lil trailed along behind as Maud inspected the bedrooms with the bug-squashed walls and broken floorboards.

"Well, you could certainly do with a do-up," said Maud when she had finished.

"What's up?" Lil demanded.

"The sanitary inspector is coming today. Here is a list of the things you need done. You make sure he sees that." She tore a piece of paper from her notebook and handed it to Lil.

"Dunno as I want no inspector prowling abaht 'ere," protested Lil.

Maud's chin came out aggressively. "Do you want to help me get Mary back?" she inquired.

"Course I do," cried Lil. "Ain't she me best friend?"

"Well, do as I say," demanded Maud. "I don't care if you never get this pigsty cleaned up, but I'll get rid of that bitch Rosie if it kills me."

"Right then," said Lil, having an immediate change of heart at the mention of Rosie.

Then Maud marched over the road to Becky who was easier to deal with than Lil.

"Sam has done a lot of repairs to this house," Becky told her, "but I'll go along with you, Maud."

"We'll demand a refund of the money you spent on her property. She ain't going to like that," said Maud. She then went on to overhaul Tim's house. She returned to her own house content. Having prepared her case she was ready for action.

"She's going to go mad when she gets the bill for this lot," she chuckled, as she settled by the window to wait for the sanitary inspector.

The outcome of Maud's plan was that Rosie, as owner of three of the houses in the alley (No. 3 was Maud's and No. 5 was Ellen's which belonged to the mission), had to make all the necessary repairs, free the drains and toilets, and repaper and paint each property.

"How come the mission owns No. 5, then?" Maud asked the young inspector.

With Maud's fiver tucked in his waistcoat pocket and nice warm brandy inside him, he was in an expansive mood.

"The original builder of this alley had a paint factory in Bow and he lived in No. 5 for many years," he informed her.

"He founded the mission and did a lot of good work about here."

"So how the devil did that old grandmother of Rosie's get hold of them?" asked Maud.

"At his death, his two sons divided the property; one got the factory, the other got the houses. Now, this is strange: this second one, it seems, was the complete opposite to his father and he took up with a dancer, quite a beauty she was. When he died, he left all the houses to her—except his father's house, that went to the mission."

"Well, that's quite a story," said Maud. "Never met old Sal, but I can't think of her as a beauty seeing as she was related to that bitch Rosie."

A week later Rosie was seen all white, pathetic and puffy eyed. According to Arthur she had been "howling her head orf."

"Look 'ere, missus," said 'Arry Smiff, when Maud came in to place her daily bet, "don't be so hard on Rosie. She just ain't got the ready cash to get them houses done up."

"You stick to your bloody gee gees. I'll decide what's what. She's got the option to sell out to me or do the repairs."

Rosie was very obstinate. She was not going to give in to "that old cow."

"Perhaps you could give me back a little of what you borrowed off me, 'Arry," she ventured timidly.

"Gawd, Rosie, how can I? Me luck's dead out. Besides, look at all the expense I've had, the wedding, then the honeymoon an' that bleeding great sparkler."

Rosie sighed. "Get young Arthur to tot up what it's all going to cost. If it comes to more than the bloody houses are worth she might as well have them."

'Arry gave her a crafty look. "'Old yer 'orses," he said, "we might even get a better price from one of them land agents."

"I don't care," sighed Rosie. "But she ain't having me shop. I'll be out in the street if she does. If she gets her thieving hands on me shop we've had it, so you mind what you're up to, 'Arry," she warned.

Maud, having caused a grand upheaval, sat back for a while to await results. "Don't any of you pay your rent," she told her neighbors, "not until she's done the repairs."

While she waited, her attention was suddenly drawn to

Bridie. The girl had been wandering about the house listlessly and missing some of her chores. Maud came down on her like a ton of bricks.

"How long is it since you cleaned the doorstep?" she demanded.

"I'll be doing it today," replied Bridie in a far-away voice.

"What the devil's wrong with you?" asked Maud. But Bridie did not reply. She went slowly out to clean the step.

Dandy, Tim and Timmo were away still, working on the Great North Road. Father and son had grown very close since Mary had left them. Timmo was now almost as tall as his father and learning a good trade as a stone mason working beside him, his long lean body stripped to the waist as they laid the curbstone end to end.

"The boy seems moody lately," remarked Tim to Dandy, one wet day as they sat beside the glowing bucket of red hot coke outside the hut where they sheltered.

"Missing his mother, no doubt," said Dandy.

Timmo, however, considered he had good reason to be moody. A mysterious note had been passed on to him by Arthur from Bridie. It seemed she was worried and Timmo was wondering what could possibly be so urgent. He sat a small distance from Tim and Dandy, frowning a little.

Tim shot a puzzled glance at him.

"Hope he's not sickening for something," he murmured.

"Could be a woman," suggested Dandy helpfully.

"Don't be a fool, man, he's only three months past his sixteenth birthday."

"You rolled plenty girls in the hay long time afore you was his age," laughed Dandy.

"No, not Timmo. He's more like Mary—reserved," replied Tim.

"Well, lad, have it your own way," said Dandy, contentedly puffing that long clay pipe.

They returned home that evening and Maud gave them a special celebration dinner of roast beef and baked spuds washed down with Irish whiskey. She was very talkative, full of her exploits and her visit to the town hall.

When Tim, Dandy and Maud began to discuss Irish Home Rule, Timmo slipped quietly out to meet Bridie in the park. She was waiting just inside the gate. The long blue overcoat gave her a kind of dumpy look but her long hair shone in the moonlight like burnished chestnut. As Timmo drew near he felt strangely excited and pressed passionate kisses on her and drew her further into the park, eager to make love. Bridie went willingly and it was a while before the subject of that urgent note was brought up.

Timmo sat up and lit a cigarette. "Why did you send me that note?" he asked mildly.

Bridie's big eyes, round like saucers, stared at him reproachfully. "Oh, you know, Timmo. Don't pretend."

"What am I supposed to know?" demanded Timmo with the thick-headedness of youth. He wanted facts. He stared at her open-mouthed when she told him.

Bridie's full lips trembled as she spoke. "Oh, Timmo, when you rushed me off my feet like that I thought it was because you wanted to wed me."

"Marry you?" shouted Timmo. "But I'm only sixteen."

"And I'm nineteen," sobbed Bridie. "So I suppose I should have had more sense."

"Now don't cry," urged Timmo, trying to gather his wits. "I do like you, but I can't get married. I'm only an apprentice and me dad will go mad if I drop out now."

"Have you forgotten that you forced me, Timmo?" said Bridie, getting a little angry.

"Maybe you could swallow something," suggested that perplexed young lad.

Bridie was most indignant. "How could you say such a thing? A good Catholic boy too! Why, I'm finished with you." She got up and ran home, her tears falling fast.

Maud glared suspiciously at her as she came in. She's been with some man, that's for sure, she thought. I'd best get rid of her. Don't want no more goings on in this alley when Mary comes home.

Early next morning, while Maud was still in bed, she heard a strange sound. She rose and descended the stairs to see Bridie retching in the sink—that hard dry vomiting. There was usually only one reason for that.

"What's wrong, Bridie?" she asked sharply.

But Bridie, clinging grimly to the edge of the draining board, was feeling too ill to reply.

Maud grabbed hold of her. "You're pregnant! You little bitch! Who is it? Is he going to marry you?" she demanded.

Bridie shook her pale scared face.

"Do you mean to say you don't know whose it is?" cried Maud.

But Bridie just broke down and wept.

"I thought you were a sexy bit from the beginning," stormed Maud. "Tell me who it was and I'll help you. But if not, out you go, bag and baggage."

Bridie's lovely eyes, so full of tears, just stared dumbly at her.

"Right," declared Maud, "you had your choice, now go and pack your bag."

Bridie put her few possessions in the straw traveling basket, as Maud gave her a month's wages. "Can't let you starve," she said, "but you'd better find the father soon or you'll be right up the creek."

Bridie, in her long blue coat, walked slowly out of the house and stood by the canal wall, looking like a lost mongrel, not uttering a sound, just standing with downcast eyes, her little straw bag beside her.

In no time at all the whole alley was roused. All eyes stared out at that lone Irish girl as the sound of Maud's raucous voice died down.

Ellen Brown watched sadly and repeated to herself: "He that is without sin among you, let him first cast a stone at her." It could have been herself standing there. If no one went to the rescue of Bridie she would find the courage from somewhere. Rapidly she began to dress.

Becky, too, was concerned.

"Go to that girl, Sam. Give her money to go home. I can't bear to see her standing there so forlorn." Sam scratched his head, unable to make up his mind.

Arthur leaped over the wall to rouse Timmo. Timmo in a boozy sleep did not wake right away.

"Maud's thrown Bridie out," whispered Arthur, "and she is headed back home."

All eyes were on Bridie and Lil's hoarse voice cried: "Why don't someone do somefink to help that poor little cow?"

Suddenly from Tim's house ran a tall lithe figure carrying a brown suitcase. It was Timmo dashing to Bridie. He took her by the hand and together they ran like mad from the alley. With a roar like an enraged bull, Tim went running after them but youth was on their side and he was unable to catch them. That was the last glimpse he had of his son for a long time.

Realizing what she had done Maud screamed hysterically and Dandy came from his bed to quieten her. Tim, in his shirt sleeves, his shoulders drooping, went back to his empty home, put his head in his hands and wept. "Oh God, how am I going to face Mary?" he cried.

The children huddled by the canal wall that day and whispered about this latest upheaval in their alley.

# *Roses in December*

ALONGSIDE THE RIVER BLACKWATER IN COUNTY Cork was Mary's mother's cottage. Her late husband had served many loyal years with the landlord farmer, so his widow had been granted this small holding to live out her life. In comparison to the rest of the folk in the area she was in a fairly comfortable position. She kept a pig and a few chickens, and planted rows of potatoes and cabbages behind the cottage. In this placid atmosphere Mary slowly came back to life. Her hair had become prematurely grey but her figure was still neat and slim. There were still smoky shadows under her eyes and a melancholy sadness about her, but mentally she was restored to health. She sat beside her mother, a white-haired old lady in her late seventies whose tiny hands worked industriously at the fine beautiful Irish lace to sell to the tourists. In a brown Holland sun bonnet little Mollie worked among the vegetables, gently drawing out the weeds with a hoe. It was two years since she had come to live in Ireland and now turned ten she had lost that pale timid look, her cheeks glowed and her skin was like roses and cream from the fresh country air.

"Will you go home, Mary," inquired her mother, "when Tim comes at the end of the summer?"

Mary shook her head. "I'll never go back to that alley, Mother."

The old lady looked worried. "I'm thinking of Timmo. It's hardly fair to him. He must be a big lad now."

Mary looked hurt. "Don't you want me to stay, Mother?" she asked.

"Oh, my darling," cried the old lady, "of course I want you, but your home and family are broken up. It worries me. And that lovely girl Mollie, what chance will she have of a husband if she stays here? Most of our young men leave to find work abroad."

"Oh, don't worry, Mother," said Mary placidly, "when Tim comes we'll discuss making a home elsewhere."

The old lady smiled gently and offered up a silent prayer that when the time came for her to go to her grave, once more Tim and Mary would be united.

The unusual sight of a postman coming down the path gave them both a surprise; very few letters found their way to this out of the way place. Tim was no great correspondent and Timmo never wrote, though Maud did occasionally. On this occasion the postman brought a four-page missive from Maud, full of foreboding. She begged Mary to return, informing her of the disappearance of Timmo and that big Tim was drunk all the time and had been thrown off the job for fighting, and things were getting worse all the time.

Mary's face paled as she read the letter, but she got up casually and said, "You have your wish, Mother. Tomorrow I start for home."

The old lady crossed herself. "I'll help you pack, dear," she said.

Maud, after months of trying to cope with Tim and negotiating with the police to find Timmo, had drawn a blank, so in desperation she had written to Mary. Maud was still at loggerheads with Rosie who showed no sign of giving in. The rents were still not being paid but apart from long letters to various departments of the council, very little had been achieved. Rosie, now that she was respectably married to 'Arry Smiff, had started a campaign to get friendly with her neighbors. 'Arry had spread out with Rosie's cash and with a bit of initiative he had installed a betting room in the back of the cafe. This was completely illegal but that was the least of his worries.

Bill Welton, having just returned from another dose of "porridge," was now narker-out and bookie's runner for 'Arry Smiff. He was onto a good thing; he spent most of the day standing on the street corner and gambled away any money he obtained. That wily bookie had Arthur installed in the back room reckoning up the bets and on the blower all day getting tips straight from the horse's mouth, so to speak.

It was Becky who gave in first and paid up the arrears in her rent. She and Sam then made an offer to buy the whole house from Rosie. Determined to keep in with the neighbors, Rosie said neither yes nor no; she just kept Becky guessing. This item of news came to Maud by way of Lil who heard and saw all that went on in the alley. Many strong words were bandied about back and forth over the cobbles. Maud declared, "Over my dead body will Becky get that house!"

"Don't think you're the only one with money," retorted Becky. "My family got plenty, they'll look after me."

Rosie leaned out of her window when Maud and Becky had a set to, and Lil from her place on the windowsill had a ringside seat.

Rosie, anxious to please the residents, organized an outing to the Derby. On the day of the race a big horsedrawn brake arrived, stacked with beer. Lil and Bill came out in their Sunday best attire followed by Arthur wearing his jaunty checked cap and a red carnation in his buttonhole. He was the master of ceremonies, the chief organizer.

Various other bodies emerged from the pub and went aboard the brake while two big dappled greys pawed the ground impatiently. A wizened little man who played the cornet outside the pub on Saturday nights was sitting beside the driver blowing his instrument lustily as all the kids from the surrounding districts gathered to watch. Rosie sat there feeling as important as a queen. She wore a black-and-white spotted dress and on her carefully coiffured hair was a huge mauve hat decorated with white plumes. She really stole the show. Even Tim in his depressed state managed to raise a feeble smile as he saw them clamber awkwardly up the ladders of the brake. Maud made loud sarcastic comments on the age and shape of the women. She was extremely annoyed and it seemed for a while as though fat butter-ball Rosie was going to be defeathered. But Maud went indoors and wrote to Mary, after which she felt much better.

When the expedition pushed off, the kids all ran behind yelling and 'Arry Smiff threw pennies out to them so that they fought each other tooth and nail in the scramble. Pat and Colleen also ran behind the brake for a while picking up the odd coins, and with the proceeds they bought themselves some bars of Nestle's chocolate—a great favorite of theirs. When they had finished the chocolate they went into Colleen's back yard and secretly, behind the toilets, they licked the red chocolate-bar wrappers and painted their lips and cheeks with it until they looked like two circus clowns. Arm in arm, they strolled to the canal wall where Lew was perched, eating a large cake.

"Give us a bit," demanded Colleen.

"Can't," said Lew, stuffing the last piece into his mouth.

"Pig!" declared Pat.

"You couldn't have eaten it anyway," said Lew in a superior manner. "It was a kosher cake."

"What's a kosher cake?" inquired Pat.

"It's what only Jews eat," said Lew mysteriously.

"Get away," jeered Colleen. "It's because you're a greedy hog and didn't want to share it." They began to kick and fight.

"Pack it up," said Pat. "Do you like our makeup, Lew?"

The girls paraded back and forth, and the fat boy almost crumpled up with laughter.

"You don't 'alf look funny," he gasped.

It was well past midnight when the brake unloaded its drunks. "Goodnight, Rosie, dear," hiccupped Lil.

Maud turned irritably in her bed. "I'll get even with that blonde bitch however long it takes me," she muttered to herself.

It was several days later when, as an unshaven, bleary-eyed Tim sat amid the muddle of his neglected house, surrounded by dirty crocks, empty beer bottles and fish and chip papers, Maud came stalking in carrying a plate of food. Placing it before him she flounced out without a word. She had lost all patience with Tim; she was sure he was slowly and surely becoming an alcoholic; he ate very little and drank from morning till night. Tim looked vacantly at the plate. He had lost all taste for food. He pushed the plate away from him and put his head on his arm, miserably resting on the mucky table. I feel so bloody rough, he told himself. I must pull myself together. Tears of self-pity came to his eyes as he slumped forward.

Then a cool, gentle voice, said: "Now eat up your dinner, Tim," and there was a soft hand on his shoulder. Mary was home again. Tim's arms went about her, his head against her warm body where his tears wet her dress.

Mary stood calm and still until he let her go. Then she called: "Come, Mollie, come and kiss your pa."

Mollie dashed in; loving arms entwined his neck. She had always been his favorite. He held her at arm's length and fondly surveyed her.

"My," he said, "you have grown up, and what a pretty colleen you are, to be sure."

With her pink cheeks, creamy skin and coal black hair Mollie was indeed a grand sight.

The news that Mary was home spread through the alley like a bush fire. Soon Maud, Dandy, little Pat and all the Weltons were crowding into that small kitchen, kissing, talking, and laughing with such excitement that had not been known for a long time. Later there came a well-dressed young man carrying a big bunch of roses; it was Arthur, and Mary wept at the sight of her little urchin grown up. He stood shyly to one side away from the boisterous neighbors, but in his eyes shone a love for Mary that nothing would ever change. Becky, Sam and Lew came over, while Lil and Maud made tea together—old scores were forgotten. It was just like old times in Mary's house.

Over the road at the cafe, Rosie's baleful eyes glared through the window.

"Cor blimey, 'Arry," she cried, "she's back!"

"Don't worry, gel, you're a married woman now," was 'Arry's comment. "And I'll see you stay that way," he added. There was a nasty glint in his eye as he made this remark. Rosie was not sure she liked it.

July was kind to the alley dwellers, with its weather, and the neighbors took many trips out together—not in Rosie's horse-drawn brake, but very respectably in the train. They went on day trips from Bow Station to Southend, with bags of food, buckets and spades. They paddled and had picnics on the beach. Maud, Lil and Mary sat on the sands and gossiped while the men went to the pub and the children romped about. For one bright summer the sun shone in our alley and most of its folks were content and happy. Maud decided to let up on Rosie for a while but, she threatened, she was not finished with her yet.

The door of No. 5 still remained shut and the dark red curtains closed. Ellen's small thin shape drifted down the alley in the same old shabby clothes, always with a book under her arm.

"She's going bleeding barmy," was Lil's cryptic comment from her usual seat on the windowsill. "Looks half-starved, always sitting there reading books." Lil would say her piece loud and clear for all to hear. The fact that Ellen still considered her as a future mother-in-law did not occur to Lil; her son George did not write to her. But he had never learned to write, he had spent too little time in school, and Lil was quite illiterate and not able to correspond with him anyway. Lil had no time for sentiment, as far as she was concerned another son had left home and that was that.

Ellen had received a couple of printed ill-spelled notes from George since he left two years ago. The first one, from the ship, was full of love and rash promises and the second, written six months later, described the place and the job. In his new life George seemed very satisfied. Since then there had been no news of him. It was now the beginning of October and Ellen was at the end of her tether. She had saved diligently over these two years; she had deprived herself of many comforts and had had no pleasures—all for this grand wedding that she dreamed of, the white velvet and the deep red roses. In her loneliness she had dwelt so often on this special occasion that it had become an obsession. She would walk back and forth to work to save on bus fares, planning and planning, almost talking to herself as she plodded along. I wonder, should I ask Maud's little girl to be a bridesmaid? she pondered. I'll have to have Colleen too; they would make an ideal pair. Red velvet for them would be nice, and white carnations perhaps. Over and over in her mind she turned her wedding plans as she walked along in a dream.

Emm, seeing her one day when she came out from the bike shed (for she rode everywhere now), called out: "Hi, Ellen!

Mind you don't get run down, walking along in a trance like that!"

Ellen smiled tolerantly, she was used to Emm's banter.

Once back home she would settle down to read, wrapped in a blanket to save fuel bills. In the last few months she had digested Huxley, Darwin and Karl Marx, Shaw and Wells, Jane Austen and the Brontës. Hour after hour she read, consuming every bit of knowledge and losing herself in the dream worlds of others.

Saturday morning was the only time Ellen made contact with the other residents of the alley. One misty autumn morning she gathered sufficient courage to go over and ask Lil if she had heard from George. I can make arrangements about the bridesmaids at the same time, she told herself, bolstering up her resolve. So far she had never been within speaking distance of her future mother-in-law, except the rude comments that Lil made on her appearance as she walked through the alley. This morning, Lil, as blousy as ever, sat in her usual position. With her arms crossed and her small eyes missing nothing, Lil sat there observing the lives of her neighbors. But when Ellen came across the cobbles and stood directly facing her she was taken aback and stared open mouthed, not knowing what to say.

"I came to ask if you had heard from George," Ellen said timidly.

Lil looked angry. "No, why should I?" she answered abruptly. "He's out in Australia, ain't he?"

"I hope you did not mind me asking," Ellen murmured apologetically.

"I couldn't care less," declared Lil belligerently. "He don't write to me. If you're still mooning over him, you're a bigger bleeding fool than I thought you looked."

A hard lump came into Ellen's throat. But she would not be bullied; her wedding must go well at all costs.

"I wonder if you would allow me to take Colleen to be measured for her bridesmaid dress and Patricia as well."

Lil exploded. "What bleeding wedding?" she yelled. "Silly cow! Don't fink he's coming back 'ere for you, do yer?" she glared at Ellen as if challenging her to dispute it. But Ellen had lost her nerve, she had had enough. She fled back home like a rabbit to its burrow.

Mary had heard Lil's strident voice through the thin walls and wanted to go to Ellen's aid. Mollie, however, with a firm hand detained her. Since her mother's illness, she would not allow anything to upset or worry her.

Colleen's big ears took in every word that was said. Indignantly she stumped past Lil to go to her friend next door and stood with her hands on hips, a small imitation of her mother. "Come out, Pat, I want to tell you somefink," she yelled.

Pat's small disgruntled face appeared in the doorway, one hand holding the long rope of hair that she was plaiting, the other hand a red ribbon. "Don't call me now," she said crossly, "you know I have to go to church with Mollie."

"Wait till yer 'ear wot I got to say," Colleen's voice rose in that same Cockney twang of her dissolute mother's.

Pat looked alarmed but she came out quietly, closing the door so that Maud would not hear.

"What's up?" she demanded.

"Well, we was going to be bridesmaids, we was, in lovely long frocks and flowers on our heads," said Colleen, disappointment in her voice.

"Who to?" inquired Pat.

"To our George and Ellen Brown, of course," Colleen replied.

"Well, why aren't we?" asked her best friend.

"Why?" screeched Colleen, mimicking Lil again. "Because me bleeding muvver's gorn and spoilt it for us, that's why."

"Hush," whispered Pat, terrified in case Maud heard her friend swearing. "I'll come over to the canal wall and you can tell me all about it." Huddled together on the wall, they discussed the terrible thing that had happened. To be done out of being a bridesmaid! Why, that was a real setback! Fat Lew was perched on the wall and he wriggled up closer to find out what they were whispering about. "Ha! Ha!" he yelled, "she won't have you because you're too ugly."

"You beast!" they screamed together and rushed at him with their determined little fists screwed up ready to punch him.

"Don't hit me!" yelled Lew in a scared voice. But he lost his balance and toppled backward over the wall straight into the canal. With a loud shout and a big splash he disappeared.

Nearby Arthur was cleaning his bike—a new-found treasure that he had bought with his wages. There he was, attired in a smart yellow pullover with socks to match worn knee-high over his trousers, and earning from his sister the nickname of "lavatory legs." As Lew went over the wall Arthur sprang into action. Dragging off his pullover, he dived in after Lew, still wearing his yellow cycling socks. The fat boy whirled around and around in the deep water which was carrying him under the bridge. In no time Arthur had hold of his collar and was dragging Lew, gasping and coughing, to the bank.

The balloon had gone up; the news that someone had fallen into the canal had spread quickly. All the inhabitants gathered down by the canal wall; the excitement and jabbering was reminiscent of an Arab market. Tim and 'Arry Smiff pressed the water from Lew's stomach and lungs, while Maud was ready with blankets and a glass of brandy for the shivering Arthur. Screaming and gesticulating, Becky ran about like a chicken without a head. "Who did it? Who pushed my Lew in the Cut?"

Lil, as usual, ready in defense of her wayward daughter, shouted: "Don't you blame my Colleen. Always the same, you Jews—don't matter abaht our kids, it's always yours, that's all that matters."

Everyone ignored Lil and helped to get Lew into his parents' house and to bed.

For his good deed Arthur got his name in the paper. There was a picture of him outside his house in a jaunty cap and holding on to his famous bike. There was talk of him getting the Royal Humane Award; not many small alleys could boast of such a hero.

Arthur cared little for that promised award. In his pocket was a letter and a half sovereign with it. The letter contained words he treasured all his life. It was from Becky Lewis thanking him for dragging her son out of the canal. It read:

4 Autumn Alley

Dear Arthur,

We owe you the life of our son. No words can express our feelings. We will always be grateful and if any day we can assist you, do not hesitate to ask.

May God be with you and give you all the luck you deserve.

Sam and Becky Lewis.

PS. Just a little bit of gold inside to buy something for yourself.

Ellen Brown had watched the whole pantomime of Lew's rescue from her window. How strange, she was thinking, how that murky green water gets involved in the life of our alley. Kids fall in it; unwanted dogs, cats and furniture are disposed of in it; and that young brother of George's, Billy, had got on a barge and sailed away on it last year and no one had heard of him since. The years rolled back and there on the canal wall was her George, his white hair blowing in the wind, fishing with a piece of string and a bent pin. She wondered if anyone ever voluntarily ended their lives in it. While this melancholy thought possessed her, Ellen walked through the deserted rooms touching the little treasures that had been her mother's only joy—velvet-framed photos, a shell basket. All the time she could hear Lil's loud voice inside her head repeating: "Yer don't fink he's goner come back 'ere, do yer?"

She put on her old red wool tam-o'-shanter and went for a walk through the park, the way she used to go with George; and as she walked she imagined her wedding, step by step, from church door to honeymoon chamber. Head bent, she did not see the party of young people who were riding their bikes toward her until they had almost run her down.

"Hello, Ellen," yelled Emm, very smart in her knicker-bockers. "Come and have tea with us at the open-air tea shop."

The young folk gathered on the lovely green lawn drinking tea and eating cream buns. They were an odd-looking bunch; youths in checked suits and natty neck bows and contrasting waistcoats, the girls in hats held on with colored veils, and hobble skirts looped up to give more freedom for pedaling the bike. They all chattered gaily. Emm, who looked like neither boy nor girl, strode from table to table, stridently putting forth her point of view.

"We've formed a club, Ellen," she said. "Get one of these contraptions and join us."

Ellen shook her head. "No thanks, I'm too nervous."

"Nonsense," said Emm, "anyone can learn."

"I'll teach you," volunteered a bespectacled youth sitting beside her. "It's not so bad once you get your balance."

"No thanks," said Ellen. "I'm saving up to get married."

The youth stared at her for a while, and then got up and wandered off to talk to someone else.

"You are a chump," Emm informed her. "Old Egghead there is my cousin, and he fancies you."

Ellen said goodbye and went home to her lonely abode.

The winter came cold and hard and still the dejected figure of Ellen tramped back and forth from home to city and back to the alley each night. The snow soaked through the thin soles of her shoes and her fingers were blue under the worn patched gloves. It was the second week in December and there was still no news of George. The thought that he might arrive suddenly consoled her; her lovely wedding could go on as planned.

There was no longer the laughing, warm and generous Emm to cheer the office now; she had gone to the college of science, determined to study photography, and Ronald had gone to America to complete his newspaper training. So life was duller than ever. Each evening Ellen buried herself in her reading and thought of George. Her common sense told her that he would not wait for her as she had done for him. But she would not allow herself to listen. She would show them in the alley; she would teach them not to mock her.

Also in the dark lonely nights the voices of her twin brothers came cold and clear to torment her. That blood-stained shirt in the lavatory, why could she not forget it? That cry in the night when that old lady fought for her life? She, Ellen, was guilty too; she had known all about the twins and had said nothing. Voices whispered and whispered close to her ears. She put her hands over them to shut out the sound.

It was Christmas Eve and in the alley preparations were being made for a real good time. Mary was back home, the men were all working. There was new paint and pretty wallpaper; Lil, Mary and Becky all had new flowered curtains. They were almost identical with just a slight variation in the shade and pattern. Lil had copied Mary and Becky had followed suit.

Pat and Colleen were busy wrapping up little parcels and

holding secret meetings with Lew to smuggle him the chocolate that was forbidden him now. He would tell fantastic stories of his new school and boast that all his friends' parents were in show business.

"Get out of it," jeered Colleen, "they're all Jew boys up at that school."

"My dear girl," Lew replied in his most supercilious tone, "don't you know that the flowers of the theatrical profession are all Jews?"

"I don't believe yer," retorted Colleen.

But Pat was inclined to believe him and said, "Don't argue. Go on, Lew, tell us."

"Shortly I'm to be in a play," confided Lew. "I might even let you come and see me."

"What's it called?" demanded Colleen, very jealous of all these new friends that Lew boasted about.

"It's from Shakespeare," said Lew airily. "I'm to play a fat fellow called Falstaff. It's not really your type of thing, it's a bit highbrow for you girls."

"Slosh him!" cried Colleen, "and get our bar of chocolate back."

So they mowed him down to the pavement, punching and pommeling him. His yells brought out Becky who was most incensed.

"My life!" she cried. "What a way for girls to behave! I'm disgusted."

The girls stuck out their tongues and ran away.

With slim black stockinged legs and long white pinafores the two friends, arms entwined, now skipped happily together outside the desolate No. 5. Inside the house lay Ellen unable to move. She was down with the flu. She lay white and shivering, wondering if the little girls would hear her if she called out. She opened her mouth but no sound came.

Soon it was dark and the lamplighter passed by. Ellen watched through the glass as he pulled the chain on the mantle with a long stick. The yellow light flooded the bedroom as Ellen thought of the long cold night ahead of her, unable even to get up to get a drink to quench her burning throat.

Outside it had become quiet; the children had gone to bed. Then Mollie and Mary came with the carol singers from the church. They stood under the lamp, their voices rang out sweetly on the still, cold frosty air, but Ellen was unable to lift her limp hand from the bedcover. Those strange things were there; they always came at night, laughing and cackling, jumping on and off the bed. She wished they would go away. As her temperature rose, her body got weaker and her mind more delirious. Those things, they talked and jabbered. "They're monkeys," she giggled. "Why not? We all come from monkeys. I am a monkey, Egghead is a monkey, Emm too. We are all monkeys." All through the night they tormented her until the gray dawn brought Christmas Day.

With crazed eyes Ellen looked about the room. The bells were ringing. It was time for her wedding. On the back of the bedroom door hung her shabby old coat and the red tam-o'-shanter. How nice! Her wedding outfit, a long white dress and a bunch of red roses. Unsteadily she rose, put the coat about her trembling shoulders and bunched up the red tammy in her hands. Slowly and very sedately she went downstairs and out of the front door. She was going to her wedding, George would be waiting for her.

Tim had risen early as was his custom. Rolling up his shirt sleeves he looked out of the front door to see what the weather was like. Suddenly he noticed Ellen. She's out a bit sharpish this morning, he reflected. Just as he was about to go indoors and close the door he heard a splash. Looking toward the canal he realized that Ellen had disappeared and on top of the wall was her red tam-o'-shanter. Tim ran to the wall and saw her head just disappearing beneath the water. The ice had cracked around her and the water closed over her head. "Arthur!" yelled Tim, as he almost fell over the wall. Slipping and sliding on the ice, he lay on the tow path and grabbed hold of Ellen, clinging on grimly as she fought like a wild cat to get free. Tim roared out again for Arthur to hurry and he leaped over the wall dressed in his fancy pajamas. But Tim had panicked and crashed his huge fist into Ellen's face so she lay white and still.

Together they pulled her out and carried her back to the alley. Her long hair was caked in mud, her eyes closed tight. They took her into Lil's so as not to upset Mary, and for once in her life Lil got moving.

Removing the wet clothes, she wrapped the girl in blankets and put hot water bottles at her feet. But there was still no sign of life. Tim looked worried.

"I hope I didn't hit her too hard. She would have drowned us both if I hadn't quietened her. Better send for the ambulance. There's no sign of her coming round."

A small crowd gathered outside Lil's house to watch Ellen's still body being transferred to the ambulance. It was one of those new petrol-driven contraptions, a blue and white shuddering thing, driven by two men in smart uniforms from the new hospital that used to be the old workhouse. Instilled in all watching was a fear of hospitals; they were regarded as places of no return. With solemn faces the adults said a silent goodbye to sad little Ellen, and the children peered at this weird thing on wheels that emitted such strange noises.

"I'll go along with her," volunteered Tim, "she has no kin and I might have to give a statement to the police, if all's not well with her."

"Never quite the ticket, she wasn't," insisted Lil, when the ambulance had left, "that's why I didn't want my George to marry her."

"Yes, better off where she is, poor little cow," snivelled weepy Rosie.

Mary stood back from the crowd with Mollie clinging to her arm. "How sad is this little alley," she murmured in a quiet voice. "They are ready to bury that poor soul before she's dead. Come, Mollie, we'll go up to church and pray for her recovery." Together they went, young Mollie now almost as tall as her mother.

Arthur sat in Maud's kitchen, clad in only a blanket, as she washed and ironed his pajamas and he knocked back her brandy. Lil still stood gossiping on her doorstep having already forgotten that once more her son was a hero. Arthur was no swimmer and Ellen, in her crazy state, could have pulled him in as well as Tim and drowned the lot, but Maud did not forget so easily. She loved this courageous daredevil, with his friendly and carefree approach to life. She also appreciated of course his knowledge of the gee gees, for it was from Arthur that Maud got all those hot tips.

Arthur sat at ease, his long thin legs spread out before the fire. Without his specs his eyes remained crossed which gave him a ludicrous expression.

"Put your specs on, Arthur," said Maud ironing briskly. "You ain't no handsome hero without them."

With a grimace Arthur found his specs and wiped them dry. "Don't rub it in, Maud. I know I'll never win no beauty contest," he grinned.

"Ah, but you're a brave lad, and that's got its compensations," she told him. "Hitching two people out of the Cut deserves some reward—I'll see what can be done."

"Tim saved her, not me," protested Arthur.

"Don't be a chump, he's so heavy he would sink like a stone, boots and belly full of beer," jested Maud.

"Don't talk like that about Uncle Tim," Arthur reproached her.

"Well, perhaps it is a bit spiteful, you may be right, Arthur," she said, handing him his freshly ironed pajamas. "They are nice, aren't they? You like smart things, don't you Arthur?"

"Not 'alf," said Arthur. "All I want from life is plenty of money to spend."

Maud smiled indulgently. "Pity you didn't go on with your education, you're a bright lad."

"Could be," said Arthur, "but now I think I'll stick with the gee gees; perhaps some of your good luck will rub off on me." They laughed together.

Meanwhile, Tim rode nervously in the horseless carriage as it almost flew along the road to the local hospital. He looked at Ellen's ashen face as her lashes flickered into life. For a brief second her lips moved. Tim leaned close and heard her whisper: "It's in the toilet, the blood-stained shirt." Then she passed out again.

It's funny what a crazed mind will divulge, thought Tim, as he sat rubbing her cold hands.

In the cold corridor of the hospital, Tim sat all day. The police interviewed him and a newspaper reporter asked for details. An attempted suicide? Did Tim rescue her? and so forth, but still no report came of Ellen.

At five o'clock a white-capped sister came to tell Tim that Ellen was still alive but in a dangerous state of shock. "You'd better go home, it is Christmas Day," she advised. "Come back tomorrow morning."

Tim left and walked toward home. It was cold and getting dark. He could do with a drink. He decided to wait a while until the pub opened and idled away the time looking over the canal wall at the freezing water, wondering what had ever possessed Ellen to try to end her life that way.

The next day Tim and Mary went to visit Ellen in the hospital where she still lay in a semi-conscious state. They had brought with them a huge bunch of red roses, acquired by Maud from a posh florist and paid for by the folk in the alley. So poor little Ellen had her roses in December after all.

# Maud Buys Up the
Alley

THE NEW YEAR CAME. AS THE BELLS TOLLED
London celebrated and the alley had a party. At midnight in
the middle of the cobbled square alley dwellers all joined
hands to sing "Auld Lang Syne." The yellow light of the one
gaslamp shone down on their flushed faces and the cobble-
stones echoed to the sound of dancing feet. There was Lil and
Bill quite intoxicated, and Tim and Dandy full of good old
Irish whiskey. Mollie and Mary stood close together, and near
them Arthur, smiling happily. All the children were there and
at the last moment Sam and Becky came from their house
very sedately to join in. Maud left her pile of sandwiches
which she had been preparing and 'Arry Smiff staggered forth
from behind a tall stack of beer crates. Around and around they
all twirled, ending in a hectic knees-up.

Only one person was absent, and that was Rosie. She had
condescended to come to the party earlier to show off the new
dress she had bought at Christmas, but 'Arry had got drunk
and danced with all the young girls, so Rosie had taken
herself off home and 'Arry Smiff spent the night on Maud's
floor.

Maud was still involved in a very complicated game with 'Arry Smiff. Every day she placed a bet, sometimes a pound note, and nearly always backed a winner. 'Arry, who dealt mostly in threepenny bets, had originally appreciated Maud's custom. But when she continued to win he got worried. Then she started to plough her winnings straight back. All through the remainder of the racing season her request was abruptly: "Let it ride," allowing all her winnings to go on to the next horse. 'Arry Smiff was quite sure that she would soon lose it all so he did not worry. But by mid-September he owed her fifty guineas. 'Arry encouraged Maud to gamble hoping her luck would run out soon but by the time the season finished and Maud demanded her winnings, they now amounted to seventy-five pounds. 'Arry was worried. "Ask her to take a check, Arthur. I might get out of trouble before it bounces."

However, the check came back and Maud with it.

"What sort of damned rogue are you?" she shouted. "I'll take it in cash if you don't mind."

"Why not let it go on, Maud?" whined 'Arry. "Might pick up a bit more during the flat season."

"Don't like the flat," declared Maud. "I'll have my money."

"Perhaps we can do business," he wheedled.

"We'd better, otherwise I'll let the police know about this joint."

"Still interested in buying the houses?" he queried.

"You know I am," she said abruptly.

"How much are you prepared to give for the two on your side?" he ventured.

"Three," corrected Maud. "I want Becky's house as well."

"Hundred quid ain't bad," said 'Arry, "and property going up all the time, and there's forty quid owing for arrears in rent."

"That's okay, I'll pay it all up," Maud said. "Now what do you want for them? No argy bargy, they're broken down slums and I know that it's going to cost you a hundred to do them up. The council only gave you till the spring. Your time's running out."

'Arry looked alarmed. Rosie had said to get rid of them if

the cost was too high, so this might be a God-given opportunity, he thought.

"Fifty quid each plus the rent owing and minus the seventy-five I owe yer," he said quickly.

"Done," said Maud, opening her handbag. "Here's your blood money, and I want it all in writing." She rattled her bag of sovereigns. "Two hundred and we're quits." He goggled. Here she was raging and storming for her money and her handbag was stuffed with gold.

But Maud was not going to back down. She stood over him as he signed the draft that Arthur made out with shaky hands. "I'll take it to the solicitors today," Maud told him, "and I don't want any funny business with that fat bitch of a wife of yours." She marched out.

'Arry wiped the sweat from his brow. "What am I going to say to Rosie?" he whimpered.

Arthur looked dispassionately at him. Because of Mary he had no sympathy for Rosie.

"You could do with the ready money, 'Arry," he told him. "Might be able to get that stand down on the track."

"Christ, you could be right, lad," said 'Arry gathering up the bag of sovereigns.

Within a few weeks it was all signed, sealed and delivered and the alley was practically the property of Maud Fitzpatrick who immediately began to make changes all around. The two pieces of wasteland at each end of the alley were included in the deeds. One was beside Tim's house, facing Rosie's cafe. It was a fair-sized piece of open ground where the carriers parked their huge wagons for their nags to munch the grass while they had a cup of tea at Rosie's. The other piece of ground was beside Becky's house and led to the canal bank.

Imagine the surprise of the residents when a brightly lit stall appeared one night on the waste ground beside Tim's house. A young man with a loud voice sold toys and household goods, and raffle tickets to help boost the sales. To Pat and Colleen it was a new-found heaven. On Saturdays they hung about that stall all day. Once Colleen won an enamel bowl in a raffle and was immensely proud of it; it was her own personal possession and no one but Colleen was allowed the use of it. Colleen would wash her lovely hair in it.

The majority of the residents did not want to annoy Maud by expressing their opinions, for she had canceled the rent they owed and installed painters and decorators to do up the houses. Rosie, however, was loud and vociferous in her protests, for the wagon drivers no longer stopped for their breakfasts. "Nowhere to leave the old nags," they explained. Rosie was losing business and she was furious. Moreover, the huge paraffin flares that lit up the stall also lit up the side door to Rosie's where the furtive ones crept in to stake a bet. "It ain't right," said 'Arry Smiff, "the coppers can see right in here now."

Maud was jubilant; she was one up on that bitch Rosie and had a nice bit of profit from the rent of the stall.

Becky was also very eloquent on the subject. "That stall lowers the tone of the neighborhood," she said. "We should have the law on her."

Immediately Maud was down on her. First she put her rent up to 7s 6d and when Becky protested Maud came back with: "Well, who's going to pay for the repairs?"

So Becky retired sulkily and Maud then had a barge unload some sacks of cement and stack them on the bank, level with Becky's back door. Becky tore over to Maud's house and demanded an explanation.

"That's not your back yard," Maud informed her. "It was a vacant piece of land. Said so on the deeds. Now it's a builder's yard and belongs to the firm of Fitzpatrick."

"I'll sue you," threatened Becky.

"Yes, you do that," grinned Maud, who was thoroughly enjoying herself. After that, along the canal came load after load of cement, all obtained on the cheap to be sold later at an enormous profit. In the "yard" there were piles of bricks, secondhand timber, windows and doors—a whole heap of unsightly stuff that grew higher and higher.

Becky wept in mortification. "I'll move," she threatened, "I'll go up with me sister at Stamford Hill." But she never did.

Maud was in her element, riding roughshod over council officials, who took to going into hiding when they saw her black flowing shape entering the town hall with more demands for proper drainage and various other improvements. The cobbles were torn up, the toilets ran free, new-fangled gas cookers arrived and lights were fitted that held a light mantle which popped when it was lit.

As Maud improved her properties, Rosie pined after them. She had lost all that her Gran had left her and now the cafe was not doing a lot of good. Red-eyed and weeping, her big moon-like, gin-filled face would be seen at the window watching 'Arry Smiff smarter and tighter lipped than ever. The tall gangling Arthur in a lop-sided cap was now 'Arry's constant companion. They were off to the races to sink what was left of Rosie's inheritance.

The long winter was very cold and the gaslights were cozy. Colleen and Pat played draughts and Ludo hour after hour. Lew had not been allowed to play with them since he fell in the canal.

"What a boy," exclaimed Becky's sister, "twelve years old already and over, but still no Hebrew instruction. Plays with *goyim* at that. What is wrong with you, Becky, eh?"

Becky loved her Lew; he was all she had. "He'll be all right, he's just a late starter," she pleaded in his defense. "He's such a clever boy, so musical and he can play anything."

"Except music," growled Sam, who had heard enough of popular songs being played by ear.

But in the end Becky was forced to give in and Lew was sent off to a Jewish day school in north London, staying with his aunt all the week and coming home at weekends. Pat and Colleen remained as close friends as ever but missed Lew, mostly for his piano playing.

Mary and Mollie went several times a week and twice on Sundays to the Catholic church, where Mollie was a child of Holy Mary and walked in procession, dressed in a long blue cloak and white veil with a very pious expression on her face. Both Mary and Mollie were deeply involved with the church and its activities and they talked of nothing else but the church. Most evenings they were busy on some church business or other.

It if happened to be a foggy or particularly dark night Arthur would take his bike and go to meet mother and daughter. With the light of his bicycle lamp, they would stroll along together. Arthur now considered himself a real man of the world and still had a "pash" on his Mary but of late his eyes had wandered in the direction of Mollie.

Mollie, however, never knew that Arthur was there; all her time and energy was taken up looking after her lovely mother.

Not far away in the local hospital Ellen Brown was slowly being restored to the living. She had received a tremendous amount of help from the ward sister whose own love life had gone and who now devoted her entire life to her career. The sister with her own memories gave all her patience and understanding to Ellen Brown and was able to pull her through the very worst days when the deep dark depression was hard to fight.

At the end of March, Ellen sat out in the glass-covered balcony looking over the forest of London chimney pots. Her hair had been cut short to prevent any more falling out, her face was thin and pale. There was an entirely different look in her eyes from before, and she no longer screwed them up nervously, they were wide and clear.

Emm came that day, freshly tanned from her Swiss skiing holiday.

"Now look here, Nell," she declared, "you're not going back to that gloomy old house. I won't let you."

"I'm all right now." Ellen spoke in a clear decisive voice.

"It doesn't look it to me," said Emm, peering at her.

"It was a bad attack of flu. I'm over it now," said Ellen.

Emm only stared at her and thought that Ellen had perhaps forgotten that she tried to do herself in. She reflected that perhaps it was better not to mention it.

"You come and dig with me. I've got old Egghead's flat now. You've got a bit saved—you could make a start on that novel you always wanted to write."

"I wouldn't like to bother you," protested Ellen, though her heart leaped at the chance to leave the hated alley and all those peering eyes.

"That's settled then," said Emm. "Give me your latch-key and I'll go and get what things you need for now. Then I'll get a cab and you can come straight to me when you're discharged, and no argy bargy. That's final."

Ellen smiled affectionately at Emm who, though not yet twenty, was so well poised and assertive.

A week later Ellen drove through the city in a cab with an excited chattering Emm, leaving Autumn Alley behind forever. The door of No. 5 remained closed and the curtains drawn tight. There were rumors and speculation. According to Lil, Ellen Brown had gone completely potty and they had taken her to an asylum.

# BOOK TWO

# The Buskers

IN THESE LAST FEW YEARS LIL HAD LOST ALL remaining traces of beauty and was now fat, square and solid. Her mousy hair was pulled back in a scraggy bun, her eyes red-rimmed. She was loud in her exclamations and slow in her gait. She always wore a print dress, never overclean, and over it a black woolen apron. She idled her time away between the windowsill and the Railway Arms, except when Mary invited her in for a cuppa. Of late, this was seldom because young Mollie did not like Lil. She hated her nasty gossiping tongue and sat looking very disapproving if Lil chanced to visit Mary.

Sweet Mary, her hair was now snow white and her face calm and gentle, those lovely eyes changing from light green to dark according to her mood. Tim, looking at her, would say: "Your eyes get more beautiful and look younger as you grow older, darling."

"Away with you, Tim, behave yourself." Gently Mary would resist his caress. Tim would obey but within him he could feel a secret hungry yearning for the happy passionate Mary of his youth. There was no other woman in his life now; as he remarked to his old pal Dandy: "It's all work and booze now, me boyo, nothing else to look forward to."

Tim had filled out and was even better looking, but Dandy, thinner than ever, was like a dry old stick, positively shrivelled. His dark blue eyes looked out into the world with a melancholy expression and his thin droopy moustache was straggly and lightly ginger from constant dangling in pints of porter. They still drank together, argued together, and worked together, stripped to the waist as they sweated laying curb stones end to end on the new road slowly stretching toward the north. They worked on piece rates, self-employed as they always had been.

Because of the persistent battles that went on at home Dandy stayed out of Maud's way; her energies were either directed against her family or her neighbors. The house was in constant turmoil, and Patricia battled daily with her strong willed mother. For Maud was now agitating for Pat to go to boarding school, and Patricia, remembering that convent she had absconded from, was refusing quite flatly to go to another crummy school.

"I want to go to school with Colleen," she screamed.

"You stay away from that common child," shouted Maud.

Then Pat rushed at her mother, kicking and screaming. She had a dreadful Irish temper. "Don't you start on my friend. You leave her be!"

Maud held her daughter until she had calmed down, then she delivered a hard clout in the right place. Stunned and offended Pat dashed upstairs and barricaded her bedroom door. Then she leaned out of the window to tell Colleen all her troubles. Her face was all blotched with crying, her hair hanging untidily down.

"I hate her," she declared.

"You can't hate your own mother," replied Colleen.

"Oh yes, you can, if you like," retorted Pat. "Let's run away," she suggested.

"But where?" asked Colleen.

"We could make out we was older and go into service," suggested Pat.

"Don't fancy that," said Colleen. "I want to go on the stage. Let's ask Lew, he might like to come too. We could make money busking, like we did when we was kids."

While they talked and planned, Maud beat angrily on the door. But no way could she get Pat to come out until Dandy came home to make peace between them.

From then on Maud tried endless tricks to bring her wayward daughter into line; she took her up the West End, brought her pretty things, and even found her a new friend, the daughter of Mr. Piggot, the sanitary inspector with whom Maud was very friendly. Mr. Piggot's daughter, Ethel, was the same age as Pat and went to a private school in Woodford. She was bespectacled and had goofy teeth. Pat disliked Ethel from the start. Maud worked like a Trojan to promote this acquaintance but it was a waste of time. Ethel played duets on the piano with her father and giggled hysterically over a game of snap. Pat eyed her with disgust, her dark eyes brooding, her mouth in a sullen droop.

The only glimmer of interest that Pat showed during her visit was that Ethel had ballet lessons at school. "Well come on, show me how it's done," Pat perpetually bullied the red-faced and perspiring Ethel. Now Maud had found a chink in her daughter's armor—ballet lessons were to be the bait. Right away the wily Maud enrolled Pat for the next term. But then Pat discarded Ethel and returned to her old friend Colleen. Having scrounged the ballet steps out of Ethel, she proceeded to teach them to Colleen. Colleen did her best to take an interest in ballet but she was not so agile. She had filled out this past year and her bosom made her top heavy. When Lew was home from school the young troupers rehearsed all day and every day; Lew would play his mouth organ or the piano, and Colleen, with true Cockney gusto, would sing "Waltz me round again, Muvver" or some such ditty, while Pat twirled and pirouetted in Ethel Piggot's tights.

Soon they decided to take this famous act to the West End. One Saturday afternoon a few weeks later they crept off, apparently in disguise. There was Lew in a pair of long shabby flannels and a jersey full of holes, with Arthur's second best cap stuck jauntily on the back of his black curls. Colleen wore an old yellow-spotted evening dress of Lil's. It was very old-fashioned with a bustle at the back and lots of braid, and it trailed behind her as she walked. Her auburn hair was bundled up into Lil's one and only straw hat which was trimmed around the brim with cherries. Pat, with a touch of drama, decided she would be a granny with an old jet-trimmed cape, a tattered old skirt, black Victorian bonnet and long umbrella, all filched from Maud's wardrobe, but underneath it all she wore her much-loved ballet dress. She pretended to be tottery and Lew supported her in an appropriate manner.

They left the alley while most of the folk were either out shopping or drinking, and they danced and sang outside the theaters from Cambridge Circus to Shaftesbury Avenue until Arthur's cap was stuffed with pennies. Then they bought fish and chips, sweets and all the things they fancied. Finally they returned home on the tram and no one had even missed them. For several Saturdays they battled their way through hordes of other buskers, having rehearsed all week for a different act each time. They were very popular. Pat's dainty figure and long slim legs brought the pennies tumbling into the hat. Colleen's fresh young voice and Lew's mouth organ accompaniment brought cries of "Encore!" from their audience who all joined in the chorus of the popular tunes the children sang. Their little act became very prosperous. When men made approaches to the girls Colleen told them where to go and between the three of them they picked up a choice vocabulary of swear words and the loud Cockney patter would draw people's attention to the performance. And all this time it was nice and quiet in the alley—the kids, according to Lil, had "gone orf to the Saturday pictures."

One Saturday night it was wet and rather cold. The threesome stood by the chestnut stand warming their fingers, waiting for the vendor to put the hot chestnuts in a bag—how comforting those bags of nuts were to little frozen fingers. They were huddling by the glowing coke can, when from a misty street came a man in blue. "Move on," he shouted. "You're not supposed to park here." The little Italian rapidly picked up his barrow and trundled it away.

The bobby looked down at the buskers with their wet bedraggled appearance and red noses. "How old are you?" he asked Pat, staring down at her long legs and short skirt.

Because she was cold, nervous and inexperienced Pat told the truth. "I'm nearly fourteen," she said.

"You mind your own business," said Colleen quickly.

A big hand grabbed her. "Oh, cheeky, ain't we. And begging under age too. You come with me." The bobby was staring down at Colleen. "You coming quietly or do I have to blow me whistle?"

Vine Street Police Station had seen many an amusing case

arrive but when the constable hustled in three kids one Saturday night, the sergeant was set with a sticky problem. He stared at their tired mucky faces. "They're only kids!" he exclaimed.

"We're all fourteen," cried Colleen, obstinately, "and we're all old enough to work."

The sergeant's stern face looked at Colleen. His eyes passed over her taking note of the dress, all muddy, and her hair falling down from beneath the straw hat.

"What are they supposed to have done?" he asked the constable.

"They was begging and what else I ain't sure, but if you ask me there is more to them kids than meets the eye—they're loaded with money."

The sergeant sighed; always over-zealous was P.C. 29.

"Busking," he said, "not begging. There is a difference. Still, they ought not be hanging about round here. We'll keep them and send for their parents."

Maud had just returned from a pleasant dinner with Mr. Piggot, and Dandy had retired with a belly full of beer. Lil was sitting in the kitchen supping her gin when the policeman called—that loud rat-ta-tat that echoed through the night.

"We have three children in custody. Will you come and collect them?"

Maud hired a cab, and with Tim and Becky went to bring home the culprits who were very pleased with their adventure. They told of how the sergeant had asked them to do their act and had applauded them. And they explained how kind they all were at the police station where they had been given hot chocolate and buns.

While the children chattered on Maud sat tight-lipped. This was the end. From now on there was to be no street raking for Patricia.

Lil was not much concerned. "Got a loverly voice, our Colleen," she said placidly.

Sam and Becky settled their differences with a screaming row in Yiddish and they decided that Lew should go back to his Auntie Sophie.

# Colleen Makes Her Debut

PROMPTLY, STRAIGHT AFTER EASTER, LEW AND Patricia were whisked off to school, Pat to Woodford with Ethel Piggot, and Lew with his cousins at Stamford Hill. All alone on the canal wall, Colleen sat swinging her long legs discontentedly. The pale early spring sunshine brought out the burnished sheen of her long mane of hair that hung down to her waist. Her tip-tilted nose was still sprinkled with last year's freckles and there was a sullen droop to her full petulant mouth. It was awful. Whatever was she going to do without Patsy Pat? She twisted her hands in her ragged pinafore, trying not to cry and banged her heels hard against the wall. She was not going to go to crummy school. Anyway, who knew when she was not there? No one cared and that harassed teacher with a class of fifty was relieved when Colleen was absent. No, decided Colleen, I'll not go to school, I'll get a job.

Having made this decision and not a lot past thirteen, she took off that grubby pinafore and put on her best navy serge dress and went down to the Roman Road market to look for a job. She hung about the stalls for a while turning over the hair ribbons and bright gaudy beads and earrings. Then she moved to a stall that sold hats. Trying on hat after hat, she admired her image in the small cracked mirror hanging on the stall until the proprietor said: "Have a heart, Ginger, you'll wear the bloody things out before I get a chance to sell them."

With a huge conglomeration of flowers and feathers perched on top of her head, Colleen gave him a ravishing smile. "When I get me wages, I'm going to have this one," she informed him indicating the gaudy headgear.

"You ain't left school yet!" he exclaimed. "Blimey, don't the years go by quickly."

Joe Fox, the stall holder, was a young man in his late twenties and had seen Colleen grow up. He had watched her with the other kids as she scrumped Saturdays down the market, as the kids were wont to do when the stalls were packing in. He was a hard grafter, liked women, wine and song, but he had a heart of gold.

"I'm just off. Going to get meself a job," Colleen said. "Save that hat for me."

"What sort of job are you looking for?" Joe asked, amusement on his face as he quizzed her.

"What sort of job you gort?" Her blue eyes stared suspiciously at him.

"Oh, you little devil!" he pinched her cheek. "You can mind the stall for ten bob a week. That suit?"

"Not 'alf," said Colleen gleefully. "Can I start now?"

So Colleen became chief saleswoman on the hat stall and Joe took a little more time off to manage those fast women and slow horses, as he told her. Colleen turned out to be a great success and was very popular with the customers. Attired in a large hat of multi-colored feathers, Colleen encouraged the customers to gather around the stall by entertaining them with songs and fast talk. She could imitate Marie Lloyd to perfection. "Proper little comedian, that kid on the stall," was the popular comment. The customers were happy with their hats, Joe was well pleased with the increased sales and Colleen was in her element; and if Joe smacked her bottom when she bent down or accidentally touched her bosom, she would just giggle or pretend she never noticed.

Lil was quite unmoved by the fact that Colleen had a job in the market. "Waste of bleeding time sending you to school because you'll never learn. Still, I was working in the flour mill long before I was your age. Give us five bob of yer wages and you can keep the rest. See if you can nick a few hats and I'll flog them to me mates." This was Lil's philosophy of life; she had always lived from day to day, without worrying about tomorrow, so she naturally supposed her daughter would.

Bill Welton, however, did look slightly further ahead. "Saucy little bugger. Ain't going to do a lot of good down there. Going to bring trouble home, she is. Can't keep her trap shut a bloody minute."

"Mind your own bleeding business," shouted Lil, and the precocious young Colleen sang out: "Boozy Bill never worked and never will."

Roaring like an enraged bull, Bill chased her the length of the alley.

Lil would collect Colleen's weekly five bob and go straight over to the Railway Arms. When eventually the school inspector arrived Lil swore on oath that Colleen had gone to stay with Mary's relations in Ireland. "Had a shocking corf, she did. Never get rid of it in this damp hole," she told the exasperated man. Mary, with crossed fingers behind her back, was forced to go along with Lil and maintain that it was quite true. "It was just to keep the peace," she explained to Tim.

"They're a funny lot," remarked Tim, "and a devil of a lot of good it's going to do that lovely child, and she almost a woman in a market full of rogues. It just doesn't seem to be the right place to me but, as you say, Mary, it'll do us no good to interfere."

Colleen was extremely happy, as was her mother. "I'm quite independent now," she informed Lew one day when he was nosing about the stall; he had come back from Stamford Hill for a while.

"But don't you still want to go on the stage?" inquired her disappointed friend.

"Well, we'll have to wait and see," Colleen replied airily. "I might change me mind."

But Colleen did not have long to wait for her debut.

The market stood on a long winding road with stalls on both sides. Right at the end was a tall, dilapidated house and outside was a board that read: "Market Trader's Club." It was known to all and sundry as "Bum Daddy's." The proprietor had been there for a number of years and in his prime had been on the stage as a female impersonator. Now retired from show biz, he managed the club and preferred the company of virile young men to pretty young women. On wet days there was always a card game in progress and fun and entertainment to be had; Bum Daddy, dressed as a vivacious blond, put on a risqué but amusing act and there were often guest artistes, who stayed in the rooms above the club. Bum Daddy's had been there a long time and most folk had lost interest in it. Joe Fox liked the club because it was near the stall if he was needed, but no female ever crossed those hallowed portals—Bum Daddy would not allow it.

Colleen became very interested in that club seeing Joe Fox disappear into it every day. "What goes on in there?" she asked him one wet day.

"Nothing very terrible," returned Joe, "just a game of whist and a glass of beer."

"They say that show people live upstairs. Do they?" Colleen persisted.

"Yes. I believe old Bum Daddy lets out a flat to some nancy boys."

"Can I come in there with you?" she inquired.

"Cor blimey," said Joe, "what the hell for?"

"To sing on the stage," said Colleen. "I know they do, because I've heard them."

Joe was tickled to death. "Old Bum Daddy would have a pink fit," he guffawed.

"Well, then?" said Colleen. "How's about it?"

Joe pondered. "You ain't got a bad voice and it would be a bit of a lark. I'll see what I can do."

Arriving at the stall the next day, Joe said: "I fixed it. Brought your outfit?"

"Of course I did," announced Colleen.

"Go over the ladies at lunchtime and dress up. I got you a booking," chortled Joe.

Colleen dressed herself in the old yellow spotted dress with the bustle and her large feathered hat. She also had a feather boa which Rosie had reluctantly lent her.

She swaggered across the road and Joe's yellow teeth showed in a grin. "You don't 'alf look a caution," he tittered. As a final touch he rolled up two large balls of tissue paper and stuffed them in her bodice. "Gotta look like ya got a lot of it, them nancy boys really look the part."

So, billed as a female impersonator, Colleen stepped onto that rickety stage in a smoke-filled room full of men. She did her Marie Lloyd act with complete confidence, then broke into the Irish ballads that they always sang at Tim's parties. Her fresh young voice trilled through the foul air; sweetly and perfectly she sang "The Rose of Tralee." That pleased the Irish navvies who came in at lunchtime and she brought tears to their eyes with "Blind Irish Girl." Bum Daddy's had never seen such entertainment. The Irish contingent cheered, the Cockney boys sang out their requests. Colleen was a great success. But Bum Daddy stared very suspiciously at her and snarled at Joe—he was not sure if he had pulled a fast one on him.

Colleen got five bob and a bit of a sore throat from that hour's performance, but she was so happy she looked like a cat that had just swallowed a saucer of cream. And she was booked for Saturday evening.

"Christ!" blasphemed Joe. "I didn't know you could sing like that, I only did it for a joke. It's a pity you ain't a bit older, I could get you a booking at some decent club."

"Who's to know how old I am?" declared Colleen.

"That's true," said Joe thoughtfully. "With makeup you would pass for seventeen, being such a big girl," he grinned suggestively.

But next Saturday the performance at Bum Daddy's did not go well. Colleen had added some new songs to her repertoire. Joe was installed at the front with all his barrow boy acquaintances and the Irish navvies were there in force. Bum Daddy was trying to wriggle out of the contract; his suspicions had been confirmed and he was not sure he wanted to break the club's tradition. But Joe Fox and his boys were very persuasive so Bum Daddy stood backstage gnawing his finger nails.

When the incorrigible young girl swaggered onto the stage, dressed in a long black skirt and Irish plaid shawl she had borrowed from Mary, her long hair hanging over her shoulders, her wide charming smile ready to greet her audience, there was a moment's silence. Then they all cheered and clapped.

It was Dulcie who triggered it all off. He was the effeminate young man who played the accompaniment on the piano. He sat at the piano, with arms folded, sulking, refusing to play a note. The audience booed and jeered and stamped their feet while Colleen stood in the center of the stage awaiting her cue. Bum Daddy began to argue with Dulcie and they quarreled like two fishwives with Joe Fox's barrow boys egging them on. Then a young Irish lad took out a mouth organ and began to play a lively tune. Colleen began to dance while the audience clapped and stamped like mad. But Dulcie was so incensed he rushed from the piano screeching like a throttled hen. "You cow!" he screamed and gave Colleen a hefty push that toppled her off the platform down amid the crowd of navvies below.

In a split second all hell broke loose. Joe Fox's gang rushed in, eager to join in the fray; the Irish fought the Cockneys and each side fought among themselves. There were old scores to settle. It was like a match to a keg of gunpowder, and the battle raged on even after the police had arrived.

Once Colleen had landed on the floor she sat there in a dazed condition, amid a sea of heavy boots, until Joe came up and lugged her to her feet. "Scarper, kid!" he said. "Don't let them bobbies catch you in here, you're under age. Run like bloody hell."

Colleen immediately took his advice. Picking up her long skirt she did not stop running until she reached home. So ended her stage career for a while.

"Blimey, what a bundle," said Joe at the stall on Monday. "The boys said they had never enjoyed themselves so much for a long time," he cackled.

"Won't be able to sing in there now," she grumbled. "That bleeding nancy boy didn't 'alf hurt me pushing me off the rotten stage like that."

"I know," said Joe sympathetically. "Get very jealous, them buggers do. But cheer up, kid, I know a good club in the Mile End, owner's a pal of mine. I'll see what I can do," he promised.

"Oh, thanks, Joe," exclaimed Colleen, brightening up. Her wide smile returned and she set about the business of selling hats once more.

Colleen's despondency at the early close of her singing career was small in comparison to that of her mother, for Lil had been deserted by Bill again. She ambled up and down the alley looking like a sick cow, her round red-rimmed eyes gazing morosely at the other residents. Not even an extra gin could cheer her up because a most unusual thing had happened to Bill Welton. The alley folk were well aware of the cat-and-dog life that Lil and Bill had lived for so many years. Since the affair of Uncle George their quarrels had been loud and bitter, and through the years Bill had frequently disappeared for days at a time. "I expect he's been nicked," Lil would comment. "Serve the old git right." But this time it was different. He had replaced Lil with a smart redhead down in Brighton and Lil moaned up and down the alley as if she had suffered some great loss.

It happened this way. Being a looker-out for 'Arry Smiff had brought a measure of prosperity to Bill Welton despite his passion for gambling. He had smartened up, bought a new suit and got his gold watch out of the pawn. At Whitsuntide he went with Arthur and 'Arry Smiff to the Brighton races where they had booked a pitch. Down the alley went dapper little 'Arry Smiff with books and papers under his arm. Beside him strolled the tall gangling Arthur carrying the collapsible stool and easel, the tools of the trade. Behind them both lumbered Bill, his stocky figure adorned in his new brown checked suit, his gold watch and chain stretched across his big expanse of tummy and his head sporting the smartest of headgear—a bowler hat. This was the last glimpse of Bill that anyone in the alley had for quite a long time.

Once the day's racing was over, it was down to the fairground and there Bill met his fate. She was Frances O'Grady, a six-foot fourteen-stone redhead, the wife of the fairground boss who was at that time doing a long stretch for grievous bodily harm. It was love at first sight and Bill never looked back.

When 'Arry Smiff and Arthur boarded the last train home they were not unduly worried that Bill was not on board. With so many drinks inside them they settled down to sleep during the long journey home. Arthur commented that the old fool had probably got himself nicked. "He'll be home in the morning I expect."

But Bill did not return. After a week's absence, Arthur went down to Brighton to look for his father and came back with quite a tale to tell. He had discovered Bill sitting outside a huge, very prosperous looking caravan, dressed in a velvet smoking jacket and brand new slippers, and smoking a large cigar. Inside the caravan a big good-looking redhead was cooking a meal. A savory smell issued from within and she sang in a full rich tone as she worked. When Bill spotted Arthur prowling about, he did not move but just snarled at him out of the side of his mouth—old lag style. "Hop it, you nosy sod. Don't come round here queering my pitch." Rather taken aback, Arthur went home to impart the news to the alley.

Lil, shouting hysterically, dashed into Mary's house. "That's 'is lot," she spluttered. "Wait till I get me bleeding hands on her," she threatened.

Mary's gentle voice reassured her. "Hush, Lil, I'm sure he'll return, there's nothing to worry over. He'll come back. He always was a rolling stone, your Bill."

"No, he don't. He don't come in here no more," cried Lil. "I'll spit in his bleeding eye if he does."

As the days went by Lil became quieter and moped up and down the alley until even Arthur got fed up with her. ("Good riddance to bad rubbish," the forthright Colleen had declared.) Lil did not go far from her windowsill until the pub opened, and then she would join her cronies, the black-shawled women who sat on long wooden benches and were full of gossip. They came from the poor back streets, and were mostly war widows or grass widows drowning their sorrows in black beer. Grotesque shapes, they were, in hats with broken feathers trailing lop-sidedly behind them, and black aprons shiny with grease, and ragged skirts. Morosely they sipped the frothy liquid and passed along little boxes filled with snuff. "Have a pinch, old dear," they would say to Lil, "'twill cheer you up."

In no time at all Lil was hooked and this dirty habit lost her the last remaining shreds of her family's affection; there were always brown stains under her nose and an unpleasant peppery smell lingered about her.

"Good God!" cried Tim, when he came back from the pub one evening. "What the devil's happened to Lil? All that time I was talking to her she was shoving some dirty stuff up her nose."

Mary sighed. "Pool old Lil, she's taken it really badly, old Bill going off like that."

"But that ain't going to bring him back, nor anyone else for that matter," said Tim, and Mary had to agree with him.

In March and April of 1914 there had been trouble on the political scene—a transport strike, a coal strike and the suffragettes were on the march again. This time it was a campaign of extreme violence and Maud was up to her neck in it. She was seen to leave the alley one day with a determined stride and a huge handbag. Maud was on her way to join a march on the house of the prime minister. With Pat away at school Maud had a field day and enjoyed it immensely. Only some sort of miracle and the threat of impending war prevented her from going back to prison. Then Tim and Dandy came to loggerheads over the job. They often employed casual labor. Tim was all for a union and refusing to employ non-members but Dandy was only concerned with getting on with the job and having it finished on time. So they argued and at one time they almost had a fight and the cheerful atmosphere of the alley seemed about to disappear. Only Becky and Sam went on peacefully, working hard seven days a week in the shop.

The spring departed and gave way to a blazing summer. Londoners put on their summer clothes, and the ladies, with straw hats and flowered dresses and little parasols to match, walked in the park. Storm clouds drifted across the sky and there were rumblings in the distance which disturbed no one. Arthur strolled in the park with Mollie and Mary. He was very proud, for they both looked so charming and attracted many appreciative glances from passers-by. Tall slim women in flower sprigged summer dresses that they had made themselves, and straw boaters trimmed with matching ribbons, they looked so sweet and so pretty. One could be forgiven for thinking that they were sisters, it seemed hardly possible that they were mother and daughter. Mollie, at seventeen, was very mature and her serious face well composed. Although her hair was now white, Mary's face was still youthful; in recent years her cares seemed to have left her.

Arthur walked in between them, as he always did, holding their arms in a very proper manner. His thoughts, however, were not always quite so proper. They passed lovers embracing on the park benches and he wished fervently that it might be him and Mollie in that close clinch.

He had often tried to get Mollie to go out with him on her own. "Not take Mother?" she would ask tartly, her fine eyebrows raised. "Why ever not?"

"It would be nice to be alone for once," Arthur would stutter feebly.

"Whatever for?" this icy young miss demanded. "You must be going off your head, Arthur. I always go out with Mother."

So it ended in failure but he would always tag along with them. Not that he did not enjoy Mary's company; all his young life he had been devoted to her but with Mollie it was different. Persistently Mollie clung to her mother and Mary was so used to Arthur being around that she had no inkling of the love he bore for her daughter.

Once a week to the cinema, and at weekends to the park, he regularly and dutifully escorted them. But not on Sundays. While they went twice that day to church, morning and evening, Arthur got on his bike and rode out to Epping Forest where he would lie in the grass in a green leafy glade and stare up at a patch of blue sky. As each fluffy cloud drifted past it formed a shape in his mind, huge boats that flew, huge airplanes, not like those box kites he had seen at Brooklands, but real ships carrying people, large flying ships with engines in them that went as fast as sound. Many years after he remembered these adolescent fancies and marveled that such grand inventions had come to pass. And he would dream of Mollie wearing his ring, her soft dark hair against his cheek as she lay with her head on his shoulder. That dream never came true but it filled in the lonely day before he returned to the alley, an alert happy-go-lucky lad once more.

One particular hot Sunday evening in July he came into the alley to find a lot of excitement at the Railway Arms. "Will there be a war with Germany?"—it was the question on everyone's lips. They had shelved the topics of Home Rule and women's franchise for a while.

"You can blame those blood capitalist warmongers if there is a war," said Tim fiercely.

Dandy, ignoring him, muttered darkly into his beer: "Got to be ready, Tim. Blow us to kingdom come the Kaiser will if we're not prepared."

Maud and Mary chatted in the parlor. "They're going to need us women very badly," said Maud, "it's time they acknowledged us as equals."

"The wars make the rich richer and the poor poorer," Mary murmured gently. "I pray to God it doesn't happen."

So it went on and the world waited with bated breath.

About this time Patricia arrived home for the school

holidays. She looked very lanky in her school slip and blazer and black stockings; her face was still very pale and her eyes dark and brooding. In fact boarding school had made her moodier than ever.

She had not been home half an hour before she was leaning out of the window to gossip with her best friend who leaned precariously out of her own window next door.

"Blimey!" Colleen said. "You've gone all posh, talking with a mouth full of peas—'how doo yoo doo?'" she mimicked.

"Don't take the mickey, Colleen," pleaded Pat. "I hate that rotten school."

Her friend was full of sympathy. "Sorry, love, I suppose you have to mix with that crummy lot so you can't help talking like them."

Pat nodded, her eyes full of tears. "Tell me about your singing job, Colleen. Make me laugh," she pleaded.

So Colleen chattered away very excitedly, telling her of her debut at Bum Daddy's, the tissue-paper tits and the irate nancy boy who had pushed her off the stage. Pat laughed until tears ran down her face. Then they were overheard by Maud who rushed upstairs and dragged her daughter from the window. There was a terrible scene from which Maud retired white and strained so great was her temper. She had locked the window and screwed it down so it was impossible to open, and Pat had hurled a tirade of insults at her.

"Jail bird!" she yelled. "I'll tell the coppers about you. I hate you!"

"Don't be a silly child. Calm down. It's for your own good; that girl next door is a bad influence."

"Who are you to judge other people?" Pat asked scornfully. "Colleen is my best friend."

Maud, unable to reason with her, left her to a storm of tears, wondering how she had managed to have such a wayward daughter—and such a pretty one as well. She was an unattractive person herself but she loved beauty and worshiped her very contrary daughter. Maud wanted so much that Pat should grow up to be a cultured young lady. Yet these continuous battles seemed to be wearing out even the tough old Maud and it was obvious right from the beginning of the six-week summer holiday that it was going to be impossible to keep Pat and Colleen apart.

Then Maud found a solution: they would take a holiday. So the next week Patricia was whisked off to Scarborough with Ethel Piggot and her mother, and Maud.

During the first week of their absence England entered a war with Germany. Cheering crowds gathered outside Buckingham Palace, and a huge march of suffragettes went to offer their services to the war effort.

Maud could not stand being away from it all. The next week she and Pat arrived home again. Pat unscrewed her bedroom window and resumed the daily gossip with her best friend next door; her mother was always down at the town hall working as a voluntary organizer for the Red Cross, and she had little time to spare for her daughter.

Colleen was simply bursting with news for Pat. She had been to Hyde Park to watch the soldiers marching. "Luvly red coats and real fur hats they had," exclaimed Colleen. "They have to guard the king and queen 'cause old Kaiser Bill's going to kill them."

Pat's dark eyes looked so sad. "Oh, I do wish I could see them," she burst out, "but she won't let me go."

"Don't worry, Patsy Pat," Colleen consoled her, "I'll take you. But you'll have to get some smart togs. I can't very well take you up west in that silly gym slip."

Pat felt very inadequate.

"Joe packed up the stall," Colleen informed her. "He's going on the run because he don't want to be a soldier. But he got me another job in a social club, singing. I'm starting tomorrow."

Pat gazed in admiration, tinged with envy. "I might run away and go on the stage," she said lamely.

"Bet you don't," jeered Colleen.

Kate Cohen's club in the Mile End Road was the spot where Colleen had acquired a job. It was well known to servicemen and to the big business boys from the nearby Petticoat Lane Market. Shops and houses were bought and sold within the gold-embossed walls of Kate's Club, robberies were planned, stolen goods disposed of and a hidden roulette wheel helped people to gamble their profits away. Most of the customers only came in for a drink but behind the smart little bar Kate attended to various other needs. Ladies were only allowed in accompanied by an escort.

"This is not a pick-up place," Kate would declare primly.

"I like to keep this joint respectable." With very white skin and small sloe-black eyes, a shiny polished hair-do and long glittering earrings, Kate was well known in the East End. In fact, her club was a kind of landmark, almost a tourist attraction. A popular feature of the place were the impromptu, rather suggestive, ditties Kate herself sang at the piano.

When Joe Fox told her he had found her a kid with a great voice—"she'll be a great asset to you, Kate"—her whimsical reply was: "Think I'm getting too old for the job, Joe?"

"Give over, Kate," grinned Joe, "but the war's going to keep you very busy. She's a good-looking kid with a fine voice and a great personality."

Kate's deep-set eyes crinkled in amusement. "All right, Joe," she said huskily, "send her along. I'll see her."

When Colleen arrived Kate was very surprised at how young and how pretty she was, and how badly she was dressed! So Kate tinkled the piano keys and Colleen, in all her finery, her hair frizzled and curled out of all proportion, bright red patches of rouge on her cheeks, sang "Bless This House."

As the notes trilled away to a sweet tender finish, Kate looked very impressed. "Let's try something more lively," she said. Her long fingers, rippling up and down the keys, struck up the popular number "Goodbye, Dollie, I Must Leave You." Colleen picked it up like lightning and they sang together in obvious enjoyment. Colleen had certainly made a hit with Kate.

"We work every night except Sunday," Kate told her. "What about your mother? Will she mind you getting home so late?"

"Oh, she's all right," answered Colleen. "Have I got it then?"

"God forgive me, ducks, but you certainly have," replied Kate.

"Thanks," said Colleen with a beaming smile, not fully understanding Kate's remark, and caring very little as long as they let her sing.

"Come with me, love," said Kate, "over to Abraham's. I'll get you some new togs. You can pay me back a few bob a week."

So Colleen was fitted out with a long black silk skirt, a cascading twist of braid all down the front, and two white high-necked silk blouses, with full sleeves and lace insets. She was also measured for a black velvet evening gown to be worn on special occasions.

"I'd sooner have red," said Colleen, pulling a long face.

But Kate was firm. "No, ducks, I want you to look older and more sophisticated, and black is always smart. You can take my advice on that. I'll do your hair for you," she told her, "and don't you paint your face, darling."

On her first night Colleen looked very pretty. Her auburn hair was smoothly combed into two shining sausage curls that hung over her shoulders and were held in position by a flat black velvet bow. The soft lacy frills of the blouse and the tailored cut of the skirt made her look much older and very sophisticated. She was popular from the start, the audience loved her.

"Now don't stand no funny business from the boys," said Kate. "Tell me if anyone gets fresh and out they go. Do as I tell you, lovey, and you'll not be sorry."

So began that relationship which was to be the making of Colleen and put her foot on the first rung of the ladder of fame. Kate Cohen had always been a lone wolf—no husband, no children, not even a regular lover—and this vivacious young girl brought warmth into her life; she was bright, young and fresh, and a dedicated performer.

The majority of Londoners had responded enthusiastically to the war. "Old Kaiser Bill's asked for it and now he's going to get it," was the Cockney attitude. Long queues waited outside the recruiting centers—eager young men most of whom had had no regular job since leaving school, all anxious to get over there and fight for king and country.

On a liner traveling toward England was a young man, blond and curly haired, hurrying home, afraid of being left out of all the excitement. It was Larry, Maud's son by her first husband. As cheeky a daredevil as ever, American college life had toughened him. He could not get into the war quick enough. "Must have a go. I'm trying for the Flying Corps," he informed the other passengers. "It'll soon be over once yours truly gets there," he jested with the nice young ladies. He was popular with them and he chased every pretty girl in sight. He had the same ungainly shape as Maud—tall and wide shouldered—but on a man it was becoming. There was the same honest twinkle in his eyes as Maud's, that same loose mouth that could shut as tightly as a trap in a temper but just as suddenly expand into a dazzling smile. He was certainly a good-looking young charmer.

At ten o'clock one Sunday morning he bounced boisterously out of a cab and knocked at Maud's front door. "Mother," he called through the letter box, "let me in, I've come to win the war for you."

Maud swept him into her arms, bursting with happiness and joy.

If the Prince of Wales had come to stay in the alley he could not have had better treatment than did our Larry. While he hung around waiting for some influential person to wangle him a quick officer-training course, it was one endless round of welcome-home parties and trips to the theater. Even Becky gave a party because Lew was so fascinated by this American boy and never tired of listening to his colorful tales of life on the college campus.

Apart from Maud, all the alley dwellers were working class, so there was not a lot to spare once everyday needs were catered for. But in comparison to the inhabitants of the small back streets behind the market they lived fairly comfortably. With Maud's assistance they now had gaslight, running water and clean, efficient outdoor privies. The sordid squalor that existed in the other slum streets had to be seen to be believed. Tall three-story houses teemed, families of eight or nine to a room. Cold, hungry, ragged children swarmed the streets and scrounged in the market begging for scraps of food. Women sat on the stone steps that led to the tenements and men idled the time on the street corner, playing cards or throwing halfpennies up the wall in a gambling game of chance.

It was on these poor people that Mollie and Mary now expended their time and energy. They collected old clothes and distributed them among the poorer houses, and gave out soup and cocoa on Friday nights in the church hall. Mollie, cool, calm and impersonal, would go into the dirtiest home to tend old folk who lay sick, and when they died she washed them and laid them out neat and tidy.

"I don't know how you do it, Mollie," said Maud. "I'm not afraid of any man but death and sickness scare me stiff."

"God provides, Aunt Maud. We get our courage from him," was Mollie's cool response.

"It's a pity you don't take up nursing," said Maud, "you have a great gift for it."

"Oh, I'd love to work in a big hospital, but you know I can't leave Mother."

"But there's nothing the matter with her now," returned Maud. "She's got an easy life."

"That may be your opinion, but it's not mine," snapped Mollie. "Mother has never recovered from losing Abby and she still frets over Timmo. Allow me to know best," said this self-possessed young woman, and Maud retired from the fray.

Still very concerned, Maud remarked to Dandy: "That girl worries me. She's going to ruin her life, clinging to her mother the way she does."

"Mind your own business," grumbled Dandy. "To be sure, why do ye have to poke yer long nose in?" That started a quarrel. Loud and fiercely they argued, bringing up old sores.

From her room Pat heard them and put her hands over her ears. "There they go again, blast them," she called to her friend next door.

After the arrival of Larry, the bickering seemed to stop. Things in the alley took a decided turn for the better. Maud was all smiles and very proud. Pat was shy but anxious to please this good-looking older brother. Larry, amid the red plush, highly polished surroundings of Maud's front parlor, entertained the neighbors with tales of life in America, and of his Peter Pan-like father who would not allow himself to grow old and was always chasing some pretty young girl. On the last occasion it had been Larry himself who had won the chase and that had destroyed the beautiful friendship that existed between him and his father.

Every day Maud went off to her various assignments for the Red Cross leaving Larry, Lew and the two girls to idle their time away. They sat in the parlor, drinking Maud's home-made wine and consuming all the available food, talking and joking as young folk do. Larry, his feet up on the best sofa, accepted their friendship as might a filmstar his fan club. They spent many pleasant afternoons singing and dancing to that gramophone with its huge trumpet, and playing the ragtime records that Larry had brought with him.

Larry made a point of looking out for Mollie as she went on her errands of mercy. She was always accompanied by her tall slim mother. Both women wore neat gray silk dresses and navy blue straw hats with wide brims, and they carried baskets of food for the needy.

In the mornings Arthur lounged on the corner, taking a few bets and keeping a look-out for coppers. Larry often stood with him.

"That's the best looker about here," said Larry as Mollie passed by one morning. "I wonder what her legs are like."

Arthur blushed scarlet. "Lay orf," he growled, "she's mine."

"You're kidding." Larry looked incredulous. Sweet Mollie and long thin boss-eyed Arthur?

Arthur was getting angry; he did not want to discuss his lovely Mollie with this flashy young man.

"Well, you'd better get a move on, lad," jested the incorrigible Larry, "that little dolly is just ripe for the picking and someone is to get her soon."

Arthur looked sad. "Nothing doing," he said. "It's got to be all upright as far as she is concerned."

"Oh, an icy one," grinned Larry. "Believe me, son, they're the hottest once you break them down."

"Give over!" yelled Arthur and fled into Rosie's to hide his embarrassment.

The next day Larry got his call-up papers.

# *Mollie's Romance*

BY THE AUTUMN THE FIRST EFFECTS OF THE WAR were beginning to be felt. Big battles had been fought and lost; homes were without sons and husbands and many people were desolate because their loved ones would never return. Maud threw all her energies into raising money to buy dressings for the wounded, and even Lil took her big backside off the windowsill and toddled off to work in the old match factory that had now turned to the production of munitions.

The younger ones still idled the days away, except Colleen who always slept late since she did not get home from Kate's Club until the early hours in the morning. The club was packed with service personnel and drinking went on long after closing time. Pat could not return to school as it had been commandeered as a military hospital and she was immensely pleased about this. She would spend hours standing on the doorstep watching Lew in his front room rattling away at his piano—Becky was always afraid to let him out of her sight.

When it became known that a Zeppelin had bombed a coastal town, the general conversation turned to air raids, and

warning systems were installed. In a tin hat and with a whistle
about her neck that she blew furiously at any sign of danger,
Maud would call out in a loud voice: "Take cover!" Then
everyone from the alley would retire to Maud's back kitchen
which was sandbagged and boarded up. At first this was
regarded as a grand joke but later, once the air raids reached
London, all the folk were grateful for Maud's diligence.

After a minor raid one night, 'Arry Smiff called in to see
Maud the next morning. He looked rather down, his face was
drawn and haggard.

Maud eyed him suspiciously. "This is a great honor. What
are you after borrowing?" she asked.

"I came to do you a favor, Maud," he replied.

"Well, let's have it. I ain't got all day," she said impatiently.

"I'm getting out. Do you want to buy the shop, Maud?"

Maud was astounded. She never thought Rosie would part
with that shop. "Why, what's up?" she asked brusquely.

"Rosie has got so bad, honest to God, if I don't get her out
I'm sure she'll land in the barmy house." He looked so
depressed, Maud felt a little sorry for him.

"Come and have a drink," she said and poured him one of
those famous brandies.

"It's terrible," confessed 'Arry. "She don't sleep, waking
me up all night worrying about the air raids."

Maud nodded sympathetically. "Where are you going?"
she asked him.

"I've got a pal up near Liverpool. He's going into the army
and wants me to take care of his racehorses for the duration.
Cottage and a fair bit of land and, after all, racing's more or
less finished for the time being."

"Hum," said Maud. Here was a chance to acquire the last
dwelling in the alley and get rid of Rosie at the same time. "I
don't want a cafe," she told him. "Got too much on my hands
with this war work."

"Thought I'd give you first chance, Maud," wheedled
'Arry. "Got an Italian down the market who's interested."

Maud positively bristled. "How much?" she demanded.

"Good little business," went on 'Arry, "flat upstairs you
can let. Three-fifty?"

"Don't want the business," said Maud. "Take that rubbish
out and sell it and I'll give you two-fifty for the building."

'Arry heaved a deep sigh. "Done," he said. "Will I get it in cash, Maud?"

"You know bloody well you will," said Maud, rummaging in her handbag.

In October it was Larry's birthday. He was twenty-five, and was at last able to handle the legacy left to him by his maternal grandfather—the money that his parents had battled over for so long. Maud was planning a special celebration. Larry had completed his training course and was now with an infantry regiment, the Royal Fusiliers, stationed in Colchester. He had been slightly disappointed about the Flying Corps but he soon settled down in the army. He arrived home smartly attired in polished gaiters, brass buttons and peaked cap and proudly sporting on his jacket shoulder one dearly earned pip.

Saturday was the big celebration night. A barrel of beer was rigged up in the back yard, and a big table groaned with food in Maud's house. It was a mild autumn evening and Lew's piano had been brought out in the alley and stood beside the canal wall. Lew, his mop of black curls hanging over his eyes, played ragtime with an air of Scott Joplin. Over the cobbles young and old danced in that clear crisp air and in the yellow light of the street lamp the alley made merry. Larry kept everyone amused with his impersonations of the army officers. Then they all lined up for an Irish set; Tim called out and Dandy scraped at his old fiddle. The young ones laughed as they all got mixed up in the grand chain.

The party was at its height when a stocky figure came walking down the alley, a sailor boy with a red face looking shy and uncomfortable. Lil was sitting on her usual perch, and he came and sat beside her. "Hullo Mum," he said gruffly.

Lil let out a wild shriek. "Oh, my Gawd," she cried. "It's Billy boy. My Billy's come home!"

The music ceased and everyone stood still looking at the sailor. Suddenly there was a general rush to greet him, to welcome the lad who had got on a barge and sailed away without farewell. He had married a bargee's daughter and she was expecting her first baby. What a fuss they made of Billy. Lil wept. Mary and Mollie came to kiss and congratulate him and for a while the limelight was off Larry who stood back in the shadows watching Mollie.

He saw the sheen on her long black hair, the white skin above the square-necked purple dress, and the white roses tucked in her bosom. Then Larry dashed in where angels feared to tread. He put an arm about Mollie and waltzed her into the middle of the road where Pat and Colleen danced with two boys from another street. They all held their breath; surely Mollie would not dance, she was too shy. But there she was, dancing with Larry, his blond head and her dark one close together. She hung her head shyly and there were two spots of bright color on her cheeks. To the further astonishment of all when they had finished the waltz, they sat down close together on the old settee outside Maud's front door talking very earnestly.

The party went on and everyone quickly lost interest in this young couple so absorbed in each other. Not so Arthur. Already half-tipsy he drank more and more, played the fool a bit more, but always keeping his eyes on Mollie and Larry. Soon the settee was empty. Larry had taken Mollie for a stroll.

At about ten o'clock it began to get chilly, so the remaining guests went into Maud's for a grand supper, and the sing song went on until early morning. When Arthur went out to the yard to replenish the beer barrel he saw Mollie and Larry standing close together. A full moon painted them silver like two ghosts lost in each other. Arthur dashed away, unable to control the tears that fell from his eyes.

It was Colleen, his perverse little sister, who found him and comforted him. "Don't cry, love," she begged. "It's just one of those things. She never loved you, Arthur, so why let it bother you. And there are plenty more fish in the sea."

Arthur took off his glasses and wiped away the tears. "All right, Colleen," he said. "I won't cry any more. But don't tell anyone, will you?"

"Of course I won't tell. What do you think I am?" declared Colleen. "You must get tough, Arthur, it's a rough old world outside this alley."

Arthur smiled and put an arm around her. "Come on, big head," he said, "let's get going."

So they returned to the party, and while he got drunk she sang for the others—Uncle Tim's favorite, "The Little Grey Home in the West."

Suddenly Maud appeared in her tin hat and told everyone to get down in the kitchen as the Zeppelins had reached London. The men went out in the street to look up at the sky, while Maud dragged Lil, who was very drunk, down into the back kitchen, chased the lovers from the back yard and collected all the kids. By this time the sirens had sounded the all-clear, so they all went home to bed, except Arthur who swung his long legs over his bike and pedaled off into the night.

In the morning Mary sat up in bed looking very thoughtful. Tim was snoring so she shook him to wake him.

"I want to talk," she said. It was seldom she held a long conversation with him these days because Mollie was always there, a disapproving look in her lovely brown eyes, taking in all they said. So it became a habit that if they wanted to talk in confidence it was done before they got out of bed.

"All right, my love, I'm awake," said Tim sleepily.

"What did you think of Mollie and Larry last night?" she asked anxiously.

"They're young," he replied, "it's only natural to want to kiss and cuddle a bit. There was a full moon as well!"

But Mary shook her head. "No, not Mollie," she said. "This is serious."

"Well," replied Tim placidly, "it's not such a bad match. They're only related by marriage and Maud's father left Larry well provided for."

"Money is not the answer," Mary said sharply. "Mollie is a very sensitive girl, she's possessive and she's led a very sheltered life."

"Well, it's time she grew up then," returned Tim impatiently.

At this Mary sat up straight, her eyes wide and staring, her mouth tightly drawn. Immediately Tim was sorry.

"Don't start worrying, love," he requested. "It might be just one of those whirlwind romances that will be forgotten in a day or two."

"It's not so," she insisted angrily. "Besides, what do you care? You destroyed this family with your boozing and your fancy women. Mollie is all I've got left to love and to protect." Getting up, she strode majestically from the room.

With a deep sigh, Tim pulled the blankets over his head

and settled down to sleep again. "Women!" he growled.
"There's no forgiveness in women."

Within the hour Mollie and Mary were kneeling side by
side in the church. The sweet smell of the lovely flowers amid
all the glowing candles, combined with their great faith, gave
them peace and drew them closer together.

On the way home Mollie pressed her fingers into her
mother's arm nervously. "Is Larry a Catholic?" she asked.

"He was probably baptized one," replied Mary, "but he's
led such a varied existence, passing from parent to parent, I
doubt if he's sure what he is now. I have never seen him at
Mass. Why do you ask?"

"I was thinking if we marry it would be nice to be wed at St.
Joseph's."

Mary drew a deep breath and tried hard to smile. "Count-
ing your chickens, little one? You're only just getting to know
each other."

Mollie looked hurt. "Oh, Mother," she protested, "I
thought that you of all people would understand."

"My dear, I'm so afraid for you," murmured Mary.

"We're wonderfully and terribly in love," exclaimed Mollie
clasping her hands together. "I'm sorry if it hurts you, but I
can't help myself."

Mary relented. "Be happy, my dear, but do be so careful."

"Don't be silly, Mother, I'm tough enough. I know what I
want from life. I am not all soft and gentle as you are," she
said with a smile.

"Well, let us pray to God that it's so," murmured Mary.

As they approached the alley, there stood Larry, all blond,
bright and breezy, his arms stretched out to welcome them.
Mary slid quietly into the house, empty of any feelings inside
her, and Mollie and her new boyfriend went slowly hand in
hand toward the park.

For the remainder of the week her parents saw little of
Mollie. She was out with Larry from morning till night,
concerned only with how she looked; did this dress suit? did
this hat match? Her cheeks were flushed, her eyes bright. Tim
tried not to look too closely at her but Mary did and always
with that anxious expression. At night Mollie would come in,
kiss them both and fly off to bed.

"Best thing that could have happened to Larry," declared
Maud. "He's been sober every night. Never known him to

stay off the liquor for so long." She shook her head. "Glory be, wonders will never cease," she muttered.

Mary only stared coldly at her. There seemed to be a change in Mary. Her shoulders drooped and there were lines about her mouth.

Next door Lil was having a good time. Her prodigal son, Billy, was spending his embarkation leave at home. He had bought Lil a new dress and persuaded Colleen to wash and tidy up her mother's hair. Billy was different in all respects from the moody aloof Arthur or the lively aggressive Colleen. He was a generous, rough diamond, sturdy and mature. Lil's snuff box did not bother him one bit. "Leave the old lady alone," he hollered. "If that's her bit of comfort, let her bung up her nose if she feels like it." Billy was also very fond of a drink and spent many hours in the pub across the road beside Lil. When they returned home, he would take off her shoes and help her to bed. "Lie down, Ma. Sleep it off," he would say. Then later on he would wake her with a nice hot cup of tea. Such comforts were quite new to old Lil who was constantly at war with the rest of her family.

Brother Billy was a real character; molded in youth by canal boats, and finished off by the navy, every other word he uttered was a swear word, and he was far from particular about his person. He told Lil about the girl he had been obliged to marry. He called her Dot. She was small, he explained, but as tough as they come and could unload a barge and steer it all night if necessary. Billy was very proud of her. Now the barge that was their home was in a Norfolk back water while Dot waited for her baby.

"Will yer write to her, Ma?" asked Billy. "Once I get back to sea, Gawd knows where I'll bleeding be."

"You know I can't write a bloody letter," grumbled Lil, "but I'll ask Mollie, she writes all our letters."

At the beginning of the week Arthur had queued at the recruiting office and been turned down because of his eyes. He was very depressed and stayed drunk most of the week unable to bear the sight of his lovely Mollie with Larry.

But generally it was a jolly time for the Weltons, who for a brief time were united as a family. At a special invitation from Kate they all went to Mile End to hear Colleen sing. Kate liked Billy on sight; she laughed at Arthur's foolish antics and stared with incredulity at Lil, who sat huge and sphinx-like, her round face like a polished apple. Kate marveled at the fresh young beauty of Colleen beside her stout, illiterate mother.

"Well, bugger me!" exclaimed Billy when Colleen came on the stage. "She looks about nineteen up there. No one would believe she ain't sixteen yet."

Kate bit her lip. She was under the impression that Colleen was at least seventeen. She would have to be extra careful with her. She did not want to lose her; at ten pounds a month she was a bargain.

The two weeks' leave was over and Billy had left to rejoin his ship. Larry's leave was also over and Mollie lay in bed weeping, as he, cold and stiff from a night of boozing, sat shivering on the mainline station, his kit beside him. His embarkation leave had ended in a disastrous manner. For the previous weeks he and Mollie had been constantly together. They had spent the time holding hands, kissing and cuddling, finding out all there was to know about each other. There had been many women in young Larry's life, young and old, some sex-starved, others just permissive. At twenty-five he had missed very little of the business of loving and living, but this time it seemed different. Maybe with Mollie it was the real thing—the true love that all men seek. She was young, pretty and innocent but at the same time strangely coy. He had noticed how she closed those big brown eyes very tightly when he kissed her, as if she did not want him to see too closely into her heart. That she was very passionate he did not doubt, nor that he touched her emotionally; he could tell from the way she pressed close to him quivering with the shiver of love that the experienced can easily recognize. But at the slightest wrong move—like the undoing of a button— she was immediately on her guard and drew back quickly with real fear in her eyes, and that lovely moment when two bodies and souls were in unison went fleeting off into the night. He would wait, he told himself, much better do that than frighten her away. He was sure that she would give in of her own free will in the end. But there was a war on and the army would not wait. He panicked, he was frightened he might lose her. To marry her might solve the problem but she was only eighteen and her parents would insist on a fair term of engagement.

One evening they had lain on the sofa in Maud's best

parlor. It was the same sofa on which Timmo had made love to Bridie, but so far Larry had not been so fortunate.

With her hair disheveled and beads of perspiration on her brow, Mollie struggled from Larry's grip. "No, Larry. For the last time, will you listen to me, it's no," she said firmly.

"You don't love me," he moaned, "or you wouldn't be so hard-hearted."

"Oh, don't be so daft," cried Mollie, putting the pins back in her hair.

"I might be killed," he said in a melodramatic manner. "I'm going out there to fight for you. Grow up, Mollie, be a woman."

"If there's any growing up to be done, it's by you. You're like a kid deprived of its sweets," she told him sharply. She stared down at him and stood up ready to escape his clutching hands but he put out a strong hand and pulled her down on her knees beside him. She buried her face in his blond curls. "Oh, my darling," she whispered, "if only you realized how much I love you. Don't make it so difficult for me."

They began all that passionate kissing once more.

"What are you afraid of?" he asked.

She half smiled. "Do you know, Larry, that somewhere in the back of my mind I want to scream and throw off all my clothes and say, 'Take me, Larry, I'm yours.' But I'll fight that feeling because I want things to go well for us."

Larry sat up looking bewildered. He wondered what his best move was. He had suddenly seen a different, more complicated Mollie and was not sure that he liked it.

Saturday was their last evening together. Larry, as pigheaded as Maud, was not going to be beaten. He planned it all—seats at the theater and a costly dinner for two up in town and, with a last throw of the dice, he booked a room in a back street hotel.

They left the alley in a cab. They were such a good-looking pair. Mary and Maud watched proudly as they left.

"Be a wedding soon," prophesied Maud.

"Not before Mollie's nineteen," returned Mary quickly.

Maud sensed Mary's unease. "All right, in the spring then," she said. "But God knows where we'll all be come the spring," she added gloomily.

"Nonsense," said Mary, "everyone says the war will be over by Christmas."

"Don't be so sure," said Maud, wagging a bony finger. "There's a big battle planned and we're losing ground all the time," she said gloomily.

"Oh, Maud, don't be so pessimistic," declared Mary, pulling her knitted shawl about her and going back into the house.

Maud was not far wrong. The worst years were yet to come.

Happily, the lovers sat close together as the old cabby trotted away through the crowded streets. Larry admired Mollie's candy pink silk evening dress and the fine lace shawl that her grandmother's dainty hands had fashioned. They went to the Gaiety in the Strand where girls danced the can-can and little men cracked funny jokes. They stole kisses in the dark and looked only at each other. After the show they dined in a candle-lit restaurant, with soft-footed waiters and gypsy violins playing from behind a curtain. Mollie was thrilled. The wine and the champagne made her head swim so much that she did not notice where they were going as he later guided her through the back streets. They crept up soft red-carpeted stairs. Larry held tightly on to her hand. "Come, darling, I want to show you something," he whispered, and Mollie went like a lamb to the slaughter. Another dark room, soft under foot, and Larry's arm tight and possessive, holding her, guiding her. Mollie held her arms about his neck, his head rested on that scented bosom. For Larry it was heaven. The battle was almost won. As they slid down onto the silken coverlet his hand took hers and held it against his own hot rising flesh. Mollie did not object, she was lost.

As quick as a flash she came back to reality—the hotel room, the strange bed and Larry's hand caressing the most intimate parts of her body.

"Oh, my God!" she burst out, and sprang up from the bed, grabbing her lace shawl from the floor. She ran from the room like a startled hare. Frantically she dashed down the stairs, past the astonished receptionist and out into the street. She crossed the road, dodging through the traffic, to the shelter of a wide shop doorway where she stood trembling, trying desperately to collect her wits.

In a few minutes Larry had found her. "Mollie, darling, whatever's the matter?" He looked white and scared too. "I would not have hurt you, darling. I'd never have forced anything from you, my love," he pleaded.

She was sobbing hysterically.

"I want to marry you, my love," he begged.

"You tricked me," she accused him.

"But it's our last night, we may never meet again." He tried desperately to play on her sympathy. She gradually grew calm but refused to go back into the hotel.

As they stood arguing a passing bobby asked: "Are you all right, miss?" But seeing it was an officer beside her he said: "Sorry, sir," and passed on.

Larry's patience was completely exhausted. His mouth dropped into a scowl so reminiscent of his mother's. "Look here, Mollie," he said, "if we stand here any longer I'll be arrested for molesting you."

"Take me back home, Larry," she pleaded.

One of London's few hackney carriages driven on petrol came chugging down the road. Larry hailed it and put Mollie inside.

She sat for a second looking at the padded seat back with its lines of brass studs. What a fool she had made of herself! But they would make it up on the way home. She was sure he would forgive her when she told him of that hidden childhood dread, the nightmare that would not go.

Larry spoke abruptly to the driver and handed him some money. "Goodnight, Mollie," he said and went off down the road. The strange-smelling shuddering cab took her out of his sight. Mollie could not believe it. She wept heartbrokenly all the way home. She dashed into the house and up the stairs and wept all through the night. Tim, lying awake, thought she wept from parting from her first love but Mary was sure she wept for her lost virginity. Both were wrong, as parents so often are.

# The Wandering Boy Comes Home

MARY WAITED ANXIOUSLY FOR MOLLIE TO COME down in the morning. Her arms were aching to hold and comfort her. But when Mollie did come down, the girl was strangely quiet, very pale and tense but not a sign of a tear.

Mary made tea and sat with the long toasting fork in front of the red glowing fire; she sat staring into the blaze that morning as she had done each morning for many years. Her thoughts wandered to her absent son, Timmo. He would be a grown man now. Her lovely red-headed son, he had always been so independent. She knew she had grown apart from him, perhaps forfeited his affection, because of her worry and concern over Abigail—God rest her soul. Tears came to her eyes and trickled down her cheeks. Perhaps she and her son would never meet in this world again.

The slice of bread on the end of the toasting fork caught fire. Mollie dashed forward. "Don't sit dreaming, Mother," she said impatiently, "you're burning the toast."

Mary was shocked by the hard tone in Mollie's voice; it was not like Mollie to reprimand her that way.

"Don't bother to make any more," said Mollie, "a cup of tea will do me this morning."

"Is all well between you and Larry?" inquired Mary.

"Everything is fine," said Mollie, in a tone that warned her mother not to question her further.

With a deep sigh Mary got up and poured out a cup of tea and handed it to her.

Mollie had now taken Mary's usual seat in the low rickety old nursing chair by the fire and was staring into the flames. There was a strained silence until Mollie said: "It's time I did my share of war work. Don't think I could tolerate a factory, I might ask to work up at the hospice; the orphans and old people are still in need of care."

Mary smiled. Whatever it was that was troubling her, Mollie was fighting it.

"That would be nice, darling," she said sweetly. "I'll come with you later on to see Sister Agnes."

The mother superior was very pleased to have Mollie. She knew she was a hard-working girl, and her presence would release a trained nurse for more important work.

So Mollie began the career she had always longed for. Calm and efficient, she took care of the old folk, nursed the sick and mothered the babies. Mary missed her terribly during the day, the house was so empty. Every evening Mollie came home, very tired but somehow fulfilled. She always looked first at the mantelpiece. "Any letters for me, Mother?" she would ask, and sadly Mary would shake her head.

Then one day it arrived, posted in Chelmsford. Mollie swooped on it and dashed upstairs to read it. It was from Larry, posted just before he left for the front. He was very penitent, begging to be forgiven. He said he wanted her and loved her and would wait for her forever.

With a quiet little smile Mollie kissed the letter. "I knew you would come back to me, darling," she whispered. Then she sat down to write the first of her long loving letters to him, those wonderful letters that kept him going while the war was at its height.

One evening Arthur came in very shyly to say goodbye to them all. He had finally found a war-time occupation in something that had always interested him; the labor exchange had secured him a post at an airplane factory. It was near Bristol and he was very glad to go. He did not find it much fun in the alley these days. With his best cap pulled jauntily over his eyes, his long thin legs went swinging out of the alley. Mary had a tear in her eye for the little urchin with the dirty nose who had cheered her life.

The year gradually dwindled—soon it would be Christmas once more. The shop on the corner was now used by Maud as a depot to collect old clothes or anything of value to be sold for her Red Cross effort. Pat sulkily assisted her, endeavoring to relieve her boredom by sorting out the old clothes. Weekends for Pat were brightened by Lew and Colleen. On Saturdays Maud would go off to the mainline station with a canteen trolley to meet the home-coming hospital trains; the wounded men were glad of some sustenance as they lay on their stretchers waiting for the ambulance to take them to the hospital. So once a week the three youngsters were left in charge of the shop. They undid the incoming parcels and sorted out the contents. There were many old-fashioned evening dresses—society dresses were more sober now that the gay Edwardian social life had disappeared. Lew could never resist dressing up. He wedged his fat body into the long dresses, stuck the large hats on his head and sang in a high-pitched voice. Pat and Colleen loved the beaded scalloped attire and would waste their time trying on all of them. Few if any parcels got wrapped on Saturday mornings because of the games they played. But from them the first Red Cross concert was launched.

The first of these concerts, organized by Maud with the cooperation of Kate, was very successful and it was held in the church hall. The audience, mostly women and children, came from all the poor streets. Admission was threepence, children half price. It was impromptu but hilarious, and everyone loved it. Lew played the piano and dressed up as the sugar plum fairy, while Pat danced and Colleen sang like a happy canary. The proceeds went to the Red Cross Fund. Pat lost her bored expression and dived into the organizing of the next concert. Maud was quite proud of the kids.

At New Year the three recruited some volunteers and put on a show at Kate's Club. The snow lay thick in the alley that night, there were no lights on in any of the houses except Mary's. Maud, Lil and Becky were all at the concert. The yellow light of the one street lamp shone on the snow, white and glistening; there was not a mark on the white carpet, as yet not a footstep had marred its perfection. Looking through that one lit window of Mary's house you would have seen Mary and Tim sitting close together, hand in hand, their heads bent, around them the relics of that past Christmas —the tinsel, the tree, the bowls of fruit. Mary would not go to the concert until Tim had come home for his meal, but then the snow had fallen, so they had decided to stay at home.

Along the alley came a tall figure in an army greatcoat. The snow crunched in a musical sound as his heavy boots made huge imprints on the ground. He was thinking of that old fellow who had been singing in the pub that famous old song of the New Year: "The log was burning brightly, 'twas a night that would banish all sin, and the bells were ringing the old year out and the New Year in." It had been the verse rather than the chorus that had filled him with nostalgia: "I gazed through the window and, there by the fire, sat my mother, and my heart filled with joy." He could stand no more and had left the pub and walked through the newly fallen snow to the alley. He looked through the window and saw his mother, her pearly gray hair which used to be so dark, and the red head of his father, now sprinkled with a kind of silvery dust.

The soldier took off his peak cap and tapped on the window pane. Mary uttered a startled cry and Tim came to the door. A six-foot-two Irish Guardsman burst in on them, almost sobbing. "Happy New Year, Mum and Dad." Timmo had come home.

The bells tolled the New Year—ushering in the second year of bloodshed. It was not a lot to look forward to but at least the ill wind of war had blown another wanderer home. Timmo was tall and broad and looked so smart in his Irish Guards' uniform. He told them that he and Bridie, whom he had married, lived just for each other and had two splendid children.

Tim inspected his son with pride. "Foine big lad for your age," he said proudly, admiring the suntanned skin and the rippling muscles.

"There's nothing like a team of shires to keep you in condition," replied Timmo.

"You're a farmer, Timmo?" asked Mary.

"No, Mother, just a laborer. My wife works beside me and we live in a tied cottage in Newark. I don't know why I volunteered for the army. I was sorry the next day but I was anxious to get into the Irish Guards. My grandfather was in the same battalion, it's in the records," he announced proudly.

Tim smiled. He had been only a young lad when his father had been killed out in India fighting in the British army.

"Well," he said, "what's bred in the bone comes out in the flesh, I suppose. You certainly make a very smart soldier."

"You will stay with us tonight, Timmo?" pleaded Mary.

"Yes, mother, and every night I'm off. I'm stationed up in London."

"Fine," said Mary. "I'll get you some supper."

Her step was lighter and those little furrows between her brows were erased. Her son was home and, above all good things, she was now a grandmother.

Mollie was delighted to see her brother but she remained rather distant from the general excitement. It was as if she lived in a world of her own. To please her parents she sat down immediately to write to Bridie and send love to the children, Tony and Tessa, from their grandparents, who also sent them three pounds in new treasury notes. Mary wept and mooned over the photographs of them and Tim said that they would go up in the spring to visit them.

Mollie wrote letters every evening; she lived at the hospice now and the evenings were sometimes lonely. She wrote first to Larry, then to Arthur (who wrote frequently to tell her his troubles), to Billy's wife in Norfolk and from now on to Bridie in Newark. With all this writing and her work at the hospice, time passed quickly for Mollie as she went through each day, living only for the time when Larry would return to her.

Nearly everyone in the alley was involved in the war effort now. Colleen, Lew and Pat planned and rehearsed for the next Red Cross concert. Tim and Dandy went to work at the Woolwich Arsenal, and Lil waddled from the pub each day up to the munitions factory. Only Mary stayed at home.

Then, in August things became very short. There had been strikes in the mines and coal was in short supply. Most foodstuffs were rationed. Mary at last found a way to make herself useful. Outside the butcher's and baker's she queued for supplies for her family and for her neighbors because

Maud was always busy and Lil was too lazy. In wind and rain she stood, a black shawl about her shoulders, sometimes for all day. Mary caught several colds and developed an irritating cough but was happy to be able to do something to help.

The second year of the war was rolling by, and Colleen went to live with Kate. Her excuse for moving in there had been the air raids, but really it was the comfort of Kate's apartment and the deep bath with real hot water that drew her. Colleen was developing very nicely under Kate's excellent tuition. She dressed well and tried hard to improve her speech but still had the same boisterous charm.

At Kate's Club there was a telephone and, as the air-raid warden, Maud had had one installed in the shop in the alley. This tubular piece of metal with the power to speak was a great delight to Pat. She chattered and giggled with Colleen at the club and spoke to all sorts of strange people. Maud was still slightly nervous of it; she would stand at a distance from it and shout down the receiver.

"There's no need to shout so," Pat told her mother.

"Well how the devil are they going to hear me?" Maud retorted.

Patricia was now almost sixteen. Apart from the Red Cross concerts she made little attempt to make herself useful and still quarreled violently with her mother. She only saw Colleen once a week.

"Let's go up the town this Saturday," suggested Pat to Colleen on the telephone one day. "We could go to a show."

"It'll have to be the first house because I must be back before ten o'clock when the club opens. Kate's very busy Saturday nights," said Colleen.

When Saturday came the two friends set off arm in arm, wearing long hobble skirts and large floppy hats, and casting side-long glances at every male who passed by. They stood in the long queue for the gallery seats of a popular show. Then they grew impatient at the wait and changed their minds.

"Let's go to the back of the Gaiety and watch the chorus girls go in," suggested Colleen. Pat readily agreed.

They cut through a small back street toward the Aldwych where the famous Gaiety show was now playing. The streets were crowded and there was a tense atmosphere. People stood looking anxiously up into the sky. There had been no warning siren but in the sky was a long shape that emitted a strange droning sound.

Pat clutched her best friend. "What's that?" she asked.

"I think it's a Zeppelin," replied Colleen, still looking unconcerned.

Everyone had begun to scamper hurriedly away. It was a Zeppelin all right, but whose?

A tall woman was walking along the street. She moved with a swinging masculine stride, and wore a long open skirt over a pair of knickerbockers. As she drew level with them, Pat nudged Colleen and they giggled. But from the air came a whistling scream—the unearthly sound of a bomb whizzing its way down to earth. The woman jumped straight at the girls. She caught them by the scruff of their necks and dragged them down to the ground as the bomb zoomed overhead and struck the back of the Gaiety. "Stay down," she threatened, lying almost on top of them. The street was filled with dust, people were screaming and there was the shattering of breaking glass. Then there was a deathly silence.

The woman picked them up and gave them a shove. "Get going!" she cried. "Run for the station and go down the tunnel."

The warning siren was now wailing and the woman went running off in the direction of the blast. Pat and Colleen tore off in the other direction as fast as they could, trying not to see the havoc and pandemonium that was all around them. An old orange seller lay in a doorway, her wares scattered in the road, her eyes turned up in death. Scared and breathless, they ran for shelter.

Once inside the station they stared dismally at the dirt on their new dresses and realized they both had lost their smart hats. People came into the shelter bringing news that busloads of people had been killed by the bomb, the first that had struck the West End in daylight. They said the whole cast at the Gaiety had been wiped out, but in fact the truth was that there were only two casualties; a call boy who went to post a letter, and that little blonde dancer, Elli Jones, who had been waiting in the foyer for a friend.

While the fire engines and ambulances dashed to and fro, the young woman who had told Pat and Colleen to find shelter stood still as a statue gazing down at the mutilated body of her friend, Elli Jones. Tears came to her eyes as she thought of her recent happiness, now lost.

As Emm stood over her dead lover, Ellen Brown was looking out of the window of Emm's costly flat wondering if her friend was all right. As she stared out at the forest of chimney pots and the sloping slate roofs all around her she felt very frightened. She had seen the long grotesque shape in the sky and heard the heavy drone of its engines; and she had jumped at the flash and crackle of red fire as the anti-aircraft guns started up.

Ellen was still thin. Her hair was worn short and a large pair of specs were perched on the end of her nose. She had been very happy living here with Emm and they had a large circle of friends. Her outlook on life, long cramped in the alley, had broadened enormously. Much of her energy was spent on her work for the paper but she had plenty of leisure to indulge in her own creative writing and she had managed to complete a full-length novel.

Emm had changed considerably since the war began. She was constantly pestering everyone of importance to get her out to France, but at that time very few unskilled women were allowed at the front. Only qualified nurses and doctors were eligible, so Emm volunteered as an ambulance driver and brought home the wounded from the hospital trains. She became strangely belligerent, often got drunk, was argumentative and smoked very heavily. She had her hair cut as short as any man's, wore overalls all day, and knickerbockers and open skirts when off duty. Ellen often eyed her curiously but she would turn away, ashamed at the confusion in her mind.

But in these last few weeks Emm had been cheerful and confident. She had fallen in love. The object of her affections, whom she showered with flowers and presents, was the giggling little blonde dancer, Elli Jones. She allowed Emm to fondle her, and in return conned her for money. It was a sordid affair. It worried Ellen but what could she do except wait for the day when Emm would need her instead? She was fully aware of what it implied. But what a fool she had been for George, and how he had used her! No! Never would she be so foolish again.

The raid was long over but Emm was still not home. Ellen

went to bed but she lay awake; unable to sleep. When she heard the key turn in the lock for some reason her heart gave a thump. Emm stumbled into the room smelling strongly of brandy. She did not light the lamp but felt her way to her own bed in the opposite corner of the bedroom.

"Oh, I'm so glad you're home safely, Emm. The raid had me worried," called Ellen.

But Emm did not answer her. She had thrown herself down on the bed and given way to frantic weeping, hard dry sobs that convulsed her body.

Ellen crept out of bed and lay down beside her friend. "Hush, hush, don't cry, darling," she soothed her.

"Oh, her poor little face!" cried Emm.

Ellen drew her closer. "Don't cry, darling," she murmured, kissing her softly. And Emm, morbid with sorrow and drink, crushed her lips passionately onto Ellen's.

# The Demise of Mary

THE TWO BEDRAGGLED GIRLS ARRIVED HOME FROM their West End jaunt, minus their hats, with holes in their stockings and their dresses torn and dirty. Their eyes were very red with weeping. Maud was furious, but she provided hot baths and sedatives, grumbling and nagging all the time.

"That's the finish. No more traipsing up town for you," she informed her daughter as she energetically plaited Pat's hair.

Back at home and warm and comfortable, Pat immediately regained her old cheekiness. "I'm not stopping in this dreary old alley every weekend," she declared.

"Well, go to the Bioscope with Lew, as you used to on Saturdays," Maud told her.

"Oh, him, fat old Lew. Who wants to be seen with him?" she argued.

"At least I'd know what company you were keeping," said Maud. She glared in the direction of Colleen who sat by the fire drying her magnificent mane of hair.

"Can't always get Saturday off, so I won't bother you much," retorted Colleen who felt exceedingly sorry for Pat. She endeavored to change the conversation. "Did you see that old gal?" she asked. "She was all squashed up with her oranges."

"Be quiet, girl!" Maud reprimanded her. But it was impossible to stop Colleen once she got going.

"I wasn't 'alf frightened. If it wasn't for that woman that looked like a man we would have been all squashed up too."

Maud sighed and tried hard not to listen.

Later on Colleen found a more appreciative audience in Kate, who listened with interest and fond amusement to Colleen's exaggerated account of her adventure on the night the Gaiety was bombed.

"I knew that little dancer Elli Jones," remarked Kate. "They say her face was almost torn off." Kate was filing her nails and she did not look up as she spoke.

"Never saw her," replied Colleen. "We didn't get that far. Some woman—well, I thought it was a fella—pulled us down."

"Lesbian," muttered Kate. "Plenty of them up in the Strand."

Colleen's blue eyes popped wide open. "A whatter?" she asked.

"A woman with masculine tendencies," replied Kate in a matter-of-fact tone.

Colleen started to giggle. "What, like them nancy boys at Bum Daddy's?" she inquired with a smirk.

"That's it," said Kate quite unmoved.

"Well, I'm blowed!" burst out Colleen. "I didn't know that women could have it off with other women," she cackled.

Kate frowned. This child could be so coarse.

"You're seventeen this October, aren't you, Colleen?" she challenged her.

"Yes, but don't tell anyone. I get away with nineteen," said Colleen.

Kate put away the nail file and closed the lid of the manicure case with a snap. It was time for this little one to grow up. She had probably been scouring the West End looking for a boyfriend in the first place, thought Kate. She did not want to lose Colleen; she had become her bread and butter. Colleen's next male admirer, Kate decided, would not be thrown out by the bouncer; she would allow the girl to cultivate him. It might solve a few problems.

Colleen loved chatting with Kate in her flat above the club. She now occupied the room next to Kate's, and she always rose early, bursting with energy, and ran down the road for the crispy French rolls that Kate was so fond of. She would have a little chat with Lew who was helping his father in the tailor shop these days, and then rush back home to make coffee and serve Kate her breakfast on a tray. With her hair in curlers, Kate would sit up in bed and together they shared breakfast. After life in the alley, living with Kate was like a Swiss finishing school for some society miss to Colleen. Kate advised her, listened to her problems, guided her clothes sense and told her how to take care of herself. Colleen would sit and absorb every word, loving Kate very much.

"How was Lew this morning?" Kate inquired one day.

"Fed up. He hates that shop and he eats all the time to pass the time away," Colleen informed her.

"He must be putting on even more weight," remarked Kate drily.

"Coo! he's like a bloomin' barrel of lard." Colleen made a wide circle with her arms in order to indicate Lew's condition.

"So you won't marry Lew then?" Kate teased her.

"No, I ain't going to marry no Jew boy," retorted Colleen.

Kate's eyebrows shot up. "I'm a Jewess," she said coolly.

Colleen's pretty face flushed in embarrassment. "I'm sorry, I didn't mean. . . . But they never marry people like me, do they?"

Kate shrugged her shoulders. "They might if they were poor. And lots of us get left on the shelf, you know," she said.

"I thought all Jews were rich," said Colleen.

Kate smiled gently and stroked her hair. "Come on, love, let's get up and get on with it," she said.

News from the front was very grim. The Germans had begun to use mustard gas and the list of casualties grew longer every day. Back at home women now worked on the trams and took over many of the jobs previously done by men. Long food queues formed outside the shops, and bread and coal were in short supply.

There was plenty of trouble in Ireland and because of it the Irish immigrant families, who worked long hours for the war effort and whose sons gave their lives for England, were resented and called traitors. In the East End many battles were fought, mostly in the lower type of pubs.

Tim, escorted home on several occasions by the police, with black eyes and a good number of whiskeys inside him, ranted and raved about the Sinn Feins and Black and Tans.

Mary sat quietly sewing. "Hush now, Tim," she said, "this is our country, and our son is at the front."

"It's the imperialist warmongers prolonging the war," cried Tim. "The people want peace."

"Calm down, Tim, there's nothing you can do," Mary pleaded with him.

Pig-headed as always, Tim took no notice and before long became involved in another fight.

The whole nasty business was too much for Dandy. He stayed at home with Maud in the sand-bagged kitchen and played endless games of dominoes with Patricia while Maud sat energetically knitting long woolly socks for the soldiers. This period of the war brought those two incompatible people closer than they had been for years.

About this time Lew had a stroke of luck. His Uncle Solly up in Leeds owned a small cinema. It was more of a magic lantern effort really, and his Aunt Esther played the accompaniment on the piano. With all the troops in town the business had picked up but Aunt Esther had fallen and broken her wrist, so the family decided that Lew should play the piano instead of her. And if Becky went with him it would solve the problem of her terrible fear of the air raids in London.

Wearing a smart suit with a bow tie, Lew came to say goodbye to the girls.

"I'm manager as well as pianist," he boasted. "I shall probably inherit the property, they have no children."

"Big talker," sniffed Colleen. "It'll have to be a bloody big piano stool to fit your fat arse."

Lew went off in a huff.

The next day an unshaven rolling-drunk soldier came down the alley. Larry had returned from the front. Mollie, home for the day to visit her mother, had seen him coming. They met at the door, arms out for each other, but the stalwart shape of Maud pushed in between them.

"Mollie," she shouted, "go out the back yard and stoke

that boiler up." Then turning to Larry, she said: "And don't you move till I get those lousy togs off you."

So weary war-shattered Larry was almost forcibly stripped and made to take a bath. He sank into the bathtub with a tired grin.

Mollie was chased up and down the stairs, to fetch clean underwear from the neat pile with its lavender bags, to fetch clean towels, to make up the bed and put hot water bottles in it. It was like a command post with Maud issuing orders all around. Then she lit a fire and burned his uniform.

"Have a heart, Mother," he called out. "It'll cost me a packet to get a new one."

"I'll buy it," yelled back Maud. "I'm not having those foreign germs in here." Then, after a hot toddy, Larry was marshalled upstairs to bed.

Hot and perspiring, Mollie gazed after him; so far they had not even exchanged one kiss. His eyes looked at her hungrily, but no one dared defy or disobey Maud.

She took off her apron with a deep sigh. "Thank God, he's home safe," she murmured. "I think I'll go and have a cup of tea with Mary." That bright twinkle came into her blue eyes. "He's all yours now, my love," she whispered to Mollie as she went out the front door.

Mollie flew up the stairs and almost fell into bed with her lover.

Larry and Mollie were married three weeks later. She was nineteen and he almost twenty-six. They made a very handsome pair. Larry wore his brand-new uniform and Mollie was sweetly feminine in a gray silk dress and floppy hat. At their own request it was a quiet wedding—just a glass of wine and a piece of cake before they left for the Lake District on their honeymoon.

All the neighbors were happy at the wedding, it was so romantic and they were a couple so terribly in love. Only Mary was rather subdued.

"Don't fink she's well," said Lil in her tactless manner.

"Bit upset at losing Mollie, that's all," said Maud, "but she'll get over it."

It was Christmas once more and Tim and Mary went up to Newark to visit Bridie and their grandchildren.

They returned in January, fresh and glowing from the

change of air, and bringing photographs of the grandchildren. Mollie, back from her honeymoon and radiantly happy, thought her mother did not look so well; she noticed that her cough had returned and that there were lines about those lovely eyes. "You'd better get advice about that cough, Mother," she suggested.

"'Tis only a cold," said Mary obstinately. "It will pass."

Then there was Tim going on about the troubles in Ireland. "For God's sake, give over," Mollie would say as Tim pontificated in slurred tones on the injustice and persecution his country suffered.

On one such occasion Mary was sewing a little dress for Bridie's daughter. It was a white sailor dress and she was stitching on blue braid. Suddenly she put down her sewing and burst into tears.

"Sinn Fein, Black and Tans, that's all I ever hear. 'Tis green I should be putting on the child's dress, not blue."

Mollie flew into a temper at the sight of her mother's tears. "Must you keep on about Ireland? You've been here twenty years, it should be your home now as it is mine," she scolded Tim.

Tim roared like an angry bull. He rose from his seat waving his arms. "Men are dying for the rights of the old country. I'll have no such talk in my house."

"All right," Mollie said, "I'll leave."

Father and daughter stood up facing each other like two angry cats. Then a sound made them turn. Mary had gone down onto the floor, her face all contorted, her mouth twisted.

Mollie dashed to get a spoon. "Quick," she cried, "she's in a fit."

After a few days of rest Mary seemed to show some improvement. "Just one of those things," the doctor had said. "Might never occur again. Probably the menopause."

Mollie was determined not to get trapped in the home now that Larry was back in France, and so she went back to live in at the hospital and to complete her training. Tim began to drink even more, and each night he would collapse in the passage too drunk to climb the stairs. Mary would cover him with an old coat and leave him until morning when he would get up, unshaven and irritable, and go off to work. Maud and

Dandy kept their own counsel, but both could see the tension between Mary and Tim.

One morning Lil went in to Mary's as she often did for a cuppa. She found Mary, not yet dressed, sitting like a statue in the old armchair by the fire. "Men," Lil cried, sniffing loudly as she sipped her tea from her saucer. "None of them is worth a bleeding light. Look at my Bill, that cow's son, took the best years of my life, then hopped it, he did."

Mary stared into the fire.

"And that Arfer," went on Lil. "Look at that sod. Not a penny he ain't sent me home and earning good wages in that airplane factory, I tell you." She wagged her finger and her tousled head in a most ridiculous manner. "All tarred with the same brush, they are. Even if old George was to come back from Australia I'd tell him to piss off. Not if their arseholes hung with diamonds would I be bothered with any of them."

Mary was slightly shocked at Lil's vocabulary; she smiled and said: "But, Lil, I thought you truly loved old George."

"Oh, Gawd, so I did!" Lil's eyes rolled.

"Knew just what I liked, did old George. But sod them, that's what I say."

Mary gave a deep chuckle. "You always cheer me up, Lil. What would I do without you?"

Lil placidly munched her toast. "Blimey, I wouldn't 'alf miss you too, Mary."

Shortly after Lil heaved herself out of the chair. "I'll just pop out and get three ha'porth of snuff. I won't be long, Mary."

Mary smiled. Her eyes gleamed and her cheeks were flushed from the heat of the fire. Lil looked back at her with a kind of hangdog affection. Mary looked so nice in that pretty nightdress that Mollie had bought her for Christmas, her hair hanging down free.

"Won't be long, dear," said Lil again as she toddled off to buy her snuff.

On her way to the shop Lil met one of her old cronies and had a long gossip. Then she went on to the secondhand shop and rummaged through the bits of clothing that Maud had arranged on the counter. By now it was almost twelve o'clock and the pubs were open.

At closing time Lil made her way home up the alley. She paused outside Mary's house.

"Marree!" she called. There was no reply. A cold wind blew down the passage and Lil shivered. "Marree!" she yelled once more. "Suppose I'd better go and see," she grumbled. Slowly she went down the narrow passage—Mary's polished lino always made her nervous, she was so afraid of slipping—but on reaching the kitchen door her knees went from under her.

"Help!" she screamed at the top of her voice; her lovely Mary lay on the floor with her head bent back, her face in the repose of death. She had had another fit, the back of the old chair had given way and she had fallen backward breaking her neck.

A black gloom descended on the alley after Mary's death. Tim went to pieces; he was drunk every day, he slept in the passage at night, and went off to work disheveled and hung over. Mollie went back to the hospital and buried herself in her work—anything to fill in those empty days—longing for the time when she had completed her training and would be able to join Larry out in France. Lil wandered fretfully from house to pub, weeping copious tears and comforting herself with the company of the black-shawled widows in the bar. Maud missed Mary more than she dared to admit and seeing the happy-go-lucky Tim in such a state of despair filled her with a forlorn air of defeat.

# The Secret of No. 5

A LOVELY SPRING CAME AGAIN. THE WAR MADE little difference; wild flowers bloomed on the blood-stained battlefields and down in the alley a soft breeze blew the blossom from the trees in the park. A fresh breeze traveled from the river down the canal removing the stench of the long winter.

The evening was floating down into a misty twilight. Patricia Fitzpatrick leaned over the canal wall and stared down at the olive green water. She dreamed of a lover, one that would come riding on a great white charger to rescue her. Her romantic young heart was filled with a deep yearning to be loved.

Suddenly she noticed a light in the back of the Browns' house at No. 5. It had been empty for years. The curtains had been drawn and it had remained as silent as a grave. But now there was a light on in the back kitchen. Pat was curious. She stood watching the front door as it opened very slowly. Was it a ghost? Should she start to run? She waited as a youngish man emerged. He was very dark and had a small beard. He was about thirty-five and wore a neat dark suit and a clergyman's collar.

As he came out, he saw Pat and came over to where she stood. White teeth flashed in a charming smile.

"Excuse me, miss," he said. "Do you know where I can buy some milk?"

Pat looked into those glowing black eyes and nearly fainted with fright.

Quickly pulling herself together she said: "I'll get you some from the house." She dived indoors and brought out a jug full of milk.

"That's very kind of you." He thanked her in a smooth polished tone.

Little thrills crept up her spine as he took the jug and their fingertips met.

All that long night she could not sleep. Her mother was out working (Maud ran the station canteen seven days a week now), and her father was snoring loudly, having spent the evening in the company of Uncle Tim. Pat sat at the window of the front bedroom looking over at No. 5. Who was the mysterious man? How good-looking he was! She was sure she had fallen desperately in love and the dreadful thing was there was no one to tell. No Colleen to share her secret with, no Auntie Mary to listen to her troubles.

At the same time, probably due to the spring in the air, her best friend Colleen was also having problems of the heart. When Kate made her decision to relax and give her protégée some freedom, she was quite unprepared for the avalanche of trouble that Colleen brought down on them. A young New Zealander called Stuart had hung shyly about the bar for several nights. He had come to the club with a crowd of colonials on their way to France. His comrades had traveled on but Stuart had remained and he stood propped against the bar every night staring at Colleen, his brown puppy dog eyes filled with ardent admiration. Kate missed nothing of what went on around her and, in the early hours of the morning when the bar closed, Stuart was invited to stay for coffee. After Kate had gone discreetly to bed, Colleen and Stuart cuddled up close on the sofa.

So Stuart continued to hang around and showed no intention of returning to his unit—he was too much in love. Two or three weeks of these nightly encounters and Colleen was no longer a virgin. She did not care; Stuart was going to marry her and take her down under after the war. Kate began to worry just how far this affair had gone, but Colleen positively bloomed and sang like a full-throated thrush.

Then one evening as Stuart propped up the bar and gazed at Colleen like a lovesick dog, the military police came and marched him away. Stuart was so wrapped up in love he had forgotten there was a war on and Colleen never saw him again. She wept many tears for her lost lover and instantly regretted her rash impulse.

Kate wrinkled her brow, but said kindly: "Never mind, darling, you couldn't help it if you loved him. Besides, it's not the end of the world. Just take a good dose of salts and forget it."

Maud was very weary after a cold night of waiting for troop trains to come in, on hand with hot cocoa, soup and cigarettes. She tumbled straight into bed and had no time to listen to her daughter's chatter about the strange man in No. 5 who had borrowed a jug of milk. That morning he had returned the jug to Pat and gently squeezed her hand in gratitude. Her young heart missed a beat and she walked on air.

A few days later he came into Maud's shop, which Pat was now left in sole charge of. He turned over some of the books, opening one here and there, pretending to read. Pat knew those strange eyes were surveying her. With her heart in her mouth she asked: "Do you live at No. 5?"

"My dear young lady," he replied, "I was born at No. 5."

"But . . . I thought Ellen Brown lived there," stammered Pat.

He came closer, folding his hands in a pious manner. "Oh, you mean my poor dear unfortunate sister."

"Oh, you must be one of those twins I heard about," Pat said suddenly.

"Nothing bad, I hope?" he smiled sardonically, a flash of white teeth above a black beard. Pat noticed a scar that ran below his cheek, almost obscured by the long unruly sideboards.

"I wasn't even born when you left the alley," she said.

He leaned familiarly on the counter. "Why, my dear, that makes me feel terribly aged."

"I'm sorry," said Pat shyly.

"It's many years since my poor departed brother and I left this place for our mission overseas."

She looked very interested so he recounted the story; of the mission in the Chinese interior, of the attack by bandits who killed his brother, he himself having escaped death only by inches, hence the disfiguring scar on his face to remind him of that terrible ordeal. Pat listened intently, attracted to him as a moth to a candle.

He left an hour later, pressed her hand to his lips. "God bless you, my child," he whispered.

Pat trembled and shed a few tears. She pressed the burning spot on her hand to her own lips and wished Colleen was home so she could tell her best friend all about him.

When she dialed the number of the club on the phone Kate's crisp voice informed her that Colleen was away for a few days. Pat was surprised. It was not like her best friend to go anywhere without telling her first. She felt betrayed.

"But where has she gone? And who with?" she demanded.

Kate was feeling rather aggrieved with Colleen and she wished fervently that she had not been so soft as to let her go with Joe Fox to Brighton for the weekend. Colleen should have come back the night before but had not yet returned.

"Look here, honey," she said, "your friend is a big girl now and she's having a few days off. I expect you'll hear from her." Then Kate rang off.

Pat was depressed but she got little sympathy from her mother. Maud thought it time Pat found a life of her own and this pathetic clinging to her old playmates irritated her.

"She's chasing some man I expect," was Maud's comment. "What's bred in the bone comes out in the flesh."

Pat scowled at her mother and said nothing.

Next day when her mother departed for work, the nice young parson came into the shop with a bag of "odds and ends." "Just a small contribution to the war effort," he said, "a few things my departed parents left behind. They'll bring in a few shillings for charity." With an ingratiating smile he placed the bag on the counter. It contained the much treasured bric-à-brac of his late mother, Hannah Brown—Victorian velvet-framed photographs, a shell basket, various vases—and, at the bottom of the bag, Ellen's old books.

Pat looked at him pathetically, so pale, so forlorn.

"Whatever's the matter, little one?" he asked, moving closer to her.

"It's my friend, Colleen, she's disappeared. I'm sure she's

been murdered," she burst out. Her wild imagination had now taken over and she started to cry.

"Now, now," he comforted her and came behind the counter. He placed his arms about her and produced a hanky to wipe away her tears. Pat laid her head on his shoulder and he gently comforted her. That he held her very familiarly she did not care, he was so manly and so sympathetic, and to cheer her up he suggested that she might visit him the next afternoon and see some of the photographs he had taken on his travels.

Pat's best friend had certainly not been murdered. In fact she was very much alive and kicking in a rather sleazy hotel down in Brighton, where at eight o'clock that morning there had been a considerable disturbance. Bad language filled the corridors, emanating from a room occupied by a young London couple who had arrived in the early hours of the morning, very much the worse for drink. The hotel manager who went to investigate found a red-faced Colleen beating Joe Fox as if he were a drum—both fists pounding him—and him with a sheet over his head, too terrified to move.

"You dirty bastard!" yelled Colleen. Her auburn hair was hanging loose and she was still wearing the same crumpled dress of the previous day. "You took me on, Joe Fox," she screeched. "I swear I'll knife you, you treacherous git."

"Is something the matter, madam?" the manager inquired discreetly. He got no answer but retreated rapidly as a hair brush sailed over his head.

It had all begun with Joe's new car, run on precious petrol filched from the army store. Colleen had mooched about the club brooding over Stuart for several weeks and had developed laryngitis and was unable to perform. Then Joe arrived back at the club after a long absence, wearing a wide-shouldered suit and smoking expensive cigars. Now Joe was a big spender, even Kate was impressed by his boasting. "Got a nice little gaming joint down south. Lolly coming in thick and fast." So Joe stayed the night and in the morning suggested to his old pal Kate that they take a trip to Brighton in his smart new automobile.

"No thanks, Joe," she said. "I can't afford to close the bar—too much competition round here."

"Well, let the kid go then," urged Joe. "With that sore throat it'll do her good."

Colleen looked at Kate expecting her to refuse. But Kate gave in. "All right," she said, "but come back on Monday. And I don't want no funny business, Joe," she warned.

"Me?" cried Joe, waving his hands expressively. "Ain't I got enough trouble on me plate?"

So off they went. Kate watched as Colleen clambered into the high seat of that bright yellow auto and fervently hoped she had done the right thing.

It was April, and a real spring day that Sunday as they cruised along at the terrific pace of ten miles an hour. In Kate's heavy overcoat with its large fur collar and a blue veil tied over her hat and under her chin, Colleen sat breathless, holding on to the side of the car as they took the bends. Bouncing up and down she waved gaily at passing carriages whose horses showed the whites of their eyes at this noisy encumbrance in their path. Joe sat beside her, completely unrecognizable in huge goggles and leather cap with long ear flaps.

As they neared the coast, distant thumps could be heard.

"What's that?" asked Colleen.

"It's the big guns out in France. You can hear them from up here," Joe informed her.

Colleen looked afraid. "You mean that that's where they're all getting killed?" She stared out over the horizon.

Joe nodded. "I'm only bloody glad it ain't me out there."

Brighton was great fun. So was Joe's club. Colleen's throat cleared up and she even sang a few songs. At midnight they left the club and went out to a party in the country. Their host, a bookmaker, had laid on plenty of food and wine.

Colleen drank a great deal of fizzy stuff that she thought at first was lemonade. "It's nice, Joe," she said as she sipped the champagne. "I don't like beer, hate the smell of it, but this is lovely."

"Not my poison," said Joe, waving the bottle of whiskey he always carried around with him. "But drink hearty, love, he's got plenty."

At three o'clock the host discovered Joe unconscious under the table and Colleen stretched out on the sofa. Obliging friends collected them and dumped them in the same bed at a private hotel.

Morning dawned and Colleen sat up in bed to find the ugly red features of Joe Fox on the pillow beside her. His nose looked more knobbly than ever in the cold light of day. Through her thoroughly muddled mind went the memories of last night but worse still of those hours just before dawn when she had put her arms about his neck and murmured: "Love me, Stuart darling," and Joe had obliged with vigor.

Colleen's face flushed. She grew hot and very angry. She leaned over to deal the sleeping Joe a hefty punch on his sensitive nose. She then proceeded to beat him with her fists as her temper ran riot. She hated him and all men. With blows and abuse she let him know just how she felt. Joe, always the cowardly type, took refuge under the bedclothes until her temper abated and she began to cry. Then shaking with sobs, she snatched up her coat and bag and headed for the railway station where she flopped down in the corner of an empty carriage of the London train looking very much the worse for wear.

Kate sat at her dressing table plucking her eyebrows. She looked up anxiously as Collen burst in at the door, red and indignant, looking a positive wreck.

"God in heaven! What happened to you?" exclaimed Kate.

Colleen opened her mouth and let out a dreadful yell. "It's that bloody Joe," she sobbed. "Got me drunk and done me, he did."

"Oh, dear," sighed Kate. "Come on, tell me all about it." She put her arms around her. "It seems to me that you're the kind of girl who can't say no."

"I'm finished with men," wept Colleen. "They only want you for one thing."

"It didn't take you long to learn that," said Kate. "But never mind, you'll get over it. Let's go and have some coffee."

# Beauty and the Beast

IT WAS SEVERAL WEEKS BEFORE THEY MET AGAIN, Colleen and her best friend Patsy Pat. In the tea shop, over tea and buttered buns, they exchanged confidences with heads close together, talking in whispers, now and then letting out a shrill giggle. Colleen's blue eyes were wide with astonishment as she leaned toward her best friend to hear Pat solemnly relate the progress of her love affair with the good-looking parson. She had spent every afternoon lately at his house.

It had all begun with the photographs. First he had shown her pictures of China and other far-away places; before long they moved on from views of landscapes to French ladies doing strange things. Then they had played Pat's favorite game—dressing up. In fact they had acted out all sorts of funny games during the past few weeks, and Pat, confused and a little frightened by it, could not help confiding in her best friend.

Colleen looked rather worried; she had ceased to giggle. "Blimey, Patsy Pat," she burst out, "he's kinky. You'd better stay away from him."

Pat's face assumed an offended expression. "How can you say that, Colleen? You know I'm in love with him."

"Christ!" exclaimed Colleen. "They're the sort of blokes what do murders!"

"Don't be silly. He's a vicar," retorted Pat.

"I don't care what he is, it ain't natural," returned Colleen. "At least that rotten swine Joe Fox done it good and proper," she added coarsely.

"Now you're worried in case you might be pregnant," Pat reminded her. "At least I'm still a virgin."

A pink flush suffused her friend's face. "You are mean, Patsy Pat. I wish I'd never told you."

"Well, don't say things about Paul," pouted Pat. "I love him, and we're going to be married."

Colleen shook her head. "He'll never marry you. He's only using you."

Pat rose, tall and indignant. "You're jealous, that's what, Colleen Welton. Take that back or I'll never speak to you again."

"Please yourself," shrugged Colleen. "But I know a kinky guy from a real man and so will you soon, Patsy Pat."

Pat stalked out and Colleen sat staring into her cold tea. This was the first real quarrel they had ever had.

On her way home on the bus Pat relived those secret afternoons with Paul. She now wished fervently that she had not told Colleen. She might go and tell her mother and spoil it all. Her mind went to the time when she had drunk the port wine he offered and she had fallen asleep. She remembered that warm feeling of soft hands caressing her breasts, the dazed awareness of her underwear being removed, the vague sensation of his hot mouth kissing her intimate parts, and her not caring a bit. She had awakened to find Paul standing beside her with a cup of hot coffee to rouse her and she had felt as if it had all been a lovely dream. She recalled dancing for him in her ballet tights, his hands fondling and thrilling her. A deep dark passion consumed her. She did not care; this was the one she loved and no one was going to stop her.

Of late Maud had regarded her daughter rather anxiously.

"Are you not feeling well?" she inquired one particular morning.

"I'm all right," replied Pat evasively.

"But you're so pale and washed out," grumbled Maud, "and never a word to say. What's up? Cat got your tongue?"

"What do you want me to say?" asked Pat crossly. "You're never here for me to talk to anyway."

Maud shrugged her shoulders and looked hurt, and went off to work.

As soon as her mother was out of sight Pat crossed the road to the shop. She went in the front door and then out through the back and over the wall to No. 5.

Paul looked rather different today. He lay on the sofa looking very disheveled, minus his dog collar. In the dark, stuffy and very smelly room she knelt down beside him.

"Boo!" she said, giggling childishly.

He opened his bloodshot eyes and looked at her as if he did not recognize her.

"Wake up," she called in his ear.

He pulled her roughly toward him. She went willingly, clinging as a child might. Then without any warning he threw her from him with such brute force that her head struck the large brass knob on the fender as she fell. For a moment she lay stunned.

"Jezebel!" he sneered, glaring down at her with an odd twisted expression on his face.

Wide-eyed and terribly scared, she looked up at him unable to believe what she saw. She struggled to rise but he was down on top of her in a flash, tearing at her clothes, biting her.

"Oh, don't!" she screamed. "It's me, Paul, it's Patsy."

But the beast had risen in his schizophrenic character. He could no longer control his instincts. Her little body he savaged and devoured beneath his great strength. She had no chance of escape. A wave of unconsciousness passed over her as he tore into that delicate young flesh.

Lil, sitting dozing on the windowsill, heard Pat's screams but her befuddled mind could not think where they came from.

Later Pat's slim figure dashed across the road. She was holding her torn dress together, her body shuddering with sobs.

Paul sat biting his nails. What had he done? Perhaps he should leave right now, not worth staying to get nicked. After all, he was only out on parole. This house had seemed a safe billet until he could get enough money to go to the States. It was a pity that he was that way with women. It was always the same, but so far at least he had escaped the looney bin. He did not want to end up like his brother, Peter—shut away for life. It had not been such a good idea to come back here. Still, on second thoughts, he'd give it one more day. That kid was stupid enough to cover up for him. He would wait and see.

"How did you get that bruise on your forehead?" asked Maud at breakfast next morning.

Pat put her hand to her head. "Ran into a door over at the shop," she replied casually.

"That was a bloody foolish thing to do," said Maud impatiently. "I don't know what the hell is wrong with you, walking about in a dream lately."

"There's nothing wrong with me," retorted Pat crossly. "Why don't you shut up?"

Maud looked into her daughter's face, and for some reason she felt very guilty. It was a pity they did not get on. She loved her and wanted so much to understand her but had never been able to. Larry she understood, yes, that happy-go-lucky nature with his sunny smile, he was easy to love. But not Pat, she was too moody, and it was not in Maud's nature to bend to Pat's strong will.

"Don't go to the shop if you're unwell," said Maud this morning.

"I'm all right," said Pat abruptly.

They would have probably dissolved into one of their violent tearful quarrels but a knock at the door distracted them. Maud went to open it and a telegram was held out to her by a cheeky-faced young boy.

"For Mrs. Dolan," he said.

Automatically she took it and opened it. Her first married name had been Dolan. The words swam before her eyes: MISSING STOP BELIEVED KILLED STOP LT LARRY DOLAN STOP.

"Oh, my God!" she screamed. "It's for Mollie. Larry's missing!" Her shrill screams rang along the narrow passage. Pat sat still and white-faced while her mother ran about like a lunatic. "Oh, my God, my lovely son. Who's going to tell Mollie? Dear God, don't let it be true," came Maud's heartbroken prayers.

Pat had never seen her mother so distressed. Yet she sat still as a statue, as if it was all happening to someone else.

Maud ran out of the house to Lil, who for once was reasonably sober. She calmed Maud down with some hot sweet tea and offered to take the telegram up to Mollie at the hospital. For this Maud was truly grateful; she had dreaded facing Mollie.

An hour later, Mollie, hatless and without her cape, was running down the alley, apron strings flying out behind her. They met at the door, Mollie and Maud, and flung their arms around each other. Their sobs came thick and fast.

By the time Dandy arrived, accompanied by Tim, their tears were all cried out and they sat pale and silent.

"Don't fret, dear," said Dandy, "he might have been taken prisoner." He tried so hard to console them.

Tim stared dumbly at Mollie, not knowing how to approach his grief-stricken daughter, and eventually he escaped to the pub.

Pat made coffee and did not say a word. Her mouth had a petulant droop as she did the evening chores when her mother went upstairs to rest.

Mollie went home to that cold empty house that had such an air of desolation about it. Beside the unlit fire was that same chair that had caused her mother's death. The back still swung loose, nobody had bothered to remove it. It stood there, a poignant and constant reminder of her mother. Dust had settled on the furniture, there were dirty crocks in the sink and an air of absolute neglect pervaded the once neat and well-kept house that Mary had resided in.

Mollie stood for a second looking about that desolate room and then went down on her knees, her head on the old chair. Sobs shook her body as she pressed her face down onto the hard seat of the chair. Then cool gentle hands caressed her brow; loving arms removed her to an armchair and placed a cushion under her head. Mollie closed her eyes in exhausted sleep murmuring: "Mother, I knew you were here."

Tim returned to find his daughter sleeping. He tucked a blanket about her and sat beside her. He had aged a great deal lately; his hair was grayer and his shoulders bowed. He seemed nothing like the Tim of the old days. He had lost his wife, his only daughter disliked him, and his son was out in France and would possibly never return. Tim was sadder than he had ever been as he sat beside the sleeping Mollie. He sat there wondering whether it was worth while to go on living.

When the thick lashes fluttered and Mollie began to stir, he got up and poured hot water into the teapot he had set ready. He dreaded her awakening, fearing the effect the shock of Larry's death would have on this emotionally young woman.

Her dark brown eyes opened and she stared solemnly at him. Taking his rough, work-worn hands in hers she said: "Be sad no more, Dad, don't grieve any more. Mother is still with us." Then she made the sign of the cross.

Poor child, her mind's disturbed, thought Tim. But Mollie, sipping the hot tea, seemed very relaxed.

"Larry's most likely been taken a prisoner," he said gently. "He'll come back, dear. Pray for it."

"No," replied Mollie, "Larry's dead. He's with Mother and they're both very near to me, I'm quite sure of that."

Tim patted her hand. He did not know what to say.

"I tell you what, Dad," she said brightly, "I think I'll leave my job and come home and take care of you."

Tim could hardly believe what he had heard. Tears welled up in his eyes.

"You'll have to stay off the booze though," she added.

"Welcome home, Mollie, darling," cried Tim. "From this day on I'm on the water wagon."

"Let's take care of each other," said Mollie gently. She got up and went over and sat on his lap as she had done when she was a little girl; and a sweet gentle spirit hovered over them, a tall dark woman who smiled sweetly.

Of late Maud did not feel so good. She still worked many long hours for the war effort dashing here and there. In her spare time she tried desperately to get news of Larry, to find someone who had seen him killed. She wrote to the various authorities to find out if he had been taken prisoner. Weeks had passed and no more information had been forthcoming. Her face grew yellow with fatigue, her temper very erratic. The mystery of the purple bruise upon Pat's forehead had never really been solved and Pat seemed more remote, tightly wrapped up in some dream world.

"What are you going to do with yourself today?" Maud inquired one morning.

"Not much," was the laconic reply.

"You never do do much lately. There's no money in the till. Is the shop not doing any trade?" Maud grumbled on.

Pat did not answer, she just pushed the plate of gray looking porridge away from her.

"Not eating either?" quizzed her mother.

"There's not enough sugar in it and very little milk, I can't eat that muck," complained Pat.

"Think yourself damned lucky to get that," declared Maud. "There's a war on. Some poor devils are going out hungry this morning."

"Stop nagging," said her daughter cheekily and prepared to leave the table.

Maud caught hold of her wrist angrily. "I'll say when you can leave the table," she shouted.

Pat struggled with her and the white silk scarf that adorned her slim neck fell off into the messy gray porridge. "Now look what you have done!" she burst out tearfully.

Maud just stared for one second in fascinated horror at the disfiguring purple mark on her daughter's neck. It glared out like a raw wound. A hot dart of fear shot through Maud's mind as Pat dashed upstairs to her room.

Her mother sat for a while completely stunned. There was no mistake that that was a love bite on her child's white neck. She began to worry. She had been unwise to leave her daughter alone all day. But who could it be? There were no young lads left in the alley, unless that bitch Colleen was up to something. Come to think of it, she had not heard much about her lately. Maud sat running her fingers through her untidy mop of hair. What should be her first move? She was not even sure. Pat was a strange obstinate child and Maud was a little afraid of her.

It was Lil who settled her mind and put her on the right track. As she sat there there was a slight tap on the back door and Lil toddled in.

"Don't like asking," she began, "but could you spare me a bit of tea? Run right out, I have."

"Some in the caddy," said Maud sharply, remaining seated. She was in no mood for Lil's meanderings this morning, but she reached out and poured Lil a cup of tea. "Here," she said, "it's still warm, might as well finish it up."

With a contented sigh Lil seated herself at the table, poured the tea into the saucer and loudly supped it up. Maud simply abhorred bad habits. She sat and scowled silently at her.

When Lil had finished her tea she stared short-sightedly at Maud. "Ain't you well?" she queried. "You don't 'alf look a funny color."

"Nothing's wrong with me," replied Maud tartly. "You'll be seeing bloody pink elephants if you don't watch out."

"I'll go then," said Lil huffily. "But I thought you might like to hear the news seeing as you are never here these days."

"All right, Lil, spill it," said Maud impatiently, "and it had better be good, because all I get is bad news these days."

Lil settled down, put her hands on her fat knees and leaned forward. "One of them twins is back."

"What twins?" demanded Maud in exasperation.

"Them over the road." Lil made a sign with a jerk of her thumb. "Got a long beard and wears a parson's collar."

Maud showed signs of interest. "If you mean the brothers of Ellen Brown, I never met them. Why, it's eighteen years since they left, before I came to the alley. It always puzzled me why the mission left that house empty."

"Funny they was," continued Lil, "all a bit mad. My Arfer swears it was them twins that done old Sal in. Now one of them's come back, and that ain't all. . . ." Lil looked very mysterious.

"Well, what else, Lil? I've got a busy day and can't stay chatting." Maud tried to dislodge Lil, but she had not yet said what she intended to say.

"It's your Pat," Lil said suddenly. "In there all day with that bloke she is."

It was as if a bomb had dropped. Maud looked horrified.

Lil looked very frightened, thinking she had said too much. She eased her fat body from the chair. "Better be going, but I thought you ought to know."

As Lil disappeared Maud just sat staring. In her mind's eye was the lovely slim neck of her daughter and that ugly purple bite.

After a while she rose and rammed on her big hat, pushing the knobbly hat pin into it. "I'll come home midday," she muttered. "I won't be persuaded by gossip. If it is true, I'll catch them." She strode off up the road to open up her canteen at the station.

Upstairs in her room Pat looked in the mirror examining the mark on her neck. She touched it with her finger. Had her mother seen it? She had gone to work as usual, so she couldn't have noticed it. Pat wished Paul would not do that. Why, her mother would have a pink fit if she ever saw the bruises on her breasts and thighs. Paul had promised her when she forgave him the first time that he would never hurt her again, but yesterday he had gone crazy once more. He said it was because he loved her so much, and told her how the devil entered into him, and how he prayed for forgiveness for himself and her. But she loved him and those strange twilight afternoons. Now she could not live without him. Her eyes lit up. She did not care; what did her old body matter? It was the mind that counted and they were joined in holy wedlock—had he not read out that marriage ceremony so many times to her? Let her mother find out, she would not give him up.

With these defiant thoughts in her mind she bathed her hurt body and put perfume behind her ears—all ready for her lover. They might play acting if he was in the mood. She would dress in that silk kimono she had found at the shop, and pretend to be his slave. She shivered excitedly at the thought.

Maud meanwhile made plans to leave her job at midday. Shortly before two o'clock she walked swiftly down the alley. First she went to the shop. Unlocking the door she surveyed the empty interior. "Never opened today," she muttered. Then she went over to the house. That was just as empty. Lil lurked in the passageway of her house, her round eyes more cow-like than ever.

"Shush!" Maud put a finger to her lips and Lil pointed to No. 5. With two long strides Maud was over the road and knocking on the door. For a long time there was no response, so she knocked again even louder. Then the figure of Paul, slightly ruffled, came to the door complete with pious expression and parson's collar.

"Can I help you, madam?" The words came slowly, smooth and suave.

But Maud moved swiftly. "No thanks," she said, "I'll help myself." She gave him a shove that sent him reeling.

Pat, hiding behind the door, saw Maud coming. She ducked under her arm and tore off down the alley, stark naked except for the kimono which was flying out behind her like a balloon.

Maud, screaming her head off, landed the dazed Paul a terrific punch on the nose and ripped off his parson's collar. "I'll deal with you later, you bastard," she yelled. Then she charged like a bull after Pat, who fled not to her own house but to Tim's, crying out: "Uncle Tim, Uncle Tim, don't let her hit me."

Tim was at work and Mollie sat sewing buttons on his neglected underwear when Pat's unclothed body catapulted into the room with Maud two yards behind her. With quick thinking Mollie sprang up and pushed herself in front of the enraged Maud in the passageway blocking her path so that she came to an abrupt halt. Mollie stood there looking so like gentle Mary that Maud's temper suddenly left her. Then she subsided into sobs—long dry heartbroken sobs. Nobody had ever seen Maud cry like this but she'd finally reached the end of her tether.

Mollie's calm hands soothed her. "I'll talk to Pat. Go home and rest, dear," insisted Mollie. Still hiccupping sobs, Maud did as she was bid.

Pat was hunched up on the sofa and stared defiantly at Mollie. "Now what have you been up to?" Mollie asked. "Your mother is very upset."

"Serve her right," said Pat viciously, "she shouldn't have spied on me."

Mollie looked astonished. "I'll get you a dress," she said, going to a cupboard.

Shivering, Pat held the flimsy kimono about her. Red and gold and covered with dragons, it was a lurid affair.

As Mollie helped her into a dress she noticed that Pat's body was covered with bruises. "Good God, who did that?" she asked.

"My mother," lied Pat. "She's always beating me."

Mollie knew that Maud had a bad temper but she was shocked. "I can't believe it! Why, Pat, some of them are old bruises, been there quite a while."

"She did it. Beats me every day, she does," insisted Pat.

Mollie buttoned up the dress at the back with trembling fingers. Whatever possessed her mother-in-law to be so violent to this frail child? "But what is it you did to upset her today?" she asked mildly.

"Just playing dressing up, that was all," said Pat.

Mollie's lips tightened firmly. "You had better stay with me, love, till she calms down."

"Thanks Mollie," said Pat with a satisfied smile.

In the evening, Maud, now recovered, came back to Mollie's house on the war path again. Pat would not leave the room. She locked herself in and refused to come out and face her angry mother no matter how much she ranted and raved from the bottom of the stairs. Mollie had left for the ward duties that she still did in the evenings. Tim and Dandy, looking very embarrassed, tried hard to calm the almost distracted Maud. Neither believed bad of Pat, and thought it was just one of her dressing-up escapades.

But Tim was suspicious of the young man across the road. "I don't know why, mate," he confided in old Dandy over their evening glass of beer (for he had not completely given up drinking since Mollie had come home), "even when they were boys, they gave me the creeps, those Brown brothers. I don't care if that one is a parson, I'll swear he's up to no good."

But Dandy said his daughter was willful but very innocent, so there was probably no harm done. Thus Maud was out-voted.

No. 5 remained very quiet and Pat kept up her stand in Mollie's bedroom. The battle raged on. The majority of the alley dwellers took sides against Maud and were ready and willing to protect Pat from her wrath. Maud, however, was by no means so easily defeated. After a big set to with Dandy, whom she lashed almost to a standstill with her acid tongue, he made a weak attempt at getting Pat to come out and face her mother, but to little avail, and Maud was off down the road to the mission.

The old man in charge, a kind and deeply religious old man, lived next door to the Hall of Friends. He listened sympathetically to this irate mother. The person concerned, he told her, did not belong to his calling but he had known the late father of the mentioned man. Mr. Brown had been a good loyal servant to the mission, but the sons had not attended since they reached manhood. The house? Well, that still belonged to the mission but only the freehold. A forty-year lease had been taken on it by the late Mr. Brown.

Thanking the old man profusely, Maud marched off down

to the local police station. She looked fairly calm now but a white hot fury seethed inside her. He was not going to get away with it, that impostor who corrupted decent young girls.

It was fairly peaceful in the local police station. A very old sergeant was snoozing in his cubby hole when a woman in a large hat banged on the counter.

"Wake up, you old rogue. Sleeping on duty, eh?"

"Well, what is it?" he asked irritably.

"I have come to make an official complaint," Maud stated loudly. "A man is masquerading as a parson and interfering with young girls."

The sergeant stared at her, his huge whiskers bristling. "I'll have your name and address first, madam," he said, getting out a big book.

"That's it, waste time," said Maud. "Give a real villain a chance to escape and persecute women. Just like all you bloody bobbies."

"Madam!" The sergeant banged his hand on the counter in exasperation. "Have you a complaint? Then give me your full name and address and we will proceed."

"All right, get on with it then," Maud said huffily.

The details were carefully entered and the sergeant closed the book and replaced his pen. "Someone will call on you," he said.

Once more Maud exploded. "Don't think I come to this bloody place for fun, do you? I want attention and I want it now—not tomorrow, then it will be too late."

The sergeant went a blustering purple, his eyes bulged. "It will be attended to," he said, controlling his temper.

Maud continued to rant and rave. "I want to see your super," she demanded, "not a bloody office wallah, sitting on your backside all day. No wonder the country is going to the dogs."

The station was indeed understaffed because of the war, and the old men retained during the state of emergency were lazy. In very definite language Maud continued to tell him so.

A man in his early forties had been sitting in a small adjoining office trying to read, but the argument going on out at the desk was distracting him. He came out of his office determined to settle the matter. His name was Angus Macdonald, known to his associates as "Sandy Mac" because of his sparse thin red hair and ruddy complexion. He had recently been invalided out of the army and was now back in the force as a plain-clothes man.

He beckoned to Maud. "Come in here," he said, feeling rather sorry for her, seeing the flushed angry face and the tired lines under her eyes. "Let me see if I can help you. Did I hear you say you came from Autumn Alley?"

"That's right," replied Maud, very relieved that at last someone was talking sense.

"It's quite a coincidence. I was sitting here reading an old report of an unsolved murder in Autumn Alley. I remember it well though I was only a copper on the beat in those days. A young lad fell off the bridge and was killed."

Maud raised a smile. "Thanks for rescuing me from the old buzzard," she said.

Sandy Mac grinned. "Well, I heard the commotion, but the mention of Autumn Alley was what caught my interest."

"It was before my time," said Maud, "but of course I heard about old Sal being done in. I own the shop now," she informed him.

"This parson who annoys you, where does he live?"

"No. 5, right opposite," said Maud. "He only came back to the alley recently and, believe me, sir, he's no parson. Why, he had my young daughter in there stripped off, practically naked."

Sandy picked up his soft hat. "I'll come back with you," he said. "I'm interested in your alley for more reasons than one."

Maud smiled gratefully. "Thanks, you won't be sorry. There is something very odd about this young man."

Later on in her sitting room they held a conference—Maud, Dandy, Tim and Sandy Mac—all having just recently retired defeated from another battle with the errant Patricia, who still stated that she had done nothing wrong, that Paul was her good friend, and that it was her mother who constantly beat her.

"I suppose we could bring a charge of indecent assault," Sandy informed them, "but if she was a consenting party it will be a job to make it stick. But I'll hang about for a while, see what I can pick up." He was anxious to help them but also to solve that murder committed eighteen years ago.

Tim remembered how he had picked up that religious tract the morning they had found old Sal's body. "I've still got that little picture somewhere," he told Sandy. "Meant to give it to Mollie, but I never did."

"Come to think of it," said Sandy, "it was me who let those blighters out of the alley on that day. There was an old lady in a bathchair with them."

"Yes, that was the Brown family," Tim replied. "An odd lot of buggers they were; the girl tried to drown herself but me and Arthur pulled her out of the Cut."

"Who's Arthur?" inquired Sandy Mac.

"Chap who lived next door. He's away on war work now. He was only a little kid when the murder was committed, and he used to go around telling everyone that he knew who did it, but no one took much notice of him."

"Sounds as if I might be on the track of something," said Sandy Mac, and he went off to keep an eye on No. 5.

At midnight Paul came creeping out minus his dog collar. He had shaved off his beard and he carried a suitcase. Sandy recognized him right away.

"Hello, mate," he said genially, stepping out of the shadows. "Fancy meeting you. Thought you were still doing time."

"You lay off me," snarled Paul, "I've done my time." His voice was harsh and brittle; gone was that cultured tone.

"I'm arresting you for indecent assault. Come quietly, or do I blow me whistle?"

"All right, I'll come, but you've got nothing on me," snarled Paul.

In the morning, accompanied by Mollie, Pat returned home. Maud was simply jubilant about Sandy's catch. She had to let everyone know about it, including Pat, even though she had promised Mollie that if Pat were persuaded to come home she would be gentle with her.

"They got your bloody boyfriend," jeered Maud. "I knew he was no parson. Jailbird he is, he's just done five years."

Pat looked hard at her mother. There were dark rings beneath her eyes, and her mouth hung in that petulant droop. Her lips barely moved but the words came out cold and clear as ice. "I hate you," she said, "I wish you were dead."

Maud recoiled as if from a physical blow.

# Case Dismissed

THERE WAS DEEP SILENCE IN THE DIMLY LIT COURT house. Its musty, dusty interior had not changed for years. It was lined with dark oak paneling, and a huge portrait of Queen Victoria looked sternly down on the folks from the alley who were waiting to hear the case of Paul Brown, holder of several aliases and a considerable list of previous convictions. They amounted to eight and included fraud, larceny, grievous bodily harm, false representation and indecent assault.

In the front row sat Maud, her usual large hat obscuring the view of those behind. Beside her sat Tim and Dandy, then there was a little space and then came Mollie, cool, calm and neatly attired, and with her sat Patricia, pale, tense and very upright, a little fur tippet about her neck. From the back row an elegantly dressed Colleen gazed down with consternation on her best friend Patsy Pat. Kate, in furs and laces, accompanied her. Halfway down sat Lil, slightly tipsy and taking up more than her share of the seat. Her lank hair hung down untidily from beneath a huge man's cap that she wore at a lop-sided angle.

The judge wiped his specs and rubbed his tired eyes. What a morning he had had. There were more petty offenses than ever, what with men returning home from the war and beating up their wives' lovers, and shoplifting rampant—mostly of food by those in dire need. He was tired. He wanted his lunch but now he had one more case to deal with: a habitual criminal—a regular customer in fact—accused of interfering with a young girl and masquerading as a parson. Never a dull moment.

The very professional prosecuting barrister, obtained by Maud, stood up. His fat stomach stuck out, showing off his waistcoat lined with pearl bob buttons. The detective who had arrested the prisoner read out the charges.

The judge sighed. Undoubtedly the prisoner was a bad character, but justice had to be seen to be done. Patricia was called to the witness box.

Paul Brown stared with arrogant hatred about the court. He looked different. They had cut his hair very short and the deep red scar on the side of his face showed up on his closely shaved chin. Pat's peaky face glowed dead white under her dark hair as she gazed with undisguised passion at him.

"Well, miss, what do you have to say seeing as you seem to be the most injured party?"

Pat quietly dropped a bombshell among them. "I wish to say," she announced very clearly, "that they are all wasting your time. I am past the age of consent and everything I did with Paul was of my own free will."

There was an excited buzz from the onlookers.

"Silence," roared the usher.

"How old are you?" asked the judge.

"I'm seventeen. And I love Paul. I intend to marry him."

"Well," muttered the judge, "for your age you are a very determined young woman. I only hope he proves worthy of you. As far as the court is concerned there is no case to offer. He did not practice as a parson, he only dressed like one, and we have no proof of impersonation. Case dismissed."

Paul's mouth twitched in a sardonic grin as he left the dock and Maud's head dropped in shame. Ignoring her parents, Pat ran toward him and he walked out of court with her clinging to his arm. Kate and Colleen went with Tim, Dandy and Sandy Mac for a drink while Mollie assisted the befuddled Lil. Maud almost ran out of court and strode home, her shoulders bent though the tears of mortification refused to fall.

"He's a rogue, right enough," declared Tim, over the rim of a frothy pint.

"Aye," came back the slow drawl of Dandy. "But 'tis no good fighting her, she'll have him, and that's for sure."

"She'll live to regret it if she does," declared the authoritative voice of Kate.

"Oh dear!" wept Colleen. "My poor Patsy Pat."

"Not to worry. I'm not finished with Paul Brown yet," said Sandy Mac. "There's still this unsolved murder and he might know more about that than we think."

"Our Arfer could tell you more about it," cried Colleen excitedly. "He was always on about it. He saw them twins come home that night, just before our John got killed by the bloody coppers."

"Have you forgotten?" said Sandy. "I'm also a copper."

Colleen smiled at him. "You seem too nice to be a copper," she said.

Sandy Mac offered to escort Colleen and Kate home and as they walked slowly toward the club he brought up the subject of the twins again.

"How about me meeting this brother of yours?" he asked.

"Can't," Colleen stated. "He's down in Somerset."

"Well, let's go on a trip for the day," he suggested. He had taken a fancy to this vivacious redhead.

Colleen gave him a dazzling smile. "All right," she said. Suddenly her face dropped. "No, I can't. Sorry, no can do," she said hurriedly.

"Why not?" Sandy asked in his most charming manner.

"One, is that I'm a working girl," she said with determination, "and the other, well, you can tell him, Kate."

They had reached the club and Colleen disappeared inside. Kate took Sandy to her sitting room for a drink and put him in the picture: Colleen was pregnant and had been left in the lurch, Joe Fox having disappeared.

Sandy was truly sorry. "Can we be pals, anyway, kid?" he asked Colleen when she returned from changing her dress. "If you need my help you only have to ask."

Colleen looked steadily at Sandy Mac. "Thanks," she said quietly.

In the meantime, when Paul had left the court with Patricia clinging very possessively to his arm, they had walked in the opposite direction to the alley, toward the City. He slouched along in his old manner and wore the thick specs that he had previously discarded. They altered his appearance but that made not a scrap of difference to Pat; this was her man, she had fought for him and won and was not letting him go.

Paul was rather confused. He had not expected to be lumbered with this young kid. He had been a loner ever since they shut his brother away, and he did not like the situation one bit.

Pat was hanging tightly on to his arm, trying desperately to keep in step in her dainty high-heeled kid boots.

"That floored them. You should have seen my mother's face," she said triumphantly. "But Mollie's on my side. I'm sure she'll help us get married."

Paul suddenly stood still. "Get married?" he gasped. "Who's getting married?"

"Oh, Paul!" Pat threw her arms about his neck. "We must get married. I can't leave you, not ever!" Tears flowed and passersby stopped and stared.

Paul was about to strike out at her, but changed his mind. "Let's go where it's quiet," he suggested. "We can't talk here."

They walked into one of the quiet green squares that are so common in London—a neat tidy flower-edged square with a couple of benches. Paul sat leaning forward, deep in thought, his elbows on his knees, and Pat snuggled up close to him on the damp bench.

No one had ever shown him so much affection before, nor had he cared for any other human being, except perhaps that poor crazy brother. She was nice, soft and dark, like a black shiny kitten. Some hidden emotion stirred within him. Her old mother owned most of Autumn Alley, he had heard. Must have a good bit of money tucked away. Might not be such a bad proposition after all, he thought. He looked down at her. She looked so content that he almost expected her to start purring.

"They'll never let you marry me," he told her abruptly. "You're under age and they'd have to give their consent."

"That's all right," replied Pat, "I'll live with you."

He stared at her in admiration. Plenty of guts, this chick.

"What? In the house in the alley? You wouldn't dare!" he challenged.

"Wouldn't I?" returned Pat. "Try me!"

Paul fondled the back of her neck under her soft dark hair. "You're quite a gel," he said. "Perhaps you and I would tick over together, who knows."

"I love you," declared Pat, holding her lips up to be kissed.

It was just a peck on the cheek that he gave her. There was no time for a demonstration of affection; there were plans to be made—the situation had altered considerably. He stood up.

"Come, let's go then," he said sharply.

So together they returned to the alley. Cool and calm, walking arm in arm, they entered the front door of No. 5.

Lil, who was watching out as usual, saw them and goggled in amazement. Panting for breath she ran to inform Mollie.

"Oh, my!" she gasped. "Maud will murder her. She's come back, the little bitch, and gone in there with him as brazen as you like."

Mollie looked very worried and stood biting her lip. "I'd better go and see Maud," she said, taking off her apron. She was very close to her mother-in-law; the sorrow of Larry's death and Maud's fondness for Mary had drawn them closer.

It hurt to see that brave woman sitting so dejected. Maud's face was drawn with worry and fatigue. Beside her was the brandy decanter. "Sorry, love, I felt I had to take a drink," she apologized to the strictly abstemious Mollie.

"It's all right, dear." Mollie so earnestly wanted to help, but even she was beginning to feel the strain.

"She went in there with him," said Maud suddenly.

Mollie dropped her gaze. "She loves him. I know she's very young, but even the worst villain can be reformed by love."

"Not him," announced Maud. "There's something very evil about him."

"Look, dear, let Pat come home and allow her to see him. Once she gets her own way she might get tired of him," urged Mollie.

But Maud shook her big untidy head. "Can't do it, Mollie. My beautiful Patsy is tied for life to that beast."

Mollie sighed. "Well, you're just as obstinate as her. Please try and be a little more tolerant," she begged. "She's your only child now Larry's gone."

Maud gave a deep pathetic moan and Mollie took that big unhappy head to her bosom and rocked her back and forth just like a baby.

"Dad and I will go over there when he comes home from work. You go and rest now," she said quietly. This kindly young woman had all the gentleness of her mother but Mollie was stronger, more ready to cope with the blows in life.

At six o'clock that evening Tim and Mollie went over to No. 5. Pat, very flushed and excited, opened the door to them.

"Well, this is an honor," she said with heavy sarcasm. "Enter the abode of love." She made a dramatic sweeping gesture.

Tim looked embarrassed, but Mollie said firmly: "Stop this nonsense, Pat, we've come to discuss the best path for all concerned."

Paul, with an ingratiating smile, came from the dimly lit depths of the front room. "Good evening, Tim. What can I do for you, Mollie?"

"Well, first thing," said Mollie sharply, "you'll send Pat back home. It'll break her mother's heart if she lives here in sin with you."

"I'm quite ready to accommodate you, Mollie," Paul answered politely. "There's already been such unnecessary friction."

"Are you prepared to marry her?" demanded Tim. Pat looked anxiously at Paul.

"If her parents will allow it," he replied.

"That was all I wanted to know," said Mollie. "Now, Pat, you come back with me and I'll persuade your parents. Is that to your satisfaction?"

"I'll stay with you, Mollie, but not with Mother," returned Pat still defiant, but slightly more amicable.

So the deal was clinched and Pat returned across the road to live with Mollie, on the condition that, as far as the alley folk were concerned, she and Paul were officially engaged. It was insult added to injury. Maud took it very badly.

" 'Tis one below the belt, my boyo," Dandy remarked to Tim.

" 'Tis a real dirty trick for fate to play. She worshiped that gel, and this so soon after losing Larry, God rest his soul."

Tim was all sympathy, even more so since Pat had come to

live with Mollie and him. " 'Tis an odd business, I don't like it one bit," he muttered, taking the clay pipe out of his mouth. "He's a wrong 'un, I'm sure of it. And she looks so strange some days, that little one, not a word to say, not a smile and no appetite. She's not the bright young miss she was, to be sure, not at all."

"They say she stops out half the night with him," said Dandy, with a melancholy nod of his head. They sat close together on that long bench in the public bar sipping huge jugs of porter. "Poor old Maud, I don't know what to say to her," confessed Dandy. "She just sits around the house; she's given up her work, and she looks ten years older."

"Perhaps it would be better to let them marry," suggested Tim.

"Maud won't hear of it," replied Dandy.

"Why not take her home for a holiday, back to the old country? It might do the trick," advised Tim.

Dandy carefully weighed his words. "You could be right, me boyo. I'll see what I can do."

At this very moment, with Mollie to back her up, Pat stood in Maud's front room, demanding that her mother should sign the official papers consenting to her marriage with Paul. Mother and daughter faced each other, anger gleaming from Maud's gray eyes, her face haggard, her hair disheveled. "I'll see you in your grave first," she screamed. "I'll never let you throw yourself away on that jailbird."

Pat, calm but very pale, held out the form. "I need both your signatures," she said coldly. "I'm getting married in three weeks."

"To hell with you," roared Maud. "Go and live with him, what do I care? You couldn't disgrace me any more than you have done already."

"All right," said Pat, "I'll apply to the magistrate for permission. Then it will all get in the newspapers again." There was a kind of cruel twist to her tone.

Mollie stepped forward and intervened. "Maud, listen to me. Don't make your own grandchild a bastard."

Maud stared incredulously at them; her mouth trembled. "Oh, dear God!" she cried heartbrokenly.

"Whatever's the matter with Pat?" shouted Mollie suddenly. Pat had put her hands over her face and sunk sobbing to the floor. They both ran to her but her mother reached her first. Hungry arms held her tight.

"Oh, my poor little babe," Maud wailed. "How could you do this to me?"

Pat sobbed. "I'm truly sorry, Mother, but I love him, I can't help myself."

As Mollie wiped away the tears, Maud took the crumpled form and put her signature to it. "Now get your father to sign," she said steadily. "Let's get it over with. You can have your wedding, my love, then I'll sell this bloody place and move away. I've had my fill of Autumn Alley."

That night for the first time in many years old Dandy held Maud tight as she cried herself to sleep. "I'll take you back to Ireland for a holiday, old gel," he said gently, "just as soon as we get this damned wedding over and done with."

# Annie Fox

THE WAR HAD TAKEN A DEPRESSING TURN. The army was entrenched and the streets were full of walking wounded in their blue suits and red armbands. Long food queues added to the problems, combined with the hazards of the air raids. Many East End shops had closed down and there had been some reprisals against the German Jews, most of whom had fled out of town—even as far as Ireland. Another who had gone to Ireland was Joe Fox whose main desire was to dodge conscription.

There was still one bright spot in town, however, in those dark blitzed-out streets of the Mile End—Kate's Club— where soldiers and sailors on leave and civilians out on a spree gathered to watch the show. Kate, as impeccably dressed as ever, sat with Sandy Mac to watch the performance. In spite of his unpopular profession, Sandy was now a regular customer. Kate chewed the end of her pencil reflectively as she watched Colleen perform. The girl was almost three months pregnant but had had not an ache nor pain. There had been no complaints from this incorrigible child who took everything in her stride. Attired in a wide crinoline and a cute Victorian bonnet and holding a dreadful rag doll in her arms, she put on a comedy act, playing the part of little Nell to perfection. "She were poor but she were 'onest, the victim of a rich man's shame," she yelled in pure Cockney. "So he took her orf to London, there she lorst 'er maiden name." Amid the roars of laughter she banged the rag doll around.

Sandy gazed at her in admiration. "Got lots of guts, that kid," he exclaimed.

"Yes, she has," agreed Kate. "She seems to be able to laugh even at her own troubles . . . but they have to be faced, you know."

"Found the bloke yet?" he asked.

"No, he's skipped off to Ireland," Kate informed him.

"What will she do?"

"She'd never have married him," declared Kate. "She's a strange kid; falls in and out of love very easily. Suppose it's natural for one her age. There's a great future ahead for Colleen, the problem is getting her over this present bad spot."

"Why don't you go and see Fox's mother?" said Sandy. "She might help, I know she's got plenty. I had dealings with his father. He was a trader down the lane. Heard he left that old lady rolling in dough."

Kate's eyes gleamed. At last someone was talking sense. She remembered her own youth and how she had been thrown out of the house into the street with a child in her arms, a little girl that she had been forced to give away. She shivered as she thought of those sordid days. She must take care of Colleen at all costs. "Get the address for me, Mac," she said.

Colleen had finished her act and came to join them. She was pink and glowing, and having discarded the ridiculous bonnet her hair cascaded down to her waist. "Gawd," she burst out, "I'm starving. Give us some sandwiches, Bill," she said to the old fellow who served at the tables.

Sandy Mac's thin lips twitched as he tried hard not to grin.

"Restrain yourself, Colleen," Kate said. "If you continue eating this way you'll get too fat too soon."

"Got to feed the poor little so and so, ain't I?" said Colleen with a wide grin. She grasped the plate piled high with ham sandwiches and tucked in.

Several days later Kate left the club, clad in her best black dress and her wide plumed hat. She did not tell Colleen where she was going.

The cab with its ancient old nag clopped its way through the narrow back streets until it halted outside a very dreary looking red brick building. A grimy sign outside told the world that this was Temple Dwellings.

"Are you sure they still live here?" Kate anxiously asked the cabby, as she stood looking at the flight of dirty steps and the crowd of ragged children who played outside.

"Quite sure, lady. The Fox family 'ave lived 'ere all their lives, they have," the cabby informed her huffily as he drove away.

Kate gathered up her skirts and climbed warily up the steps. Inside the door were more stone steps and attached to the wall was an iron rail to make climbing more bearable. The walls on each side were stained and dirty. A little boy rushed past almost knocking her down. Kate began to doubt the wisdom of this trip. Then, on the second floor, she spotted a reasonably well-painted door with a brass plate which stated that these were flats three, four and five. Above that, in large letters, was the name "Annie Fox." A strange smell pervaded the air. It was not unpleasant but rather exotic. Kate knocked lightly. To her amazement a young woman wearing the attire of a maidservant opened the door. "Come inside," she said softly in broken English.

The small, very cramped hall had dark embossed wallpaper on the walls and at the far end a hatstand that was full to overflowing with hats and coats. Kate stood waiting and could hear the mutter of voices through the half-opened door. She could see a very old lady sitting by the fire, very upright and quite motionless. A lamplight shone on her silver hair. The door was opened wide suddenly and Kate looked around at the size and splendor of the long room within. It had three big windows with velvet drapes, plush furniture and satin cushions, brass lamps, and candlesticks. In the center of the room another old lady was seated at a round table which was covered with a deep pile red-and-gold tapestry tablecloth. The lady was stout and her hair black and shiny. There were diamonds in her ears and around her fat neck. Her small hands, laden with rings, were busily crocheting a wide shawl, and her eyes, black and speculative, looked hard in Kate's direction.

"Well?" she asked. "What can I do for yer?" The Cockney intonation was strong.

"I wish to speak privately to you, if I may," returned Kate.

"That's all right, take no notice of Momma, she's deaf as a post. Get on with it, gel, sit down."

Kate sat down because her knees had gone weak. All those grand well-rehearsed speeches had flown, but she need not have bothered, for Annie Fox shot her a shrewd glance.

"Come about Joe, ain't yer?" she inquired.

"Well, yes, how did you know?"

"Don't miss much up here," commented Annie, still twisting and turning the white thread through her fingers. "What's he done this time?" she demanded.

"It's about a young girl who works for me," replied Kate. "He's got her into trouble."

"*Shiksa?*" inquired Annie with a shrug. After a pause she said: "It's that singer, ain't it?"

Before Kate could reply she continued: "I know you got a club in Mile End. Good business that." She relapsed into thought once more.

Kate got on her high horse. "You may or may not know all about me, but don't get it wrong about Colleen. She's a good, and was an innocent little girl until that son of yours did the dirty on her."

Annie Fox put down her crocheting and the light in her eyes warned Kate that she was prepared to do battle.

"I know what Joe is so I don't need you to come here to tell me. Also, I know the kid; she worked for him on the stall. But what do you expect me to do about it, eh?" She stuck out her chin in Kate's direction.

The wisdom in Kate made her retreat immediately. "There's not much you or I can do. I know that Joe's already married, but this kid hasn't got a cent. Surely you can see to it that he gives her something to tide her over till she can work again."

"Fair enough," muttered the old lady, "but, my life, what I put up with from him. Always been a trouble he has, and been much worse since his father passed on, God rest him."

Kate felt a qualm of sympathy. Amid all this luxury, the mother was ashamed of her only son.

"Have a glass of wine?" offered Annie. "You're a Yiddisher girl yourself, ain't yer. I remember your folk, I do," she added.

Kate nodded assent as a tray of wine and cheesecake was brought in by the servant.

"Go and get Esther," Annie ordered and the servant left quietly.

Ten seconds later she was back bringing with her a stout dark young woman and two little girls, identical twins with black curls tied with white ribbons and lovely dresses, all frills and lace.

"This is Joe's wife," said Annie. "Deserted her, he has, she's from Germany, and now those lovely babies are left to my care and responsibility. Come on, darlings." She held out podgy arms to the children and cuddled them close.

Kate smiled at the children. Annie sipped the wine and insisted that her guest sample her cheesecake. She rambled on all the time about Esther, who sat very silent. Her small deep-set eyes looked as if they had wept an ocean of tears.

"So ain't I got enough on me plate?" asked Annie, waving her hands. "This gel here"—she jerked a thumb in the direction of her dejected daughter-in-law—"she can't speak English and don't want to learn either. That Joe, he spent all her dowry. Less than six months it took him. Gave her two kids, now he don't want to know her any more."

Kate nodded sympathetically, thinking how lonely this German girl must be—unpopular with the Londoners and an embarrassment to the Jewish community.

Annie went on talking and munching all the time, crumbs each side of her mouth. "Joe's a no-good, always was," she declared emphatically, "never kept up his true faith, mixed with all them boys down the market—it killed his poor father it did."

There was a moment of respite while Annie went over to the old lady by the fire to give her a piece of cake. "That's me old mother-in-law," said Annie. "Ninety-two, she is. As yer can see, I got me plate full."

Kate agreed and began to think about leaving. She fidgeted with her furs and drew on her gloves.

Suddenly Annie's black eyes fixed on her face. "How much was you thinking of getting for the kid?" she asked.

"I hadn't really thought," Kate replied.

Annie waved her arms. "That Joe, that bloody Joe, now there's another poor little bastard to worry about." She lapsed into a long ramble of Yiddish that was unintelligible to Kate. Then she said: "I'll give the kid a hundred quid to see her through her confinement, and if it's a boy I'll do more."

Kate was so surprised she was momentarily speechless. "Why, that's a very generous offer," she gasped out at last.

Annie cuddled the two little girls close. "Not to worry," she said, "money's the least of my problems. Besides, it might be a boy. Might be luckier with him, even if he is born on the wrong side of the blankets."

She dived deep into her pocket for a bunch of keys. The servant took them and returned with a large old-fashioned polished wood stationery box. Annie unlocked it, counted out a bundle of notes and handed them to Kate.

"Get me a bit of paper," she ordered and Esther rose slowly and handed her an old envelope.

"Just between you, me and the girl," Annie told Kate, "no one else involved." She wrote slowly with a thick stump of pencil: "Paid to Joe's woman, one hundred pounds."

"Put your name to this, love. I like to keep things business-like."

With a subdued smile Kate wrote her name on the small piece of paper. It was then put back in the box which was relocked and with almost ceremonious style carried out again by the servant.

Kate rose to say goodbye to this family of females. She felt mixed emotions: some amusement and some admiration for this true Yiddisher momma.

"I got a bed I support in the London Hospital," Annie Fox remarked as Kate left. "She can go in there to have her baby. Like that I'll get the news quicker."

When Kate got home she told Colleen about the money. To Colleen it was of little importance. In fact, she was not even interested in Kate's account of her visit to Annie Fox. "Bloody yids," she grumbled, "think they can buy everyone with their lousy money."

"But, Colleen," Kate remonstrated with her, "this money was given generously with your child's interest at heart." There was a good deal of Lil in Colleen. She had a kind of bulldog obstinacy when it suited her.

Kate looked at her sulky face and shrugged. "Well, at least it's a worry off my mind. And if you're fortunate enough to bear a son he'll be well taken care of."

"I'm having a girl, I don't like boys," pouted Colleen.

"I think you've still got a lot of growing up to do, my dear," said Kate. Then she dismissed the subject.

The thing that was troubling Colleen at that moment was not the child in her womb but the fact that Patsy Pat was being married in a lovely white dress, and because of this unsightly lump on her tummy she would not be able to be her maid of honor. She scowled and sulked, and mooched about the house all day. At night her performance lacked enthusiasm. Kate began to wish that she would go back to the alley till the baby was born. Suddenly, out of the blue her wish was granted, though not in the way she would have wished.

Several weeks had passed. It was midday and the lunch break and the children were playing out in the school playground. From a blue cloudless sky came a by-now familiar droning sound and in the Mile End Road people stopped to stare up at the sky at a black sausage-like shape. Then came the sudden explosion of the guns. But it was too late; in broad daylight a German Zeppelin had broken through.

Old Sam Lewis came from his shop to look up at the sky. Becky was still up north with Lew, so Sam camped out in his shop most days and nights. The sirens blew but were drowned by the whistling sound of bombs streaking down, the crash of breaking glass, and the scream of the people as they ran for cover. The force of the explosion threw poor old Sam up in the air.

Kate ran to find Colleen and together they went down to the cellar underneath the club. They could hear the crash and thump of the bombs hitting the surrounding streets. They crouched close together, showered by plaster and breaking bottles.

The last bomb was a direct hit on a local school. Mothers left their jobs and ran to the school. Some lucky little ones survived, but not many. The East End wept tears of blood and hatred. The Kaiser would pay for this bloody deed.

Colleen and Kate, very scared and very dirty, emerged from the cellar at the sound of the all-clear. Kate wept as she surveyed her lifetime's work in ruins. The mirrors were broken, plush seats ripped and overturned, and the whole place was covered with dirt and debris.

"Oh my God!" she cried.

Colleen just stood there, white and shivering. "I wanna go home," she wailed childishly. "I wanna be with Mollie and Patsy Pat."

Kate surveyed her impatiently and felt slightly sad that Colleen did not want her mother as girls often did in times of despair. But Colleen did not want Lil, she never had.

"Perhaps I'd better take you home," Kate said, putting a coat about Colleen's shaking shoulders. "Never know, damned Jerries might come back, blast them."

As they walked along the main road, women with tear-streaked faces passed them. "Oh, my God, those poor little kids," murmured Kate, when she heard what had happened.

Amid all this chaos it was hopeless to wait for a bus, so they took the short cut to the alley through the park. It was cool, green and unusually quiet there; the birds still sang but no children played on the swings.

Kate began to consider the future. If London was to be subjected to these daylight air raids, it would be impossible to keep the club open, and once she had handed Colleen over to Mollie's care she would be more or less free. Perhaps she should do something for the war effort: most women of her age worked in munitions. No, not that, she thought, she could not stand all the grease and dirt of a factory at any price.

Lost in her own thoughts, Colleen was thinking how nice it would be to be with Patsy Pat once more. Her baby would be about three months younger than her own. They might both have girls and it would be fun to dress them up, and put a blue ribbon in her own baby's hair and a red one in Pat's baby's hair just as they had when they were small. Lil would probably create a big scene when she heard about the baby, but Arthur would be home soon for Pat's wedding and he would protect her. Just as well she was going home. She was quite looking forward to it.

They came out of the gates at the end of the park and turned toward the alley and Mollie's house.

Mollie was more than willing to take care of Colleen.

"There's no need to worry about the expense. I have a hundred pounds in care for her," Kate told Mollie.

"She'll not need it. I'm far from being poor. Put the money away for the child," replied Mollie.

"You're a very nice person," said Kate quietly. She felt she must try to express her gratitude to Mollie who so far had not uttered a word of reproach. "I'm very sorry it happened when Colleen was in my charge."

"It would have happened to Colleen anyway," replied Mollie sadly. "But don't worry, I'll take care of her."

Thus Kate went on her way feeling very relieved, confident she had done the best thing possible for her protégée.

Mollie went upstairs to tidy the bedrooms and move her belongings into the small spare room. Colleen could share with Pat in the double room until Pat got married next week.

As she made up her own bed in that small boxroom, in her mind's eye she could see a small white cot under the window. Would Colleen let me keep the baby, wondered Mollie. How I would love to take care of it.

Downstairs Pat and Colleen laughed and giggled. The toffee apple man had just passed by, and they sat on the old sofa licking their toffee apples as merry as two debs.

Mollie's dark eyes surveyed them. They were just two kids and about to bring two more into the world. It did not seem fair somehow. Mollie, hardly three years older than they, felt old and mature.

It was not long before Lil appeared to upset them all. She was slightly tipsy and she had taken to wearing that man's checked cap all the time and it gave her a most absurd appearance.

"So yer 'ave come 'ome, 'ave yer?" She crossed her fat arms and stood in the doorway, confronting her daughter.

Colleen put down the huge wally she was now consuming. "What's it look like? A bleeding ghost?" she retorted.

Lil blew out her cheeks and assumed a belligerent stance. "Got yourself in the family way," she shouted, "now yer come 'ome bringing yer troubles to my doorstep."

"Give over, Muvver," yelled back Colleen.

"Oughter punch yer bleedin' head in, I did," said Lil, waving a grimy fist.

"Why don't you go and clean up that pigsty of a house instead. Arthur's bringing his posh gel home tomorrow," warned Colleen.

Lil looked slightly vacant for a moment, but then she

suddenly remembered that Billy might be coming home for the wedding. He had said he would try. A light came into her faded eyes.

"Arse 'oles," she roared at Colleen as she turned and went toddling off.

They all began to laugh, even Mollie; Lil's bark was always worse than her bite.

Armed with a bucket and mop and perspiring freely, Lil set about her neglected chores. "Never mind abaht that toffee-nosed Arfer," she told Maud, from whom she borrowed sheets and various cleaning materials. "My Billy Boy might come home. Fighting for the likes of you, 'e is."

# Winkles for Tea

ON THAT SATURDAY MORNING OUR ALLEY SPRANG back into life. It began with the arrival of Arthur, brimming over with fun and good humor. Time and absence had matured him. In fact, that funny looking youth was now a rather distinguished, good-looking young man. Expensive horn-rimmed specs seemed to have corrected his eyes and a private dentist had done wonders with his crooked teeth. He spoke the king's English clearly and precisely, wore well-tailored suits and was engaged to the boss's daughter. It was quite a big step up the ladder for this unwanted little Cockney lad who could not even get in the army.

This boy with an untrained but quick-thinking mathematical mind, who had wasted his time reckoning up tuppeny bets, had fitted in perfectly in the burgeoning aircraft industry. Then he had met Hortense. She was no beauty but, like Arthur, had a surplus of brains. It was Hortense who suggested that Arthur should have English and elocution lessons; she also found him good lodgings, and taught him to play tennis and to ride a horse. In fact she seemed to have taken him over, lock stock and barrel, once she had made up her mind that she would marry him.

Arthur admired her but he did not love her as he had loved Mollie. Yet Hortense was an ideal partner in many ways, and he was content with their relationship.

The problem of his family and background always worried him, especially when they were making plans for an autumn wedding. Her father had approved and was generously having a house built for them.

"How about your mother, Arthur?" said Hortense. "We can't have a wedding without a mother-in-law."

Arthur looked worried. "It would be useless to ask her," he said. "She has never left the district we live in and I doubt if she ever would."

"Nevertheless, I'll invite her, and the rest of your family and friends down in that dreadful alley," she informed him.

While Arthur was still considering whether it would be wise to introduce his obese mother to his well-bred fiancée, an invitation came from Maud to Patricia's wedding.

"It'll be nothing like anything you have been used to," he warned Hortense. I know it's awful to say it, but I am bloody well ashamed of my mother."

Hortense stroked his wiry hair, flattening it as she always endeavored to do. "Now, darling, behave yourself," she admonished. "Let's get this mystery over and done with, it has stood between us for too long."

"I know you are right, darling." Arthur turned to her affectionately. "Whatever would I do without you?"

So that Saturday they traveled up to London.

"I'll book us in at the Great Eastern Hotel," suggested Arthur as they came out of the station.

"You will not," said Hortense firmly. "Get a cab. We'll stay in the alley come what may."

To begin with all went well; the return to the alley was not as embarrassing as Arthur had feared. Lil was clean and fairly sober; Colleen had washed and curled her hair for her and Mollie had cleaned and pressed her best dress—the one that her Billy had bought her. The parlor table was laid with Mollie's best embroidered tablecloth and Mary's dainty china. On the sideboard bottles of drink were stacked—this was Tim's and Dandy's contribution to the welcome-home for Arthur and his bride-to-be.

Everyone liked Hortense on sight, even though they were a little shy of her. And her smart tailored suit caused quite a stir, the skirt was daringly short—calf length, as it was described in the fashion pages.

"It's come from Paris, that suit," whispered Colleen to Pat.

"Oh, it's lovely, isn't it?" sighed Pat dreamily as she eyed it.

Hortense's cheerful laugh and frank manner impressed Mollie and Tim, while Maud greeted her like a long lost sister, making a terrific fuss of them both; Arthur had always had a special place in her heart. But also she recalled how she herself had come as a stranger to Autumn Alley, and it did not seem so long ago. Lil said very little, she just gazed silently, moon-faced, at this tall fresh-looking young lady.

Arthur and Hortense went over the road to visit poor old Sam Lewis, who still had not recovered from the shock of the bomb blast that had destroyed his shop. Becky, much stouter and blooming rather like a ripe fruit, had returned from the north to take care of him, leaving Lew to carry on making a name for himself as a comedian in the northern clubs.

With overwhelming affection, Becky greeted Arthur and Hortense. "Oh, such a handsome young man he is. Look at him, Sam, he looks like a doctor don't he?" She flattered and embarrassed Arthur and showered compliments onto Hortense, who was forced to listen to the exploits of her famous son.

"They are very sweet," remarked Hortense, as they came back hand in hand across the cobbled street.

"Rather too sugary," commented Arthur drily. "But they aren't so bad. I always have got on well with our alley folk; we used to be a very closely knit community. I suppose it was being down here beside the canal, shut off from the main road."

"Is that the canal?" inquired Hortense, looking over the wall into the green slimy water.

"We call it the Cut. Remind me to tell you some funny stories about it." Arthur leaned long and languid back against that nostalgic wall. "I once hooked Becky's son out of that water. She wrote me a wonderful letter. I always keep it in my wallet, I've got this funny feeling that it brings me good luck." He opened his wallet and brought out the old letter, yellow and faded with age.

Hortense read it silently, then folded it carefully and

handed it back to him. She put her arms through his. "I've always known you were a brave lad, that's why I chose you," she said contentedly.

"Rotter," replied Arthur, giving her a kiss.

Then they entered Lil's best parlor where the feast was laid out. Ready and waiting were all the family and the neighbors, except Tim and Dandy who would arrive later when the bottles were opened.

No one had thought to advise Lil about the menu. Normally in the Welton household they had scrappy meals eaten picnic fashion. Lil's idea of the grand life was high tea on Sundays when the folks as could afford it had shrimps and winkles and watercress. So on the table were huge mounds of tomato-and-watercress sandwiches and a large bowl of shrimps—all pink and whiskery—and another bowl of those snail-like creatures, winkles. To complete the spread there was a huge shop-made fruit cake. Her face red and shiny, her blue dress fitting tightly over her ample bosom, Lil proudly presided over the feast she had prepared.

Maud's eyebrows shot up when she surveyed the table, and Colleen burst out: "Crikey, Muvver, couldn't you think of anything better than shrimps and winkles?"

Lil, suddenly all riled up, was about to say her piece when the situation was saved by the arrival of the honored guests. For some moments there was complete silence; they all sat sipping tea, very much on edge. Arthur, striving to make someone relax, said loudly, slipping back into his Cockney voice: "Give us some of them bloomin' snails, I ain't seen none of them for years." So pins were produced and they all began to attack the winkles.

Hortense sat petrified, hoping she would not be expected to try them. Lil saw that her plate was empty and called out: "What's up wiv yer? Arfer, give the gel some winkles." With a grin Arthur loaded up Hortense's plate, handed her a pin, and left her to get on with it.

The general chit chat began to warm up around the table. The girls giggled at Arthur's jokes and Mollie blushed at his compliments. Beside him Hortense struggled valiantly to get one of these strange creatures from its shell. At last she succeeded; it was a grayish color and wore an odd flat hat. She stared at it in fascination, dangling there on the end of the pin. She could not put that in her mouth, no, not if her life depended upon it. So she sat and stared and wondered what to do with it.

In Lil's house there lived a black cat—a descendant of old Tigger who had resided with Mary. Now he sat on the shabby rug looking balefully at the unusual sight of people consuming something that had a nice fishy smell. With tail erect he came forward to investigate at the precise moment when Hortense had decided she would lose this winkle, pin and all, by dropping it on the floor under the table. The cat dashed forward. He was not going to miss a nice titbit. There was a dreadful squawk as he grabbed the winkle and the pin got stuck in his gullet.

"Christ!" yelled Lil. "Old Tigger's swallowed a flaming pin."

The cat was chased, grabbed, held up by the tail and banged on the back by Arthur. The pin with the winkle still attached shot out onto the rug. The cat broke free, shot up the curtains and out of the top of the window and was not seen again for a week.

By now the ice was broken as everyone screamed with laughter. The bottles were opened and the party really began. Tim and Dandy arrived, the old fiddle was brought out and the old square dances stepped out in fine style.

Maud was strangely keyed up. She danced like a young girl and drank lots of brandy and sat very close to Dandy. "I'll be glad when it's all over," she murmured.

Dandy held her hand. "It won't be long now, old gel, and then it's the ould country for you and me."

Pat stood outside looking up at the sky. Where was Paul? Why had he not come to the party? There had been a light air raid; she wondered if he was safe. She twisted her hands together nervously. Hurry up, next week, she thought, she could not wait for that day when they married—then she would feel more sure of him.

Colleen was calling: "Come in, Pat, we're going to play forfeits." So the fun went on until the early morning.

In Lil's best bedroom Hortense cuddled up to Arthur. "You'd better go down now, Arthur," she said. He, for propriety's sake, was sleeping downstairs. She kissed him goodnight. "They are wonderful people," she said. "How could you be ashamed of them?"

Arthur smiled and felt very happy. He was so pleased that Hortense's introduction into Autumn Alley had been a success.

Lil had become rather subdued as the evening wore on. Several times she muttered: "Billy Boy never came."

"Stop worrying, he'll be here for the wedding," Mollie consoled her.

"I'd have liked him to be here," she said forlornly.

With just one week to the wedding preparations were in full swing. Maud had very little to say to her daughter and so far had not addressed one civil word to her future son-in-law. All the negotiations had been done through Mollie. Paul avoided the alley folk by staying out all night and sleeping all day, and Pat was happy in the company of her old playmate. They took trips up to town with Arthur and Hortense, visiting Selfridges and Madame Tussauds.

Maud had given Paul the wherewithal for redecorating that dreary house, but so far no progress had been made—there were no signs of any improvements. "Oh, I expect he will get around to it," said Mollie cheerfully.

"I'll be lucky," replied Maud. "Bookie's got most of that money by now."

"Oh, I wouldn't say that," returned Mollie. "I think he's working nights in a club or something. A croupier, I think he did tell me."

"Oh, I know all about his nights out. Don't take me for a fool, Mollie," said Maud bitterly.

Mollie looked very distressed and Maud was immediately repentant. "Take no notice of me, I'm a mean old body," she said. "But she's making a hard bed for herself, and as far as I am concerned she can lie on it."

This undercurrent of feeling that coursed through the alley worried Arthur. He knew he could not confide in Hortense; there was a deep stubborn pride in this close-knit community and Hortense was still a stranger. So he discussed the affairs of the two young girls with Tim and Mollie.

"It's pretty obvious that they are both pregnant. It doesn't surprise me about Colleen—she never had any proper guidance at home. But I'm shocked at Patricia, and her marrying that damned rogue over the road!"

Mollie sat placidly knitting little white jackets for the new generation. "He's not so bad. You know what they say about giving a dog a bad name."

"I know I was only a little kid, but everything that has happened in this alley is as fresh in my mind as if it were yesterday." Arthur's keen gray eyes looked right into her face. "I remember that family. They were all a bit mad. I remember how we used to call out to the old father."

"Yes, and a lot of little nuisances you must have been," returned Mollie.

So Arthur retired defeated. But not even Mollie's cool insistence could win him over; he disliked Paul intensely.

Tim rose from his seat by the fire. "Come on, Arthur, let's go over the road for a drink."

"Only one," warned Mollie as they left.

Once over at the Railway Arms Tim relaxed with his pint of porter. "'Tis bad business, lad," he confided to Arthur. "I'm every bit as worried as you are. He's twice her age and not even of her own faith and that's enough against him."

"He must be about eight years older than I am," said Arthur. "He was about eighteen when old Sal was done in. Same age as our John."

"Don't I know, lad," returned Tim. "Wasn't it me who held him at the last? And found old Sal wallowing in her own blood? It takes some forgetting, scenes like that."

"Yes, I still see that picture in my mind," agreed Arthur. "I was looking through the letter box and I saw them coming down the street. The police never searched their house and it was funny that they disappeared soon after."

"I've still got the bible picture I picked up that morning. If you remember they always carried those huge bibles about everywhere with them."

"I wonder what happened to the other brother?" pondered Arthur. "And that skinny sister . . . we never saw the going of her, did we?"

Both men stood still and silent, wrapped in thought, looking out of the open door of the pub. In the doorway of No. 5 they spied Patricia with her arms locked about her lover. Both men turned away in embarrassment.

"Better let sleeping dogs lie," said Tim. "Come on, drink up, Arthur, we'll have another."

* * *

Maud had seen Pat go creeping into No. 5. He would be in bed most likely, she thought. She felt a burning rage within. Pull yourself together, she said to herself. She'll learn the hard way, the same as you did. History had a way of repeating itself, but if she had had a mother she might have listened to her and things would have been different. Maud poured herself a drink and sat down by the window. I could have prevented her marrying him, she thought. I need not have given in, but it was to give the child a name. But then what's in a name? The bad blood in him will ruin any good name. She put her hand over her eyes as if to shut out those bitter thoughts.

"Oh, God! how am I to face this wedding?" she exclaimed out loud.

She stood up, blew her nose and wiped her eyes. "Better get some work done," she muttered. "No good giving in. I haven't been to the shop for ages." With sudden decision she grabbed her coat and marched off down the road to the shop on the corner.

The shop looked very derelict. There was dust on the windows, and dumped on the doorstep was a pile of parcels that someone had presented to charity. "Soon get this lot straightened up," she told herself and set to work with a will.

There had always been a depressing atmosphere in this shop. "This is the first bloody place I'll get shot of," muttered Maud as she busied herself opening bags, sorting the rubbish in them.

She picked up a brown paper carrier that had been dumped behind the counter. Pat was not one for keeping the place tidy. Maud emptied it out on the counter. Inside were small pictures with velvet frames, some containing photographs of very severe-looking Victorian ladies. "God knows who sent this junk," she muttered. She rummaged in the bag. At the bottom were some old books. "Might be more use," she murmured. Turning over the leaves she noticed a familiar name. In a clear hand was written: "This book belongs to Ellen Brown, 5 Autumn Alley." The book was called *Science of the Mind*, and had belonged to Paul's sister. Now that was a coincidence. Among the other books was a large bible. When she picked it up, the cover fell off and some loose leaves fell out. It looked as if it had been badly knocked about. Inside the cover in large black letters she read: "To Paul Brown from his father at Christmas." The words swam before her eyes. At the bottom of the page was a large red thumb print. It was blood. She shivered. The book fell from her hands. Looking down she saw the same dried blood marks on the shiny cover. Oh, how horrible! How did it get blood all over it? Was it some sort of omen? She sat down, sweat on her brow. The dark corners of the shop seemed more shadowy than ever. Her mind was in a whirl.

Suddenly she rose, found a piece of tissue paper, wrapped up the bible very carefully, closed the shop and walked up the road to the police station to find Sandy Mac.

Sandy looked at Maud with sympathy. "I can't really say if this is evidence," he told her. "It's for the experts to decide. It could be too old to be identifiable," he explained to her.

"I've got a feeling in my bones," said Maud.

"If you feel sure this man is a murderer why don't you stop the wedding?" he asked.

Maud shook her head. "She would never forgive me."

"Well, perhaps she won't forget if this proves to be true," argued Sandy.

"I'll chance it," said Maud. "I've got a feeling about that bible. I was meant to find it."

"Well, by right I shouldn't tell you, but I've traced the other twin. He's in an asylum for the criminally insane. He's in there for murdering a girl, a servant in a house that was burgled. Witness swears there were two of them. So who knows? We might be able to get him there."

"Oh, my poor little girl!" burst out Maud. "Whatever shall I do?"

Sandy patted her head. "Keep silent, that's the best thing you can do. I'll be around. As a matter of fact I'd like to come to the wedding."

"Oh, yes, of course. You'd be very welcome. But get him before he does my little one real harm."

She did not seem so tall as she hurried back to the alley without her big hat, her shoulders bowed, and her coat flying out in the wind. She had not one word of greeting or a smile for anyone. She just sat by the fire waiting for news.

"What's up with Maud?" asked Lil of Mollie. "She don't 'alf seem to be acting funny."

When the Saturday morning finally dawned it was a really beautiful day. The wedding guests had begun to arrive. The previous evening little Bridie, very homely in country attire, had returned to the alley with her tall red-haired Timmo, now a sergeant in the Irish Guards, and with them four-year-old Tessa and eight-year-old Tony who were to be attendants at the wedding.

Mollie's house was a hive of activity. She loved it, absolutely thriving on the atmosphere of being needed and having children running around the house while she attended to the final arrangements. There was no sign of Maud.

Bridie and Colleen helped Pat into her expensive bridal gown. Pat, disregarding all traditions, had insisted on a virginal white ceremony, and Mollie had arranged for there to be bells, music, flowers and candles—all the usual trappings. The old priest had been difficult at first; Paul was not a Catholic. But for Mollie's sake some of the difficulties had been overcome. The reception was to be held in a large room over the pub, and a select firm of caterers had been called in.

All this expense was to be met by Maud, but she showed little interest in the proceedings. She still sat by the fire, yellow-faced, a brandy bottle at her side.

Dandy had begun to lose patience with her. "Pull yourself together, old lady," he pleaded. "We'll be off to the ould country as soon as this is over."

Slowly Maud put on her new outfit. It was a great change from the bossy energetic woman they were all used to.

Dandy had begged Timmo to stand in for him and give the bride away. "Not up to it, lad," he said. "I've got to keep my eye on the old lady."

The guests held their breath as Patricia came down the aisle on Timmo's arm. She was so composed, tall and slim. Her face was pale and her hair black and shining as a raven's wing. A crown of orange blossom with a halo of white veiling framed her beauty. Holding the long embroidered train were Tony and Tessa. Sturdy Tony was in tartan and a snow white shirt—such a contrast to his auburn curls—and Tessa wore green and white, and her long corn-colored hair gleamed in the sun. A pink rose nestled on top of her head, and matched her rosy cheeks.

Paul stood awkwardly at the altar looking rather seedy. His

best man stood beside him, his one and only pal—a little man with a bad leg called Bertie Harris, but known to the underworld as Sparsie. He claimed to have been recently invalided out of the army, but the only front line he had ever seen was the cold gray wall of Wormwood Scrubs.

Many local people filled the church. This had been a much discussed wedding because of the scandal caused when the local newspaper published the account of the recent court case.

It was a lovely ceremony. Everyone agreed that, even though Paul was not a soldier, they made a handsome couple. Colleen wept and Mollie busied herself with the children. Maud sat as still as a statue in an extra large hat with a long white plume and an expensive black suit. Not a tear, not a smile, just a kind of mask devoid of emotion.

The reception was an unusually swell affair for the alley folk. Waiters served them soup, chicken and white wine. But there was a lack of the spontaneous gaiety that usually attended their functions.

At six o'clock the bride and groom departed for the station. A weekend in Brighton was to be the extent of their honeymoon—Paul having got rather low on funds. As the guests waved farewell to the bride and groom Maud, who had been so silent all day, broke away from the little knot of guests and ran after the cab, arms outstretched, screaming: "Patsy, my darling. Don't go, come back, Patsy, my love."

Tim and Dandy went to her aid. She broke into hysterical weeping as they escorted her back to the alley. It put a damper on the remaining guests so the party soon broke up.

Arthur sat for a while, chatting with Kate and Sandy Mac. "Didn't like to see poor old Maud so cut up," remarked this kindly young man.

"She was distraught. Must have a great deal on her mind," said Kate.

"More than any of you know," joined in Sandy.

"You in the police force?" Arthur questioned him.

"That's right, plain clothes," replied Sandy.

"Tell me the truth, then. Have you got anything on him?"

"I'm not allowed to discuss it really," said Sandy. "What I've got is only circumstantial evidence, it'll do me no good. But I've been waiting to talk to you about it for a long time."

So they began to discuss the alley murder when old Sal was battered to death and robbed of her life's savings. Arthur told the old story of how he had spied through the letter box and seen the twins returning home.

"I'll tell you what," said Arthur, "if you could find that sister of his I bet she knew what was going on. She tried to commit suicide some time after."

"It's an idea," declared Sandy eagerly, taking out his little notebook. Arthur described Ellen for him. He even remembered the name of the paper she had worked for and Sandy Mac noted it all down very carefully.

By Sunday afternoon the excitement of the wedding had abated and everyone began to leave. First to say goodbye were Arthur and Hortense, extending invitations to Colleen and Lil to visit them. Then at five o'clock Maud and Dandy said their farewells. Maud was subdued and still very depressed as they went off to catch the early morning boat train to Ireland. At six o'clock Mollie and Tim left with Bridie, Timmo and the children, for a week's stay with them while Timmo was on leave.

Everyone had gone and Colleen was down-hearted now that the alley had emptied of all her close neighbors and friends. So at eight o'clock she moved back into her old home.

Lil sat around the fire looking very much the worse for wear, having filled herself to the brim with gin at the wedding.

"Oh, so yer 'ave come back, 'ave yer?" she snorted at Colleen.

"Only until Mollie comes back. No sense in staying in there on my own."

Lil suddenly began to weep, loudly and morbidly. "He never came," she sniveled, "he said he would. Oh, poor Billy, where is he?"

"Perhaps he couldn't get leave," said Colleen casually, but Lil continued to grizzle.

"Oh, for Christ's sake shut up, Muvver," shouted Colleen. "Go up the road and have a beer. I'll give you some money."

But Lil refused and just sat there, a fat lump of morbid depression.

"Well, this is bloody happy," declared Colleen. "I'll go and get my room in order and go to bed. If I stay down here we'll both end up with the bleeding hump." Tugging her suitcase with her she marched up the stairs to the little back bedroom that used to be hers.

Billy Boy was at that moment out in the stormy North Sea aboard H.M.S. *Hampshire,* sailing with its escort toward the icy Arctic waters. Many a swear word had been uttered when the liberty boat had brought him back to the dock, recalled at the last moment. It was enough to make a saint swear, and he was going to a wedding—fat lot that jammy lot of bastards cared. But once they set sail Billy Boy was back to his old good-humored self. On a secret mission; that would be something to tell the folk in the alley when he returned. Lord Kitchener on board and lots of other posh blokes.

At dawn he was on watch, banging his frozen hands together, and thinking of his young wife and baby in Norfolk. How silent and misty it was. They moved slowly, awaiting the escort destroyers, which seemed to have gone out of sight, to catch up with them.

Suddenly it happened. There was a blinding flash and a loud roar of the explosion that ripped the decks apart. Billy Boy went into the icy water. Violently he fought the icy waves, swearing loudly between gasps of breath. Around him in the gray dawn were others fighting for survival—great men, important statesmen—now it was time for them as it was for Billy. The last four letter word rang out into the Arctic mist and the icy waters closed over his head.

Back at home in the alley, Colleen was sound asleep dreaming she was a film star in a long flowing gown, but someone was calling. "Colleen! Colleen! Go down and open the front door," her mother's voice was shrill and tense. "Hurry up, you silly cow, Billy Boy is knocking."

Colleen dashed down to the front door and opened it. No one was there, only the cold still moonlight and the yellow glow of the street lamp. Not even a shadow stood there.

Colleen ran back upstairs and Lil stood at the top in her large white nightgown, a curious expression on her face.

"There's no one there," said Colleen. "Go back to bed, you look like a bleeding ghost standing there."

"I heard him knocking. He called me," Lil insisted.

Colleen, trying hard to be patient, said: "You were dreaming. Go back to bed, Muvver."

"No," said Lil obstinately. "I'm going down to wait for Billy Boy."

"Go on then," yelled Colleen and flounced back to bed.

Suddenly there was a loud knock. She sat up as she heard female voices in the passage. It was not Billy Boy. Once more she went down.

Becky was in the passage, weeping and very distressed. "It's Sam," she cried, "he's had a bad turn. I need someone to get the doctor for me."

"All right," said Colleen, "I'll go." Putting a coat over her nightie she raced down the road to the doctor's house and returned with him. He went off with Becky to attend to old Sam.

It was daylight by now, and Lil still sat waiting. "I wonder if he knocked and went away again," she muttered. "He might come back later on."

"Blimey, what a night!" said Colleen.

"He might come. Not like Billy Boy to say he's coming and not turn up."

"Oh, my gawd!" declared Colleen, and went back up to bed to catch up on her lost sleep.

At midday she rose and was having a cup of tea in the front room when the paper boy rushed by shouting out the hot news as he always did. "Lord Kitchener dead. Ship hits mine." Colleen looked out of the window at the placard he carried with him. She read: "*Hampshire* Lost." She drew a quick breath. Billy Boy was on the *Hampshire*. She dashed out and bought a paper. With trembling hands she read the headlines: HAMPSHIRE LOST, ALL HANDS. Perhaps he was on leave, she consoled herself. Better not let Lil see it. But Lil was behind her. She had heard the paper boy's cries. She snatched the paper from Colleen. Lil could not read but from those large headlines she knew. "Billy, Billy Boy!" she screamed, and like a mad woman pulled her hair.

"Be quiet, Muvver," begged Colleen. "You don't even know yet, it's not been confirmed. He could be picked up among the survivors."

"I know, I know," wailed Lil. "Wasn't he calling me last night?" She trailed over the road, still weeping, to the comfort of those black-shawled women in the public bar to share with them her grief for her Billy Boy.

Once she had left, Colleen suddenly felt very tired. She sank into the old armchair and stared down at her swollen tummy and around at the disheveled house. She felt that she must either smash something or have a good cry. But a shadow darkened the doorway and a jolly, familiar voice called out: "Arise, Cinderella, you shall go to the ball. I am your fairy godmother." Lew had come back to the alley.

"Oh Lew!" Colleen ran to him, almost bouncing off that mound of flesh. He was still fat but had grown tall and was now a fine figure of a man. He still had that mop of black curly hair, those merry boot-button eyes; he had not altered a lot. Colleen was certainly pleased to see him again. She hung about his neck kissing him. Lew had learned a thing or two up north, and he returned her caresses and they surprised each other as their lips met.

"Now, Lew," said Colleen, breaking away, "behave yourself. Come on, sit down and tell me all the news."

"Not so good," he informed her. "My old father is very sick, that's why I've come back home."

"I am sorry," she said. "It was me who ran down for the doctor last night."

"Yes," he said, eyeing her strangely. "Mother said to thank you."

"What a night!" sighed Colleen. "Now this morning there's this news about Billy Boy. The ole lady's gone all to pieces."

"Was Billy on the *Hampshire?*" She nodded assent. "He might still be picked up," he said, trying to console her. "Come here, Colleen, come and sit on Lew's lap."

She was about to, but suddenly hesitated. "Cheeky beast!" she declared. But he pulled her toward him and held her tight. She lay passive in his arms as he fondled her red curls. Colleen felt very safe and very comfortable.

"Do you remember when we was kids, we used to say we was going to marry each other," said Lew.

"Kids' talk," scoffed Colleen, "life's not so simple as all that."

"Come back up north with me, Colleen," Lew whispered. "I'll get you in our show."

"Exactly what would be my little contribution?" A hardness crept into her voice.

"No strings attached," spluttered Lew.

She pulled away from him. "Well, it seems your luck is out, mate. Someone else had the same idea and now I am four months' gone."

This did not seem to surprise Lew. "I've got eyes, I can see," he answered cheekily.

"Why, you flaming liar!" yelled Colleen. "I don't even show all that much yet."

He looked sheepish. "But I do know. Jews have got their own grapevine. Joe Fox, wasn't it?"

She flew at him, fists waving. "Why, you fat, nasty-minded old devil."

But Lew held her close, quelling her struggles. "Don't lose your temper, Collie, I don't care."

"Well, what the hell do you want of me?" she demanded.

He grinned. "I thought a slice off a cut loaf would not be missed, that's all."

"Why, you beast!" exploded Colleen, but suddenly the humor of the situation made her laugh.

"Come on, love, let's be pals," wheedled Lew.

"All right," she said, giving in gracefully.

She sat on the arm of his chair while he boasted of the part he had in the seaside show.

"I'd like to run my own show," said Lew. "How about joining me, Collie? You've got a magnificent voice, and who knows, we might make the perfect team."

"It's not a bad idea," she agreed, "but what about this kid?"

"Nothing to worry over," said Lew. "You can always get a kid minded if you got the money."

So Colleen began to smile again and Lew cuddled her close.

# Hardly a Honeymoon

THE *BRIGHTON BELLE* WAS VERY POPULAR WITH honeymoon couples. In wartime the wedding had to be quick and the honeymoon short and often just a forty-eight hour pass must suffice. So many Londoners chose Brighton, and there were always confetti-scattered couples on that train. Today they included Pat and her new husband.

Paul Brown seemed to be a little on edge. Earlier, his blue eyes had scanned the platform, and now he stared at the other passengers suspiciously. In the station waiting room on the platform lurked Paul's friend and partner in crime, Sparsie— this name was given to him on account of his much-used expression of always being down to his last farthing. He had watched Paul and his bride go aboard the train. He would wait for the next train. Never know, the cops might be tailing Paul. He had taken a long chance in marrying that young bird.

Pat was quiet during the journey but quite content even though her groom seemed very preoccupied. Once they had arrived in Brighton and were alone in the hotel bedroom she threw her arms passionately about his neck. "You are mine!"

she cried dramatically. "At last you belong to me. I simply can't believe it."

Paul stood mocking, looking down into her face. That angry ugly scar across his cheek stood out and it was very unattractive, but she dismissed it from her mind and snuggled up to him.

"Better get dressed," he said, pushing her away, "we're having a swell dinner tonight. I'll go down and get some cigarettes."

Pat tidied her hair, changed her dress and sat patiently waiting for him. He was a long time coming back and washed hurriedly. They went down into the hotel dining room for that special honeymoon dinner. It was a cheerful convivial atmosphere. Several other newlyweds were there, all enjoying themselves. But Pat's husband did not smile or return the greetings and, while others danced to the orchestra, Pat and Paul walked silently along the front. The sea was rough and the wind blew her nice hairdo to bits, and still Pat did not complain.

Finally he said: "It's getting late. You go in, I won't be long."

So she went to the honeymoon chamber all alone. She put on her dainty nightie—hand embroidered, a present from Mollie—and she lay there sadly waiting for him until sleep shut out her sorrow.

At the first light of dawn he fell drunkenly into bed beside her, fully dressed, and was still snoring when she rose in the morning. She ate breakfast alone, and lunch, making excuses for him all the time. She should have realized he would not like this hotel with all these people. He liked being alone. He would settle down once she got him back to the alley. She had all the rest of the days of her life, so why be so miserable over one weekend?

Paul woke at four and asked her the time.

"We'd better get going," he said. "Don't want to make it too late."

Once more she packed her pretty things and they boarded the train that was to take them back to London. At the ticket barrier he handed her a small suitcase. "You take care of this," he said, "I'll see to your luggage."

She did not remember seeing this small black suitcase when

they had traveled down, but she asked no questions. It was very heavy so she lugged it into the carriage. Paul seemed to dawdle at the barrier for a while, but eventually he settled down beside her and the journey was tedious and uneventful. Within three hours she was turning the latch-key in the door of No. 5. A smell of damp pervaded the hall and an air of gloom swept over the young bride.

"Put the kettle on," ordered Paul, as he knelt to put a match to the fire. "I'm gasping for a cuppa."

The firelight flickered casting shadows about the old-fashioned untidy room. Suddenly Pat wanted to cry, but bit her lip and went out into the filthy kitchen to make the tea. Paul had almost snatched the black suitcase from her grasp as they entered the house and had dashed upstairs with it. She poured tea into thick cups. There was nothing to eat in the cupboard. She would pop over to Colleen. She'll find us something nice for supper, she thought.

After gulping down his tea, Paul had his coat on again. "Won't be long," he said. "I'm going out." The front door closed with a bang and Pat was alone in the dark gloomy house.

She looked about her nervously. She must not be foolish, she had to be brave, she told herself, and opened her suitcase and started to unpack. She supposed she ought to go up and see the bedroom. She had never been up those forlorn musty stairs.

Pat was standing at the bottom of the stairs too nervous to venture up there when a loud knock on the front door made her jump. Her nerves were so frayed that her body gave a convulsive jerk. Looking very scared she opened the door. Two men stood on her doorstep; one face was familiar though. It was Sandy Mac. Relieved, she smiled sweetly at them.

"May we come in?" they asked.

"Of course you can." She pulled the door wide. "We've only just got home."

Sandy looked apologetic. "Is your husband home?" he asked, knowing full well that he was not.

For a moment Pat looked bewildered, then she said sweet-ly: "Paul's gone out for a while. He'll be back soon. Would you like a cup of tea?" she inquired. She stared wonderingly at them. Why did they want to see Paul?

Sandy looked down at the open suitcase with all the frillies sticking out. "Is that your luggage?" he asked.

She giggled. "Oh dear," she said, pushing the undies back inside, "I was just going to unpack."

"Where's Paul's luggage?" Sandy asked abruptly.

"He's taken it upstairs," she replied.

Sandy snapped the suitcase shut. "I'll carry this upstairs for you," he said.

"Thank you," returned Pat.

In a swift moment Sandy Mac was up the stairs. The other young policeman stood looking at Pat in embarrassed silence and she stared very puzzled back at him.

Sandy was back soon. "Sorry to bother you, love," he said, "we've changed our minds, we'll not wait."

Once outside the door, Sandy said: "It's all there, mate. Pop down to the station and get a warrant. I'll nick that swine when he comes back."

After they had gone, Pat left the front door open and ran over the road to her friend Colleen who was hobnobbing with Lew in Lil's parlor. Pat rushed forward to welcome Lew and forgot about the front door and the visit from the police.

Twenty minutes later the sound of quick footsteps came hurrying down the alley. Pat put her hand to her mouth in terror. "It's Paul! I forgot to shut the front door." She ran quickly from Lil's house to her own just opposite but she was a fraction too late. Paul towered over her like an avenging angel, or maybe devil.

"You bloody silly bitch," he snarled. "You went out and left the front door wide open."

Pat stood like an embarrassed schoolgirl looking pathetically up at him.

"Get inside," he said coldly and his hand came out to deal her a slap on the side of the face. Then with his boot he helped her inside the house.

Colleen and Lew, spying from the window, could not believe their own eyes. "Not bad for newlyweds," exclaimed Lew with a smile.

"Lew, the slimy beast hit her!"

Inside No. 5 Pat stood in the hallway, hands over her face, sobbing bitterly as if her heart would break. Paul dashed upstairs then down again in a second. His face was purple. He grabbed his wife viciously by the throat and proceeded to bang her head violently against the wall. "You stupid idiot!" he screamed. "Who's been in here?"

"I was going to tell you," she sobbed. "Two men came."

"And you let them in and showed them around the house, I presume."

"No, it was only Sandy Mac. He took my suitcase upstairs for me," she wept.

"You stupid little fool." Filthy words poured out in a torrent, he hit her with his fists and his knee crashed viciously into her stomach. She broke free, screaming in terror. Running toward the back door she fell over the step, crashed down on the path and lay still as two stalwart figures leaped over the wall.

Soon three men were fighting and struggling in the small back yard. Sandy fought desperately to hold Paul still long enough to clap the cuffs on him but he seemed to have the strength of ten men, and was screaming and foaming at the mouth as he struggled. A whistle blew and soon more police came running and finally Paul, almost insensible, was overpowered.

It was Lew who got to Pat first. He picked her up in his massive arms and carried her over to Lil's. She lay limp and still, her face bruised and blood-stained.

Paul, white, exhausted and sobbing, was eventually handcuffed to Sandy and driven off in the police wagon. He was to be booked not only for murder and assaulting a police officer, but also as an accomplice to the notorious cat burglar, Bertie Harris, alias Sparsie.

Sandy had got the idea at the wedding. He had taken a good look at Paul's diminutive best man, and then returned to the station to consult the rogues' gallery. There he found that Bert was famous for his exploits as a thief, climbing into the most inaccessible places. His method was to rob country houses—usually when a party was in progress. He had been caught and had done time, but none of the loot was ever found because Sparsie had an astute accomplice who always made off with it.

Seeing Sparsie in such a peculiar setting as a church made Sandy's copper's mind tick over. He put a tail on them and it paid off. On this occasion Sparsie had handed the loot to Paul who in turn gave it to Pat to carry home. Sandy had been prepared to wait and now he had no intention of letting him go until he coughed up, possibly to several unsolved murders.

Great care and attention was lavished on Pat; even old Lil forgot her own misery temporarily to aid the poor wounded girl. She was put to bed in Lil's front room and they waited for her to come around and for the doctor to arrive.

Soon Pat sat up and began to cry. "Where's Paul? I want to see him."

"Where he won't do no more bleeding harm," growled Lil.

Colleen cuddled her best friend tight, her tears mingling with Pat's. "Don't think about him, love," she whispered. "Colleen's here with you."

But she lay down again, flushed and restless, holding her hand to her stomach. Lil eyed her with concern, then she turned back the covers and saw the thin trickle of blood.

"Blimey! Colleen, go and hurry up the doctor. She's going to miscarry that baby."

The doctor eventually came. He carefully examined Pat and slowly shook his head. "Don't like the look of things. Must have had a terrible blow to her abdomen. I'll send her up to the hospital."

The ambulance was called and took that stricken child to the hospital. As soon as Pat was admitted an emergency operation was performed. That vicious kick from Paul had injured the unborn child and her young body as well. Lil and Colleen waited in the cold corridor for news. Colleen walked up and down anxiously.

"Sit down for Christ's sake," snappped Lil irritably.

"We ought to let her mother know," said Colleen. "Do you know where they are, Mother?"

"In Ireland," said Lil, "but Gawd knows where. I think I'll go to Mollie's house and see if I can find Bridie's address. I'm fed up standing in this bloody corridor."

Colleen stayed on, and later Lew joined her. They went in to visit Pat who was lying white and still; she had lost her baby. Her dark eyes looked sadly at them. They tried to cheer her up, but all she would say was: "Did Paul come home?"

Together, arm in arm, Lew and Colleen walked back home to the alley.

"I might not go back up north," Lew informed her.

"Why not?" she asked.

"Well, the old man's not so good. That blast affected his lungs. He's got to go into a sanatorium," Lew informed Colleen in a very subdued tone.

"Oh dear," sighed Colleen, "everything's going wrong at once. What will you do?"

"One thing I must do is to keep that darned old tailor business going. It's all they have to live on."

"But you can't give up show biz, Lew," cried Colleen, "you've worked so hard for success."

"Well listen, my love, this is my plan. I was thinking of working the clubs like we did in the beginning. Old stage folk are retiring all the time and most of the young ones are working for the army. It might be easy to get a good spot—of course I'll have to run the shop in the daytime."

"Sounds great to me," replied Colleen. "Only wish I could do the same."

"But you can, Collie," he said eagerly. "There's lots of time. Why, some of the old timers worked right up to their time and dropped the baby backstage."

Colleen started to laugh. "Oh, shut up, Lew," she cried, "you make me feel awful. But it must be a great life," she added with a deep sigh.

"Don't you worry, love," he consoled her, "you and I will be head-liners one day. Momma is going with Pa to Bournemouth, so we can rehearse at our place and get a really good number going."

"Oh, Lew," cried Colleen, "it all sounds lovely. I'm so glad you came home."


When Mollie received the telegram from Colleen she came hurrying home alone. Tim was enjoying the company of his son and that of his grandchildren even more and he had no intention of cutting his holiday short.

It was not long before Mollie was sitting by Pat's hospital bed, still wearing the suit she had traveled in.

"Shall I send for your mother?" asked Mollie.

"No, don't do that," said Pat quietly. "Mother has had enough of me. Let her enjoy her holiday."

Mollie agreed that it was probably the best thing to do and promised to get news of Paul. That was not difficult. In the morning the appearance of Paul Brown and his accomplice

Bertie Harris in court was reported in the local paper. They had been remanded in custody pending further inquiries.

"Well, at least he's out of the way for a while," commented Mollie without much feeling.

Lil and Colleen, who were in for a cuppa, both looked amazed. "I thought you liked him," declared Colleen.

Mollie's small mouth twitched slightly at the corners. "Colleen," she said, "what I do for those I love I do because I think it's what they want, but whether I like him or her is a very different matter."

Lil and Colleen looked at each other. It was quite clear that they did not understand; black was black and white was white as far as they were concerned. It was right or it was wrong, there were no gray patches.

Mollie sat down to write that dutiful letter to Maud telling her Paul had been arrested and that Pat had lost her baby but was making a good recovery.

Three days later Maud received the letter. She hurried home to the alley with the light of battle once more in her eyes. Colleen was there when she visited Pat in the hospital. Pat was now sitting up. She was white-faced and sulky, and her hair fell all over the place. Tears came into her eyes when she saw her mother but they did not fall.

"Hallo, Patricia," said Maud brightly. She sat down beside the bed, produced a brush and a scarlet ribbon and slowly and carefully brushed those long tangled locks and tied them back with the ribbon. Pat leaned back and closed her eyes; for the first time in a long while there was peace in that harassed young face. Colleen dashed out into the corridor, put her head against the cold marble wall and began to weep. Lew came to find her.

"Come on, Collie, let's go home. I booked a spot for us tonight and we ought to rehearse."

"Lew, how wonderful!" Colleen wiped her eyes as he put a gentle arm about her, and they went home to the alley together.

Soon the air rang with the beat of the old piano, the tap of dancing feet and voices blended in song. On her seat on the windowsill Lil sat gloomily waiting for the pub to open. "You'll drop that lot, you silly cow, if you keep jumping up and down like that," she yelled coarsely over at Colleen.

But her daughter never listened; she danced with carefree abandon.

Mollie, briskly cleaning her little house, also heard them and wondered how the little one would fare if Lew and Colleen decided to get together.

And in the hospital Maud sat contentedly beside Patricia as she slept with the scarlet bows on her dark hair.

A month later, a happy and rejuvenated Maud was discussing her plans with Mollie. Pat was now convalescent and Paul still languished in Wandsworth Prison, awaiting trial.

"It was my intention to sell up and leave the alley," Maud confided in Mollie. "But at the moment I can't decide. I wanted to get Pat away from here just in case he only got a light sentence. But somehow I don't think he will. . . ." Her voice trailed off. In her mind was the evidence still to come—that blood-stained bible.

Mollie listened placidly. "Are you sure you'll be able to keep them apart?" she queried.

"By God I will," cried Maud, "even if I die in the attempt."

Mollie bent over her knitting but made no further comment.

"If it wasn't for those damned German submarines I'd send her to the States," declared Maud. "I've a sister-in-law who'd take good care of her."

"There's a rumor that America will come into the war," remarked Mollie.

"Then it will go on for another year at least," said Maud, "and I'm not sure that I'd get the true value of the property with a war on. Honestly, Mollie, I'm at my wit's end. I'm not very sure of anything any more."

Mollie's thick lashes obscured her eyes as she counted the stitches. She never wanted Maud to leave the alley and certainly not Patricia. They were all so close; this was her family. But now Maud was talking of selling the alley. She had every right of course. Maud's voice broke in on her thoughts.

"What the devil's up with old Tim? How long does he intend to stay up at Bridie's? Timmo must be back in France by now."

Mollie looked unconcerned and said placidly: "I expect it's the children holding him up there."

"Can't expect Dandy to keep his job open forever," grumbled Maud. "Business costs money to run and there ain't a lot left in the kitty now."

Maud was certainly back in form, decided Mollie. "As a matter of fact, according to his letter, he should have returned yesterday."

"Got on the booze, I expect," sniffed Maud.

Mollie looked unhappy. It had not taken her mother-in-law long to get back her old tactless domineering ways.

"I hope you'll consult me before you sell my house," she said gently.

Maud looked surprised. "Why, Mollie, I naturally thought that you and Tim would come with me if I took a large house just outside London."

Mollie shook her head. "I shan't leave this house," she said. "My mother is still with me while I live here."

"Oh dear," sighed Maud, "let's not get into that argument again, Mollie."

Mollie's small mouth was set in a stubborn line. "All I ask, Maud, is that you give me the opportunity to buy my own house. I won't have strangers living here."

"Be sensible, Mollie," pleaded Maud. "Surely at your age you'll not chain yourself to a pile of bricks and mortar."

"I've informed you of my reason," said Mollie coldly. "Just promise you'll do as I ask. I have money, just name your price."

Maud was offended at Mollie's cold tone. She drew herself up to her full height. "I'm sorry, Mollie. I'm too fond of you to allow you to become a dried-up old spinster. You've got to get out in the world and find yourself another husband. You can't stay here all the rest of your life in this moldy backwater, shouldering other folk's troubles."

Mollie put down her knitting and stared straight at her mother-in-law. "Larry was your son, how can you say such a thing?" Her face was pale and distraught. Larry was dead, but for Mollie he would always live in her memories, bound up in some way with her own lovely mother Mary.

"Oh, Mollie, Mollie, don't let's quarrel, dear," begged Maud.

"I've no wish to quarrel with you, Maud," replied Mollie, "but I'll tell you now, once and for always, I'll live my life how I please."

Maud sighed and retired defeated. "As you wish, Mollie, and if you want to buy this house from me, it's the price I paid for it."

She began to walk out, but she stopped in the passage and started to laugh very loudly. Mollie came out to see what was so amusing. There, on the doorstep, stood Tim, arrayed in khaki and grinning broadly. He held his hand to his forehead in a mocking salute.

For a while pandemonium reigned. Maud, still laughing, demanded the reason for his get-up. Lil came waddling in—she was not going to be left out of anything. And Mollie stood silent; she could not believe that her own father, almost forty-three, had joined the army.

"Took ten years off my age, I did," boasted Tim, "and they believed it." He seemed much younger in every way. "I'm in a non-combatant unit; the Pioneer Corps it's called. We're being trained to build bridges and repair the roads and get in and clear up after the air raids."

"Well, they must certainly be getting short of recruits," said Maud drily. "I wonder what old Dandy will think of it."

Tim twisted the ends of his moustache that was now waxed in an appropriately military fashion. He took off his hat, and polished his cap badge with his handkerchief.

Mollie watched him silently. She had not seen him so happy for a long time; he had been dull company since he lost his wife.

"I'm going over the road for a beer," he informed them. "Not got a lot of drinking time; have to report to base tomorrow." Lil waddled off behind him knowing that there would be plenty of free drinks in the Railway Arms that night.

Maud folded her arms and surveyed Mollie. "Well, my lady, what are you going to do now?" she asked.

"Nothing has changed," said Mollie decisively. "I'll still go my own way."

Maud shrugged and stomped out.

There was a big send off for Tim the next day. He was very drunk, as was Dandy who was almost in a stupor, so full was he of porter.

To Mollie, Tim had been apologetic. "Sorry, my love, I had to do it, seeing all them Irish lads up there in the guards' barracks. You take care of yourself now, my love, and get back up to the hospital to your work. Don't hang about in this dismal old alley."

Mollie only stared scornfully at him and did not reply.

Once Tim had departed for France, the alley went on as before. Mollie would sit knitting, while in the back yard Lew and Colleen rehearsed most afternoons. They had begun to get regular bookings at the smaller music halls—the Royal, the Collins and the London—and also at some of the working men's clubs. They were really beginning to find their feet.

The war had hit the profession very hard but the old established music halls had managed to keep going, in spite of the lack of talent, and they brought a little brightness to people's lives.

The old music hall troupers welcomed Lew and his lovely singing partner to their number and did all they could to encourage them and get them bookings.

Colleen had begun to get fat, but she was still full of vitality and more prettily flamboyant and more appetizing than ever. On stage, dressed in a full skirt and carrying a basket of roses and a parasol, she would sing, in harmony with Lew, "If you were the only girl in the world and I were the only boy." They sang just as if they really meant it and when they had finished the audience stood and cheered—men on leave from the mud and blood of Flanders out with the loved ones for that one precious night. Lew did a solo act; one moment a tough sergeant, the next a namby-pamby officer. His jokes were coarse, but the audience loved it that way.

As stage partners Lew and Colleen became very close. It was a platonic relationship, though both of them knew that if it were not for her predicament things would be very different.

"You know, Lew," she said one night, "I'm beginning to hate this kid inside me."

They were in a gloomy dressing-room, getting ready for the night's show. Lew was trying in vain to hook her dress up at the back—she had put on so much weight that it would not meet. Eventually a large safety pin secured it.

"It won't show," Lew assured her. "Put that little shawl on, it'll cover it up."

"Oh, I'm fed up," moaned Colleen. "Why did it have to happen to me?" Her lovely red mouth puckered up as she clamped her elbows down hard on to the dressing table.

Lew looked very anxious. "Oh, Collie," he begged, "don't give in, you promised you wouldn't let it worry you."

"Don't be a chump, Lew," she said, "how can I forget it? Look at the size of me!"

Lew looked concerned; his mind was on the future bookings. But he cuddled her and said: "Don't fret, my dickybird, just go out there and sing your heart out."

# The Arrival of George

AT THE END OF THE MONTH, MAUD BROUGHT A sad-looking, painfully thin daughter back to her home in the alley. The doctors had warned her to be very careful. They had told Maud that Pat was still emotionally distressed, and that Maud should not push her. Maud took Patricia under her maternal wing, treating her like a piece of precious fragile china, but Pat's dark eyes only stared at her with hostility again. She had not one word of gratitude or even a welcome smile for her mother.

There had been an awkward moment as the cab slowed down and Maud and Dandy helped her out. Pat had stood perfectly still staring over the road toward No. 5. The dark red curtains were drawn, it was as silent as the grave.

Her hesitation was only momentary for her father gently took her arm and escorted her into Maud's house. Lew and Colleen were there to welcome her and in the kitchen Mollie was making the little jam tarts that Pat was so fond of. Colleen, as loving and boisterous as ever, dashed forward to kiss her. Pat's eyes strayed to the lump on her friend's tummy.

"Oh, don't look at me," burst out Colleen, "I look a sight."

She covered her large stomach with her hands.

But in a soft gentle voice Pat said: "I think you look lovely, Colleen." There was a slight embarrassed silence broken by Lew who took off his jacket and laid it on the floor.

"Step this way, your majesty," he cried.

Then they all began to laugh and chatter. Pat was back home with her playmates in the alley. Everyone was careful not to discuss Paul's forthcoming trial and newspapers were kept out of sight.

Pat graciously accepted the undivided attention her mother gave her and the new dresses that she bestowed on her, but she continued to regard her mother with that brooding hostility.

One day Maud went weeping into Mollie. "I can't stand it much longer," she cried. "I want to shake her and say, 'I'm your mother, the one that bore you, your own flesh and blood.' This coldness is breaking my heart."

"Try to be brave, Maud," urged Mollie, "she still has a lot to face. You must be patient with her. Things will be better when the trial is over."

"Oh, why don't they get it over and done with?" cried Maud. "It'll be better for all concerned if they finished him."

Mollie was shocked. "Surely, Maud, you don't mean they should hang him?"

"I bloody well do," stormed Maud. "Do you think I want him to do a couple of years inside then come out and destroy her life again?"

Mollie was trying hard to conceal her feelings. "Well, I hope they find him insane, as I feel sure he is," she said calmly. "I'm against capital punishment, we all pay for our sins once we leave this world. Only God is our judge."

"Oh, Mollie, you really exasperate me," cried Maud and dashed out of the door.

Pat and Colleen were happy to be together once more and made light of their problems. They went to the cinema or wandered down the market, then spent the evenings rehearsing the weekend show with Lew. Pat was a very appreciative audience. The color came back into her cheeks—though most of it was rouge provided by Colleen who loved to paint her face and dress up.

"What will you do when the baby comes?" asked Pat one day as they sat re-styling their long hair.

"Honest to God, I don't know. I hate even to think about it. Now that I can't get into my dresses, it's really getting on my nerves. And sometimes it kicks me so hard it nearly knocks me over. One of these days I'll hit the deck out there on stage, with one of those rowdy audiences looking on."

"But don't you feel for it?" queried Pat. "Love, I mean. It's really part of you."

"Give over, Patsy Pat," declared Colleen, "don't you start. Why, it's this bloody kid that's holding me and Lew up. We could have gone up north for the panto season, but how could I go looking like this?" She stared down with a rueful expression at her large tummy.

Pat sighed. "If I had kept my baby I'd have loved it," she said; her voice was remote and dreamy.

"Oh, don't, Patsy Pat," cried Colleen, "don't have regrets, darling." They held on to each other very tightly.

"After the baby's born, let me come with you and Lew," pleaded Pat.

Colleen's round blue eyes stared straight at her, then she said: "It's a good idea. I'll see what Lew has to say about it."

Lew was as easy going as always. "Why not?" he said. "Feel up to it, Pat?"

A lovely smile appeared on Pat's face. "Oh thanks, Lew!" she cried. "You're a pair of darlings."

All the next week was spent discussing new numbers. Time flew by on golden wings. Lew put his arms about the girls and said to Maud: "What do you think of my two dancing dollies?"

Maud smiled gratefully back at him; she knew Pat was on the mend once more.

At the Old Britannia that Saturday night Pat danced in and out of Lew's comedy act, wearing long black tights and a short frilly dress which drew many a wolf whistle from the gallery. Lew's near-to-the-bone humor brought roars of laughter, while Colleen sat like a beautiful picture in a beautiful golden frame, and the audience wept tears of pleasure as she sang.

The little show continued right through till October. Then one Saturday night Colleen said to Lew: "I've got a flaming backache. You better go on with Pat tonight." She went to see Mollie.

"You won't be long, dear," Mollie said, her gentle hand

feeling Colleen's tummy. "Are you still sure you want me to attend you?"

"Oh, Mollie," cried Colleen tearfully, "you won't make me go to that Yiddisher maternity home, will you? I don't want anything from old Annie Fox. All I want to do is get it over and go up north with Lew."

"All right, darling," said Mollie, "I'll send down the road and let old Doc Sullivan know. He probably won't be needed, I can take care of you myself, but it's better to be safe than sorry. Here you are—a little job to pass the time away." She handed her the little woolly vest she had just finished knitting. "It's ready to have the ribbon put through the neck."

Colleen folded the garment on her lap, confident and content once more. Mollie went upstairs and put on her white apron. She pushed her dark hair under a snow white cap and then went into the little spare room where there was a clean white bed, a tiny cot, jugs and bowls—all in readiness for this moment. Mollie had made complete preparations for the new baby.

Later that day old Doctor Sullivan called. "No worries there, lass," he said, "she's a fine healthy specimen. Call me if you need me."

At midnight the baby was born. Colleen had ceased yelling and Maud held her hands as the little head pushed its way into the world. With expert hands Mollie held him upside down and with a gentle pat on the bottom there came the first tiny cry which got louder and louder and ended with a great healthy yell. Colleen had given birth to a lovely bonny boy. Flushed with excitement, Maud held the little new-born, wrapped in a blanket, while Mollie attended to the exhausted mother. Lil was in her element and bustled about getting the bath ready—friends and neighbors all united in this hour of need. They stood watching Mollie expertly wash those fine sturdy limbs and saw the curly head emerge from the water.

"Why!" declared Lil. "He's got hair just like my George."

Mollie put a woolly vest and a flannelette nightie on the baby and handed him to Colleen. She held out her arms. "Oh, ain't he loverly," she cried.

Their eyes wet with emotion, the rest of the alley folk agreed.

"You know," said Colleen examining him very closely. "He does look like our George; that's what I'll call him."

"Well, it's a right royal name," remarked Maud.

So baby George became prince of the alley. He had so many aunties to love and fuss him, and a proud grandmother always handy and a mum who loved every hair on his blond little head. After Colleen's attitude to her pregnancy, most of them were very surprised at her delight and solicitude for her baby son. Lil celebrated over at the pub and boasted of his size and beauty. Maud went up the market to buy him the latest thing in perambulators, and Mollie loved him, washed and bottle-fed him as diligently as if he were her very own.

When George was three weeks old, he had a visitor; a short dark middle-aged lady, clad in a fur coat with diamonds in her ears. From the doorway she shrewdly surveyed Mollie who held the child in her arms, while Lil hovered open-mouthed in the background. Then she looked at Colleen who stared insolently back at her.

"I'm Annie Fox. Isn't anyone going to ask me in?"

Realizing how ill-mannered they all seemed, Mollie apologized profusely, and invited Annie Fox into her little parlor.

"No need to look at me like that, gel," she informed Colleen. "I ain't come to see you, just to take a look at Joe's boy." She took the baby on her knee and studied his funny little face. His eyes were such a dark blue, they could do little else but turn brown as he grew, and his nose was rather prominent, though flat and squashy as babies' noses are before they begin to develop. "He's Joe's," she decided. "Looks like him when he was born. Going to bring him up Jewish?" she asked.

It was as if a bomb had dropped.

Lil dashed forward. "Hi!" she shouted. "He ain't no Yidderboy. Just like my George, he is."

"Please yourself," said Annie, "but I keep my promise, I'll see to him."

Colleen snatched her child from the old lady's lap. "He's mine," she cried, "and he don't want no charity. And you can tell that swine Joe Fox I said so."

"Please yourself," said Annie once more. She got up to leave. "Keep in touch," she said to Mollie, "he might need me yet." Then, kissing the babe on the top of his head, she said goodbye and left.

"She's got a cheek coming down here," declared Colleen.

"Bloody sauce, that's what I call it," announced Lil.

Only Mollie was silent. She knew little George would need someone as soon as the novelty had worn off.

"That old lady is rolling in dough. You'd be wise not to offend her," advised Maud.

"I've got my baby. I don't need her," retorted Colleen.

Standing quietly to one side, taking it all in, was Patricia. So far she had not fussed the baby. In fact, she tried to avoid it and when Colleen showed the baby off she felt sick with jealousy. She would be glad when the panto season started in a few weeks. Lew had already promised to take her up to Leeds. Once she left this alley, she would never return; she had had her fill of it all, she would get free of it—break out into the world on her own.

When Colleen got to hear of the proposed move up north for the pantomime season, she had her own ideas. Lew was not going without her, that was definite.

"But what about the baby?" asked Pat quietly.

For a moment Colleen looked distressed. Then she said: "Mollie will mind him. I'm coming with you and that's that."

So with much kissing and weeping she handed her son to Mollie. Then the three bright stars left the alley in November to tour the misty north in *Mother Goose*.

Christmas time came around again very quickly and, since there were not many of them left, Maud suggested they all muck in for the festive season. So Mollie and Lil spent Christmas with Maud and Dandy and little George. They played cards and talked about the Christmases of the past when the alley was full and happy. The cold waters of the Cut drifted by.

The New Year brought another year of war, but the tide had turned; London was full of Australians, telling the Cockneys how they had come from down under to win the war for them. Now that we had fighter planes and tanks the news went around that at last we really had Jerry on the run. In the distance the faint flicker of the dawn of peace began to brighten the lives of the war weary.

A smart little woman left her office in the city and wended her way home to her cozy flat in the Grays Inn Road. She had bought a newspaper on her way and it was neatly folded under her arm as she tripped along. Slim and dainty in a long skirt and a blouse with a sailor's collar, she wore her hair drawn neatly back in a bun under a brimmed felt hat, and a pair of specs on the end of a small nose. She was miles away, creating as she walked the next episode of the novel she was writing. It was Ellen Brown from Autumn Alley. Time had matured her. She had never been a good-looking young maid but now she had become a very comely young woman, and there was a certain air of self-possession about her.

Entering her house by the side door she climbed up to the fifth floor. There she paused, hesitating, for sitting at the bottom of that last flight was a man, evidently waiting for someone.

Cautiously she tried to edge past him, but he rose and took off his hat.

"Have I the pleasure of addressing Miss Brown?"

She did not reply but stood silently weighing up the situation. Experience, however, had taught Sandy Mac that he had at last found that elusive Ellen Brown whom he had searched so diligently for.

"Don't be alarmed," he said and produced his identity card.

"Police?" she stuttered. "What's wrong?"

"Nothing is wrong," he assured her. "I'm here on behalf of your brother, Paul."

She paled slightly, then she put the key in the door of her flat. "You had better come in," she said.

Sandy was rather surprised now he had met her—having heard such strange stories from the residents of Autumn Alley. He followed her into the flat. It was neat and tidy, and full of pot plants and books.

"Please sit down," she said. "I've just come home from the office. I'll make some tea if you don't mind."

Sandy lolled in a comfortable chair and looked around the room. It was tastefully furnished, there seemed to be no lack of funds here.

She returned with the tea tray, poured him a cup and as she handed it to him he caught a glimpse of those clear hazel eyes behind the thick specs. "What did you say your name was?" she inquired.

"I'm Detective Sergeant Macdonald—known to the East End as Sandy Mac." He gave her his broad charming smile.

That usually did the trick, but she did not smile in response. She just removed her large specs and rubbed her eyes as if they ached.

"You are the sister of Paul Brown, I presume?"

"What is it you want of me?" she said pathetically. "I thought I'd left that part of my life behind."

"Have you read tonight's paper?" he asked her.

She shook her head.

"Well, everything has gone against him. More than likely he will hang."

"What do you care?" For the first time she showed a flash of spirit. "It was you who arrested him, wasn't it?"

"It was my job to do so, Miss Brown," he answered apologetically. "I followed your brother's career for a number of years and even you must admit that he is an habitual criminal. But nevertheless I don't particularly want to see him hang."

"He's more to be pitied than blamed," she whispered and sank into a chair regarding Sandy with those strange eyes, fear and suspicion intermixed.

"It's not easy to hound a man to his death, even if he is guilty," said Sandy. "That's why I've called on you."

"Living in this world is punishment enough," said Ellen. She began to talk about her home life in the alley, that unbearable household, and the life she as a little girl had led with a fanatical father, her cruel brothers and a weak, ailing mother. Sandy listened, his face soft and mellow, his eyes full of sympathy.

"And now," she said, "I'm free. I live only to learn. I've no faith unless it's in my writing."

Sandy sat silent as she finished speaking.

"Well," she said, abruptly, "have you got what you came for?"

Sandy fidgeted, got up and took his hat from the chair. "I'm sorry if I've distressed you, Miss Brown, dragging up old memories. But if you would tell that story in court it may save your brother's life."

She looked dismayed. "No, no! I couldn't, not in public."

"There isn't one soul in all the world to defend him, that's why I wanted to help him. I've visited the other twin . . . he's in Broadmoor. Did you know?"

Ellen lowered her eyes. "Paul would be better off dead than locked in an asylum for the rest of his life."

"Couldn't you at least visit him, acknowledge him," pleaded Sandy.

"Sit down again," she said. "It's not entirely my decision. I have another to consider. In a moment you'll understand— that's Emm coming up the stairs now."

The door of the room burst open. It was as if a whirlwind rushed in. There stood a tall figure in uniform, long skirt and heavy boots. Her short hair was brushed straight back from her face. In a loud hearty voice she shouted: "Hellooo, Nell." She grabbed Ellen and swept her off her feet, twisting her around and around. "I did it, Nell," she cried, "I'm going over at last!"

Sandy Mac sat staring incredulously at the way this newcomer kissed her companion, and the possessive way she held her. Surely it was a masquerade, a man dressed as a woman. Ellen calmed Emm down, indicating that they were not alone, and Emm turned to look at Sandy, her arms akimbo, staring down at him, suspicion written all over her rugged face.

Ellen introduced them. "This is my friend Emm, and this is Sergeant Macdonald."

Emm poured herself a cup of tea. "What's he want with us?" she inquired, not overfriendly.

"Oh, sit down, Emm, and do listen," said Ellen impatiently. "It's about my brother, Paul."

Emm seemed to panic. "Nell!" she cried, "you can't afford to get mixed up in that affair, you've left all that behind."

"But, Emm, he's my own flesh and blood," protested Ellen gently.

Emm dashed toward her. "My God, Nell, those bloody papers will crucify you. For God's sake, one word of our life together and they'll sling all the muck and filth they can find at you. No, Nell, I beg of you, don't be such a fool."

To Sandy the situation had become very clear. He stood nonplussed, wondering what to say. Oblivious of him, they were arguing in earnest, heads together. Ellen was trying to console Emm.

"Don't worry, I'll not do anything indiscreet," Ellen said.

"But they'll hound you, those damned newspaper blokes, and I won't be here to protect you," Emm protested.

"All right, if it upsets you so, I'll not get involved," said Ellen finally.

She came over to escort Sandy to the door. Her neat shape preceded him down the stairs. In the square hall with its well-scrubbed linoleum, she looked anxiously up at him.

"Now perhaps you do understand, Mr. Macdonald, it's not entirely up to me."

Sandy looked bewildered.

"Emm and I are very happy together. I don't expect you to understand, and least of all approve, but even if I could save Paul I would not do it at the risk of hurting Emm. Now it's up to you. Betray me if you wish." There was a note of defiance in her voice. Then she relaxed a little. "I think you have some insight into the history of my family—none of us are quite the ticket. Goodnight, Sergeant." She closed the door almost in his face.

The trial of Paul Brown had been in progress for three weeks and was now drawing to a close. The news boys ran about screeching out the latest stop-press news. In London even the war news took second place to this sensational case of the Brown twins who had robbed and murdered all their adult lives. Now one of them stood alone in the dock while the defense pleaded for his life. Insanity had not been proved. The prosecution insisted that each case had been premeditated: the little servant girl who caught them breaking in, only to be murdered; the prostitute who had survived the beating and who had insisted that her attackers looked so alike. And there was yet another unsolved murder of more than sixteen years ago that could possibly have been committed by those twins.

Maud had not missed a moment of the trial. Each day she sat in court taking it all in. She was often accompanied, not by Dandy (who had refused to get involved), but by her old friend Mr. Potts, who was now town and planning surveyor for the local council.

The accused seemed to care very little about what went on around him. In fact, in the last few days he had been strangely withdrawn. Counsel and doctors argued that he was not really fit to stand trial, but there were others who disagreed. And now it was up to the jury to decide. The jury returned to give their verdict. The judge placed the fatal black cap on top of his wig. There was an ominous silence while the judge pronounced sentence, and then a stampede of newsmen from the court, all anxious to get the story to their editors before the evening's deadline.

Maud dashed jubilantly home to the alley, passing the church where Mollie knelt reverently in prayer for Paul's soul. Sandy went up to Kate's flat and got blind drunk. All alone in her flat, now that Emm was in France, Ellen put her head down on the desk and her tears washed over the newspaper headlines: PAUL BROWN TO HANG.

Far away in a little seaside town in the north of England, two young, good-looking women were having a cup of tea in a tea shop. The sky outside was gray and overcast and they looked out of the steamy windows onto the deserted sea front. Deck chairs were piled high under canvas covers, and there were only a few hungry gulls to disturb the silence of the sands. Pat and Colleen were resting after twelve weeks in pantomime with Lew, having all three in turn been Mother Goose and the back legs of a panto horse. Now Lew had received his call-up papers and gone to register for the army and his two dancing dollies sat having a cuppa wondering what was going to happen to them if Lew got called up.

"We'll get by all right without him," said Colleen. "Don't suppose they'll even have a uniform to fit him."

Her companion smiled. Her pale face was enhanced by the purple velvet turban she wore, and the large gold loops in her ears. Pat had become rather a natty dresser, but still those dark-ringed sad eyes looked out with moody weariness onto the world.

"What shall we do, Colleen?" she asked. "We could join the chorus line."

"Don't fancy that," replied Colleen. "We could go home to the alley and try the London night spots," she suggested eagerly.

Pat dismissed it. "No, we're not good enough without Lew."

"Speak for yourself, Patsy Pat," retorted Colleen rudely. "I'm every bit as good as Lew and he can't sing as well as I do."

Pat sighed. She was not going to be drawn into an argument. She had witnessed too many battles between Lew and Colleen. "You can go home to the alley, Colleen," she told her. "I'll stay up north. I'm never going back to that Autumn Alley."

For once Colleen was silent. She was not sure if she wanted to persuade her. Suddenly her eyes caught a glimpse of a headline in the newspaper that someone had left on a chair beside her. She read: PAUL BROWN TO HANG. A frightened gasp left her lips. Quickly she pushed the newspaper under her bottom, plonking down on it quickly, her face pink with exertion as she gazed at Pat to see if she had noticed it.

Pat stared gloomily out of the window. "Dreary hole, up here in winter," she remarked.

But the owner of the newspaper had returned. Looking puzzled, he said, "Excuse me, madam, but you're sitting on my paper." Colleen sipped her tea and ignored him.

"Wake up, Colleen," Pat said, "you're sitting on his paper."

Colleen shifted reluctantly, hoping he would take his paper and leave, but he sat down and opened the paper wide— looking for the racing page, no doubt. There before Pat's eyes swam those fatal headlines. She snatched the paper from him and began to read. A heartbroken wail came from her. Then she dashed out of the tea shop.

Colleen gave the astounded newspaper owner a violent shove and raced after Pat. She caught her by the shelter, and they stood in a tight embrace. The cold north wind from the sea blew around them as Colleen tried hard to comfort her friend as she sobbed heartbroken with shock and grief until Colleen hailed a taxi to take them to their lodgings.

For the next two hours Colleen plied her with everything she could think of: hot tea, whiskey, but Pat was still distraught even when Lew returned.

That evening Lew had come home feeling very pleased with himself. A smile lit those pleasant fat features, he was actually going to swap that daring check suit with smoke pearl buttons for a suit of khaki. Now it had happened he did not mind; he was rather looking forward to this new adventure. He confessed he had tried to dodge conscription, and had pretended to have all the diseases you could mention. But the army medical board had declared him perfectly fit. "Too fat," said the doctor. "Much too fat. But then they'll soon whittle some of that off you." He had pleaded he must stay to care

for his ailing parents, but had cheered up when the army
recruiting sergeant said: "Don't know what you're beefing
about. You stage blokes always get a cushy number. Report
back in seven days. By then we'll have a uniform to fit you."

So Lew had gone back to his dancing dollies feeling quite
cheerful. He marched in singing "We are in the army now,"
then striking a Shakespearian pose, he roared: "Hail the
conquering hero comes . . ." But no one took the slightest
notice of him. Colleen's eyes were red with weeping and Pat
lay on the bed as still as a statue, staring up at the ceiling.
There was an air of despondency quite uncommon in this
happy little flat they all shared.

Colleen sniffed a bit and wiped her nose. Then she
beckoned him outside the door. He followed her onto the
small landing that served as a kitchen—just a minute yard of
lino, a gas cooker and a shelf for the crocks.

"What's up, Collie?" he asked in bewilderment.

"Have you read the evening paper?"

"No, not yet. Why?"

"Listen, idiot, and I'll tell you what's wrong," said Colleen.

Lew stood anxiously awaiting the bad news.

"They're going to hang him," she whispered.

"Hang who?" he asked, still very bewildered.

She pointed frantically to the door. "Hush, don't let her
hear you. Her Paul, they're going to hang him."

"Best thing they can do with him," replied Lew callously.

"Why, you nasty beast." Colleen flew into a temper and
they argued in whispers, Lew's fat tummy jammed into that
small space while Colleen had her say. It was always this
way—they never agreed for long but Lew's good nature
always came uppermost in the end. He always gave in first.

"Sorry, Collie," he said. "Give us a kiss, I'm off to be a
soldier next week."

This was the last straw. Colleen burst into a loud howl and
threw her arms about his neck.

"Hi! Stop it!" cried Lew. He was leaning against the rickety
bannister. "This bloody thing'll break and my bloody neck
with it!"

Colleen released him, smiled a little and rested her auburn
head on his wide shoulder. "Oh Lew," she sighed, "what
would I do without you?"

The next day they said goodbye to Lew who was off to

London to see his parents before he entered the army. The two young girls, his constant companions for the last three months, stood looking forlorn as he purchased his ticket. It was damp, wet and gloomy in the station. Stray papers blew about the platform; a woman and child said a tearful farewell to a sailor dad.

Colleen pulled the collar of her fur coat up to her chin and wished she was getting on the train with Lew. She thought of Mollie, warm and welcome, and of soft tiny baby hands on her face. A lump came into her throat. She must not let Pat see her crying.

Pat was cold and very calm. Not a hair was out of place. A passerby might have thought: what an attractive girl, what a lovely face. But in a close-up it was like one of those bad photographs—stark and strong, cold dark eyes and a white face. She held Colleen's arm very tightly. Every now and then her fingers gave a convulsive twitch as if she cried inwardly. "I feel awful, Colleen. I know you want to go home and you're only staying here because of me."

"Don't be such a doughnut," replied Colleen. "I'm going to have a good time once we get rid of old fat podge."

Pat dropped her gaze not wanting her friend to see how relieved she was. She knew she could not get by without Colleen.

At the final parting Lew kissed Colleen and they clung to each other.

"Be a good girl, Collie, and wait for me. The war won't last for ever."

Two big tears that had been welling up for so long rolled down her rouged cheeks. "Give our love to Autumn Alley. Kiss Georgie for me," Colleen said sadly.

The train got up steam and Lew leaned out of the window, holding on to her hand.

"Come back safe, Lew," yelled Colleen. Picking up her long skirts she ran down the platform with the train, her legs moving with perfect grace.

Pat stood silent and watched from the other end of the platform. A small crowd of servicemen who had previously alighted from the down train, stood and stared with interest at the slim silk-clad legs of Colleen as she raced after the train, her little hat to one side, her auburn hair blowing in the wind.

Pat came toward her. "Come on, Collie, those soldiers are having a good laugh at you."

"Let 'em, sod 'em," wailed Colleen. "I want to go home with Lew."

Firmly Pat took her arm. Lew had gone, her worries were over. Colleen would not leave her now.

# Home Was Our Alley

THESE DAYS BECKY WAS NOT HERSELF. HER HAIR had gone iron gray and her face was careworn and lined with sadness. Sam's accident and long illness had really aged her. All her married life he had sheltered her, put up with her whims and her bad temper, and taken all in a kind calm way. Other Jews, the ones they had been brought up with, seemed to have made a pile of money out of the war, but Sam had just struggled on with his little business and his only reward had been to be blown up into the air and have his lungs destroyed. Tenderly Becky cared for him, wheeled him around the park in a big bathchair, but it had all begun to tell on her. The fire in her had sunk very low. Sadly she lived through each day knowing only too well that her Sam would never again be the man he once was.

This particular bright morning there was a breath of spring air once more and Georgie was out in his pram. He sat up now, and his hair was a mass of golden curls. He cooed and gurgled at all who passed by.

Becky paused beside his pram and poked a work-scarred finger at him with loving affection. " 'Ow is you this morning, my little one?" George dribbled with exuberant joy. "Just like my Lew at his age," she said proudly.

Lil sat sphinx-like, but ever-watchful in her usual place on the windowsill.

"Don't see how 'e can be," she argued. "Was always so fat, your Lew. That George ain't; he's all muscle, is that boy, be a six-footer when 'e grows up, 'e will."

Becky had learned through the passage of time not to argue with Lil. No longer enemies, they fussed and chattered to George, who sat up and demanded undivided attention.

Mollie came bustling out of her house. She was neat and trim in her nurse's uniform, having gone back part-time to the local hospital. Her intention was to work for a sister's cap.

"Now, keep good watch on him, Lil," she warned. "Make sure that the pram straps are secure and give him his bottle on time, it's all ready. At lunch let him nibble a rusk." She fussed over the pram, straightening out the covers. "I'll be home at four. Go into Maud's if anything worries you." Then, with a smacking kiss on top of baby's fair brow, Auntie Mollie went off to work.

"Anyone would fink I never brought up five kids," Lil complained to Becky. "Makes me bleeding sick, she does— 'Wash yer 'ands!' 'Don't do that!'"

"I'll give eye to him if you want to go for a drink midday," offered Becky.

"Shush!" said Lil. "Don't let 'er 'ear yer." She jerked a thumb in the direction of Maud's abode. "I might take him over wiv me," she pondered. "He likes it over there, and yer gets the sun on that side in the mornin's."

"I'll mind him," said Becky eagerly. "Sam loves him."

"I'll bring him over if it rains," said Lil, "but wait till she's gorn aht."

She was referring to Maud who had once found George parked outside the pub and wheeled him away. Lil had appeared after finishing her glass of beer to find her beloved grandson gone and all hell had been let loose.

"Bleedin' cheek! Said I neglected him, she did. Don't hurt him, a little drop o' Guinness. Just to dunk his biscuit in, that's all, and she goes and tells that Madam Mollie."

Becky nodded in sympathy. She did not drink and could not understand Lil's need for the Railway Arms, but she

loved giving an eye to George whom she fed with scraps of
cake, and it cheered Sam up immensely to see this happy
baby boy.

From the house next door emerged Maud, all dressed up in
black as usual: jet beads, jet earrings and a large hat with a
white pom-pom.

"Gawd," said Lil in a loud voice, " 'ere comes the duchess
of our alley orf to meet her fancy man."

Maud ignored Lil, fussed over little George, said a polite
good morning to Becky, then went on her way up town.
There she was to meet Mr. Potts; together they were negotiating to buy up slum property. Maud was now fully back in
circulation; she had obtained a good road contract for Dandy
who was away in Dover, in charge of a big road-widening
scheme which was to accomodate the big guns and the troops
who embarked from there; and Maud herself was up to her
neck in private real estate deals with her close friend, Mr.
Potts, who was in the know. Maud had antagonized Lil by
interfering with the upbringing of her grandson and Lil now
retaliated by putting scandal about that Maud Fitzpatrick had
a fancy man.

"It ain't right, yer know," said Lil, sipping the froth from
her beer in the Railway Arms while little George sat in his
pram outside. "It's only a few weeks since they hung that
poor bugger. She put him away, you know, I couldn't rest in
me bed if it was me." As usual, her audience, the old women
in the pub, grunted and nodded. Lil thoroughly enjoyed
herself but she kept a careful eye on darling George who
waved a sticky fist and gurgled happily.

" 'Ark at him, ain't he beautiful" cooed Lil, and because
she bought them beer the old women felt obliged to agree.

Returning home, looking very tired, Mollie collected her
charge and put him to bed in his little cot. In the evening she
put her feet up, got her knitting out and sat dreaming of the
future, of the day when little George would run to meet her
or when she would take him to his first school. Diligently she
put money by each month to make sure that he would get a
good education. After the war she intended to make the
necessary arrangements and officially adopt him. Mollie was
happy and content now that that little rose-bud mouth and
those tiny warm hands filled her life. She wanted nothing else;

in all respects he was her baby. Colleen had her career—she would probably marry and have other children later on. Castles in the air Mollie built about herself in that neat little house.

On the mantelpiece was a fine photograph of her late mother, Mary, holding little Abby close to her cheek. Those great wondrous eyes seemed to follow Mollie about the room. She often stood to say a little prayer in front of that picture and there was always a vase of fresh flowers beside it.

Apart from the necessity of her work at the hospital, the world outside the alley did not exist for Mollie any more, except for the visit to Mass on Sundays. Her life was as regular, sweet and holy as that of any nun in the convent, and Mollie was not yet twenty-two.

On Saturday morning in Autumn Alley everyone set about doing their chores, preparing for the weekend, when a boy on a bicycle rode into the alley bearing a telegram. Work ceased and everyone watched to see which house it was going to; telegrams were more often bad news than good in those days of war. On to No. 4. He knocked at Becky's, pretending not to notice that all eyes were on him.

When Becky came out waving the telegram excitedly, the three other front doors immediately opened and Mollie, Lil and Maud stood waiting to hear the news.

Maud took the telegram and read it out loud: COMING HOME TODAY STOP LEW.

"It's from the children," cried Maud. "They're coming home. How wonderful!"

Lil sniffed. "First I've heard of it. In Colleen's last letter she said she'd joined a new show, didn't she, Mollie?"

Mollie nodded her assent. It was always her task to translate the contents of Colleen's letters to Lil.

"But surely Lew won't come home alone," cried Maud, her face almost exposing the despair behind her brave mask. "No," she said, "if one comes, they all will. I'd better start getting things ready."

Hastily she pushed her fears away and went inside to make preparations for her daughter's homecoming. She aired Pat's bed, and put on fresh sheets and lace-edged pillow slips. Then she went down to the kitchen and began to prepare a homecoming feast.

"Would you mind taking the baby in to see Sam?" Becky asked Mollie. "I don't like to leave him alone too long. I'd better go and tell the family that Lew's coming home. And I'll bring back a nice bit of apple strudel. How he'll like that!"

Mollie willingly carried George over to see Sam who was sitting in the front parlor, as pale as tissue paper and equally thin.

Twilight had descended on the alley and the gaslamp had been lit. Mollie sat in Maud's parlor watching her mother-in-law's tall figure bent over the table, her large hands carefully smoothing the white tablecloth, her face flushed from baking, her hair awry. From the kitchen she brought large plates of sausage rolls and some of those little jam tarts that Pat was so fond of. In the center of the table was an iced cake, decorated with scarlet bows and much loving care. On Mollie's lap George bounced and jiggled. Without a trace of sleepiness, he jumped up and down clutching at Mollie's long braids of hair, and waving a large wooden spoon as he tried frantically to get at the goodies on the table.

Presently Maud stood back and admired her handiwork. "How's that, George boy?" she asked. "All those sweeties are for you and Auntie Pat."

George gurgled in a most appreciative manner.

"I'll go and tidy myself up a bit," said Maud, "give me a call, Mollie, when you hear the taxi."

Mollie did not reply for she had already heard Lew arrive. From over the road came the buzz and drone of excited voices as Becky and her family welcomed Lew. But there were no other sounds—no Colleen's loud voice or Pat's gentle giggle. A small crease appeared between Mollie's fine brows; something was wrong, Lew had come home alone. Poor Maud, how disappointed she was going to be. Mollie pressed her lips to George's soft curls and anxiously awaited her mother-in-law's return.

Maud came hurrying down in her best lace dress and rows of beads. Her eyes met Mollie's. "Lew's back," she said, "I can hear them cackling over there. Where are the girls?"

"Perhaps they'll follow on later," suggested Mollie timorously. But Maud's steely glance challenged her; in her heart she knew as Mollie knew, that Pat would not come home to the alley any more.

"I'll go and put the baby to bed," said Mollie. She felt she had to leave; she could not face the desolation in Maud's eyes.

When George was finally asleep she picked up her knitting, knowing full well that Maud sat in the window looking down the alley anxiously waiting for her little girl.

On Sunday morning Mollie returned from Mass to find the smiling boisterous Lew waiting on her doorstep. "I hope you said a few prayers for me, Mollie, me darling."

"Depends on how much you need to be prayed for," returned Mollie drily.

"Oh, I do, love. I'm a great sinner, but I'll come in for a cup of tea, if I may."

He almost filled Tim's big armchair by the fire.

"Good God," declared Mollie, "I do believe you're fatter than ever."

"Have a heart, love," he said, holding out his large hands in an expressive gesture. "I'm off to be a soldier, be kind to me."

"I can't believe it," she cried incredulously.

"Nor can I," said Lew, "but believe it or not they're going to whittle me down to the size of an average uniform." He burst into that infectious laugh. Unable to control herself, Mollie joined in. Over a cup of tea he told her of the girls—how Colleen had wished so desperately to come home and of Pat's refusal.

"I'm not at all surprised," said Mollie, "but Maud is heartbroken."

"How's our baby?" inquired Lew.

An odd expression appeared on Mollie's usually pleasant face. She resented that remark "our baby" but made no comment. "He's with his grandma," she replied, "she takes him while I go to Mass."

After Lew had said farewell, Mollie was very thoughtful. So the dancing team had broken up. Colleen might not settle down with Lew now. Inside this good-living young woman was a terrible feeling of guilt. She did not want to share baby George, not even with his own mother—let alone a stepfather. George was hers and always would be.

She sat down to write a long letter to the girls, urging Pat to visit her mother, or at least to write to her. "She's taking your absence very much to heart and I don't like to see it. Your father is away working and it is a lonely existence for someone who loves you and needs your company. Think it over carefully, Pat. We only ever have one mother."

Mollie still kept up her correspondence with all the family and friends of the alley dwellers. She was never known to miss a birthday or a Christmas or any occasion, sad or happy. Today she also wrote to Bridie who was nursing her Timmo—he having lost a leg in his last battle. But Bridie had her husband home once more and was thankful. Mollie sent the usual postal order in the letter for which Bridie was always grateful—it enabled her to buy a few extras for the children. Then Mollie wrote to poor Billy's wife in Norfolk. Then a letter to her father in France, along with long woolly socks and a balaclava helmet, instructing him to keep warm and not to drink too much, and to be sure to say his rosary beads before he slept.

The following weeks were rather dreary for Pat and Colleen. The weather was cold and windy, and the little seaside town that depended almost solely on holiday makers for its prosperity was a bleak place out of season. They had managed to hold down their jobs in the chorus line at a third-rate theater which was struggling to keep going through the long winter. Pat was depressed and put little enthusiasm into her work and Colleen hated being one of the crowd, so there was a series of squabbles with the management and the rest of the cast.

"Damned peroxide blondes," remarked Colleen. "Stringy-necked lot of cows, don't know one foot from the other."

Each night when they returned to the flat it felt so empty without Lew. Colleen fussed over Pat in a motherly fashion, and while she ran down to the chip shop for their supper Pat would sit finishing off Lew's gin, for which she had acquired quite a taste. The big problem was the shortage of money. Previously Lew had handled their finances; he had taken charge and managed everything, done all the shopping, paid the rent and taken them out several times a week to dine after the show. Now, however, at the end of three weeks they were hungry and broke, and they still had a week to work before they collected any pay.

"I'm so fed up with chips," moaned Colleen. "I wish Lew was here to take us out to dinner."

Pat, her face flushed after several gins on an empty stomach, said: "I'm not hungry, Colleen, you can eat mine."

"Of course you ain't hungry," grumbled Colleen, "you drunk all Lew's gin. Anyway, the bottle's finished now and I'm glad."

Pat looked pathetically at her friend. "Got to have a little something to keep me going," she murmured.

"No need to become a bleeding lush. I hate the smell of that stuff," declared Colleen.

"It's all right for you," cried Pat tearfully, "you've got plenty of courage. I can't stand this life as well as you can."

Colleen went over to her and cuddled her. "I know, love," she said. "Let's go home. I'm right fed up and we're completely broke."

Pat covered her face with her hands. "Oh, no, Colleen! Don't make me go home." Tears trickled through her fingers.

Colleen gave a deep sigh. "All right, we'll stay till the end of the month. But when we get our wages I'm footing it out of this dump. We'll go to Blackpool for the summer season. I've heard it's great there—plenty of life. I'm not staying here and that's definite."

Pat wiped her eyes. "All right. I don't care where we go as long as you stay with me."

The next day there was a terrible rumpus at rehearsals. The stage manager—a very effeminate young man recently up from London—swore at Pat and was not particular in his choice of words: "Not like that, you silly whore."

The words had hardly left his lips when a raging tornado struck him. Colleen came charging toward him and landed him a punch square on the nose that sent him bouncing over the footlights into the stalls. In a matter of minutes there was uproar and it ended in the instant dismissal of Pat and Colleen and the forfeiture of their pay. After much argument Colleen did manage to dislodge a few pounds from the manager. Then they left the show.

Once Colleen's temper had cooled, she and Pat went for a walk along the front. The wind had dropped and the evening was mild for the time of year.

"What are we going to do, Colleen?" asked Pat.

"I'm not quite sure," replied Colleen. "I don't know yet if we'll have enough money to get us to Blackpool, and if we don't, how are we going to live till we get another job?"

Pat had no answer. She just stared at Colleen in dismay.

"I'll write to Mollie, I think," said Colleen.

"Oh please Colleen, don't do that. *She'll* come up and get me if she knows I'm stranded."

"She's the cat's aunt," retorted Colleen rudely. "If you mean your mother, why don't you say so?"

But Pat's lip was set in an obstinate line. "You go home, Colleen, I know you want to. I'll get by."

"Nuts!" said Colleen briskly, and they walked on in silence. Suddenly Colleen said: "Look at all those soldiers. Where have they all come from? The bloody town is full of them!"

"They're Americans," said Pat casually, "they've just arrived. They're in the war now."

Colleen gazed with interest at the young men lining the seats on the esplanade. The men whistled and looked at the girls in admiration.

Pat and Colleen strolled past the brightly lit Queen's Bar; tinkling piano music came out on the night air.

"Let's go in," urged Pat. "I really fancy a drink. It'll cheer us up."

Colleen looked at her aghast. "We can't go in there alone, not without Lew." She had worked in a bar but had never gone into one for a drink. "Besides," she told Pat, "unescorted ladies don't get served."

Pat's mouth dropped into that disconsolate line. Colleen hesitated; she could hear the music, that drew her, not the drink. They were standing looking at each other when across the road came four young men. Before the girls knew, the Americans had taken them by the arm and whisked them through the glass doors. "This way, ladies," they said. "Let's buy you a drink."

What a night to remember that was! How generous those young Americans were and how delicious that slap-up meal had been when the girls had been so hungry.

From then on it was Queen's Bar every night. Pat drank more than she should but Colleen kept a watchful eye on those charming young men and drank only soft drinks. But she did acquire a long cigarette holder and began to smoke, and the lads kept them supplied with cigarettes.

One evening one of the Americans sat down at the piano and began to play some of the jazz tunes that were all the rage in the States. Colleen stood beside the piano, her feet tapping to the music, watching his slim fingers ripple up and down the keys. Then he played some of the old Negro spirituals and Colleen's fresh young voice joined in. She hardly realized she had an audience. Urged on by the others, they went from one popular tune to another, ending with the Irish melodies she sang so well. Everyone clapped and cheered, demanding an encore.

"Like a job for the season, Ginger?" asked the landlord, an astute Geordie. "Going to get busy with all these troops in town."

"How about my friend?" asked Colleen. "She don't sing but can dance all right."

"I'll give her a job in the bar."

"No thanks," retorted Colleen. "She's no barmaid."

"Well, what about a hostess job. She's bright and pretty. I'll give her a percentage on the drinks the boys buy."

"Done," said Colleen briskly.

They were booked for a whole summer season at the Queen's Bar. Pat, cool, immaculate and smiling, played hostess to the American officers and persuaded them to spend their money, while her red-haired friend sang for her supper. The dancing dollies were on their feet again.

That was a great summer; mad parties and ardent young men who wanted to live for a while, madly, badly, before going to the front. Lew was forgotten, even Autumn Alley became dim in their minds, for there was no time to stand and wonder. Colleen put on a little weight and her hair became a brighter red gold in the clear salt air. Pat smiled again and that cute little giggle returned; her skin lost that pallid look which greasepaint and footlights had not improved and she now sported an attractive suntan. They fell in and out of love by the week; there was always a new admirer with a pocket full of banknotes. It certainly was a good summer.

Early one morning they sat up in bed and over coffee and toast they exchanged confidences. "I don't mind being nice to them," said Colleen, "but when they start pawing me I feel sick. Don't think I'll ever sleep with anyone else again, not after that rotten Joe Fox. I get kind of scared."

"Sometimes I hate all men," said Pat bitterly. "I expect you and I will end up old maids."

"Well, we've both got jobs and we're having plenty of fun, so as long as we keep our legs crossed we will get by," pronounced Colleen coarsely.

So hearts were broken, faces slapped, and as men tired of them more green ones arrived. When the summer blaze died down and a cool autumn breeze drifted along the promenade, the Yanks sailed for France, leaving many happy memories for the dancing dollies.

One Saturday night it was very quiet in the Queen's Bar. They were sitting at a small table contemplating their next move when a bandy little man who had been listening to Colleen sing came over to them. His face was cheery, brown and wrinkled.

Colleen stared insolently at him.

" 'Ow's Autumn Alley getting on then?" he asked in a shrill Cockney voice. "Yer look like yer muvver," he went on blithely. "Gawd blimey if yer ain't the image of Lil!"

Colleen's mouth dropped open. Someone knew Autumn Alley, though she didn't care to be told that she looked like her mother.

"I'm 'Arry Smiff. Mean to say yer don't knows me? Rosie in the cafe—remember?"

Colleen began to laugh. "Of course I remember you. What are you doing up here?"

He turned his gaze to Pat.

"Well, Christ! If it ain't little Patsy Fitzpatrick. What a beauty! To think you was only a scruffy little pair of kids when I left the alley. Can I bring me mate over?" he asked, beckoning to another man who was even shorter than he was, younger—about twenty—dark-haired and smartly dressed. He had deep blue eyes and spoke in a thick rolling brogue.

"This is Stevie O'Toole, me stable companion," beamed 'Arry.

Stevie put out his hand and stared at Patricia like a rabbit transfixed in the beam of a torch. An embarrassed silence went around the table.

"Hi, let go that filly!" roared 'Arry. "A real thoroughbred, that one, and this 'ere red-headed beauty is from the same stable."

The way 'Arry referred to them as though they were horseflesh amused Colleen. She took to 'Arry right away.

"Lorst me missus," said 'Arry, "poor little Rosie. Went to

pieces in no time. But I still got a nice little number going, looking after a racing stable while the owner's in the army. Got a few good little gee gees of me own too. Getting 'em ready for after the war. He licked his lips at the thought of it. "See that boy?" he said to Colleen. "Going to be a champion jockey, young Stevie is. Wizard, that boy is, I tell yer."

'Arry drank a great deal of whiskey and persuaded Colleen to sing all the old songs in memory of those riotous alley parties.

Pat was very quiet and little Stevie seldom spoke. He just gazed at Pat and his fingers softly stroked her bare arm. Pat's eyes were almost closed, the gin, the warmth of the bar and the presence of this gentle man beside her gave her a peaceful feeling. It was so good to be with someone who did not expect to be entertained.

They all went back to the flat for coffee. Patricia and Stevie were an oddly matched pair, she tall and willowy, he small and sprightly. Watching them together, Colleen thought she had not seen Pat so serene for a long time.

Pat hugged up close to Colleen in bed that night. "Wasn't that little man sweet," she said.

"If you like little men," replied Colleen. "But I don't."

She had begun to think about Lew, and Georgie and Mollie, and even Lil. She was homesick for Autumn Alley. Lew had not written to her; it was six weeks since his last letter had arrived and in it he had complained of the hardship of the training camp, the cross country runs, the meager food, and he said he was considering making a bolt for it. Colleen had replied, telling him not to be a fool. Perhaps she had offended him for that was the last she heard. But she still missed him; no one could really take his place.

The next day Stevie and 'Arry drove out to collect them in a smart pony cart. 'Arry wanted them to go out and view his "spread," as he termed it, a big farmhouse with magnificent stables. 'Arry had his own cottage and a very droll but homely Welsh housekeeper who nagged and fussed all the time.

"They're such dry old buggers, the Welsh," commented 'Arry. "Give me my fat Rosie any day."

After dinner Colleen played brag with 'Arry while Stevie took Pat for a stroll.

Pat came back that evening very starry eyed and Stevie

more in love with her than before. Colleen could not believe what her own eyes beheld. She began to get worried.

"Surely, Pat, you're not gone on that little squirt?" she said sharply when they got home.

"Yes, I am," replied Pat. "As a matter of fact I think I'm in love with him."

"Crikey!" exclaimed her friend. "He's more a bloody leprechaun than a man."

"Don't be so unkind, Colleen," Pat reproached her. "He's very nice."

"My gawd!" cried Colleen. "You ain't 'alf got it bad."

The Queen's Bar seemed particularly hot and stuffy that next Saturday night. Colleen was not her usually happy self. She would not be sorry when the evening was over. A big detachment of the Scots Guards, home from France, had hit the town. They were a rowdy lot and most of them too drunk to enjoy the show.

Pat was absent. She had been missing all day. Colleen was worried about her. She did not trust Stevie. He was supposed to be giving her horse-riding lessons, but you did not take riding lessons after dark and it was now ten o'clock.

After the performance Colleen went straight home, dodging out the back door to avoid the drunken soldiers. Pat had not returned home and Colleen began to get very apprehensive. All sorts of anxieties went through her mind.

She removed her dress and sat in front of the mirror looking at herself. What had 'Arry Smiff said? That she reminded him of Lil. It filled her with dismay. She examined her trim waist, patted her full hips. Oh no, surely she would never look like that. How long did it take to get wide and dumpy like Lil? She took off the little corsets she wore and proceeded to tighten up the laces. She patted cold cream on her face to remove any sign of fading bloom. Then she threw herself on to the bed and began to weep very loudly. How miserable she was! Pat was missing and she was getting fat and ugly. It was a cold hard world and she wanted to go home.

A movement at the door went unnoticed as she pressed her face into the damp pillow. A rough chin rubbed her bare shoulder and a familiar voice said: "Crying, Collie? What's wrong?"

She rolled over and threw her arms about his neck. "Oh, Lew, darling. I can't believe it's you."

There was a loud thump of army boots being dropped beside the bed and they entered a dream world together.

In the morning Colleen rose with the lark to make tea and to kiss that close cropped head on her pillow—the army had made short work of Lew's curls. She hummed a tune as she waited for the kettle. She had made up her mind to stay with Lew; she had never been loved like that before. Then she realized that Pat had not yet come home. Why should I worry? she thought, and climbed back into bed with Lew.

They sat up in bed like a married couple and Lew dunked biscuits into his tea. He was much thinner and looked a good deal fitter. His skin was no longer spotty but clean and fresh looking, and he had the same merry humor and toothy smile.

"You'll have to marry me now, Collie."

She giggled. "I might not," she replied.

"You've got to, you seduced me. I don't know what me Momma's going to say." Lew kept up this banter and they began to lark about as they used to do. Suddenly he asked: "Where's Pat?"

"I don't know," said Colleen. "She's gone off with some bloke she met at the bar."

Lew looked concerned. "What? Stayed out all night?"

"Yes, that's why I was crying when you came in."

"Well," he said, "we'd better start looking for her." He slipped on his pants and dived under the bed for his boots.

Colleen was looking at him. He had lost so much weight; that big tummy and the rolls of fat around his neck had all gone. "It really suits you, Lew. You look lovely," she cried.

"Thanks for the compliment, but you'll never know what I've been through to get down to this size. I deserve a more positive reward," he said with a grin.

She moved closer and rubbed her chin on his. "You ain't done so bad so far," she whispered.

"I know, darling, I always knew that you and I would get together some day. Let's get married while I'm on leave."

"What about your parents, Lew?"

He looked serious. He thought of that pale thin face of his

father and that husky voice saying: "Get a nice Yiddisher wife and I'll hand over the business to you, son." Then there was Becky's formidable host of relatives—all closely connected with the synagogue. For a moment he looked dismayed.

"It don't matter, Lew, we can live together. I don't want anyone else."

"No, Collie, we'll go back to the alley and face them. They might be a little shocked but it'll be no surprise. They know I never had eyes for anyone but you."

Colleen was snuggling close to him when Pat walked in looking rather disheveled but exceedingly happy.

"Come in, Steve," she called to the small figure behind her. "Lew, welcome home," she cried, delighted to see him again.

Over tea and toast they discussed the future. Steve's dark blue eyes never left Pat's face as she coolly informed them she was going to Ireland with Steve to see his mother.

"I know you're longing to get home," Pat said to Colleen as they stood in the kitchen, "so I'm glad that I won't be standing in your way."

"I slept with Steve last night," she whispered.

"I slept with Lew," giggled Colleen.

The Queen's Bar gave them a good send-off and the next morning, with passionate goodbyes, the two girls parted company. Like a river that suddenly divides, Colleen and her best friend, Patsy Pat, went their individual ways. Colleen, glowing with health and happiness, in a new pink dress and a feathered turban to match, sat next to Lew in the second-class compartment of the train speeding homeward to that smoky city they loved. Pat, as cool, smart and aloof as ever, was traveling in the opposite direction to Liverpool where she was to stay with Stevie until he was free to travel to Ireland.

With a far-away look in her eyes, Pat was dreaming of Autumn Alley; of the grand welcome there would be for Lew and Colleen; of her mother's steely blue eyes that could light up so affectionately; of her father with his slow drawl and long thin moustache. She buried her face in Stevie's shoulder.

"Don't cry, me darlin'," he said with deep concern.

"Be good to me, Stevie," she begged. "I'm going to miss

Colleen so much. We've always been so close, just like we were sisters."

"Now, now, pet," whispered Stevie, "we'll be home next week. It's so peaceful in Limerick, all your cares will fly away like the birds in the air." In his soft lilting voice he consoled and soothed her. She closed her eyes. "'Twill bring the peaches and cream to your lovely face, me darlin'."

# The Parting of the Ways

IN AUTUMN ALLEY THINGS WERE HAPPENING. Mollie and Becky sat beside old Sam who was propped up in bed, gasping for breath, the pallor of death upon his ravaged face. Becky rocked to and fro in her sorrow while Mollie held the spittoon to his cracked lips and wiped the sweat from his brow. In the front parlor, a cluster of women had gathered, weeping and muttering. They were Becky's relations—aunts and sister—waiting to share her grief, as was the custom. The rabbi came and silence descended on the alley. In no time it was all over.

Across the road Lil anxiously rocked little George in his pram outside her door. It was the concern of them all. Had they not been close friends and neighbors for many years? When old Sam finally died they all closed their doors and drew their curtains and mourned the passing of this gentle hard-working old man.

An hour later the silence was broken by Colleen's merry laugh as she and Lew strolled hand in hand down the alley. They were met by a bevy of aunts who, with loud cries, told Lew the bad news. It was not the homecoming they had expected. Lew was suddenly enveloped by his relations and almost pushed into the house. Colleen stood shyly outside in the street. But Lil spied her and came barging from her house.

"Oh! yer come 'ome, 'ave yer?" she demanded, almost grabbing her traveling case.

"Hello, Ma," said Colleen, and two big tears of disappointment ran down her cheeks.

"Don't stand there gawping," said Lil, "they got trouble over there, old Sam just died."

So Colleen, as docile as a lamb, turned and went into the dark musty smelling passage of her childhood home, and there, sitting up at the table in a high chair, was her son George. His mop of curls was rather grubby and there was jam sticking to his baby chin. He waved a sticky crust in the air and called out: "Nan, Nan." Colleen caught him up in her arms, careless of her lovely dress, and smothered him with kisses. His sticky hands clutched at her hair and her tears fell on top of his curly head. "Oh, Georgie," she sobbed, "it's lovely to be home."

Lil stood amid all the muddle of toys and nappies, arms akimbo, with a very satisfied expression on her moon face.

"Where's Mollie?" asked Colleen. She hadn't expected to find Lil taking care of Georgie.

"Gorn to light a candle. Yer know what she's like when there's a deff," replied Lil.

A tall shadow filled the doorway and there stood Maud. "I heard your voice, Colleen." Her eyes roved the room.

Colleen put the baby back in his chair and made an attempt to remove a sticky spot from her dress. But she was forced to raise her face to Maud's questioning glare.

"We came alone, just Lew and me," she said. "Pat's not with us."

Maud's mouth tightened and she held on to the doorknob as if to steady herself.

"All right," she said, "tell me, Colleen. Where is she?"

"She's gone to Ireland."

Maud looked surprised. "In a new show?" she asked.

"No, with a man," replied Colleen bluntly.

Maud's knuckles showed white as she gripped the knob of the door.

"She's all right," explained Colleen. "He's going to marry her. Lew will tell you, he's seen him." Desperately she tried to placate Maud and defend her friend at the same time.

"Don't make excuses for her," said Maud bitterly. "I'm her mother."

"But honestly," continued Colleen, "I've never seen Pat so ate up with anyone before. He's a jockey, a famous one."

"Well," said Maud, "it would have been nice to have heard it from her. But never mind, I've received my answer." She turned and went home, slamming her own front door as she went in.

"Cor blimey!" announced Lil. "That daughter of hers done it this time."

"She wouldn't come home," exclaimed Colleen. "She never wants to see Autumn Alley again."

Mollie returned brisk and efficient and took George back under her wing. She told Colleen all the latest alley news as she gave Georgie his bath, pouring water over his fat rosy limbs. He chuckled away happily.

"What religion would you say I was, Mollie?" asked Colleen.

"Well, that is a funny question coming from you." Mollie's fine brows rose in astonishment.

"Well, I'm worried," explained Colleen. "Lew and I want to get married and he's afraid his family will be against it. But seeing as I ain't got no proper religion I might just as well be a Jew."

"Jewess," Mollie corrected her. "It's for you to decide, Colleen," she told her. "After all, you've had no religious upbringing."

"I don't believe in anything, but I'll die if I lose Lew."

"I believe you could have a civil wedding and make up your mind later on. But, Colleen, it's up to Lew. It won't be so easy for him."

"Well, that's all right then," announced Colleen. "After the funeral and the mourning is over, I'll tell Lew I don't mind being the same as he is. After all George's father was a Jew. Perhaps I'm destined to be one."

Mollie frowned. Did Colleen plan to take the baby away from her? She and Lew had their careers, a baby would be a definite drawback. She would not let her mind dwell on such a dismal future; her baby was safe with her for the moment.

It was a week before Lew came over. He had grown whiskers—not being allowed to shave while in mourning. He looked very harassed. His leave had been extended because of his father's death but now the army had recalled him urgently.

"I'll write when I get back, Collie." He kissed her hurriedly.

After he had gone Colleen sat about for days with a gloomy expression on her face. "Oh dear, Mollie," she wept, "I don't know what to do next."

The tall sycamore trees in the park scattered their winged seeds across the paths. Colleen sat on a park bench, the baby in the pram beside her. He slept peacefully clutching a little toy animal. She gazed idly at the sycamore seeds strewn about, her memory going back to the days when Lew, Pat and she had tossed them into the air to make them fly, laughing and screaming with sheer exuberance, as free as the lovely soft breeze that blew across the park. Her normally pink cheeks were rather pale and her long braids of hair untidy.

That morning she had quarreled with Lil as she often did but this time it was serious. Lil, back on the booze, had laid into Colleen about Georgie.

"Bleedin' glad of me, wasn't yer, when yer was orf flying yer kite."

"Oh, give over, Muvver," yelled Colleen.

"Don't shout at me, you saucy little bugger," cried Lil, dealing Colleen a box on the ear that sent her spinning.

Colleen was so shocked she did not know whether to laugh or cry, but she dashed from the house, wheeling the pram with Georgie inside it, and fled to the park.

Lil stood at the door and hurled a tirade of insults after her. Then she marched off to the public bar to regale her cronies with her many grievances. "Luvs him, I do," she wept, "looks after 'im. Wot fanks do yer get? She doesn't give me nothing. Even Mollie give me something for a little drop o' beer, but not a bleedin' penny does *she* part wiv."

"If it was not for you now, little one, I'd hop it," whispered Colleen, sitting all alone in the park. She smiled affectionately at the sleeping babe. "Might as well go up the 'Dilly on the game. They take what they wants and it's 'so long, pal.' Oh, I wish you were here, Patsy Pat." Tears welled up in her eyes but she bit her lip, got up, and began to push the pram around the pond, watching the ducks and wondering why Lew never wrote. Small boys, dirty and ragged, were fishing with a stick and a bent pin. It did not seem long ago since her brothers had done the self-same thing, all out in the world now, except poor Billy.

Colleen pushed the pram out of the far gate and turned toward the market where she had had her first job. She passed the old club, Bum Daddy's. It was a grim, derelict old ruin now. Broken windows like sightless eyes stared at her. She shivered. There were very few stalls in the market these days. There were big spaces in between the ones that were there. Most of the stallholders had been called up and those that still traded had women in charge of them. They sold bruised-looking vegetables, bits of bric-à-brac and second-hand clothes.

Colleen came to a stall that had sold children's clothes. She turned them over idly, remembering how she and Patsy Pat used to buy ribbons off this stall—red for Pat, blue for herself. She was examining a little jersey, still miles away, when a voice broke into her thoughts.

"That's very fine. Good quality. Have it as a present from me." A quick hard-worn hand loaded with rings reached for a paper bag, thrust the woolly inside and held the package out to her.

Colleen's blue eyes opened wide in astonishment as she looked up and recognized Annie Fox. Joe's mother surveyed her shrewdly and then bustled around to the front of the stall and leaned over Georgie.

"My life, what a boy! So like my Joe! How much does he weigh? Got any teeth yet?" She threw questions like darts at Colleen who, being caught unawares, never said a word. But the tears she had held back for so long trickled down her cheeks.

"You're upset," cried Annie. "Don't cry, *liebling.*"

Colleen clutched the paper bag in one hand and the handle of the pram in the other. She stood helpless, unable to speak. She felt so unhappy.

"Boy! Boy!" yelled Annie and a ragged boy came from a corner. "Give eye to the stall and don't nick nothing," she ordered. "I'm going for a coffee."

She led Colleen over the road to the cafe. "Now we can chat," said Annie. "Park the pram in the doorway."

Sitting at the marble-topped table with a hot mug of coffee in her hand, Colleen began to tell Ma Fox her troubles. "I love my baby but I'm not domesticated," she said sadly, "and me mother nags me all the time because I don't bring no money in."

"What did you come back for?" demanded Annie. "I thought your baby was better off with Mollie, and you were doing all right on the stage." Those shrewd black eyes gazed fixedly at her. "Besides, what have you done with the cash I've already given you?"

Colleen was offended. "It's still in the post office. He don't want your money, and nor do I."

"All right, so you don't want my help? Suits me." The old lady waved her hands expressively. "But if I was you I'd go back to work. Nothing like your own bit of independence."

Colleen put her chin in her hand and stared hard at the ring of grimy condiments in the middle of the table.

Ma Fox sipped her coffee. "Joe's in the States," she informed her, "and doing very well, I heard."

"I don't care if he's in hell," declared Colleen.

The old lady pursed her lips into something resembling a grin and said: "Well, that's where he'll end up, no doubt. But, you listen to me, gel, for the last time. Let that nice clean gel—what was her name? Mollie, ain't it?—let her mind him and I'll get you an introduction to a fella I know. Got a West End show opening soon. He owes me a few favors."

From a large pocket in that shiny alpaca apron she took a stub of paper and a grubby piece of paper. Laboriously she wrote on it: "To Samuel Enstein," and underneath a long sentence in Yiddish. Folding up the paper she put the address on the outside: "5 Frith Street, W.1, Enstein Productions, second floor."

"Do you know where that is?" she asked.

"I think so," Colleen stammered.

"Now go, gel. Tog yourself up and go today. Never put off for tomorrow what can be done today," Annie Fox counseled her. "I know you've got a good voice—heard you last year up in the London Music Hall."

"Do you mean you're finding me a job?" asked Colleen, still unable to believe it. "Did I hear you right?"

"You did, gel," said Annie briskly. "And if *he* likes you,

you'll go places, believe me. Knows the ropes, does old Sam."

"That's awfully kind of you," she said. She felt suddenly excited. She had heard of Samuel Enstein, who hadn't? To think this funny old woman was a friend of his.

"Kind?" said Annie. "It ain't kind of me, gel, it's necessity. After all, you are the mother of me only grandson. Can't have you hanging about down here getting into more trouble."

Colleen sped home like the wind. In the alley Mollie was busy polishing her windows and Lil dozed boozily on the windowsill.

"Oh, Mollie, I believe I've got a real break at last."

Mollie picked up the babe who was now awake and fretful. She cuddled him close as she listened to Colleen's enthusiastic chatter.

"I'm very pleased for you, love," she said. "Wait till I give baby his feed and I'll come and help you get ready."

At four o'clock, looking more like her old self, pretty and carefree, Colleen was sitting in a dusty office awaiting the return of Samuel Enstein from a late lunch. With her fingers crossed she prayed fervently that her luck would hold. At four-thirty, accompanied by several hangers-on, Samuel Enstein waddled in. That's the only way to describe it. He was so short and fat that he was almost as wide as he was high. He had a huge belly and a dome-shaped head that was completely bald. He smoked a long cigar that he puffed vigorously between thick lips. Colleen, who had built a picture of this famous man in her mind, felt cheated. How could a man whose name was on all the cinema screens look like that?

He had spotted her and two beady eyes surveyed her. "Hello, dolly, what are you after?" He had a hoarse but kindly voice.

Colleen stood up and handed him the note that Mollie had carefully put into a clean envelope. He opened it and his face creased with amusement as he read it. Then he let out a great roar of laughter. Colleen wished she had been able to read those Yiddisher words. He looked her up and down and her knees quaked.

"Come in here," he said and directed her into another room where a big untidy desk and a piano were the main furniture. A young man with thick specs lolled about on a chair.

"Been in showbiz?" quizzed Sam.

"In panto and a small variety act," Colleen replied.

"Walk about a bit," he ordered. "Hold you arms high above your head. Good. Now lift up your skirt and give us a dekko at your legs."

Colleen did as she was bid, her face flushed pink. He felt her calves with his podgy hands.

"I'm a singer," she told him.

He took his cigar from his mouth. "So you can sing. I don't want singers. I got all the singers I need. I'm looking for showgirls. You'll pass." He tore a slip of paper from his notebook and handed it to the languid young man. "Here, Solly, take her round the corner and introduce her to the rest of the girls. And get some candy and flowers for old Ma Fox, will yer," he shouted after them.

Colleen did not know whether she was on her head or her heels. At last she was in a real live West End show. She did not mind the hard work or the long hours of rehearsal, sailing across the stage with a huge headdress of feathers and artificial fruit on her head and wearing little else but a few discreetly placed feathers. It was all new, shocking and daring, and Colleen loved it. She began to enjoy life again, and daily grew more beautiful, her body streamlined by the exercise.

Colleen shared a flat with two other girls. Her wages were good and meals were mostly taken out in restaurants. Boyfriends queued for attention but Colleen, regal as a queen and as ambitious as ever, kept them all at bay. The rather common young girl from the alley began to disappear as a very confident young actress emerged, like a butterfly emerging from its chrysalis. Sam liked her and bestowed many favors on her. He introduced her to influential acquaintances and she fluttered about the night life of London's theater land.

On Christmas Eve Lew arrived at the stage door. Colleen was brusque with him, granting him a quick interview. "You can wait for me if you like," she said, "and take me to supper."

Lew, grasping at straws, said: "All right, Collie, I'll go and book a table."

Later they argued across the dinner table.

"Don't let's quarrel," he pleaded. "I'm going overseas after this leave."

Lew hung about for the rest of the week and Colleen made it plain that her career came first. The following Tuesday he sailed for France with only a photo of her in a flimsy costume to console him.

The news that Colleen was in a West End show had swept the alley. Mollie told Bridie, and Lil informed the locals. Maud went to see the show—the only one who could afford to—and thought it shocking.

"Young girls almost naked wiggling all over the stage with huge baskets of fruit on their heads. What a waste of money," she declared. "Though I must admit, young Colleen looked very nice. But she has a fine voice, it seems a pity not to continue her singing career."

Mollie was busy buttoning little George into his rompers, and smiled that secret smile of hers. "It's what she likes doing and they say those showgirls are all the rage in America."

"You're probably right, Mollie," agreed Maud, "but the way *she* shows off next door you'd think her daughter had a star part."

"Well," said Mollie, "Lil always was a trifle overbearing." She giggled. "Now Colleen sends her money every month, she's bought herself a new suit. I've never seen Lil in a complete new outfit before."

"Well, live and let live, I suppose," returned Maud. "But I've got some other news for you, Mollie . . . did you know Becky is giving up her house?"

Mollie put George in his chair and gave him the spoon he loved to play with. "Doesn't surprise me," she said, "she's only been home once since Sam died."

"She's going to live with her sister—Becky was always one for her family," announced Maud. "But I was wondering if I should re-let her house. I shan't stay here much longer myself. I've been to view a big house right at the top of Muswell Hill. I wish you'd come with me, Mollie."

Mollie's mouth tightened. "I'll not leave this alley, Maud, but I'll miss you and Dandy. It won't be the same without you."

Maud looked at her sorrowfully. "I know, dear, and it was

a hard decision to take. But Patricia will never come home again while I live here, and that's the hardest fact to face."

The spring had come once more to the alley. It was a dawn of peace, for this was the last year of the war. Food was still in short supply as were coals. There had been a great spring offensive—the biggest bloodbath the world had ever known.

Down in Autumn Alley, little George, clad in calico petticoats and white boots, trotted from Aunt Mollie's to his nana's, wherever he considered himself most popular. His fat little legs carried him, laughing and chuckling, from one house to the other and back again. He was full of mischief and he plagued these women who loved him so. There was Nana Lil, always ready to dip his dummy in her tin of condensed milk, and Aunt Mollie making such a fuss of him. Sometimes his lovely mum came, bearing chocolate bars or a big cuddly teddy. She smelled nice but that red stuff on her lips tasted funny. He wished she would not keep hugging and kissing him.

Today, however, he was not getting quite so much attention. He chewed at the dummy attached to his pinny by a string and intently watched all that was going on. Outside Aunt Maud's house stood a big cart and two gray horses who stamped their feet and tossed their gray manes. Two men carried out pieces of furniture and stacked them on the cart. George's nana sat on the window ledge watching, her eyes round, her face solemn, and Aunt Mollie was in there helping Aunt Maud to move. It was all very interesting. Then when the house was emptied and everything was loaded on the cart, Uncle Dandy, staggering a little, climbed up onto the high seat beside the driver who shouted: "Gee up!" The great dappled grays heaved on their collars and the cart rumbled forward with a rattle and a chink of harness. Aunt Maud, sobbing violently in a great sunshade of a hat, grabbed up George and kissed him. Georgie did not like such demonstrative displays of affection and he yelled and struggled to be let down. Then Aunt Maud hugged Aunt Mollie who also appeared to be crying, and Nana Lil came forward and in a hoarse voice said: "I wish yer luck, gel." Then she gave Maud a kiss on her tear-stained cheek. It was all very strange to young George.

After Maud left the alley it assumed a forlorn air, as if it were brooding for past memories of happy family parties, of Irish dancing on the cobbles, and children playing down by the Cut. Now only Mollie, Lil and little George were left. One side of the alley was completely empty, some of their windows were already broken; the houses were slowly sinking into dereliction. Only cats did their courting in them now and each day they seemed more depressing.

"It gives yer the creeps," was Lil's comment.

"I wonder if she intends to re-let Becky's house?" pondered Mollie. "And now her own house is empty." So far Maud had given no inkling of her plans for her old well-kept home, or for the big piece of wasteland between Becky's and the canal which was still stacked high with timber, paving stones and bags of cement. The remaining inhabitants of the alley were naturally concerned but they had never heard of slum clearance or Mr. Potts's pet scheme for the area. Town and country planning? Slum clearance? Who understood such things? Who cared? Lil and Mollie were too busy with the welfare of little Georgie. In fact Maud had already received a big advance from the council, enabling her to buy the big house she had always dreamed of; it also helped to back a big business venture for Dandy—a large-scale road-building scheme.

As the great dray went slowly from the alley Dandy, perched high on the seat beside the driver, for a second looked back and twenty years went fleeting by into time. There were Lil and Mollie, standing close together, and Dandy could see his lovely Mary between them. It was as if her glorious green eyes came right up close to his face. Dandy's droll dry features crinkled with emotion.

As he sat there, hunched up, engrossed in thought, his memory recalled the day that he and Tim had first found the alley, and had dragged that dirty old bug-ridden mattress from Sal's backyard to sleep on. How happy Tim had been larking about with the ragged urchins next door—those Welton boys. Now Dandy was leaving it all behind to live in a posh house in a middle-class neighborhood. Money was not scarce now, Maud certainly had her head screwed on all right, contracts and subcontracts—it meant very little to him. When he got too old to handle the heavy mason's hammer they could put him six feet underground. He had worked hard all his life, and had no wish to end his days sitting on his backside in an office. He should have gone with his pal Tim into the army. At least Tim had the little house in Autumn Alley to come home to and the Railway Arms to drink in.

At that very moment in a little war-destroyed town in France, Tim, wrapped in a mackintosh cape, a tin hat on his head, was squelching in the mud and blood of the battlefields, cold, wet, and sick of the sight of dead stinking bodies, that it was his task to bury. Now at last they were all marching back to the base for a well-earned rest. Very weary, muddy, bloody and even a little lousy, Tim's thoughts turned to home, to his old pal Dandy Fitz standing at the bar of the Railway Arms drinking pints of foaming porter. Tim half smiled. He wished he had not been such a fool and so anxious to join up; he might be over the road with him now. Then came a mental flash of a shining grate, a roaring fire in that little home in the alley. He could hear Mary's soft gentle brogue and smell her hot potato cakes. It was all too much to bear.

Soon the company halted for a while and took shelter in a derelict church. Other companies on the move were already installed and they sat there, cold and dejected. No one spoke. Close to Tim was an old soldier with brush-like whiskers. He coughed and swore alternately, and there was something familiar about him. Tim took off his tin hat wearily. His shock of red hair shone out in the light of the candle stuck in the bottle.

"Well, damn me, if it ain't old Tim!" exclaimed the old soldier. His stout shape catapulted in Tim's direction, a rough hand grabbed hold of his.

It was Bill Welton in the flesh, the same old Bill who had been his next-door neighbor in Autumn Alley. For a moment Tim could not speak, but Bill had plenty to say, liberally sprinkled with curses and oaths. He cursed the army, the Jerries, the war, the mud and the rain. Everything that had happened to him since he had left the alley he poured into Tim's ear.

"Come rahnd the corner," he whispered suddenly. "I've got a bottle of wine hid up."

The wine and Bill's boasting patter soon cheered Tim up. The surroundings disappeared, the half-demolished buildings, the whine of shells grew faint. Memories of Autumn

Alley had taken over. They talked together of the parties, especially the one at the Weltons' when the floorboards had given way when they were all having a knees-up. They laughed about the time they had challenged the locals to a fight in the Railway Arms, and backed horses and drank beer.

"Right couple of stupid gits, you and me, Tim, ending up out here," declared Bill.

"I wasn't thinking of it going on all this long when I volunteered," replied Tim.

"Well, it's nearly over now, mate," said Bill. "Keep out of trouble and we might see Blighty yet."

"How did you come to get back in the army?" Tim inquired.

"Well, between you and me, Tim, I ducked out of the last lot and they had their hooks in me. So it was the war or the nick. But I tell you what, mate, I ain't done so bad out here. Picked up a nice few bits of jewelry after we been in to clear up after an air raid."

Tim felt disgusted. The same old Bill, robbing the poor devils he dug from the debris.

"It ain't no good to them, poor sods, they can't take it with them," Bill went on. "We're due for a spot of leave when we get back to base—then I'll show you how to get a good time, mate. Nothing like a few sparklers to bring on the birds!"

Tim was astounded. He had lived like a priest since he lost Mary and now here was old Bill, who must be well over fifty, talking of getting a woman. He started to laugh, that hearty deep-throated chuckle of his youth, and old Bill cackled away beside him. They made plans to go on leave together—two old soldiers or two dirty old men?

Several weeks later, well scrubbed and clean shaven, Tim was on a train bound for "gay Paree." With him was Bill, already well boozed and involved in a shady card game with some of his fellow travelers.

It was in Paris that Tim met the lovely Marie. It was all rather hazy, their meeting—a smoky café, the gabble of strange voices and large amounts of wine and cognac consumed. As Tim was only used to beer the strong liquor went straight to his head. While Bill was chatting up some middle-aged woman in the corner, Tim sat looking very lost, wondering what the hell was wrong with his legs; he seemed unable to control them.

"Tim, me old mate," Bill had said when they first set out on their tour of the bars, "follow me, cock. I know just what we need and where to find it. No queuing up at brothels for us—look at the silly gits." He pointed at a line of servicemen who queued under a red light. "Come on. I know a little café down the back streets run by a widow, just the stuff to give the troops! But first let's have us a drink or two."

So Tim had followed Bill from bar to bar, and drunk more than his fill. Now Bill had got his widow and Tim had come to a standstill. When Marie appeared and wriggled herself into a seat beside him, he stared drunkenly at her.

"I am Marie," she said, "the sister of Thérèse who is with your friend. He says I must come and take care of you."

Tim nodded dumbly and took the hand she offered. With a slight stagger, he allowed her to guide him into a dimly lit back room where she gave him some supper. She sat watching him as he ate, the soft candlelight dancing on her black wavy hair and snow-white neck.

"You will feel much better now you have eaten." Marie's white even teeth shone in a smile.

Tim took her hand and pressed it to his lips. "Oh, I feel foine now I've found you," he said.

"I am not a woman of the streets," said Marie very sharply. "I only take care of you because my sister Thérèse thought you had had your share of drink."

"I know, darling," muttered Tim, still holding her hand. "Where did you learn to speak English?"

"My father was English," Marie informed him, "but he died when I was very young and I lived in an orphanage in London until I went into service when I was thirteen. After I married I came home to live with my family."

"Where's your husband now?" asked Tim.

"He was taken prisoner on the Russian front but he was killed trying to escape," said Marie bitterly.

Tim, almost sober now, was intrigued by this lovely young girl. "Let me come home with you," he said quietly.

"Yes, all right," replied Marie.

They walked home in the moonlight. As they stood close together in her doorway, he bent to kiss her and she returned his kisses with equal passion. Tim had never experienced such warmth before, not even with Rosie. He had loved Mary intensely but she had turned cold and unresponsive, always so afraid she would get more children. Marie was totally different. She made him feel like a young man again. On that little day bed in Marie's one-room flat, Tim spent the next seven nights and most of the days with her.

He returned to the battlefield feeling that once more life was worth living. He promised he would return to her and his heart ached whenever he thought of her.

# The Winds of Change

ONE MONDAY MORNING THE COUNCIL MEN CAME and nailed up the doors and boarded up the windows of the empty houses opposite. The men informed Lil, who naturally went to investigate, that they had been purchased by the borough council to be pulled down after the war.

"Why, the crafty old cow!" cried Lil, and went storming into Mollie's. "Never said a word did she? Must have made a packet of money from them. Wonder what's she going to do with her own house on this side?"

"I don't know or really care," returned Mollie. "I've bought my house and paid for it, so no one can tell me to go."

Lil stared back at her, eyes rounded in terror. "Oh gawd!" she cried. "What about me? I ain't bought mine. Do you think she'll chuck me out?"

"Oh, don't be so silly," Mollie replied placidly.

But Lil waddled off to the pub looking very serious. Mollie put George to bed and sat down to catch up on her correspondence.

At ten o'clock Lil came home, very drunk, shouting and singing.

"Try chucking me out, you old cow," she yelled threateningly at Maud's empty house. "Lived all me life 'ere I 'ave."

With an impatient sigh Mollie helped her indoors, took off her shoes and put her to bed. Big tears fell as Lil blubbered drunkenly.

"Only you and me left, Mollie. Oh, me lovely Mary, why did you have to die?"

Mollie sat by Lil until she fell asleep. Then she came out, closing the door quietly. She paused for a moment or two to look down the deserted alley. How strange, she thought, not one man left, only Lil, the baby and herself. What happened to that hive of happy folk? Maud could be right, it might be time for them all to go. She entered her own bright little house and stood by Georgie's cot, where he slept, fists clenched, smiling in his sleep. No, she decided, she would stay, this was her home and he was her baby—the future generation. The alley would come to life again, she felt sure.

Mollie plodded on through each day. Lil took care of Georgie while she went to the hospital to work, and Georgie played in the puddles and climbed up on the canal wall while Nana dozed on the window ledge. Lil stuffed him with sweets and took him to the pub where he sat on a little stool consuming arrowroot biscuits dipped in beer. Then came November and the Armistice. Fighting ceased and London went wild; flags fluttered and there were welcome-home parties everywhere except in our alley, for Mollie's man would not return, nor Lil's favorite son. So it stayed very quiet. Lil drowned her sorrows and Mollie kept busy.

A month later Mollie read out to Lil the long letter she had received from Tim, telling her he had met Bill Welton and had gone on leave with him, and that he was as hail and hearty as ever.

"Why the old bleeder!" cried Lil. "He needn't think he's coming back here now it's all over, 'cause he ain't."

"But listen to this," said Mollie, continuing to read the letter. "'I have met a young woman called Marie. I wish to marry her if she will have me.'"

With the letter was a photograph; there was Tim in uniform with Marie beside him sitting on a wall. He looked much younger and very happy. The girl's dark hair had blown out in the breeze and her tight dress clung to her magnificent figure.

"Crafty old sod," Lil commented, examining the picture. "But she is pretty and Frenchie too—hot stuff they are!"

Mollie had gone pale, her lips drawn tight in anger. Damn him, she thought, how dare he forget her lovely mother. She would not bother to answer the letter. Let him stay in France with that girl who was young enough to be his daughter. And it didn't help that she had the same name as her mother.

The following spring Arthur and Hortense paid another visit to the alley, bringing with them their baby son Algernon. "Christ, what a mouthful!" cried Lil.

It was not a successful visit. They had both become rather snobbish and would not use Lil's bedroom but booked into a hotel instead. Hortense's father had recently died and left Arthur his interests in the aircraft factory and a nice bit in trust for the new baby. Lil was boozy, cross and aggressive toward them. She resented their superior attitude and Georgie added to the disaster by his somewhat belligerent treatment of his cousin Algernon.

At first he was nice and friendly. He found that sticky old dummy he was so fond of, dipped it in the condensed milk tin, then, as soon as the baby opened his mouth to cry, he popped it straight into that toothless cavern. Hortense's horror, combined with the scolding from Mollie, annoyed him so he landed a punch on his cousin's squashy little nose.

They did not outstay their welcome; one day, and they had left for home and safety.

"Good riddance to them, Georgie," cried Lil when they had gone. She eyed with hostility the bunch of flowers that Hortense had presented to her. "Who wants bleedin' flowers?" she grumbled. "Do them more good to put their 'ands in their pockets and give us a few bob."

"Bleedin' flowers," repeated Georgie after her.

Another visitor that week was Maud, who came to see Mollie one afternoon. She looked very smart in an elegant suit and a large feathered hat and carrying a real leather handbag and rolled umbrella. Mollie remarked how nice she looked, but Maud never smiled, her face remained grim. Her eyes were dark ringed as if from lack of sleep.

"You don't look too happy, Maud. What's the matter?" inquired Mollie as she poured out the tea.

"I must talk to you, Mollie," she whispered. "Where's Lil? I don't want her to know."

"She's over in the park with Georgie," replied Mollie. "What's wrong? Don't you like living at Muswell Hill?"

"No, Mollie, it's not that." Her tone was apprehensive. "It's me. I think there's something wrong with me, something serious."

Mollie listened carefully as Maud recounted her symptoms. "Well, it sounds to me as if you're more than likely a couple of months pregnant."

Maud's mouth dropped open. "I can't be, I'm fifty-three this year."

"It's still not too late."

Maud wiped the sweat from her brow. "I can't believe it, it's not possible," she argued.

With obvious amusement, Mollie said: "Well, you're the only one who can answer that question."

Maud recalled those first weeks in the new house, how lonely she had been and how depressed Dandy was. They had grown much closer for a while, each one trying to comfort the other.

"Why, the old devil!" exclaimed Maud suddenly. "At my age! Whatever shall I do?"

"Well, stock is as good as money," said Mollie dryly. "You'd better come up to the clinic and be examined."

It was proved that Mollie had been right. Maud was three and a half months pregnant.

"My God!" cried Maud when she heard. "But I feel quite relieved. What I went through not knowing what was wrong. I wonder what old Dandy will say."

Dandy was very pleased. "It'll be nice if we have a son, old gel. We're comfortable now; think of the grand education we could give him. And that's going to be the most important thing in the future."

"I think I'll write and offer your sister Agnes a home," said Maud.

"She'd make a grand nursemaid," said Dandy. "She's sick of living in the convent."

From then on the new house did not seem so large and inhospitable. These middle-aged folk planned for an addition to their family, and they discussed the improvements to be made to the house and the nursery they wanted. For a while the apple of their eye, the wayward Patricia, was forgotten.

Then, three months later, Pat suddenly walked in on her parents, announcing that she had left Stevie O'Toole because he thought more of horseflesh than he did of her. It seemed that in Ireland she had been left with Stevie's old mother while he toured the country to ride in all the races he could get.

She stared in horror at Maud's extending tummy. "You're going to have a baby? How disgusting!"

The summer came with a vengeance that year and London lay frizzling and frying in a heatwave. But down in the alley it was cool and shady. Georgie played out in the street with a pet tabby kitten, his constant companion, who was often clutched tightly in his fat little arms. When the ice-cream cart approached, however, Georgie would throw the cat to the ground and dash into his nana for money. Holding the halfpenny carefully in his chubby hand he would toddle off to meet the dark Italian with his brightly colored cart. The ice-cream man often carried on his trade at the corner of the alley and sometimes Georgie would sit beside his cart for hours.

"Once that old Italian pitches on the corner, I can't get Georgie to come in," Lil complained to Mollie.

"It's all right," said Mollie, "as long as you watch him. I don't want him wandering off. After all there're no other children in the alley for him to play with."

Georgie's soft white curls had grown much longer, and were tied at the back of his sturdy neck in a cute little bunch. His deep-set eyes were so dark, almost black, and they twinkled as he laughed. He was big and tall for his age. His most distinctive feature was that broad squashy nose which grew in prominence as his features formed. "Gawd!" Lil exclaimed. "I fink he's going to have a big conk, just like Joe Fox."

Mollie snatched Georgie up and covered him with kisses. "Don't you dare say a thing like that, Lil," she said angrily. "I never want this boy to know of his heritage."

"Don't see how you're going to hide it," returned Lil, "too many people knows abaht it, bound to come out."

Mollie was distressed at this and more determined than

ever to adopt George and give him her name. But little Georgie only cared for his new love, the ice-cream man, who sang and whistled merrily at the street corner and who gave him tasters and talked very rapidly waving his hands all the time.

His lovely mother rarely visited him now. Occasionally on Sundays she would arrive loaded with presents for all, vivacious and beautiful, brimming over with life. She had deeper tints in her hair and her face was perfectly made up. She was now getting singing parts in revues, and was slowly climbing the long ladder of fame. Lil still argued and got very aggressive with her daughter, but was secretly very proud of her. Lew had now departed overseas on occupation duties to finish out his time. Apart from an infrequent twinge of conscience, Colleen dismissed him from her mind, and made good use of her string of admirers—young men with money to spend.

One day in August Mollie came home from work at the hospital feeling rather tired. Her feet ached and it had been a frustrating day. She discovered Lil waiting on her doorstep with a melancholy expression on her face. Immediately Mollie's mind flew to Georgie, but he was all right, she could see him playing over by the canal wall with a little toy engine.

"She's done it," cried Lil in a sepulchral voice. "I knew the old cow would."

"Who's done what?" asked Mollie patiently.

Lil handed her a letter very solemnly. It was in an official buff-colored envelope, unopened. It was addressed to Mrs. L. Welton. Mollie surveyed the letter.

"But why didn't you open it Lil?" she asked.

"Because I know what's in it, that's why," replied Lil truculently.

"Oh, how can you if you haven't read it?" sighed Mollie, opening the letter.

"Don't have to read it out to me," said Lil obstinately. "She's chucking me out. That's a notice to quit. I told yer she would."

Mollie smiled as she read the letter. "Well, I never! Lil, it seems you've been left a legacy."

"Ooer!" proclaimed Lil, mouth wide open.

"This letter's from a firm of solicitors. It seems that Uncle

George has died out in Australia and has made provision for
you. You have to go to their office for further information."

"Cor blimey!" burst out Lil. "Poor ol' George. Funny, I
got another letter as well. I know that one's from my George
but I was waiting for you till you had time to read it to me."
She produced a grubby missive from her apron pocket. She
chuckled. "Christ! That other letter had me frightened. I
thought the old cow had given me notice for sure. Got a little
bit behind with me rent I 'ave, see."

"Come in and have a cuppa and we'll read this one," said
Mollie.

Her son had written from Australia to inform her of the
death of his uncle. He had left a thriving business to young
George but had also made provision for Lil, which was in the
hands of a London solicitor. It was not a very enterprising
letter, cold and dutiful, but Lil was not worried.

"That'll be a smack in the eye for her ladyship," she said
gleefully. Once the initial shock was over, she began to get
used to the idea of having an income. "I'll buy me own house
I will. I'll say I want this bleedin' house. Tell her where to go,
I will."

"What bleedin' house?" inquired Georgie in his parrot
fashion.

"Now, Lil," said Mollie, "I asked you not to swear in front
of the child."

But Lil was too excited to listen to Mollie. She held
Georgie on her lap, her legs spread wide, her fat waist
encircled by a greasy black apron. "Buy yer a nice little sailor
suit tomorrer, love," she told Georgie, "and a woolly dog."

Georgie, clambering all over her, grabbed hold of her
wispy hair and planted a big wet kiss on her cheek.

Sitting at the table Mollie felt very sad. He obeyed her and
depended on her but he never showed her the spontaneous
affection that he did to his fat untidy nana who stuffed him
with sweets and taught him to swear. She pondered on the
fact that blood was thicker than water. How could she
begrudge Lil this freely given love from her grandson, she
who had so little affection from the five children of her own
she had borne? Now this old woman had been left a legacy.
Mollie began to wonder what changes it would bring. She
shuddered as if a gray goose walked over her grave. The

silken ties that bound her to this child were becoming taut and precarious; yet something had told her that this baby would be hers to love and protect, to fill the void in her life the loss of Larry and her lovely mother had left. Mollie reached out for her knitting bag and the needles clicked furiously. Over them could be heard Lil's untuneful voice, singing as she rocked Georgie to sleep.

Overnight there came a remarkable change in Lil. First of all she went to the newly opened ladies' hairdresser in the market and had her hair washed, trimmed, and dressed in the latest style. She got all this on credit, having allowed the news to travel that she was now a woman of means. Then down to Bletson's, the most fashionable costumier in the area, where she bought herself two dresses—one a very dashing purple silk and another a kind of plum shade gaberdine trimmed with bows and plenty of braid, and a three-cornered hat which was also a shade of plum.

There was a sailor suit for Georgie and a little straw hat to wear with it, cheap earrings and beads and a new handbag—all purchased on the strength of the solicitor's letter which was now produced for all to examine. The news went up and down the market like a bush fire. "Fancy old Lil Welton being left a fortune . . ."

Lil went back home to the alley and proceeded to dress herself and Georgie in their finery. Hand in hand they paraded along the main road and stood on the corner waiting for the pub to open. Then, obtaining an advance from the landlord, she began to treat her very thirsty companions to beer and shorts—money was no object. Young Georgie, looking very smart in his white sailor suit, trotted in and out of that forest of legs and feet. He scrambled about in the wet sawdust on the floor, occasionally guzzling the dregs of the empty bottles left near enough for him to reach. The celebration became rowdier; there was a burst of song and a bit of a knees-up. When Georgie got bored he left the party, unnoticed by Lil.

Out into the deserted street Georgie went, straight down to the canal wall. Scrambling up on to it, he walked along the top, tightrope fashion, hands outstretched. Suddenly he overbalanced and disappeared from sight. He landed on a muddy bank just a few feet wide, inches away from the cold slimy waters of the Cut. "Fishes," he babbled, trailing his hands in the water. Catching a stray stick that floated past, he began to poke and stir up the muddy water. No one saw him, no one even missed him, but some divine providence took care of him as he stretched out beside that cruel green water that had claimed so many lives. Wet and muddy, he suddenly tired of fishing game and toddled along the tow path. He spied the big pile of bricks stacked in Maud's back yard and began to climb it, scraping his knees and tearing his best suit, until he reached the top. Georgie was king of the castle, and his high-pitched voice asserted that this was so.

An old bargee, walking wearily beside his horse, spotted Georgie. "Come dahn, yer little sod," he hollered. But Georgie only waved his baby hands in delight. With the aid of his more agile young son, the bargee rescued George, who came down protesting. He received a whack on the backside from the irate bargee and was deposited back over the canal wall. Georgie, wet, muddy and bedraggled, dashed off to find his nana.

He found her sitting on the floor just inside the dim passage that led from her front door. Lil was paralytic with drink, unable to move. She had just managed to clamber over the step before collapsing, her fat legs wide apart and her new dress all crumpled. She blubbered pitifully, having just discovered the absence of her lovely grandson. Muddy and bloody from a cut on his knee, Georgie clambered all over her, planting wet kisses on his dear old nan.

"Zat you, George?" she slurred. "W'ere yer bin?" And she passed out again.

Georgie sat beside her for a moment. Then, deciding she must be having a nap, he went off to get his favorite tin of condensed milk. He sat down beside her again, and with a big spoon ladled huge quantities into his rosy mouth, now and again spreading a bit on the wall.

At four o'clock Mollie returned from work and discovered them. Her horror and annoyance at the sight of the messy George and the drunken Lil knew no bounds. She was sick with disgust and fright. Anything could have happened to her lovely baby, and God knows what he had been up to, the mess he was in. Lil was still so drunk that Mollie had to call a man passing by the alley to help her lift the old woman onto her bed. Vigorously she scrubbed George clean, telling him that he was a very naughty boy. He yelled and screamed with

temper, and had to be forcibly held down to get his nightie on
him before being packed off to bed. This can't go on, Mollie
told herself. If Lil's got money she'll be continuously drunk.

Once the initial shock was over, Maud was pleased to see her
daughter—her much-loved child once more—after almost
two years of separation. Her own aches and pains were
temporarily forgotten and Pat was welcomed home. The big
gloomy house seemed to come alive as Maud chased about
seeing to its decoration, acceding to Pat's choice in everything. As selfish as ever, Pat sat back and absorbed the wealth
of love and attention that her mother showered on her.

At night Maud sat beside Pat's bed and brushed her long
braids, tying them with scarlet bows at the end, as she had
always done. She had a soft smile on her haggard face and
wore a big print overall to hide her swollen tummy. She tried
desperately to keep the fact from her daughter that she did
not feel as fit as she used to. This baby seemed to be taking all
the life and energy from her. Her body no longer functioned
as well as it had. Already the doctors had warned her to take
more rest and better care of herself. Now her beloved
daughter had returned to the fold, as beautiful and demanding as ever, refusing to accept the fact that her mother was
pregnant. Patricia just ignored any remark made on the
subject, holding her mother in a completely selfish embrace.

Maud ran the contracting business, coped with Patricia's
whims and kept their large house in order. Once more Dandy
took a back seat. There were no pipe and slippers waiting for
him these days. Maud was always too busy or out shopping
with Patricia.

"What about this husband of yours? Is he coming over,
Pat?" Dandy ventured timidly to ask one day.

"He's in Australia at the moment," snapped Pat, "and
that's a long way off." No more was said.

Maud's legs became very swollen, her gait much slower,
and her purse emptier as she gave Pat all she wished—
dresses, lovely undies, all sorts of presents, including a
strange thing called a phonograph which played scratchy
tunes from a record that went around and around. Maud was
afraid of it and its whirring sound affected her nerves and
gave her a sick headache. Pat danced to it until late into the
night. Dandy grumbled, groused and stayed out late, coming

in staggering drunk. Maud began to look so weary that her face was yellow with fatigue, but Pat just looked coldly at her.

"I'd better send over for Aunt Agnes," said Maud one day when she was feeling very tired.

"Why?" demanded Pat. "I don't want that old frump living here."

"But Patricia, I shall need help when the baby comes," exclaimed Maud, "and Agnes is a good girl, she's lived in that convent a long time."

"Please yourself," retorted Pat, "but if she comes here I shall leave." So Maud put off sending for Agnes and wearily plodded on.

Time ticked by and soon she was in the last week of the eighth month and feeling very down.

Pat had been out all day and Dandy was late home; he had taken to going all the way back to the alley to drink in the Railway Arms. Pat had been spending a lot of time with Colleen lately, often waiting for her after the show.

However, this night Pat came in at nine o'clock. She dashed in looking very elated and ran straight upstairs. Maud slowly followed her and to her amazement she saw that Pat was packing her suitcase. All those pretty undies Maud had bought her were being rapidly rammed into the case.

"Whatever are you doing, Pat?" she demanded.

"I'm leaving," replied Pat. "Going to share a flat with Colleen. They may be off to tour the States soon and I could go with them," she babbled excitedly, dragging her dresses from the wardrobe.

Maud grasped the door jamb and gazed vacantly about the pretty bedroom she had prepared for her daughter's stay.

"I've got a taxi waiting," gasped Pat, fastening her suitcase. "I might get in on the show too—isn't it thrilling?" With a swift peck at her mother's cheek, she said: "Ta-ta! I'll write to you from the States." Downstairs she dashed, and with a rustle of silk and a waft of expensive perfume, she was gone, leaving Maud too astounded to even move.

Bracing herself, Maud went slowly down the stairs. Her head was swimming. Suddenly her foot missed a step and she toppled over and over, crashing to the bottom of the stairs in a crumpled heap. She lay on the tiled floor looking up at that high elaborately decorated ceiling and those gold-embossed walls; the portraits of nymphs bearing Grecian urns looked down at her staring aghast. No sound came from that silent house or through the colored glass windows of the front door. This was not Autumn Alley; outside the road was empty, and there was no friend or neighbor nearby to come to her aid.

Maud could not get up, an excruciating pain held her like a vice. But, always so brave, she slowly crawled toward the front door, pulled down the latch and lay over the front doorstep calling for help. A passing cabby heard her and called the doctor who immediately ordered her to the hospital.

The next day a baby boy was stillborn. Maud's spine was injured, and the news that she might never walk again was not easy to bear.

During the six months that Maud spent in the nursing home she pined endlessly for her lost Patricia.

# Down but Not Out

ONCE THE LEGAL TRANSACTION OF LIL'S LEGACY was settled to everyone's satisfaction Mollie's worries decreased. Of the four hundred pounds left to Lil, she owed fifty. Maud let her buy the house from her for one hundred and fifty pounds and the rest Mollie persuaded her to put into the post office and then just to draw a little each week. Lil became very popular in the district, in fact, almost notorious, having set herself up as an unofficial money lender to the poverty-stricken population of the back streets behind the main road, lending five bobs and ten bobs here and there and charging a steep rate of interest. This blood-sucking horrified Mollie, but Lil was queen bee, and sat on the windowsill in her best dress haggling with her prospective customers.

The problem of George was solved. Now that he was three, Mollie had got him into a small private nursery school in one of the big houses facing the park, run by a very respectable lady. Lil was allowed to go and meet him and bring him back for tea, providing she kept fairly sober. So at two o'clock in the Railway Arms Lil would explain to her cronies: "No more, ducks. Got to go meet me little George up at that posh school."

When Lil collected him they would walk through the park together and Nana would let George have a go on the swings, and buy him an ice-cream. It was the highlight of the day for them both.

Then several happenings, all tied up together, changed this peaceful pattern. Lew had returned from France and was back in show business. Colleen, unable to get rid of him, had graciously allowed him to share her flat where Patricia was also living. So the three troupers were together again and they began to work on an act of their own. Then Colleen paid a fleeting visit to the alley announcing that she was going to marry Lew and become a Jewess. Lil was incensed.

"Well, I never heard the bleedin' like of it," she cried. "I'll see my Georgie don't be no Jew boy!"

"There's nothing you can do about it," declared Colleen. "He's my baby."

Mollie listened and wondered if it was the right time to approach Colleen about her proposal to adopt him. But always in a hurry and annoyed by Lil's attitude, Colleen flounced away back to the West End.

The death of Annie Fox caused quite a stir. It was hot news that a fortune had been left, and most of it to her errant son in America, but the rest to her illegitimate grandson on the condition that he be brought up a Jew. Since his mother was one of London's most popular entertainers, the newspapers had a field day. Victory marches and the presentation of medals were forgotten temporarily to make room on the front page for a picture of them both—Colleen and her fine son, George, who had been hastily collected from school to pose for the photographers.

When Lil arrived at the school one afternoon there was no chubby smiling face to welcome her. A letter addressed to Mollie was handed her. "His mother collected him and left this note," explained the headmistress. "He's going on a ship, so she informed us. I do hope it's all right, he is such a darling."

Lil's florid features lost their bloom, as the blood flowed from her cheeks.

"Gone?" she cried, and she fled breathlessly back to the alley with the note from Colleen clutched in her hand. Mollie met her halfway. She was worried—it was nearly half past four.

"Is Georgie at home?" gasped Lil.

"No, where is he?" demanded Mollie.

Lil passed her the note, gabbling all the time. "She's done it, she's took him. Going on a big ship."

Calmly Mollie read the letter. She noticed that it was not Colleen's handwriting, it was too neat for her illiterate hand.

Dear Mollie,

Lew and I got married today. We are going to the States and we have taken Georgie with us. Sorry, Mollie, but Lil would have made such a scene, we thought it best this way. Pat is coming with us as well.

Thanks for everything.
Colleen and Lew

Mollie did not utter a word. She just walked slowly into her house, letter in her hand.

Lil waddled behind her, blustering and crying. "The bitch, the little bitch! Not your baby, she said. Going to be a Jew boy, he is. We must do somefink. I'll get the coppers, that's what I'll do."

But Mollie put an arm about her shoulders. "It's no good Lil, we've lost him," she said, and pale as death she proceeded to take the little baggy plaid pants from the line in the kitchen and fold them neatly. Lil stormed off wailing and crying to the bar to drown her sorrows. Left alone, Mollie put her head down on the table and wept heart-broken tears.

It was a sad-faced young woman who visited Maud in the nursing home. Maud saw Mollie coming down the long room, tall and neatly dressed in a long navy tailored coat and smart felt hat with a brim. Maud was shocked at the sight of Mollie's face; it was so much thinner and her velvet-brown eyes were ringed by dark circles.

The younger woman stood momentarily still as she looked at Maud—that once tall strong woman was now bent and gray, and huddled in a wheelchair. Her face, which had never been attractive, seemed to have shrunk, and her hair seemed thin and sparse. She looked many years older, but those steely blue eyes were still alert and sharp and there was a humorous grin on her wide generous mouth.

"Oh, Mollie, darling, it's so good to see you again," she cried. Their hands reached out to each other and they held on tight, each unable to express the depth of their feelings, life having dealt both a knock-out blow.

A nurse brought a tray of tea and Mollie removed her hat, placed it on the bed and began to pour. On the windowsill was a pile of books and papers; from the nursing home and the confines of a wheelchair Maud still kept the business's affairs in order; Fitzpatricks was expanding daily thanks to Maud's astute brain.

Maud's legs hung weak and useless and, according to the well-paid and best doctors, they always would. Mollie's look showed her sympathy but Maud said brightly: "Don't worry, love, it's not so bad, I can still get around." She indicated the wheelchair. "I'll be going back home soon. Tell me, love, how is our Autumn Alley?"

"You know they took Georgie from me," said Mollie glumly.

Maud nodded. "Try to get over it," she said. "It had to come. You're not yet twenty-five—all your life is before you. Marry again, have a bloody football team!"

Mollie shook her head. "I'll never marry again, Maud. Larry was and still is the only husband I'll ever have."

"Well, get out of that damned alley. Travel the world, do something with your life," pleaded Maud. "Please don't shut out living, Mollie, none of us know what's ahead of us. Look at me, a bloody cripple, and deserted by my daughter."

"I don't want to leave the alley," said Mollie obstinately. "Besides my father may return soon."

"I shouldn't worry about Tim," said Maud. "He's like old Dandy, no good till he is chock full of beer. Oh, God, Mollie," cried Maud, "don't make one setback a life's burden as your mother did, God rest her soul."

Mollie's head came up and her small chin stuck out determinedly. But then she softened and said quietly: "I'm made of sterner stuff than my mother, Maud. I'll wait for my father to come home and then I shall take up a specialized form of nursing—in an orphanage or a children's hospital."

"Good," cried Maud, "that's what I wanted to hear!" She put an arm about her shoulders. "We'll show them. We're down but not yet out, my love." She grinned, that daredevil grin reminiscent of the alley days. They began to gossip about the old days—about Lil, Becky, and Tim, all the folks they had known.

When eventually they said goodbye, Mollie looked more confident. Visiting Maud had brought Mollie's own courage to the fore. Maud accompanied her to the front gate, maneuvering the wheelchair with expert hands, stopping to chat with a gardener who surreptitiously slipped her an evening paper. Mollie smiled. Maud was up to her old tricks again—a little flutter on the gee gees.

They parted affectionately and Mollie promised to spend some time with her at Muswell Hill in the summer. She boarded the train to Bow and sat quietly in the corner, wondering where little Georgie was and if she would ever see him again.

When she reached the corner of the alley she stopped dead. There was a light on in her sitting room! She went forward quickly. Hearing voices and laughter drifting into the night, she peered through the window. Inside were four people, gossiping and laughing heartily. Her father, his red hair gleaming in the gaslight, lolled in an armchair. On his knee sat a young woman, very dark, very drunk and slightly disheveled. Facing them was Lil. She was sitting bolt upright, arms akimbo, her face flushed with drink, and she seemed to be giving someone a piece of her mind. Mollie's startled gaze swept over them to the fourth person—a thickset man in a khaki uniform sporting a huge bushy moustache. It was old Bill Welton!

Mollie's face grew red and angry as she watched them. Bill stood at her lovely polished table cutting a long sausage and a longer loaf of bread into chunks with a large jackknife. Then, placing huge chunks of sausage on the bread, he handed it to the others. Mollie could not believe it, it seemed like a bad dream. The loud excited voices gabbled on as they all munched the bread and sausage, washing it down with whiskey from a bottle, crumbs and grease scattering everywhere.

Quickly she pulled herself together and dashed into the room. "Good God," she cried, "whatever are you all up to? Look at the mess on my table." Quickly she began to gather up the debris, her face white with temper.

Lil was coughing frantically; the food had got stuck in her throat at Mollie's surprise entrance. Bill, his whiskers laden with crumbs, glared at Mollie aggressively.

Tim rose, almost tipping the giggling Marie onto the floor. "Well now, well now, Mollie darlin', 'tis a foine welcome you are giving your old dad."

Mollie looked coldly at the tipsy young lady clinging to Tim's arm and reached for her little brass crumb tray and brush that hung beside the fireplace and proceeded to brush the crumbs from the table without saying a word.

"Well now," continued Tim, "that's not very nice, Mollie. I want you to meet Marie. She is now my wife and your stepmother."

Mollie stiffened slightly and gazed with even more hostility at Marie who leaned on Tim in an effort to keep her balance. "Perhaps we had better waive the introductions until she's sober," she said, her voice hard and bitter.

Marie burst into tears and the veins on Tim's forehead swelled as he tried to keep his temper. Lil got up and lumbered toward the door; sensing trouble, she was making a quick getaway.

"Goodnight, Lil," called Mollie sarcastically, "and kindly take your old man with you."

"Don't bleeding want him," shouted Lil. "Let him go to his old tart."

But Bill had taken the hint. He grabbed his bottle of whiskey from the table and rammed it into his haversack. "Don't worry abaht me," he growled, "I'm pissing off right now." He followed Lil's fat form out of the door and their voices echoed through the alley as they stood under the street lamp arguing.

Tim was comforting his young wife who, with her head on his shoulder, was sobbing violently. "I expected a slightly better welcome than this, Mollie," he said reproachfully.

"I suppose you'll want Mother's bedroom," said Mollie, without an ounce of contrition in her voice. "I'll get it ready."

Her mother's room was just as neat and clean as it had always been. On the big brass bed was the snow-white crocheted quilt that Mary had brought from Ireland. It was on this that Mollie's dark head rested as she slipped down and hot tears poured down her cheeks. Oh, dear God, she prayed, send my mother's spirit to comfort me, I can stand no more.

On the shelf the photograph of Mary, which Mollie had placed there, stared down at her with such sadness.

Later that night Mollie lay in her little room and pressed her face into the pillow, trying not to see the empty cot in the corner, or to hear the sounds of violent lovemaking from next door.

Soon after sunrise Mollie was up, washed and dressed looking very smart in her blue striped ward dress with its stiff white collar. She took her best pieces of china from the sitting room and put them in the desk in her room and locked it. Then, packing her suitcase, she locked the door of her bedroom, put the key into her purse and crept quietly down the stairs. She placed an envelope on the kitchen mantelpiece and then softly closed the front door. She had given up her house in the alley. Her intention was to volunteer for night duty and sleep in the nurses' home.

At eight o'clock Tim rose, bleary-eyed and hung over. He tried to read Mollie's letter while Marie shouted loudly that she wanted a cup of coffee.

"There's only tea," he shouted back. "Mollie doesn't drink coffee." With a worried expression he perused his daughter's letter. It read :

Dear Dad,

For the sake of Mother, I am leaving you this house. I could never live with that woman you have married. You can pay me a pound a week in rent and I still want the use of my small bedroom when off duty. If you wish to contact me I am at the nurses' home.

Mollie

Tim sank into a chair, looking thoroughly miserable.

"What's the matter, love?" asked Marie.

"It's Mollie. She's gone," he replied.

"Good!" exclaimed Marie. "I'm glad. I don't think she would ever have approved of me."

"But this is her house, she owns it. I feel as if I've done her a great injustice. She loved this house. She's seldom left it since her mother died. Used to say she felt close to her here, as if her spirit still lingered."

Marie's dark eyes opened wide in terror. She glanced around the room in fear. "Oh, shut up, Tim!" she cried. "What a thing to say! You scare the wits out of me."

"No need to be afraid of Mary," mused Tim. "She was the most kind and gentle being that ever walked this earth."

But Marie moved closer to him. "Oh, be quiet, Tim. I'm terrified of ghosts."

"All right, darlin'," he said, placing a protective arm about her. "But I think I'll go and try to persuade Mollie to come home."

"But you promised to take me to Petticoat Lane," pouted Marie. She clasped him around the neck and held up her lips to be kissed.

Tim swept his young bride up in his arms. "You win, me darlin'. We'll go to Petticoat Lane."

After breakfast, the sink still full of dirty dishes and the beds unmade, Marie put on her best hat, a bright red floppy straw with ribbons hanging down the back, and walked proudly beside her Tim to catch the bus that would take them to that huge East End market where on Sunday mornings you could purchase anything from a needle to an elephant. They mingled with the noisy crowds and Marie reveled in the din. London to her was some undiscovered earthly paradise.

It was mysteriously quiet in the alley that Sunday morning —not a sound, not even a swear word came from Lil's house. For Bill Welton had actually wheedled his way into Lil's bed and they both lay sound asleep on their backs snoring like two badgers.

"Don't send me dahn the doss'ouse, Lil," he had begged her. Lil, in her boozy belligerent way, had stared closely at him, at the wrinkled brow and the pepper-and-salt whiskers, and gradually weakened. After all, this was her old man home from the war. "All right you can sleep in the armchair, and no funny business."

But in the dead of night, Bill had left the discomfort of that battered old armchair and crept in beside his old gel. Grasping her aging breasts he had whispered: "Come on, Lil, be matey, let's have a cuddle." Still pretending to protest, Lil had accepted his clumsy lovemaking and now, with the purpose of restoring her lost energy, she was sleeping it off, her mouth open, her hair hanging in greasy strands.

Soon Bill awoke, sat up and looked at his spouse. "Gawd," he muttered, "what a sight for sore eyes."

He climbed out of bed and was standing in his long khaki shirt looking for his trousers when he spotted Lil's straw shopping bag, the one she always carried with her. He pulled on his pants, leaving his braces dangling, and taking the bag from beside the bed he crept into the kitchen. His eyes gleamed in anticipation as he began to investigate its contents. First of all he brought out a battered old purse. He grinned, remembering how he had won it in a raffle years ago. He opened it and inside were two pound notes and some coins. He slipped one note out and put it in his pocket, then he peered down into the murky depths of the bag, not really expecting to find much else of interest. But, at the bottom were several little parcels, all wrapped up in newspaper and tied with string. Curiosity got the better of him. Listening intently in case Lil should stir, he started to open them. The first one was a mystery. Inside were a few other such packets and each one had money in it and written on a slip of paper in a very bad hand was a kind of code: F. OW 1 BOB. D. OW 2 BOB. PAID FOUR BOB. In the next parcel was a bundle of pawn tickets that Lil held as security for the few shillings she had lent the owners. Last of all there was a notebook with lists of unintelligible words written in it and a definite $Q$ beside each one. This was Lil's version of $P$ meaning "paid up." Bill was nonplussed, then he suddenly hit the jackpot; a bundle of notes, a post office savings book and the deeds to Lil's own house. There was also a letter from George in Australia. All her worldly goods were in that old shopping bag that she carted everywhere.

"Why, the crafty old cow!" burst out Bill. "She's loaded!"

Replacing every parcel carefully, he crept into her room and put the bag back beside the bed. Then, whistling cheerfully, he made a pot of tea.

"Come on, old gel, have a nice cuppa," he said, handing her the steaming drink.

Lil struggled to rise, snorted at him, her glance going straight to the straw bag. "Changed yer bloody ways—never give me a cup of tea in bed before. Bin pokin' and pryin', ain't yer?" she accused him.

"No, honest I ain't, Lil. Strike me dead if I did. Just got up and made yer a nice cuppa."

Lil poured her tea into her saucer. Supping it very loudly she stared at him suspicously over the rim.

On Monday morning, cold, gray and raining, Mollie retired to her uncomfortable bed in the nurses' home after a long stretch of night duty and thought wistfully of her soft downy bed at home, of the smooth linen sheets in her warm house in the alley.

Tim had risen early leaving Marie asleep, cuddled up like a little black kitten in the large double bed. "I'll be off early," he had informed Marie the previous night. "I've got to find old Dandy. He'll give me back my job. Funds are getting low, can't go on honeymoon forever." So he slipped out just after dawn, leaving Marie all alone for the first time since she had entered that house in the alley.

From next door came the raucous sounds of Lil's voice echoing through the paper-thin plaster walls. She had woken up in a decidedly irritable mood and she had had a change of heart about the old man. A terrific thump shook the house to its foundations as she gave him a determined shove and Bill rolled out onto the floor.

"Get up yer lazy git," yelled Lil, "go and get a job, you ain't goin' to ponce on me."

"All right," said Bill, sitting on the cold floorboards, "don't get so narked. I'll go and make a cuppa."

"No, yer won't," shouted Lil. "Get orf up to the labor exchange and get a bleeding job."

It is strange but true to relate that Bill, that once so aggressive little fighting cock ready to challenge all comers, gave in very gracefully. He got dressed, washed and shaved. Looking very spruce he popped his head around the bedroom door and said; "Yer ain't got a dollar to lend me, 'ave yer, luv?"

"No, I ain't," growled Lil, "but there's two bob on the shelf for your bus fares."

Meekly and mildly Bill actually went out in the cold to look for work. As soon as the door closed after him Lil reached gleefully for her straw bag and put it under her pillow, taking out a bottle of gin. She took a good swig at it and then, with a fat smirk on her face, lay down to sleep again.

Marie had been disturbed by all the noise next door and turned restlessly in bed. She put out her hand to the place where Tim should be. There was no warm spot, it was icy cold. Tim had left a long time ago. She sat up looking nervously about her, at the heavy mahogany wardrobe whose door hung slightly open, at the large gilt mirror on the wall that made her face look fat and distorted, and then to the photograph of Mary whose eyes seemed to bore into her soul.

"Tim! Tim!" Marie called out. "Are you there?"

There was no reply, but someone was downstairs, she could feel it. She sat on the edge of the bed shivering. She was afraid to stay in that bedroom, but even more scared of what might be downstairs. Marie muttered a prayer.

The footsteps downstairs now began to ascend the stairs. She gripped the sides of the bed. There was sweat on her brow and she stared wide-eyed at the door.

"Who's there?" she whispered. "Tim, don't play the fool. Come in, Tim."

She got up, dashed to the door and pulled it wide open. There was no one there, just a steep flight of linoleum-covered stairs leading down to a dim-lit hall.

"God in heaven," cried Marie, "pull yourself together, girl." She rushed frantically about the room straightening up the bed, closing the wardrobe door. Then with a sudden nervous movement she turned the picture of Mary face down on the shelf. "Sorry, Madame," she said quietly.

Lightly and more calmly she went down the stairs. At the bottom something made her turn and look back up the stairs. Her heart stood still. At the top of the stairs stood a youngish woman, tall and dark, her long hair flowing to her waist. She wore a nightgown and on her face and neck was a long dark bruise. She was smiling a lovely gentle smile, and her magnificent deep green eyes stared kindly down at Marie. Marie let out a shrill scream and went dashing out of the house and in next door, almost falling on top of Lil who now sat enjoying her breakfast in the kitchen.

"Cor, blimey!" cried Lil. "What's up wiv yer, Marie?"

"A ghost," jabbered Marie, "I've seen a ghost!"

Lil looked annoyed. She hated to be disturbed so early in the morning. "What bleeding ghost? We ain't got no ghost. Too much gin ain't good for those what ain't used to it."

"But I saw it," blabbered Marie, "as plain as you are sitting there. A woman, tall and dark, with long hair to her waist. And those eyes . . . just like her photograph."

Lil had gone pale, her round eyes almost popping. "It's me lovely Mary," she cried hoarsely, and she began to weep noisily.

Marie was very frightened and stared at the door as if she expected Mary to walk in. No persuasion on Lil's part would get her to return to her house. She sat there all morning in Lil's dirty kitchen, where the cooker swam in grease and the tablecloth was newspaper.

At twelve o'clock Marie borrowed a tattered old cardigan from Lil to put on over the thin cotton dress she wore. Together they went over to the Railway Arms. Marie, squeezed in between Lil and another equally rotund woman, was treated to several large glasses of port and to a potted history of the alley—old Sal battered to death in that shop over the way; the death of young John as he fell from the railway bridge, "just outside this bleeding door," as Lil colorfully described it; and the passing of Mary, whom everyone loved. "Never left us really, she ain't," sniveled Lil. Marie sat sick and frightened, too full of port to move.

It was almost three o'clock when Tim came home, strolling leisurely through the alley feeling on top of the world. He had spent the morning with his old pal and cousin Dandy Fitz who had done very well out of the war. He had several big contracts in force and employed hundreds of men. He had welcomed Tim with open arms. They had wept beery tears of joy together and Dandy had offered Tim a job as a foreman. Tim was content and happy as he passed the Railway Arms. Time for a quick one before they shut, before going in to give Marie the good news.

Speechless he gazed across the polished bar, through the glass screen of bottles, into the snug where his young wife, wedged between Lil and her drinking companions, sat with half-closed eyes and a face the color of beetroot.

"Marie! What are you doing? Get off home at once!" he roared.

Lil, looking very scared, got up and hustled the dazed Marie to her feet and headed for the door. But like some dark avenging angel Tim was obstructing the doorway. He looked at his wife, the faded tattered old woolly she wore, her uncombed hair, her unwashed face. She was drunk in the middle of the day. He caught her by the arm and began to drag her home, Marie screeching like a fishwife and cursing him loudly in French and English.

But Tim stood no nonsense from his youthful wife. He caught her by the back of the neck and, with a firm hold on her backside, he hustled her across the road to the house. As soon as he let go of her, she rushed at him, kicking and screaming in temper. He tried to restrain her but to no avail. She dashed into the parlor, throwing open the cupboard that held some of Mollie's china, the pieces that had not been locked away. She grabbed the dainty cups and hurled them one by one across the room at Tim. Each time he ducked and the cup struck the wall behind him, splintering into small fragments. After the cups went the milk jug, the sugar basin, and then the saucers until Mollie's tea-set had almost completely disappeared. Tim, ducking and dodging the hail of fire, eventually got near enough to bring down Marie with a kind of rugby tackle. She crashed to the floor with Tim's heavy body on top of her. For a second they lay there, he held her arms stretched out and stared into her stormy tear-stained face. With a sob Marie subsided.

"Oh, Tim," she wailed, "I'm sorry."

They lay there, locked in a passionate embrace, amid the broken china, and oblivious of Lil's moon face peering through the window. They were lost to the world.

That was the first and in no way the last of their desperate battles which always ended the same way—in a bout of very passionate sex.

Nothing could persuade Marie to go upstairs again or to sleep in Mary's bed. So Tim borrowed some money from Lil and bought Marie a fashionable wooden bed of her own. Mollie's pieces of furniture and knickknacks were all removed to make way for this enormous double bed which filled the little front room, leaving very little space for anything else.

For a while Marie was reasonably happy. She decked out the room with frilly drapes and pink bows, though she never bothered to dust it.

Tim had been back at work several months now and was looking tired and drained. Marie seemed to exhaust him mentally and physically and he was beginning to wonder if it had been such a wise move to marry one so much his junior.

However, Marie now insisted that she was pregnant and Tim was carried away with pride and joy at the fact that at the age of forty-five he could be so virile. Marie was loving, warm and generous with her favors—so different from Mary's coolness —but Marie's vivid imagination and her excitable temper were things Tim had not bargained for. With a bit of luck and firm handling he hoped she would eventually cool down. At least that is how he consoled himself.

"Aye, 'tis all in a lifetime," he sighed, as he confided in his old mate Dandy over a Sunday lunchtime drink.

Dandy now wore a stiff white collar, having been deprived of his old red choker by his wife who still ruled him with a rod of iron even from her invalid chair. His blue eyes shone bright with affection as he looked at Tim. One bony finger eased the stiff collar about his Adam's apple, then he picked up his tankard and swallowed his pint of beer. "Ah, 'tis good to have you home again, me boyo," he said.

# A New Baby in the Alley

No one could say that Marie did not try to settle down in Autumn Alley. She did try exceedingly hard, but the easy going life she had led in the back streets of Paris with her permissive sister, Thérèse, did not help. Charmingly she asked the tradesmen in, offering them a cup of tea, and then found to her dismay that these stolid working Englishmen thought they were on to a good thing and had no intention of leaving until they had obtained it. How often she had gone running into Lil's, complaining that she was in danger of being raped! Once Tim returned to find a tallyman sitting in his chair, and he threw him out through the window.

So poor little Marie was constantly in bother, hating the house, and never liking to stay in it alone. She would stand at the front door, her arms folded, her hair hanging in soft curls on her shoulders, her eyes dark and brooding. Forbidden to go over the bar with Lil, she idled her time away on the doorstep, and the house looked more and more neglected. Mollie's white lace curtains were drab and dirty and her shiny windows were now very dull. In an old black dress with her stomach growing daily bigger, Marie stood hour after hour on the step waiting for Tim to come home from work. He would come plodding down the road, footsore and weary, his slouch hat pulled down over his forehead, and wearing heavy corduroy breeches with a leather strap about the knee, his heavy boots covered with cement dust. Marie would run like a little girl to meet him, throwing her arms about his neck. Her man was home, for her the day had just begun. She was lost in this gloomy alley, and breaking her heart for the cheery back streets of Paris.

On Saturdays they went to the Railway Arms with Lil and Bill. Then Marie would liven up. She made herself look nice, brushed her hair and put on those gold loop gypsy earrings. Her hair was crisp and naturally curly and small wisps of it curled about her face. Her charm was always the cause of trouble. Men were attracted to her like bees to a honey pot and Tim was madly jealous. So most Saturday nights the two of them fought tooth and nail, and the noise of breaking china kept the Weltons awake.

"I'll be pleased when she's broke the bleedin' lot," muttered Lil, "might get some peace then."

One day Mollie came walking very sedately down the high street. She was looking very smart in her sister's cap and a long navy raincoat. She had made great progress in her nursing career and was now sister-in-charge at the local hospital.

She had visited the alley very occasionally on her off-duty periods. She would enter the house, wrinkling her nose disdainfully at the dirt and squalor, and go straight up to her small room. There she spent the next couple of hours writing letters. Then, having placed fresh flowers beside her mother's picture, she would return to the hospital. Lil and Marie received only a cool nod of recognition.

This particular day she came very early in the morning. As she turned into the alley she could see a group of women gathered around the front door of her house. She could hear Lil's hoarse voice rising above the others, and see her father hovering about anxiously.

Marie had refused to attend the hospital clinic, having insisted that her child must be born at home. She was convinced that she knew all there was to know about childbirth—had not her sister Thérèse had seven and all of them born at home? So the bowls and towels were all laid out ready and Lil kindly offered her services. But something was wrong, for Marie had been in labor for a night and a day. Tim had gone to work and Dr. Sullivan could not be found for some time and when he did arrive he was drunk, for he was slowly going downhill, the old alley doctor. He had fumbled around, feeling her tummy, coughing and spluttering. "Got a long time yet," he said. "I'll come back later," and left.

By this time poor Marie was in a bad way. She was almost exhausted, screaming her head off one moment, whimpering the next, kicking up such a shindy that the whole neighborhood was aroused. Lil, perspiring badly, wore a worried expression. She had fetched a couple of scraggy old women from the bar to examine Marie, and they all stood in the doorway loudly discussing Marie's predicament while Marie called loudly on the Virgin Mary, God, her sister Thérèse—anyone who would release her from this dreadful agony.

Then suddenly an angry stern-faced woman descended on them like a ton of bricks.

"Get out of here at once, you damned old hags!" Mollie ordered.

The women shuffled away, muttering among themselves and Mollie closed the front door with a slam.

Angrily she glared at Lil and Tim who both cowered before her. "What's been going on here?" she demanded. "It's like Waterloo Station, everyone in and out. And what's wrong with Marie?"

"She's in labor," replied Lil. "Been at it for hours. I ain't never seen the like of it. I'm getting really worried about 'er."

Impatiently Mollie turned and went into the untidy bedroom where Marie lay, her lips flecked with blood, bitten in agony, the bedclothes torn and dirty. With cool disdain Mollie looked down at her. Then lifting the grubby nightie she felt the swollen tummy. Marie was too far gone to care. With glazed eyes she murmured: "Oh, Mother of God, someone, help me!"

"Why didn't she go to the hospital?" Mollie demanded of Lil, but noting the look of helplessness on Lil's face she did not wait for an answer. "Fetch my bag. It's by the door," she commanded. "Then get out into the kitchen and scrub your hands with plenty of soap. And keep all the kettles boiling."

Without a glance at Marie, Mollie drew back the curtains to let in the light. Then she turned back the bedclothes and proceeded to massage and manipulate Marie's extended stomach, her face hard and unemotional.

Within an hour a baby girl was born. With her expert hands Mollie helped this little life into the world, her own half-sister, but she showed not a flicker of affection or feeling. She thrust the smelling salts under Marie's nose, propped her up in bed and handed her the neatly wrapped well-washed bundle. Marie, overwhelmed by all she had gone through, began to weep, so Mollie returned the child to its crib, picked up her bag and walked out.

Lil was skulking in the doorway as Mollie bustled past her. She watched her out of sight and then dashed in to Marie.

"Ow, poor little cock, don't cry." Her fat arms cuddled the dejected Marie.

Tim was delighted with his lovely golden-haired child. "We'll call her Angel. I've never seen a baby who looked more like one."

Marie pouted in disappointment; she had planned to call her Thérèse after her sister, but Tim would brook no arguments. So the baby was baptized Angel Mary.

Tim fussed and loved his little daughter and picked her up constantly until she became so spoiled that Marie began to lose all patience with her. "Shut up you squalling brat," she would shout and bounce her rather roughly in her cot. It seemed that this little baby knew exactly how to annoy and frustrate her highly strung mother, but she was as sweet as sugar when Tim was around. From the very beginning she pushed Tim and Marie apart. After a hard day when the baby squalled most of the time Marie was very relieved when Tim came home to take over. He would pick up his lovely daughter and fuss her, love her and play with her, while Marie's dark eyes stared at them full of jealousy. At night, as soon as Tim put his arms around Marie, the baby awoke screaming to be picked up. Tim would walk back and forth with her, crooning Irish lullabies while Marie wept tears of resentment into her pillow.

Marie began to get even more slovenly, and became addicted to the milk stout that Lil smuggled in from the bar for her. "Does yer good," said Lil. "Makes milk, that does." Marie took to it and it made her put on weight.

Since the birth of the child Mollie had not come home

again. The only information Tim received on inquiring at the hospital was that Sister Mollie Dolan was away on a nursing course at a teaching hospital, and it would be quite a while before she returned.

So life went on and Lil still sat on the windowsill outside her house. The general depression, the aftermath of the war, had caused Lil's money lending business to flop. "It ain't no good lending," she was heard to say, "the poor sods can't afford to pay back, they're all out of work."

Bill's recent exemplary behavior had continued though he had failed to get a job. He had wheedled Lil into starting him up on his own. She had bought him a coster's barrow which he loaded up with fresh fish from Billingsgate; the line of smoked haddock returned to the passage and once more that fishy odor pervaded the air. Bill was doing nicely and trundled his barrow around the streets calling out: "Fresh bloaters! Nice 'addicks!" At the weekends he removed his greasy fishy clothes and, attired in his best suit and a white silk choker, stood on the alley corner, rolling fags, chatting to passersby and waiting for the bar to open.

# *Marie's Secret*

ANGEL WAS TWO YEARS OLD WHEN MOLLIE REturned to alley. She stared disdainfully at the small child who sat out in the street in a kipper box lined with a pillow. In the doorway stood Marie as disheveled as ever and gossiping with Lil who sat on her windowsill. Mollie marched straight past them and went upstairs where she proceeded to pack the remainder of her things. Then she went out once more. For the last time, she told herself. At last she had managed to break the chains that bound her to Autumn Alley. She had obtained a position as assistant matron in a hospital for the rehabilitation of the war-wounded in Nottingham—not far from Bridie.

"I'm sick and tired of whining women and crying babies," she told Bridie, "and I'll never go back to the alley again."

Bridie, now mature and middle-aged, thought it was a great pity that Mollie had grown so hard and bitter. She herself was now a prosperous farmer's wife with a comfortable home, and she was always pleased to welcome her sister-in-law. Besides, the children loved Auntie Mollie.

It had been generally accepted that once the war was over life would return to its prewar prosperity. But those happy-go-lucky Edwardians were in for a big shock. King George was now on the throne, and the old way of life had completely disappeared. On every street corner stood hordes of shabby-clothed men, idle and down at heel; it was almost impossible to hold down a regular job. Outside the labor exchanges long queues formed—many of the men wearing their army great-coats. That winter was long and bitterly cold and to add to the discomfort the coal miners were on strike.

This ill wind of depression had blown down the alley but so far had not begun to bite. Tim still held his job with his cousin Dandy, and Bill Welton still trundled his coster barrow, though on cold days it was parked outside the Railway Arms while Bill kept warm and dry inside—those that could afford 'addicks knew where to find him. Lil and Marie whiled away the time on good days on the doorstep, and in Lil's back kitchen when it was cold. Her big fire blazed and crackled with burning fish boxes. On the grubby rug sat Angel, a small girl with thin arms, thin legs and a small freckled face. She had lanky sandy-colored hair and a small turned-up nose. "She's as good as gold," Lil would remark, "plays for hours, she does, with bits of wood and old newspapers making up little games and jawing away to herself."

Marie, now thin and listless, would look down absent-mindedly at her small daughter, completely uninterested in the child. Lately Marie had seemed remote and very far away. She was always going off somewhere leaving the child alone for hours on end.

"Have you got yourself a fancy man?" Lil demanded of her crossly.

"Don't be silly, Lil," Marie replied. "I told you, I go to visit my friend, the one in service near Kings Cross." Her dark lids lowered over sorrowful eyes.

"Well, it ain't right to leave that kid all alone," scolded Lil. "Don't know what she'd do if it wasn't for me being next door."

Lil nagged and grumbled but it made not the slightest impression on Marie. She still slid off on these mysterious expeditions, returning bright and starry-eyed, a secret smile hovering about her full sensuous lips.

Lil would snort loudly and stare at her with utmost suspicion. "Don't let Tim catch yer, he'll murder yer and that's for sure," she warned.

But Marie went her willful way. Her little daughter's straw-colored hair always looked as if it could do with a good wash, her pale face was mucky and the little red nose was always streaming as if she had a perpetual cold. She would play with her lonely little games until the evening when she would trot up to the corner to meet her dad when he came home from work. He would grab her in his big strong arms, and whirl her high up in the air, and give her a rough whiskery kiss. Later he would sit her on the table while he brewed the tea and lit the fire, and then she would sit in his lap in the big old armchair, and her cornflower blue eyes would shine as he hugged her very tight.

Marie would come bursting in at the door full of excuses. "I've just been up the road," she would say, placing her basket on the table. "Had to get some proper bread, can't get anything decent around here." She was always full of incredible excuses for her absence.

Tim would glance about the untidy room and at his dirty bedraggled little daughter. "Look here, Marie, this has got to stop. Do your shopping round here or take the child with you."

Then Marie would lose her temper, start shouting and screeching, and cups and ornaments would come flying in all directions. As her parents fought each other Angel would run to Lil who would rock her in her big comfortable lap and sing funny Cockney songs to keep the child's mind off the racket next door. These performances were repeated week after week and bleak unhappiness pervaded what was once a bright happy home.

In the spring, the council sent an army of men to knock down the empty houses on the other side of the road. They tore off the face of our secretive little alley, leaving it exposed, its dismembered body for all to view.

There was no Becky to bewail its fate, no gentle, firm Mollie to protect it or Maud to aggressively defend it. There was only fat lazy boozy Lil and she was as usual incensed. "That's it, I've had enought, no bleedin' privacy, all these navvies digging up our alley."

It had suddenly ceased to be an alley; the huge slum-clearance scheme was making a slow start. The council's intention was to widen the road and build a new school—a three-story monstrosity that eventually dwarfed the last three remaining houses—Maud's house now being an office for Dandy's firm.

Angel played outside the house, looking down into the big holes the workmen had made. The strange brown sticky clay they dug up was useful for making mud pies.

Lil, still grousing and grumbling, staggered to and from the bar, some days shouting and swearing: and still Marie disappeared every day. Recently she had obtained a very smart suit from the tallyman; "Only two bob a week," she informed Lil.

"Tim won't like it," Lil told her. "Don't have nothing on the weekly, Tim won't." She stared dubiously at the bright emerald green suit that Marie was arrayed in.

"To hell with Tim," retorted Marie.

"Why, you nasty little bitch. You've got a good husband, treats you well, he does, bloody little bitch, better than he treated my poor Mary."

"'Mary,' 'Mary'—that's all I hear in this stinking alley," sneered Marie.

Lil gave Marie a proper piece of her mind.

"You wicked bugger!" she cried. "Why, a cat's got more feelin' for her kittens than you 'ave for that little child. Starve, she would, if it were not for me, running abaht wild all day while you, you're off to meet your fancy fella. Hope the Ripper gets yer," hollered Lil. "Found stripped and murdered, you'll be, 'afore yer much older." In Lil's mind Jack the Ripper, who had never been caught, still stalked the East End streets ready to pounce.

Marie was quite unconcerned by this tirade. She put on her new suit and hat, poked her tongue out at Lil and minced off down the road followed by the wolf whistles of the navvies working on the road.

While this quarrel had been in progress, Angel, with her hair hanging over her eyes, sat on a kipper box, holding a clothes peg doll—one of Tim's efforts to amuse the little child. Angel's keen eyes followed her mother up the road. Then she began to shake that little wooden doll violently. "Naughty girl," she cried, "now I am going to make you dead." She buried the doll in a heap of clay on the pavement.

With flushed face and tears that were near to falling, Lil gazed in a puzzled way at this little unwanted child. "Oh, my gawd," she burst out, "you're a funny little bugger." She took

Angel's hand. "Come over the bar with Auntie Lil, I'll buy you a nice arrowroot biscuit."

At eventide Angel waited on the corner for Tim. Her small figure shivered in the cotton dress, stained with clay.

Tim hoisted her high in the air. "Hello, my colleen, where's your hat and coat? It's too cold for you to stand up here without it."

Angel did not answer, she just pressed herself close.

Marie did not return that night and as the next day was Saturday Tim was off work. Together he and his little daughter made their breakfast. Tim toasted the bread and with a blunt knife Angel spread the margarine, and carefully cut the slice in half—one piece for her and one for her dad. She was so tiny, she hardly reached the table, but standing on a small homemade stool she carefully put one spoon of sugar and one of condensed milk into the cups and Tim poured the tea. Then Angel stirred it. Marie was not mentioned and not once did Angel ask why she was not there.

With red-rimmed eyes through lack of sleep and shoulders bowed, Tim stared into the fire. In his rough work-worn hands he held the same long brass toasting fork that Mary had used. He held the slice of bread against the bars of the grate, engrossed in his thoughts. Where was Marie? Had she left him? That there was another man he did not doubt, but to just disappear leaving her child all alone, it was unforgivable. Angel's squeaky voice broke in to his thoughts.

"Mind, Dad," she squealed, "you're burning the toast."

"Be jabbers! So oi did," said Tim, taking the blackened slice from the end of the fork.

"I'll do it," she said, and crouching beside him close to his knee, she held the long fork—now with a new slice of bread placed on it—up to the fire. Tim thoughtfully fondled her long straggly hair.

Lil came ambling in, bringing with her a letter she had got from the postman. She was anxious to know its contents as she had recognized Marie's handwriting. She stood in the doorway, her round eyes popping with curiosity. Tim slowly slit the envelope and read the letter. There was a mixture of expressions on his face, but finally he looked up, sadness in his eyes. Slowly he handed it to her.

"You know I can't read, Tim," said Lil reproachfully.

"Right," he said. "I'll read it out to you." In a cold hard voice he read:

Dear Tim,

Please forgive me for tricking a man as kind as you. My own husband was not officially killed, only missing. I wanted to live in England that was why I married you. Last year he came home from prison camp and came here to find me. He lived at Kings Cross and worked in a hotel, but now we are going home as I cannot stand the strain of cutting myself in half any longer. Once again I beg of you, forgive me and forget me. I leave you our child. She was never really mine. From the day she was born she came between us. Forget me, I was not worth your generous love.

                                                                Marie

"Cor blimey!" burst out Lil when Tim had finished reading. "Rotten little cow." She looked down at Angel sitting by the fire. "My gawd!" she wailed, "that makes her a bastard, just like my little George." Lil began to howl "just like a banshee," as Tim remarked to Angel after Lil had left to transmit the news to her cronies at the pub.

Tim sat cold and unmoved, his little daughter at his knee. "This is one little woman that no one will take from me," he whispered as he cuddled her close.

Through the gloomy years of depression, Tim and his little Angel remained very close, in fact, they were almost inseparable. Tim had grown thinner and there were streaks of gray in that luxuriant red hair.

He still worked for Dandy Fitz, whose firm of road contractors had now made their first million but Dandy had developed arthritis and did not go to work anymore. He spent the days in his large garden, digging the flowerbeds or laying paths—a kind of busman's holiday. Saturdays and Sundays he spent down the alley with Tim; on Sundays they met at Mass, and afterward had a few drinks in the Railway Arms; on Saturdays the two men would sit in Tim's back kitchen, consuming large jugs of bitter, talking and remembering the old times. Angel crouched in an armchair, her nose glued to her library book or one of those highly colored penny dreadfuls from the secondhand bookshop, always willing and on hand to get those big jugs of beer refilled.

At eight years old, Angel was still thin and undernourished; a tiny doll-like face with its sprinkling of freckles, her hair in a straight fringe that hung low on her forehead, her mouth always serious and unsmiling.

Tim had been off sick for a month. It was the first time in his life he had need of the doctor.

"Just a touch of flu, sir," Tim said to the young doctor who had replaced the old Doc Sullivan. "Just give me a bottle of the old cough mixture and I'll be right as ninepence."

"You've got bronchitis, man," the doctor told him. "Stay indoors in the warm or you'll kill yourself."

It had been a severe blow to Tim but common sense told him he must take notice, for who would care for Angel if he were gone? Angel trotted in and out with hot toddies of whiskey and milk, laying newspapers soaked in some putrid stuff called camphorated oil on his wheezy chest—Aunt Lil had said it was "a cert" for curing a bad chest. Now he was up and convalescent but the house still reeked.

Saturday came, bringing with it old Dandy Fitz who hobbled down the alley with the aid of a blackthorn walking stick. Beside the fire they sat, bleary-eyed with beer, talking over the good old days, arguing politics and the rising troubles. The more they drank the thicker their voices became until eventually they both dozed off. All this time Angel sat with her colored comics, bought at the bookshop with the coins that Dandy gave her.

Later on she would go over to Bill Welton's barrow for two nice hard roe bloaters. These she would fry and set beside two big mugs of tea. Tim and Dandy would really enjoy that Saturday afternoon treat. Dandy, wiping his lips with a big red spotted handkerchief, would say: "Oi, that was foine, Angel. Best meal I had all the week."

"Aye, she's a foine cook," Tim would answer.

Then there would be a general exodus to the bar until ten o'clock, when Tim would return home singing his rebel songs and a taxi would come to a halt outside the pub and the bystanders would assist old Dandy into it. (Maud, to solve the problem of having Dandy brought home by the police, had devised this method of getting him back to Muswell Hill on Saturday nights in one piece.)

Most Saturday evenings Angel sat reading her paperbacks, *Magnet* and *Gem*, and giggling at the antics of Billy Bunter. Occasionally, when Aunt Lil had the money to spare, they went to the pictures and for the immense sum of fourpence for Lil and twopence for Angel, they sat right in the front row. Angel was tremendously thrilled by those Saturday nights out. As soon as that silver curtain went up and the band began to play, Angel left the world of reality. She swooned with Mary Pickford; lay on the railway track awaiting death with Pearl White and escaped in the nick of time; she laughed and cried with Charlie Chaplin until she almost wet her knickers. Aunt Lil beside her did not see too well and could not read the words, but sucked acid drops noisily and made loud comments, only to be silenced by the shushing of the audience behind her and the flashing torch of the chucker-out.

As she aged Lil grew very placid. Tim and little Angel were her chief concerns, even old Bill took a back seat these days. She drank less, but her eyes had got very bad, and she wore thick pebble lenses all the time. But always there was little Angel to run errands, to thread a needle, to read out loud to her from her paper comics, so Lil was content.

The last two houses in the alley were by now badly in need of repair. Directly opposite was a huge barrack building—the new school. It stood on the spot that used to be Becky's home, the Browns' and that fatal shop on the corner. Tall ornamental iron railings surrounded the playground which was filled twice daily with a horde of ragged screaming kids from the surrounding district.

Angel loathed this school and dreaded Monday mornings when, with two bits of bread and margarine wrapped up in newspaper, Lil would take her by the hand and deposit her at the school gate. Then all the children would stand in a long line, often cold and shivering with apprehension. They would wait until the headmistress blew her whistle, then away they would all march, like a line of convicts, up the stone steps along the gray corridors to be jammed tight in airless rooms with more than forty others, for four hours on end.

For Angel school was a nightmare. It had begun on that very first day, when the frosty-faced teacher with pince-nez poised at the end of her nose had stared disdainfully down at little Angel with her heavy lace-up boots and her old-fashioned dress with half the buttons missing.

"Tell me your name, miss," she had demanded.

"Angel," came the rather defiant reply from this thin little girl.

"Angel?" retorted the teacher sharply. "That's not a name. Now tell me what are you christened. Is it Angeline or Annie?"

Angel's thin lips set in a straight line and her freckled face looked back at the teacher obstinately. "I am christened Angel Mary Murphy," was the sharp reply.

"Oh well, I'll call you Mary," said the teacher. "I can't call you that other ridiculous name." She pursed her lips in disapproval.

"If you do I won't answer," said the small thin voice of the child.

Miss Cornish was most upset and disobedience must needs be punished. So Angel stood behind the blackboard that morning and most mornings during her first year at school, refusing to answer the register unless they called her Angel as her father did. Soon a more witty teacher hit on the idea of just calling out "Murphy." That became a huge joke with the rough boys at the school who in time altered it to "Spud" which pleased Angel still less. In the brief period that Angel attended the council school her life was made miserable because of her lovely name. They called her "Sandy," and then "Freckle Face," and each name to this child was a direct insult. So it was that she made few friends and fought continual battles with her classmates who would say when Tim came to meet her: "Your Grandad's outside waiting for you."

"That's my father," Angel would cry and run to meet him, hurt because they were laughing at her lovely dad.

Tim had aged a lot since his illness. He remained unshaven throughout the day and was often out of work as he seemed less able to get up early like he used to. There was now a new man in charge at Fitzpatrick's. He was young Mickey Flynne, an Irish cousin. He had no time for sentiment; times were bad, work was scarce and many were jobless so when they got slack Tim was laid off with the rest and after that seldom held a regular job. He was very proud and refused to go begging to

Maud who was still boss at Fitz's in spite of her age and disabilities. So time went by and things went from bad to worse. Sometimes they went to bed hungry and Tim very bad-tempered, having no money even for the beer that he had always relied on so much. One Saturday when Dandy came there was no sixpence to buy bloaters for their tea, so Angel had to ask Bill Welton for credit and get the jugs filled at the bar by promising to pay when Dad got his dole money. Angel was sworn to secrecy—on no account must she let Dandy know that they were broke.

It was Lil who let the cat right out of the bag. She had taken charge of the barrow while Bill went for a drink when the pale worried face of Angel appeared.

"Please, Dad said could you trust him with two bloaters for Uncle Dandy's tea."

Impatiently Lil sorted out that long string of fish that hung over the barrow. "What's bleedin' Tim worried abaht *his* tea for? I don't know," she grumbled. "That mean old bastard Fitzy's rolling in money. Wouldn't give yer the drippings orf his nose."

Angel's little face creased. She hated it when Lil started hollering and swearing.

Lil wrapped up the two fish in a piece of paper. "Wait a bit, cock," she said to Angel, "I'll come on over." Marching determinedly in front of the child, she carried the two bloaters as if they were an offensive weapon, and walked straight into Tim's kitchen.

Old Dandy sat beside the fire with Tim, the jug between them.

Lil banged down the bloaters on the table. "Ere yer are, Tim," she declared, "that's six bob yer owes me and who knows when I'll get paid seeing as yer ain't bin at work for six weeks."

Silence prevailed and Tim looked at her with an embarrassed, hurt expression. Dandy's mild eyes looked very shocked.

"What's the bleeding good of havin' friends on the firm," hollered Lil, "if yer can't bleedin' get a job? Can't even feed yer bleedin' selves, without stuffin' that old git." Having delivered her final blow she marched out, passing little Angel cowering nervously in the passage.

Lil's outburst did the trick. Dandy had not bothered to find out if his cousin Tim had been laid off. He had taken it for granted that his pal had a job with the firm for life. There was hell to pay in that big house at Muswell Hill when Dandy arrived back home.

The next week there was a special invitation to Maud's house for Tim and Angel and a grand slap-up turkey dinner.

"Just like Christmas, it was," said Angel, in her account to Lil. "What a loverly lady! She had all shiny beads and earrings and no legs."

"'Ansome is as 'ansome does," sniffed Lil.

"She gave me this loverly dolly, all dressed in pink silk. I've never had a dolly before. I am going to call her Anita. Do you like that name, Auntie Lil?"

"Gawd bless yer little heart," said Lil as she cuddled her, "what a poor little cock yer are."

Tim was offered a nice cushy job as yard foreman in the gradually expanding wharf beside the canal. In this way he could work and give eye to Angel at the same time.

The enterprising Mickey Flynne had devised a plan to store building materials now that times were bad, in readiness for the future recovery of the industry that must eventually come. So his wharf and huge pile of paving stones extended almost to Lil's back door. When the depression began to ease up he had stables built to house the wide-backed mares which had formerly pulled the barges, and a fleet of brightly painted little yellow tip-up carts transported the building materials to various jobs.

Angel loved those well-groomed horses. It was a great thrill for her to visit them. She gave each great beast a name, and waved goodbye to them in the mornings when, all spruced and shiny, each one went off to do its day's work. After school Angel was there to meet them. She knew each one's likes and dislikes, giving one a present of a piece of bread, another a lump of sugar.

"Stay away from those stinking stables," Lil would warn her. "Be getting trampled on by those bloody great beasts one day, mark my words."

"Don't be so foolish, Auntie Lil," Angel would reply very seriously, "they're all my friends, they won't hurt me."

"Fed up with the bleeding stink, I am," groused Lil, "I'll sell this house, I will." She was always threatening to move but no one took any notice of her.

Tim was content at his new job, and he had fewer worries regarding the welfare of Angel. Dandy still came on Saturdays, and on Sundays after Mass he would come home with Tim in time for Sunday dinner. He always brought a shopping bag with him on Saturdays and shyly he would say to Angel: "There's a nice bit of bacon for Sunday dinner, darlin', and I put in a head of cabbage with it."

With a slight little twitch of her lips that might have been a smile (but she seldom smiled), Angel would take Dandy's offering saying: "There'll be the two of you for dinner tomorrow, then?"

On Sundays she scrubbed a large pot of potatoes and boiled them in their jackets. Then she put the bacon in a big pot, and when it was nearly cooked popped in the big head of cabbage. As it slowly cooked the odor pervaded the air. Angel would wrinkle her little nose in disgust—how she hated that smell of boiled bacon and cabbage.

Punctually at two o'clock Tim and Dandy returned, having visited several pubs on the way home from church. Tim would remove the large pot from the stove and put it on a piece of newspaper in the middle of the table. Then the cabbage was drained into a large colander, the spuds put in a dish, and, with great ceremony, Tim would take out the bacon and place it on a big willow-patterned plate that had belonged to Mary. Thick lumps were carved off and set on the individual plates. Then the feast would begin; huge fatty lumps of bacon, potatoes and cabbage, all swimming in grease. Amid the talk, the beer swilling and the hearty eating, the little girl sat as quiet as a mouse, not uttering a word, just dreamily sitting and listening.

"Don't they feed that old sod up in that big house?" was Lil's caustic comment.

"Of course they do," Angel would defend her old men, "but Uncle Dandy likes Irish food."

"Well, it ain't right," Lil would say dogmatically, "you cooking and waiting on them. Cor blimey, you ain't more than two pennyworth of coppers high."

Angel would become very offended and retire to the shabby old armchair and those highly colored paperbacks.

Sunday after Sunday the conversations of her father and his friend droned on and on, and with heads nodding they both began to snooze until the pub opened again in the evening.

Little Angel had no complaints to offer the world; dearest Dad, Uncle Dandy and Auntie Lil, and even old Bill Welton next door, she loved better than anything in the outside world. Thin and pale, somewhat cold and haughty, at nine years old Angel made her own decisions, and kept her own counsel and was happy enough.

# BOOK
# THREE

# A Silken Web

THE SKY WAS VERY BLUE THAT SUMMER DAY AND all was peace and tranquility in the beautiful English countryside. It was twelve years after the war and still there was terrible poverty everywhere. But in this little corner of rural England life had stood still. Mollie lay back in a deckchair under a wide-spreading branch of an apple tree, enjoying the soft summer air and all the beauty that surrounded her. She was glad she had decided to give up nursing. It would be rather nice to settle down here, near to Bridie and Timmo, and the children.

From the farmhouse nearby came the sound of singing— that Gaelic low crooning tone as Bridie, up to her elbows in flour, set about her weekly baking. An appetizing smell of cooking came from the kitchen and a large red setter yawned and stretched on the lawn.

Mollie got up and patted her dark braids of hair. At thirty-four she was still a little vain.

From now on, she thought to herself, she would be free as the air; it was good to dwell on such a promising future.

Suddenly the dog leaped to his feet and with a loud bark raced toward the front gate.

"Come back, Rusty," called Bridie, "it's only the postman." She came out of the house, leisurely wiping her hands on her apron and went down to collect the mail. "Why there's one for you, Mollie," she said. She handed Mollie a buff-colored legal-looking envelope.

Mollie opened it rather gingerly. She paled slightly as she read it and her mouth assumed a hard line.

"Not bad news, Mollie?" inquired Bridie anxiously.

"It's from the solicitor in London. He looks after the house in the alley. It's due for slum clearance soon now and a prospective buyer is offering me a good price for the freehold land."

Bridie looked very solemn. "You must go up there tomorrow," she said, looking hard at Mollie.

"No, certainly not," declared Mollie. "Let the agent handle it. Why should I be bothered?" she added petulantly.

"But you must go," insisted Bridie, "you can't let your father and that small child be turned out into the street."

Mollie's dark eyes flashed with temper. "I said that I would never return home when I left Autumn Alley, and I meant it," she snapped.

Tears flooded into Bridie's eyes. "Well," she cried, "I'm shocked at you, Mollie. That's your own father and you haven't visited him for years." She turned and went back into her kitchen.

Mollie paced the green lawn biting her lips in agitation, turning over in her mind the contents of that letter. What a nuisance it all was. She had never taken a penny rent, she had left him the house to live in, what the devil did they expect of her? She had sworn never to visit the alley again, how could she force herself after all this time? How could she return to that dirty slum, the gloom of the alley and its poignant memories of her mother and her own young husband? The humiliation of it all when her father had brought back that young French bride from the war, a girl younger than herself. It had been a bitter pill to swallow. That she had deserted him and left him to bring up that brat was no concern of hers. Why should she allow herself to be involved? Her own future had never looked brighter, she had a good nest egg in the bank and was retiring at the height of her career.

Mollie clenched her hands. A cold fear passed over her.

She wanted so much to be free, but she couldn't stop herself. She kept thinking about her loving mother, her red-headed boisterous father, that gallant young Larry, her lover-husband killed in the war. Almost mechanically she went upstairs to pack her bag.

"Timmo will be glad," said Bridie. "Many a time he's begged Tim to come up with the child but he's always refused. Tell them there's a home here if they want it."

Angel skipped along on her way from school. She was playing her favorite lonesome game—stepping on the lines and avoiding the center of the pavement—this way she seemed to get home quicker. Now turned ten years old, very tall for her age but still painfully thin, she had a long mane of straw-colored thatch that hung down to her waist and an untidy fringe that hung low on her forehead. Two blue eyes stared out solemnly from beneath heavy sandy lashes. She had a peaky freckled face and thin lips that seldom smiled and she looked as if she carried all the world's burdens on her shoulders. Better hurry, she thought, must get the kettle boiled for Dad's cup of tea. For her old dad did not look well lately. His red hair was fading and there were wrinkles on his brow, and Angel was worried, she did not like to think about him getting old.

Down into the shadow of the alley she skipped. Suddenly she stopped and stared at the front door. Something was different today. The door was open and inside was a neat shiny brown suitcase. She peered into the dim passage very nervously and looked at the suitcase that sat on the faded lino. It was then she heard a soft sound from upstairs. She tilted her small freckled face and listened intently. No one ever went up there. She had heard Lil say it was haunted. But Angel did not believe in ghosts. She had often looked up those stairs and listened and never heard or seen a thing. Now someone was up there. She ran lightly up the stairs to see what the intruder was up to and who it was.

Standing in a room full of old furniture was a tall smart woman in tailored tweeds and brown well-polished shoes. Little Angel stood hesitating at the top of the stairs, looking shyly at this sister that she had never known. Mollie stooped and irritably picked up an overturned chair, one of several that had been thrown higgledy-piggledy about this once pleasant room. Turning slightly she noticed the little girl.

"Where's your father?" she demanded abruptly.

"He's still at work," replied Angel, advancing to Mollie's side and looking up at her.

Mollie tried to avoid the gaze of those steady eyes. "Go and tell him I'm here," she demanded impatiently.

Angel had grasped the situation immediately. "You must be my sister Mollie," she said in her confident manner. "Come downstairs and I'll make you a cup of tea. Dad'll be in at five o'clock." She held out a tiny hand as if to guide her down the stairs but Mollie ignored it.

"I can't wait long," she declared crossly. "I have a train to catch."

"Well, I shouldn't stop up here if I was you," Angel informed her in a loud whisper. "There are ghosts up here, that's why we never use it."

Mollie paled slightly. "Nonsense!" she cried. "What a dreadful thing for a child to say."

Angel eyed her shrewdly. "Are you coming down for tea or not?" she inquired.

Mollie suddenly felt like a naughty child about to be smacked, but nevertheless she followed the child down into the kitchen.

Without a word Angel offered her a chair, and went solemnly about her task. Mollie sat uncomfortably on the edge of the chair, watching this confident young girl. The qualified nursing sister, wise in the ways of the world, felt suddenly inadequate in dealing with this untidy looking child.

Solemnly Angel stoked up the fire, placing the huge black kettle on the flames. Then from the dresser she produced three sad-looking mugs and a tin of condensed milk. She lined up the mugs on the bare wooden table and slowly put a teaspoonful of the milk into each. Then tea was put into the blue enamel teapot that Mollie recognized as having belonged to her late mother. The kettle had started to sing and Angel's tiny wrists seemed likely to break under the strain as she held the teapot under the spouting kettle and wet the tea. Mollie sat mute; for some reason she could not think of anything to say.

The tea having been made, Angel was now examining the glass sugar bowl, scraping it carefully with a spoon. "There's not much sugar left," she said. "How much do you take?"

"None, thank you," replied Mollie.

"Good," said Angel, "that leaves one for me and one for Dad."

Angel passed her the thick mug of hot tea and stood back and watched her drink it. Mollie sipped it and put the cup on the table. It was dreadful but she did not want to offend this strange child whose keen eyes surveyed her.

"Why don't you like me?" Angel suddenly asked. "Is it because I'm a bastard?"

Mollie gasped in shock.

"I'm not swearing," explained Angel. "I was only telling you that my mother and father were not legally married."

Angel moved a little closer, her little finger examining Mollie's wristwatch. "What's the time? Nearly five? I'll pour Dad's tea, he'll be home in a minute."

With tear-filled eyes Mollie got up to greet her father. After all these long years of absence, she was unable to suppress a sob when she saw how old he looked. Angel placidly filled the last mug with tea. Those thin lips of Mollie's did not smile but a kind of secret glint in her eyes betrayed her happiness.

Mollie did not stay the night but went up to the hospital to stay with an old friend from her probationary days. She had to think very clearly, but all she could think of was that neglected home which her mother had always kept so neat and the bed in the kitchen that was little Angel's with drab army blankets and no sheets. She visualized the pale undernourished face of the child and the sadness in her father's eyes. They would be memories she could never erase, no matter how far from Autumn Alley she traveled. She sat down to write a long letter to Bridie, explaining her reason for not returning. "Someone must care for that child, and Dad needs me."

The reunion of Tim and his daughter Mollie was a great success, and with Angel it was slow but very sure; there was great obstinacy and determination on both sides. Within that pale-faced slip of a child Mollie encountered a great deal of intelligence, and with all her hospital experience of tactful advance the cold calm Mollie began to soothe that stubborn pride. Little by little Angel gave in to her though Angel would brook no interference between her and her dad. She still made his tea and cooked his bloaters, and sat on his lap in the evening while he read the paper.

There were many improvements after Mollie came. First there was the joy of leaving that dreadful school. No longer did Angel sleep in the shabby old camp bed in the kitchen. She had her own little room next to Mollie's. In it was a shelf for her books and a table to do her homework on. And now, clad in a smart bottle-green uniform, Angel went on the bus to the convent school. Then there had been exciting trips up to town with Mollie—once to buy a party dress—where they had tea and cream buns in a real restaurant.

She had worn the party dress when they all went up to Muswell Hill for dinner at Maud's and sat around a table that gleamed with candles, lovely glasses and flowers. Dad wore his best Sunday suit and Mollie looked very smart in a long tight-waisted skirt and a chiffon blouse, and poor Uncle Dandy, red-faced and fed up in a big stiff white collar and a little black bow tie, had "looked like a donkey gazing over a whitewashed wall," according to Tim.

Aunt Maud reminded Angel of a queen. She sat so upright in a kind of padded throne with wheels, her white hair gleaming, her long earrings glittering and swinging in the candle light glow. It had been a lovely evening and Angel sat dreaming about it for days after. She giggled when she remembered how Mickey Flynne, who had escorted them home, had tried to put his arm about Mollie's trim waist; the look she had given him it was a wonder he did not freeze on the spot.

There was now only one house left in the alley—only Mollie's faced the wind that blew over the park. Angel had been sad to see Auntie Lil's house pushed down but Lil liked living down in the market and owning a fish shop. According to Mickey Flynne who was always hanging around, they were going to be electrified, and Angel was puzzled about it, wondering whether it would be such an improvement. Where Lil's house had stood, the new offices of Fitzpatrick's were being erected, and Mickey Flynne, in charge of these im-

provements, had promised Mollie he would install for her a
real hot water system with a bathroom. The lovely horses had
all gone; motor lorries were now used to transport the
building materials. Angel missed those old beasts of burden
but, as Mollie had reminded her, they had all retired to a farm
to live out their lives. Yes, Angel thought it would be nice for
them to live in the country and not to have to work any more.
The Cut still flowed placidly by, but fewer and fewer barges
ruffled its oily water, and no children played down there now,
it was silent and depressing. A long line of factory sheds had
gone up on the opposite bank. Angel sat on the wall and
dreamed, and in this way the years between ten and teens
drifted away.

Mollie stood her ground, no developer would get her
house. The windows shone and the brass knocker on the door
gleamed, and Mollie put up a brass plaque that proclaimed
that this house was No. 1 Autumn Alley.

So Autumn Alley did not die, and for Mollie at least its past
remained fresh in her memory.

"Tell me another story of the alley," Angel would demand,
her blue eyes shining as she listened to the tales of the alley
folk.

Mollie, at forty, was still as serene as ever, her dark hair
flecked with silver. While her knitting needles clicked away,
she would tell Angel of her own mother Mary and of Larry,
her husband, and of George, the lost baby—all the heart-
breaks and all the fun of years gone by. Angel, whose
straw-colored hair was now neatly bobbed, would fill endless
exercise books with stories of the alley in a strange kind of
spidery writing.

"God knows why you waste your time with all that
scribbling, Angel," said Mollie, "you really ought to be doing
your homework."

"I'm writing the story of the alley," Angel explained.

"Well, no one will be able to read it, only yourself. Your
handwriting is dreadful."

"Never mind. I enjoy it," was Angel's bland reply. "I just
feel that I want to find out all about the people who lived in
this alley before me."

"All right, my little genius, you do that," Mollie fondly
replied.

Tim and Dandy still met as regular as clockwork each Saturday and Sunday. Dandy was now a dried-up little man, and there were deep lines of pain on his face. He suffered dreadfully from arthritis and limped along supported by that blackthorn stick. Tim now sported a beard and his keen blue eyes were as merry as ever, and they would talk continually of the old days over that big jug of bitter. Dandy's once small business, Fitzpatrick Ltd., was now an international concern. But Dandy just lived for those weekend trips to the alley to drink with Tim.

With her window open and her exercise book handy, Angel would lean, elbows on the sill, listening to the slow drawl of their voices as they sat outside, moving slowly through the years of memories.

At the beginning of the year Lil had died, having had a bad fall in that dirty greasy fish shop. Mollie and Angel had gone to visit her. Propped up in that old-fashioned brass-knobbed bed, a bottle of gin beside her, her large moon-like face pallid with the approach of death, valiantly she fought for her breath and said to her little pet Angel: "Nah, don't yer cry, cock, I'm done for, so it ain't no good worrying over it."

But Mollie and Angel wept many tears. They sat beside old Lil and talked of the alley and of her friend, Mary.

"Wonder if we do all meet again?" she gasped, holding on to Mollie's hand.

She was laid to rest in Bow Cemetery, quite near to Mary and her son John. Bill Welton and the only three remaining alley dwellers attended her funeral.

Bill followed Lil much more quickly than anyone would have realized. Without Lil he was lost. He drank heavily and it affected his liver. Tim and Dandy paid their last respects to old Bill as they laid him beside his partner. The cemetery was now full. A notice stated that no more would be buried there, and it was soon to close. No more alley dwellers could be laid to rest there.

"Bedad, me boyo," Tim exclaimed, "there's no room for us, old mate!"

Dandy replied: "'Tis back home for me, old friend. I want to be buried in Kanturk, the home of our ancestors."

"Well, then," joked Tim, "I'd better come wid yeh."

Progress destroyed the cemetery, ploughed through all those old bones and built a big motorway across it—an approach to the Blackwall Tunnel that the men sweated and toiled to construct. And that fine new road, stretching down to the coast, was constructed by the famous firm of Fitzpatrick Ltd.

# Dear Old Dad

ANGEL WAS NOW A TALL, GOOD-LOOKING STRAW-berry blonde. At sixteen she was meticulous in her dress, but still glum and unsmiling.

She went to and fro each day to St. Mary's College in the Mile End, having sailed through all her exams from high school to college. She had completed her commercial studies and now typed very well and was neat and accurate in shorthand. But still she dithered in her choice of career; she did not want to go to university or to sit in a moldy office all day.

"Well you had better hurry up and decide, Angel," Mollie said, "these things need planning."

Angel was bright and clever and Mollie had great hopes for her, but was slowly losing patience at her indecision. There was still a little nest egg tucked away if Angel wished to further her education—law school or medical school, Mollie had suggested.

"No, what I'd like to do," Angel told her, "is to travel all around the world and write books about it, but you know I'd never dream of leaving you and Dad."

Tim was just recovering from another bout of bronchitis and sat by the fire in the same old chair in the same old spot. He gave a wheezy chuckle as he heard this last remark. "You do as you want to, me darlin', I'll be away with old Dandy soon." He was still depressed at the death of his old pal the year before.

Angel literally flew to his side. "Oh, Dad, don't say such things." Impulsively she threw her arms about his neck.

He coughed, choked, wheezed and spluttered. "Take it easy," he gasped. "Are you trying to finish me off?" In spite of the discomfort caused by his illness, there was still a merry twinkle in those sea-blue eyes.

Angel released him and sat on the arm of his chair gently stroking his head. "Don't you dare talk that way," Angel scolded him. "You're going to live till you are a hundred, I'm sure."

Mollie had been watching this little drama with sardonic interest as she laid the cloth on the table ready for supper. She joined in with her sarcastic humor. "Well that will be nice," she said, "then he'll get a telegram from the king." Her words were like a red rag to a bull.

"Oh, Mollie, how could you!" burst out Angel reproachfully.

"Be jabbers," roared Tim, banging the floor with his stick, "he knows what he can do with his telegram and be damned. When I think of those children back in the ould country— dropping dead in the fields of starvation. Who did that, eh? And the foine Irish lads who swung on the end of a rope?" He gazed wildly about the room and went off in a tirade about the troubles of Ireland. He held the kings of England personally responsible for it all.

"Why, you wicked old man," cried Mollie, "you've lived here the best part of your life and got a good living, and there's not one good word you have to say. The Irish problems are over and past."

"Go to the devil!" roared Tim. "Why don't you go off and marry that damned Orangeman that's always hanging about here?"

"Mind your own business," retorted Mollie angrily.

"I'll not be spoken to like that in me own house," shouted Tim.

"Whose house?" argued Mollie.

"I'll go. I'll leave this instant," cried Tim, struggling to rise, but Angel was there to comfort and restrain him.

"Please Mollie, give over," Angel begged. "Why do you insist on upsetting him so?"

Mollie, tight-lipped but with an amused look in her eyes, went back into the kitchen. The battle was over. Soon she returned with whiskey and hot milk for Tim and peace reigned once more.

Tim had quietened down and Mollie sat placidly knitting so Angel retired to her corner and her journal. As she scribbled she reflected. How strange are humans, how complex was this family. The thought of losing her dad simply terrified her; surely Mollie was not jealous of her love for him. According to Mollie, Mickey Flynne had asked her to marry him five times. Pity he was a Protestant, Mollie was quite fond of him.

Next morning as Angel wheeled her bike out of the alley, Tim watched her from the window. She had just reached the corner, and threw the end of her striped college scarf over her shoulder with that characteristic swing, then popped her leg over the bike and with a final cheery wave rode off to school. Tim's day would be long and dreary without Angel. Mollie was good to him but she was always busy and getting very bad-tempered as she grew older. He reached for his little clay pipe and with old trembling hands relit it. The blue eyes stared out dreamily toward that low brick wall and past it to the slow moving green water of the canal. So many nostalgic memories were there—that old strip of oily water had flowed on past this house for almost the whole of his life and now he was getting near the end of the road. Almost the three score years and ten allotted to man, it was a good age; his only regret was that he might not live long enough to see his little Angel settled to a career or a husband. Slowly his eyes closed and he drifted away to that land of lovely dreams of youth as old men are wont to do.

Angel cycled through the narrow streets of Bow on her way to college thinking earnestly of her father. How tired he was lately and how cross Mollie seemed to get with him. Her lovely dad, she would have liked to stay at home and take care of him, but Mollie had insisted on this college education. Her nose was red, and her freckles stood out on her face even in the winter time. She pedaled swiftly through the mucky streets thinking of green fields and snow-covered mountain scenes she had always dreamed of but never visited. I'll take Dad home to Ireland in the spring, she decided. We'll go to that little village in Cork he always talks of . . .

She cycled through the college gates. Students stood about in groups talking and laughing. Angel rode straight on; friends were a luxury that so far she had not acquired.

Later in the large lecture hall, the learned professor waved his arms and ranted and raved as was his custom. No one took much notice of old Dr. Loski. All agreed he was very clever but eccentric. However, Angel listened to him very seriously.

"There's no need to go seeking beauty," roared the professor, "it is all around you."

Little titters went around the class and some wag said: "Where, sir? In the Mile End Road?"

"All right," he said, "let us take the Mile End. The stalls are bright and varied, the proprietors are descendants of many countries, loud and colorful in attire and accents, the houses . . ." He was about to continue when he was interrupted.

"I don't doubt that the language will be the most colorful," proclaimed that perverse student.

"All right," the professor said angrily, "I'll give you a holiday assignment on the East End. Take your notebooks and pencils and get out among the people.

"Angel," he called, "you've lived in this district all your life. What's the name of that obscure backwater you live in?"

"It's called Autumn Alley, sir," replied Angel.

"Just listen to that!" cried Dr. Loski. "Why, even the name conjures up mystery! There are many such old interesting places about here. Let me see you get on with it. Angel, kindly escort some of these illiterates around your district." With that he left the class.

The tall youth who sat next to Angel had seemed very bored, but suddenly he perked up and looked at Angel.

"This alley you live in, is it between Poplar and Bow?" he asked. "And does the canal run alongside it?"

"Yes, that's right," replied Angel. "Why are you so interested?" she queried.

"Well, I've promised myself a visit to that alley ever since I came to London. My father was born there, and I'll always remember how fondly he talked of Autumn Alley."

Angel stared at him with interest. "What's your name?"

"Welton," he replied and blushed deeply. "It's Algernon, but everyone calls me Algy."

"Why you must be a relation of Aunt Lil's! Was your father's name Arthur?"

He nodded assent and a broad grin crossed Angel's face. It was like a flash of sunlight.

"You must come home with me," she told him, "my Dad will be thrilled to meet you, all he talks or thinks of are the good old days and the grand neighbors who lived in our alley."

Angel burst in at teatime breathless with excitement. Behind her came a nervous-looking youth. "I've brought a friend," she cried.

Tim looked up and his fading eyes mistook Algy for Arthur. "Well, blow me down, hello, me boyo, long time no see." He pumped the lad's arm up and down in that firm handshake.

Algy joined the family at high tea. It took a while to convince Tim that this was not Arthur but his only son. Nothing would make Tim believe that his eyesight was fading. After tea they all sat around the fire, Tim in his big armchair, Mollie sitting upright busily knitting and Angel by her dad's knee as Algy told the story of the last years of his own father's life.

Arthur, the happy-go-lucky talented boy who had gone stepping smartly from the alley to make a name for himself in the world, had died a hero, as those who knew him thought he would. Algy's soft, well-spoken voice circled in among them as they sat about the glowing coke fire. Mollie and Tim dreamily watched those memory pictures in the fire as Angel considered how this earnest young man could be the grandson of uncouth Aunt Lil.

"Dad went down in the airship disaster," Algy informed them. "Did you know that?"

"No," replied Mollie apologetically, "we lost touch with Arthur during the war."

"That's because my mother was such a snob and still is," declared Algy. "But Dad and I were great pals, there was such a lot of fun in him, my life has been empty since I lost him." For a second his voice wavered a little.

The audience retained a respectful silence until Algy

continued once more. "My grandfather left Dad a fairly sound business but he squandered the capital—always seeking some new invention. Then after the war he got this bug for airships and that was how he managed to be on that maiden flight, when the R101 went down."

Angel's mind flitted back several years to 1930 when she had stood outside that grimy old fish shop with Auntie Lil and they had watched a tremendous airship sail over London. They could clearly see the number on the side. Aunt Lil had panicked. "Come in, Angel," she yelled at her, "the bloody Jerries have come back." Little did she know that her son was up there, sailing away to his death.

"Dad," went on Algy, "used to love to tell me of this alley, but not when Mother was around. We used to spend school holidays fishing and he used to chat about Mary and her beautiful daughter who broke his heart." He smiled at Mollie he spoke.

Mollie discreetly took out her hanky and wiped her eyes.

"I remember so well," said Algy, "the morning Dad left on that trip. Mother was not in favor of his going, so he crept out quietly early in the morning, but on the dressing table he left this." From his breast pocket Algy produced a battered old wallet. Mollie recognized it immediately, she had given it to Arthur for Christmas many years ago.

"The strange thing is," said Algy turning the wallet over in his hands, "that Dad had never left this out of his sight, and when Mother saw it lying on the dressing table she started to weep. So I took charge of it hoping to give it to him when he returned . . . but I never got the chance."

Tenderly he opened the wallet and took from it a letter yellow with age. He opened the faded sheet of paper and passed it around for all to see. At the top of the letter was Becky's address—4 Autumn Alley—it was Becky's note thanking Arthur for rescuing Lew from the canal.

Mollie's tears were falling fast; Tim took out a big red spotted handkerchief and gave his nose a good blow. Then a little faded photo of Mollie was produced with long ringlets and holding a bunch of pink roses, carefully cherished all these years in that tattered old wallet.

"Be Jasus," muttered Tim, "get Arthur a drink. Ain't there a drop o' whiskey in this house?"

Mollie got up and bustled about. The old ones were overcome by emotion and trying not to show it.

Angel moved up close to Algy. "Poor boy," she whispered. Algy's brown eyes looked down into hers with affection, and as Angel returned his gaze, she saw both an image of the alley's past and a glimmer of light that she knew could brighten her own future. Softly, without Algy being aware of it, she placed a gentle hand upon his shoulder and looked once more into the depths of the fire.